ARGOSY
ALL-STORY WEEKLY

VOLUME 198   CONTENTS FOR SEPTEMBER 29, 1928   NUMBER 2

SERIALS

COMPLETE STORIES

OTHER FEATURES

This magazine is on sale every Wednesday throughout the United States and Canada

THE FRANK A. MUNSEY COMPANY, 280 BROADWAY, NEW YORK, and
LONDON: HACHETTE & CIE.,   PARIS: HACHETTE & CIE.,
16-17 King William Street, Charing Cross, W.C. 2   111 Rue Réaumur
WILLIAM T. DEWART, President and Treasurer   RICHARD H. TITHERINGTON, Vice-President and Secretary
PUBLISHED WEEKLY AND COPYRIGHT, 1928, BY THE FRANK A. MUNSEY COMPANY

1 A

Classified Advertising

The Purpose of this Department

is to put the reader in touch immediately with the newest needfuls for the home, office, farm, or person; to offer, or seek, an unusual business opportunity, or to suggest a service that may be performed satisfactorily through correspondence. It will pay a housewife or business man equally well to read these advertisements carefully.

Classified Advertising Rate in The Munsey Combination comprising:

Munsey's Magazine
Argosy-Allstory Weekly
Detective Fiction W'kly
Minimum space 4 lines.

Combination Line Rate $3.00 Less 2% cash discount

Nov. 3rd Classified Forms Close Oct. 6th.

AGENTS & SALESMEN WANTED

MAKE $45 TO $100 WEEKLY—full or part time—and liberal bonus, selling BETTER QUALITY all-wool made-to-measure suits and overcoats. Save $18.50 per suit. No experience necessary. Commissions paid in advance. We furnish handsome large swatch samples and complete instructions FREE. Write today! W. Z. GIBSON, 500 Throop St., Dept. W-409, Chicago.

Wonderful "Whisper-it" Mouthpiece For Telephones; gives secrecy in conversation. Every telephone user a prospect. Details $1.00. Liberal profits. Write for full selling proposition. Colytt Laboratories, Dept. M. 565 W. Washington St., Chicago, Ill.

WE START YOU WITHOUT A DOLLAR. SOAPS, EXTRACTS, PERFUMES, TOILET GOODS. EXPERIENCE UNNECESSARY. CARNATION CO., 1040, ST. LOUIS, MO.

Big Pay Every Day, showing Nimrod's All-Year Sellers! Dress, Work, and Flannel Shirts, Overalls, Pants, Sweaters, Underwear, Pajamas, Leather Coats, Lumberjacks, Playsuits, etc. Experience unnecessary. Big Outfit FREE. NIMROD CO., Dept. 55, 4922-28 Lincoln Ave., Chicago.

Sell Things Needed Daily in Every Home—Soap, toilet goods, remedies, food products. Lower prices. Higher profits. Better quality. Quick sales. No experience needed. Spare or full time satisfactory. HO RO CO, 2702 Ho-Ro-Co Bldg., St. Louis, Mo.

Genuine DuPont Fabrikoid Tablecloths. No laundering. Wash right on the table—look like beautiful linen. $75 weekly, also bonus. DOILETTE CORP., 1018 Wabash, Chicago.

66 Miles on One Gallon—Amazing New, Wonderful Vapor Moisture Humidifier—Gas Saver—and Quick Starter. For all Autos. Factory Agencies wanted everywhere. 400% profit. 1 Free to introduce. CRITCHLOW, KI-427, Wheaton, Ill.

DO YOU WANT AGENTS AND SALESMEN TO SELL your merchandise? Men and women who are educated in personal salesmanship and know the house-to-house, office, and store canvassing proposition. These advertisers are getting them year in and year out, and there are thousands more for you among the readers of the Munsey Magazines. Our Classified Service Bureau will gladly show you how to use this section most profitably and at the least cost. Write to-day to the Classified Manager, Munsey Combination, 280 B'way, New York.

AUTHORS—MANUSCRIPTS

WRITE THE WORDS FOR A SONG. WE COMPOSE MUSIC. OUR COMPOSER WROTE MANY SONG HITS. MONARCH MUSIC COMPANY, 236 WEST 55TH ST. (NEAR BROADWAY), DEPT. 209, NEW YORK.

MICHIGAN FARM LANDS FOR SALE

MONEY MADE IN MICHIGAN POTATOES. $10 DOWN NOW AND EASY TERMS BUYS LAND NEAR MARKETS, LAKES, STREAMS. WRITE TODAY. SWIGART & CO., M-1276, FIRST NATIONAL BANK BUILDING, CHICAGO.

PHOTOPLAYS WANTED

$$$ FOR PHOTOPLAY PLOTS. STORIES ACCEPTED ANY FORM. Revised, criticised, copyrighted, marketed. Estab. 1917. Booklet free. UNIVERSAL SCENARIO COMPANY, 209 Western & Santa Monica Bldg., Hollywood, Calif.

TOBACCO

TOBACCO HABIT BANISHED. NO MATTER HOW LONG YOU HAVE BEEN A VICTIM, no matter how strong your craving, no matter in what form you use tobacco, there is help for you. Just send postcard or letter for our Free Book. It explains everything. NEWELL PHARMACAL CO., Dept. 845 Clayton Station, St. Louis, Mo.

HELP AND INSTRUCTION

EARN $120 TO $250 MONTHLY, EXPENSES PAID, AS RAILWAY TRAFFIC INSPECTOR. WE ASSIST YOU TO A POSITION AFTER COMPLETION OF THREE MONTHS' SPARE TIME HOME STUDY COURSE, OR REFUND YOUR MONEY. WRITE FOR FREE BOOKLET CM-30. STANDARD BUSINESS TRAINING INST., BUFFALO, N. Y.

HELP WANTED—MALE

FIREMEN, BRAKEMEN, BAGGAGEMEN (WHITE OR COLORED). Sleeping Car, Train Porters (colored), $150-$250 monthly. Experience unnecessary. 836 RAILWAY BUREAU, East St. Louis, Ill.

FARM LANDS

LAND FREE IF PLANTED TO BANANAS. BANANAS BEAR A FULL CROP THE SECOND YEAR. $5.00 MONTHLY WILL PLANT A FIVE ACRE ORCHARD, WHICH SHOULD PAY $1,500.00 PROFIT ANNUALLY. AS BANANAS RIPEN EVERY DAY, YOU GET YOUR CHECK EVERY 90 DAYS. RELIABLE COMPANIES WILL CULTIVATE AND MARKET YOUR BANANAS FOR ONE-THIRD. FOR PARTICULARS ADDRESS JANTHA PLANTATION COMPANY, 410 EMPIRE BUILDING, BLOCK NO. 26, PITTSBURGH, PA.

EDUCATIONAL

YOU READ THESE LITTLE ADVERTISEMENTS. Perhaps you obtain through them things you want; things you might never have known about if you had not looked here. Did it ever strike you other people would read your message—that they would buy what you have to sell; whether it is a bicycle you no longer need, a patented novelty you desire to push, or maybe your own services? Our Classified Service Bureau will gladly show you how to use this section most profitably and at the least cost. Write to-day to the Classified Manager, The Munsey Combination, 280 Broadway, New York.

PATENT ATTORNEYS

PATENTS PROCURED; Trade Marks Registered—A comprehensive, experienced, prompt service for the protection and development of your ideas. Preliminary advice gladly furnished without charge. Booklet of information and form for disclosing idea free on request. IRVING L. McCATHRAN, 205 Owen Bldg., Washington, D. C., or 41-J Park Row, New York.

PATENTS—Write for our free Guide Book, "How To Obtain A Patent" and Record of Invention Blank. Send model or sketch and description of Invention for Inspection and Advice Free. Reasonable Terms. Prompt Service. Highest References. VICTOR J. EVANS & CO., 762 Ninth, Washington, D. C.

PATENTS. BOOKLET FREE. HIGHEST REFERENCES. BEST RESULTS. PROMPTNESS ASSURED. SEND DRAWING OR MODEL FOR EXAMINATION AND ADVICE. WATSON E. COLEMAN, REGISTERED PATENT LAWYER, 724 NINTH STREET, WASHINGTON, D. C.

INVENTORS—WRITE FOR OUR GUIDE BOOK, "How to Get Your Patent," and evidence of invention blank. Send model or sketch for inspection and Instructions Free. Terms reasonable. RANDOLPH & CO., Dept. 412, Washington, D. C.

PATENTS AND INVENTIONS

INVENTORS: SEND DETAILS OF YOUR INVENTION OR PATENT AT ONCE, OR WRITE FOR INFORMATION. IN BUSINESS 30 YEARS. COMPLETE FACILITIES. REFERENCES. ADAM FISHER MFG. CO., 249 Enright, St. Louis, Mo.

ARGOSY
ALL-STORY WEEKLY

| VOLUME 198 | SATURDAY, SEPTEMBER 29, 1928 | NUMBER 2 |

The battle lasted for over an hour

The Masked Barmaid

Out of the sea came the Goulds—and with them a web of treachery,
mystery, and deadly intrigue that was to create sad
havoc and suspicion on the Mary Louise

By DON McGREW

CHAPTER I.

ADRIFT.

THOUGH the events involving the masked barmaid occurred after I had reached the age of thirty, I must needs hark back to the year 1771, and the mysterious tragedy on the schooner Mary Louise, which took place when I was a lad of twelve, bound on a trip from England across the Atlantic to join my widowed father in Boston.

The Mary Louise was owned by my father, then a builder and shipper in Boston. She was sailing under the command of Captain Andrew Randall, a dour, spare Yankee, about forty years of age, with gaunt, dyspeptic features;

and we were about halfway between Bristol and Charleston, our first port, when, having weathered a heavy storm, we sighted a tossing speck upon the distant waters.

The skipper, with Roaring Bill Gentry, the mate, was standing near me on the poop at the time. Randall studied the speck for a moment through his glass, his thin lips drooping bitterly at the corners. He had a long, clean-shaved upper lip, and a bony, uplifted chin, with a sharp-pointed beard beneath it which made me think of the tuft worn by a cantankerous billy goat.

" Hell!" he said at last, lowering the glass. "Looks like a lifeboat." His cold, furtive eyes shot a glance at Gentry from under his lowering brows, and he went on, gruffly; " I suppose, Mr. Gentry, we'll have to stand in closer to see if anyone's aboard her." Upon which he favored me with a queer, side-long glance, and went below.

Beyond a brief, "Aye, aye, sir, Gentry made no comment—save that he gave me a glance on his own account, and the shadow of a wink. He was a huge and terrific man, who strode about the decks in a great blue coat, with shining brass buttons, and his breath hanging behind him on the cold morning air, like tobacco smoke.

His bronzed, clean-shaved features were as craggy as granite. Even then, though he was but thirty, the lines from nostrils to mouth-corners were deeply indented, while the skin on his cheeks resembled heavy folds of pig's-hide; and his eyebrows, jutting out to either side of his fierce, horny nose, were so long, and so thick, that he had twisted them into spikes, and bent them up-wards, like a devil's horns.

Yet, when he smiled at me, with the merriest of twinkles in his keen blue eyes, I smiled in return; for while Captain Randall had the aspect of a man with many secrets and no confidants, and seldom spoke, save to snarl out an order through his long nose, Gentry had proved, from the very first, to be the best of company. He was an accomplished mimic, could imitate a dozen and one birds and animals, and was also a raconteur to bring the eyes of any lad popping from his head.

Sometimes he would poke me in the ribs with his thumb, call me " Old Sober Sides," and ask me if the cat had taken my tongue; sometimes he would " wall" his eyes at me, and twitch his spiked eyebrows in a way to make me shiver; but always, when I quailed, he would laugh uproariously, and reassure me with a slap on the back. Hence I was quite sure by this time of Roaring Bill Gentry, and felt that he and I shared identical opinions of the crusty, furtive skipper.

"That's right, Davy!" the mate cried, noting my smile. " Let a reef out of that jaw tackle—it's allus best." Then, as we drew nearer the little boat, and he raised his glass again, he swore mightily. " Why, by the Flying Dutchman!" he cried. " There is people aboard—and—" He broke off, and stared again. " Yes, by thunder!" he went on. "A woman and a babby, too!"

" A baby?" I cried.

" Look for yourself," he said, handing me the glass.

And, in a moment, I was athrill with excitement, and begging Gentry to crowd on more canvas; for there with three men sat a woman hugging a bundle close to her breast.

We soon had them aboard. The baby, whose name was Virginia, was not quite a year old, and had apparently suffered comparatively little from her travail; but the mother, Mrs. Jonathan Gould, a tall, slender woman, with calm gray eyes, and a wealth of dark tresses, was very weak.

With them were two sailors, and a man named Anthony Gould—a tallowy fop, with pale eyes, and a drooping, sensual mouth. And they proved to be survivors from the Glory of the Ocean, a brig in which the Goulds had been returning to England from the Bermudas. Jonathan Gould, the baby's father, had gone down with the ship. He and Anthony were cousins.

From the very first I disliked Anthony Gould, for he had no word of thanks for his deliverers, was forever finding fault with this or that, and was about as pleasant, on the whole, as some flabby dank fish. And Gentry once confided to me that the man gave him the "squeejie-meejies." Moreover, it soon became apparent that Mrs. Gould shared our opinion of Anthony. From the time she came aboard she never uttered one word of complaint; she was always kind when addressing me or Roaring Bill; but, weak as she was from exposure, her eyes flashed fire at sight of Anthony.

MRS. GOULD grew steadily weaker instead of stronger; and often I caught her looking at me strangely. I also saw her studying the faces of Captain Randall and Gentry at different times. And finally, when we were alone one day, she beckoned to me.

"David," she said, "I want the first mate."

I returned shortly with Gentry; and, when the door of her little stateroom was closed, she said, without preamble, "Mr. Gentry, I'm not going to live."

"Never say that, m'lady!" Gentry cried.

"I *know!*" she replied. "And this baby will be the only heir to her father's estate—*if she lives.*"

"Lives, m'lady? Beggin' your pardon, but she's a healthy little tyke."

"Praise God for that! You see, if she dies, that creature Anthony would be next in line for the estate."

"A-h-h!" said Gentry, with a slow nod.

"And I don't *trust* him! Now you've an honest face, my man"—here Gentry reddened—"and I'm going to ask you to accept a mission."

"If so be it I can, I'm your man, m'lady," Gentry answered promptly.

She thanked him, with evident emotion, and thrust a heavy wallet, and an oilskin packet into his hands. "Put them away—quickly!" she whispered, with an apprehensive glance at the door. And, when Gentry hastily complied, she went on, in low tones, "There are ample funds in the one, and letters and a birth certificate in the other."

Here she lifted the coverlet, disclosing the baby's right cheek; and on the temple, merged with the hair line, close to the ear, we saw a purple birthmark, not larger than the ball of one's thumb, and shaped somewhat like a violet. "Once I grieved horribly over that," she continued. "Now I am grateful for it. She was born in the Bermudas, you see, and none of her relatives—except that wastrel, Anthony—has seen her. With that mark, identification shouldn't be difficult."

Mrs. Gould then explained that she wanted the baby delivered to her sister, Gertrude Channing, who lived near London, on Bromderry Heath; and she assured Gentry that he would be well reimbursed if he could arrange the trip.

"Why, m'lady," said Gentry, heartily "I'll do it, if so be it I can."

She sighed with relief; but immediately her chiseled features became grave again. "There's another thing," she resumed. "I've made a will. My husband's will, which was placed on file in London, leaves everything to me. The will I have written leaves everything to my baby, and the estate—with some shipping interests—is valued at over a half million pounds. I have named my sister Gertrude as executrix, to be baby Virginia's guardian until she reaches the age of twenty-one.

"But in case Virginia dies—there is still another journey across the Atlantic, too—I have provided that Gertrude, or her heirs, will come into the estate. Otherwise Anthony—in case the baby died—would come into the property as my husband's next of kin. And I want to sign this will now, with two witnesses."

"Cap'n Randall and myself, perhaps?" Gentry suggested.

"No!" cried Mrs. Gould. "I don't trust him, either. Can't you think of some honest hand aboard?"

Gentry thought a minute. "I'll get the coxsw'n, Tom Norton," he said at last.

"Can he keep his mouth shut?" she asked. "You understand, of course, that Anthony must not dream of this will until it is safe in Gertrude's hands."

"Tom Norton's silent as the grave, m'lady," said Gentry.

"Very well, then. I know David will be, too. He's a knowing lad, is David."

And then, Gentry returning shortly with Tom Norton, the swarthy coxswain, the situation was briefly sketched to him. The will and order were produced and duly signed by Mrs. Gould, with the scrawling signatures of Gentry and Norton attached, as witnesses. I remember well how Norton chewed his tongue as he seized the quill, and how he finished the last letter with a little "curlicue," shaped somewhat like a bird's tail.

"There!" Mrs. Gould exclaimed, sinking back on her pillow and handing the papers to Gentry. "I trust that will frustrate anything Anthony Gould may have in mind." And she placed some sovereigns in Norton's hand.

"Understand me," she continued, addressing Gentry, "I don't fear actual murder—at least aboard this ship. He wouldn't *dare*. What I fear is that he will take charge of the baby when you get to Charleston and go ashore with her, and then—no one will ever see her again. I'm giving you an order, Mr. Gentry, placing the baby in your charge till she's delivered to Mr. Waltham or my sister."

"And you're not going to tell Anthony about this, m'lady?" he inquired.

"No," she said.

"But, m'lady," Norton put in, "if he knows 'bout this here docyment, right off, he'd never do anything, would he? What good would it do him to harm the baby or lose her, in which case he'd not get the property nohow?"

"You're not safe in harbor yet. Best insure the safety of the baby and the will by waiting till you get to Charleston."

This being agreed on we left her; but all of us started a little when we emerged into the main cabin, for Anthony Gould had entered, and was now seated beside the table under the stern ports.

CHAPTER II.

CONSPIRATORS.

THE big first mate wore an abstracted air as we came on deck.

He pursed his lips and looked at Norton in sidelong fashion.

"I don't think he could've heard anything," he said presently.

"Right you are, sir," said Norton. "Cap'n may be wonderin', though."

"Let him," Gentry grunted. "And now, remember—mum's the word."

"Aye, aye, sir," said the coxswain, and went forward.

"See you don't forget that, too, Davy," Gentry said to me.

"I won't, sir," I replied fervently.

"Why," said he, "I tell you, sonny, I wouldn't put it a fathom past that swab to cut that babby's throat, I wouldn't."

"Oh, I believe that!"

"Why, by the Flying Dutchman!" he exclaimed, "take a look at them deadlights o' his. That there estate's vallied at over half a million pounds, sonny. You keep mum, that's your cue, and I'll keep my weather eye on that swab, in case m'lady slips her cable."

I assured him heartily that I would do his bidding.

True to her predictions, Mrs. Gould died two days later, and she being consigned to the deep, the rôle of nurse-maid fell to my lot. Gould showed no disposition to concern himself with the infant's care, and the greasy cabin boy had other duties and was quite out of the question.

There were other occupations on board that would have appealed to me more, but whenever I thought of the danger that hovered over her, I began to regard myself as one of her guardians.

"Ha!" cried Gentry, catching me playing with her toes one day. "Well, now, you needn't fly the red ensign, my lad. Nothin' sweeter than a gal babby, by the Flying Dutchman!" And he looked down with a smile as the baby closed one hand around his big, horny finger. "But you see here, Davy," he continued, "mum's the word—now you remember. Keep a silent tongue."

I nodded energetically, for a new circumstance had arisen to increase my apprehensions. Whereas the captain had kept to himself for the most part, before the rescue, he and Gould had come by now to be as thick as thieves. They were often engaged in guarded talk. If I approached they fell silent; if I lingered near by they frowned me off or moved away; and one night, when I came on deck unexpectedly, I heard Captain Randall say:

"No! and an end to it. It's twenty thousand pounds or nothing!"

Just then I turned to go down before they should sight me; but the captain heard me and called to me quite sharply.

"Look here!" he demanded, seizing my wrist in a fierce grip, "why are you prowling around at this hour o' the night?"

"Sir," I said, "I had to feed the baby."

"Ah!" he said, in a softer tone, Then his grip tightened again, and he bent over to peer menacingly into my face. "If—" he began—but here Gould coughed, and Randall released me, say-ing, "Best go below now, sonny; sleep makes a boy grow."

Thoroughly aroused, and filled with fresh terror, I reported this happening to Gentry at my first opportunity. His eye watched me narrowly; and when I mentioned the sum the captain had named, he gave vent to a low whistle.

"Twenty — thousand — pounds!" he said, slowly. "Something big's afoot, I'll be bound." He thought a moment. "Well, I can't fathom it yet, but we'll bide the time, and maybe we'll strike bottom yet."

We received some glimmering of light before many days had passed. When we were one day out of Charleston, our first port, the baby was suddenly taken ill, with cramps. Thereupon Captain Randall ordered the after-cabin cleared.

"I'll have to quarantine her," he announced. "This may be cholera."

As soon as possible I sought the mate. "Mr. Gentry," I cried, "do you think they've poisoned her?"

He rubbed hard at his cheek. "Why, as to that I can't say," he replied, looking away over the water, with a frown. "If I was sure, I'd step up in a brace of shakes I would. But you see how it is, Davy: I'm on'y mate; he's cap'n; and I can't charge him with crime when I ain't got no manner o' proof, now can I? No, says you, I can't. Well, then, what I say is this: We'll just have to stand by, like, to see which way the wind blows."

We were soon to know. That night Captain Randall came out of the after-cabin, and announced that the baby had died.

"Ah, and a pity it is!" said Gentry, shaking his great head sadly. "Well, cap'n, I suppose we'll bury her right off?"

A heavy fog had fallen shortly after sundown, and I could not see Captain Randall's features clearly.

"No," he said. "Mr. Gould wants to bury her ashore." He turned to mount the poop. "Oughta make it into Charleston by to-morrow, less'n this fog holds," he said.

"Well, but look here, sir," Gentry persisted, "you wouldn't take chances with that cholera, would you?"

"The damage is done, if it is cholera."

"Better fumigate, though, hadn't we?"

"No!" Randall snarled. "Had to expose myself, anyway. Not going to change *my* quarters at this late hour. Fumigate that cabin when we gets to Charleston." And he mounted the poop without further words.

Gentry and I were no sooner alone than I burst into tears. But the big mate threw a great arm across my shoulders, and led me to a spot in the dark waist, just abaft one of the gigs, on the starboard side.

"Avast there, Davy!" he cried. "There may be no cause to cry yet. Now you wait here a minute till I gets the coxsw'n."

Wondering what more he could possibly have in mind, I waited impatiently until he returned with Tom Norton.

"Now, see here, Tom," said Gentry, "what do you make of this?"

"Why," said Tom, "if that babby's due for coppers on her eyes, why don't he send her to Davy Jones to-night?"

"Right you are," Gentry cried. "And why not fumigate that there cabin?"

"Well, if you asts me, sir," said Tom, "it may be that the babby's still alive."

"*Alive?*" I cried, incredulously. "Why, how—"

"Cap'n may have some scheme to get rid of her in Charleston," Gentry cut in. "Anyway, we'll find out, if you has the nerve to try something, Davy."

My heart went flopping into my boots, but I spoke up, at once.

"Ah, that's the lad!" cried Gentry, enthusiastically. "There is his daddy's boy, by the Flying Dutchman!" Then

he explained that he would show me the way from the after-hold into the cellar, from which I could go up the companionway, and into the main cabin.

"The space between the top of that cargo and the deck is too narrow for me or Norton, or one of us would go," Gentry explained. "But you won't be in no danger, Davy. Cap'n's taking his trick on watch—and, anyway, if he starts to come down off the poop while you're gone, I'll keep my deadlights on 'im. If he tries to foul your hawse I'll heave to in the offing, cap'n or no cap'n."

In spite of these assurances my heart was beating wildly as I worked my way back over the barrels and bales below decks. But I reached the cellar under the cabin without mishap; and, when I had at last mounted the ladder, and cautiously pushed up the hatch, inch by inch, I saw that the main cabin was empty.

There was no sound in the room save the creak of the brass lamp which hung suspended from a beam, and swung with the lazy pitch of the ship on the swells; so, after a moment of hesitation, I pushed the hatch further up, and, stepping on deck, ran quickly to the little stateroom on the starboard side where I had left the baby. Bending over the bundle of clothing I found there in the bunk, I distinctly heard the baby breathing. It was slow, stertorous breathing; but the fact remained that little Virginia was not dead, but undoubtedly alive.

CHAPTER III.

A MURDEROUS ATTEMPT.

WILDLY elated, my first impulse bade me pick her up, and rush with her to Gentry, using the cabin door as an exit. I was certain that neither Gould nor Randall would dare to harm the baby or me once we reached the open deck and Gentry's protecting arms; but when I ran to the cabin door I found it locked. Then, as I turned back, I heard footsteps in the companionway.

Scurrying for the cellar ladder, I barely had time to drop the hatch over my head before a key grated in the lock of the cabin door, and some one entered.

Being sure that it was either Gould or Randall, I went down that ladder step by step, holding my breath for fear of making the slightest sound; but the man above me must have heard the hatch drop, or some other sound of my movement, when he was unlocking the door; for he ran first into the baby's little stateroom—as I judged by the sound—and then dashed for the hatch.

Abandoning caution, I released my hold on the ladder and dropped to the cellar deck. As the hatch was thrown aside, and the fitful rays of the murky cabin lamp lessened the darkness of the hold, I scrambled over a hogshead and into the narrow gaps between the cargo and the upper deck, through which I had worked my way aft but a short while since.

Nor was I any too swift in my movements; for the man above me, though he could not see me, heard me scrambling; and, as he cursed viciously, I recognized the voice as that of Captain Randall. In the next second he had dropped into the hold, and began beating about here and there with a belaying pin.

"Come out o' that, you swab!" he yelled. And I knew, by the sounds, that he was striking into the black spaces behind various hogsheads and crates. "Oh, shiver my sides!" he cried, "why didn't I bring a light?"

Safely wedged, by this time, between a hogshead and the upper deck, and beyond his reach, I lay quite still; and after a moment of muttering, Captain Randall moved over to the ladder.

"I'm going aloft to fetch a glim," he gritted. "Better come out now, and take what I give you. If you don't,

by thunder! I'll give you three hundred lashes, and keelhaul you besides, or my name ain't Andrew Randall."

He paused for a moment, waiting for an answer; then, snorting viciously, he ran up the ladder and into the cabin.

Long before he came back I had crawled far forward; and when at last I reached the upper deck I hurried to the spot in the waist where I had left Gentry and Norton. There I found Gentry, but no sign of Norton.

"What did you find, Davy?" Gentry whispered fiercely. "What did you find?"

"The baby's alive!" I gasped, when I could get my breath. And I recounted my adventures to him.

"Well, by the Flying Dutchman!" he exclaimed, when I had finished—and it seemed to me that his eyes flared like lamps in the fog! "So *that's* it!"

"*What's* it?" I asked.

"Why," he said, in easier tones, "looks to me like cap'n drugged her, maybe. He's got a medicine chest, you know. Also looks like they didn't have the nerve to finish her, out and out. Figgers to cast her adrift somewheres ashore, I shouldn't wonder."

"But you can stop that!" I cried. "You can walk right in and *demand* that baby. Mrs. Gould gave you the right."

"No," he said, "I can't. A mate's a mate, and a cap'n's a cap'n, while at sea, my son." Then his tone changed. "But you see here, now: I'll take care o' her, soon as we drops anchor. They don't intend to murder her, now you can lay to it. Otherwise they would have finished her, out and out. Yes, sir; she'd be food for fishes by now, and you can lay to it."

"But I'm afraid!" I cried. "Where is the coxsw'n? He'd think as I do, I'll wager."

"Oh!" he said slowly. "Well, now, maybe two heads *is* better'n one, at that. He went for'a'd." He lifted his head and listened as some one stumbled along the deck, working his way aft.

Although he passed within a few feet of us, the fog was so thick by now that we could not see him. " You stay here a bit till I gets Tom," Gentry then went on.

" I'd rather go with you," I said nervously. " Suppose Captain Randall suspects that was me in the cabin, and he comes prowling about, looking for me?"

Gentry laid a reassuring hand on my shoulder. " Like as not when he gets done lookin' over that cellar he'll figger it was rats he heard. We've got 'em aboard big as a rat terrier dog, about. 'Tain't likely he'll fathom that dodge—you goin' through the hold, I mean. No, sirree—and he'll think quite awhile, anyway, I take it, afore he lays his hooks on a son of ship's owner. But in case he does come lookin' about, Davy, you just lay doggo here, and duck behind the gig. I'm off to get Tom."

WITH that, Gentry left me; and for a space I stood there, crouching beside the bulwarks, and starting apprehensively at every footfall on the deck. And I was still crouching there, listening for Gentry's return, when the seaman beating the warning bell yelled in sudden fright, and dropped the bell to the deck.

Simultaneously the lookout bellowed hoarsely; a tall, ghostly ship loomed up out of the fog on our port bow; and the Mary Louise, with her booms swung to starboard, struck an outbound square-rigger, the Hespion, a glancing blow amidships, and slithered along her port side with a fearful crashing of spars.

Fortunately, there was little breeze, and neither ship was making more than headway through the long ground swells, or the sharp bows of the Mary Louise might have crushed the Hespion's side. As it was, the Hespion's lower spars overlapped the schooner's port side; and pandemonium reigned. Spars snapped; shrouds were ripped away; blocks came tumbling down, along with tangled ropes and billowing canvas; and above all the shouting and cursing there rose the terrified wail of a lookout as he pitched out and downward into the sea.

At the first sound of the collision I was gripped in a panic of terror and indecision. If I remained where I was, one of the falling spars might crush the gig, and me with it; if I went overboard to escape the missiles I might not be picked up; and if I ran along the deck to one of the companionways I might be crushed while *en route*. And in my extremity I yelled aloud, calling for Roaring Bill Gentry.

My yell was still quavering in the air, so to speak, when something came whipping out of the fog and struck the bulwarks close to my head. At the instant I thought it was a small block from the rigging; but even as I dodged I realized that it was a belaying pin, thrown with murderous intent.

Instantly I turned to dive between the gig and the bulwarks, being now certain that my yell had disclosed my whereabouts to Gould or Randall— either one of whom, I was sure, would welcome this as an opportunity to throw me overboard under cover of the confusion. But I was not quick enough for my enemy.

Iron fingers caught the back of my jacket; I could not repress a scream of fright; and then my scream was cut off sharply as my throat was gripped savagely from behind. In the same second I was caught at the trouser leg and flung over the starboard side and into the sea.

Luckily for me I had long since learned to swim. So in an instant I had stripped myself of my jacket, and had kicked off my low shoes; and, thus lightened, I began swimming about in the wake of the Mary Louise, searching for any bit of floating débris that might help me keep afloat. Nor was I long in finding what I sought; for my hand fell on a broken spar end, which I seized eagerly. Then I began calling out for help.

There were at least two others in the water making the same appeal at the time; moreover, the men aboard the Hespion and the Mary Louise were shouting at one another, or chopping away with axes at the tangled rigging, and either did not hear or had no time at the moment in which to put over a boat.

For that matter, Captain Randall never did put a gig over the side. The Mary Louise sheered off almost immediately after the collision, and went limping off into the fog; and it was not until ten or fifteen minutes later that a gig from the Hespion picked me up. One of the Hespion's crew was also rescued from the waters a moment later.

Once I was safe in that gig, I began to hope that the Hespion would have to put back to port for repairs. But in this I was disappointed. She had cleared for Rio, out of Charleston, and was well supplied with extra spars and an extra suit of sails. When daylight came, and the fog cleared, the Mary Louise was not in sight; we reasoned that she was now well on her way to Charleston; and, as for the Hespion, her repairs were well under way, and she was wheeling away to southward before noon observation.

Captain Mathews, the Hespion's skipper, was a fair man; I never met a fairer; but he was also a strict taskmaster. After listening to my story, he said: " Looks to me like that skipper heaved you over, sure enough. He must've figgered it was you worked your way back to that there cabin, sonny, and saw that kiddie alive after he says she's dead. Plain as print to me he means to help that Gould get the estate. But to-day's to-day, sonny; bein' as I'm shorthanded, you goes to work in the galley."

Hence, when I finally reached Boston, after eight months or more of adventuring, I was sick to death of sousing bilges, greasy pannikins, and foul-smelling quarters; and I vowed I would never put to sea again.

CHAPTER IV.

FACE TO FACE.

WHEN I reached home at last, and was nearly crushed against my father's broad chest, I learned that the baby had been reported dead and buried at sea, just before the Mary Louise reached the port of Charleston, and that Gentry had never mentioned the will to my father!

" That isn't all, either," my father declared. " Tom Norton was logged as ' missing overboard ' same night you were."

" Then Gould *must* have heard something about that will when he came into the cabin that day !" I cried.

" I don't know, I don't know!" my father muttered, striding about his study like one possessed. He was a very large and violent man, with thick, black eyebrows that moved with every emotion; an exclamatory, impetuous man, with a quick, high temper, but the most generous of hearts.

" No, sir," he went on, " I can't say as to that. I put the Mary Louise back to Bristol—Gentry, Randall and Gould all with her. When they dropped anchor here, I read the log, and everything was there. So I never thought for one instant but that you'd been knocked overboard in that collision. But see here: will you tell me why Gentry never said one word to me about his suspicions, or sending you into that cabin?"

I shook my head. It was beyond me.

" Well, I'll tell you!" my father cried. " I think he decided to profit by that will himself. At any rate I'll be certain of it if he doesn't turn the documents over to Mrs. Gould's sister. Don't you see the possibilities, my boy? Randall said the baby was dead; you told Gentry she was alive. That made Gentry certain that they shied at murder, but intended to drop her somewhere ashore. But even before that —why, what was to prevent *him* from knocking Norton overboard while you were in that cabin?"

"I couldn't believe it of him!" I cried.

"Well, you can see the opportunity he had, can't you? No one knew of the will but you three—you, Gentry, and Norton. If Gentry could get rid of you two, he had the chance to sell that will to Gould, or blackmail him with it. Yes, sir, I'm going to believe they're all in it now, till I get proof to the contrary."

Much as I hated to believe it, father's conclusions seemed close to the mark; for, by the time the Mary Louise had returned to Boston, after a return voyage from Bristol by way of Rio and Havana, father had written to Gertrude Channing, Mrs. Gould's sister. and received a reply saying that Anthony Gould had established his claim to the estate. Captain Randall's log had been accepted as proof of the demise of Mrs. Gould and the baby Virginia.

Gentry, she said, had not visited her, nor made any report whatsoever concerning the will. And her barrister had informed her that she could, of course, do nothing without that all-important document.

"There!" said my father. "I knew it. Maybe I can't prove anything—but wait until I set eyes on that pair. Just wait!"

I was with father in his office some three months later when the Mary Louise put in, and Captain Randall and Gentry were ordered to report. Randall was admitted first, while Gentry waited in the anteroom. The skipper stopped dead at sight of me, and swallowed with a horrible, choking sound; and my father, who was breathing so hard his breath fairly whistled through his nostrils, launched into a tirade before the man could regain his composure.

But as a lawyer my father would have been a failure; for he fired my whole story at Randall, interlarded with oaths. Then he demanded:

"Well, what have you got to say to *that?*"

"I never dreamed that boy had been back in the cabin!" were Randall's first words. He licked at his lips, shuffled his feet, and twisted his hat about in his hands. "I never dreamed but what your boy had been knocked over by a falling spar, or something, sir, I tell you."

"Who did you think *had* been in the cabin that night?"

"Didn't know as anybody had. Did think I heard some one in the cellar —thought likely it was the cabin boy, stealin' raisins, maybe. Only a kid could've worked his way back over that cargo."

"What about that will? Do you mean to tell me you knew nothing of it?"

"Yes, sir, I do. How could I know anything about it? Gentry never yaps to me. Neither does Norton or this boy here."

My father snorted. "Will you deny that the baby was alive when David went into the cabin?" he cried.

"Certainly!" Randall declared, with more assurance. His eyes were sickly, and furtive, but they gleamed now with defiance. "I'm not crazy!" he snarled. "That baby was dead as bilge. I ought to know. I—"

"Yes, I guess you should!" my father cut in. "You got panicky that night, *after* you heard some one in the cabin, and finished the job right. That's my belief."

"Them's hard words," Randall declared with growing truculence. "You can take your damned billet for all me —I'm done with you. But there ain't a thing wrong that you can prove on me, I know that. I buried that baby myself, that night, all open and above-board—and any of the crew can tell you so."

"Probably you did—but it was a foggy night."

"What's that got to do with it? I had the watch piped, all regular—read the service, and dropped her overside. Of course, I could have buried her next day, afore the whole company— but I was afraid of cholera spreading, if it *was* cholera."

"Why didn't you let the carpenter sew up the body?"

"Why," said Randall, "it's like I told you when I came in. I didn't want to expose any more than had to be to that cholera."

"Bah!" my father snorted. "*You didn't want any one to see the finger-prints on that poor baby's throat.*"

"That's a lie!" Randall cried.

M Y father could restrain himself no longer. He leaped at Randall like a tiger; struck him a fearful blow on the jaw; picked him up and smashed his fist into the man's ribs; and then, with a mighty heave, he tossed the man aloft, and brought him down with a crash on the floor. There he lay quiet, a broken and bloody lump of motionless flesh.

"Oh!" I gasped, fearfully. "You've killed him!"

"No such luck, sonny!" my father cried—and he tossed the inert body into a corner. Then he threw wide the door, and called Gentry in.

The big mate was quite collected, though his face was grave. He started a little when he noted me; took in the captain with a glance; then faced my father squarely.

"Well, sir?" he said, quietly.

"What did you do with Mrs. Gould's will and packet?" my father demanded bluntly.

"It was stolen off me!" replied Gentry, as quick as winking.

"Ah! Then you won't deny having received it?"

"Why should I? Worse luck for me, it was given to me—and I never had intention of denying it."

"Then," said my father, "why didn't you tell me about it when the Mary Louise put in here after coming up from Charleston?"

"Plenty of reason, sir," Gentry replied. "Them papers weren't *your* business, sir—all due respect to you. They was for Mrs. Gould's sister."

"So? Well, you don't mean to say you couldn't trust me with the knowledge that you had it?"

"It wasn't that at all, sir," Gentry declared. "Didn't I have reason to believe the fewer knew about them papers the better? But way down below that there was another reason. It—"

"Wait a minute," my father cut in. "You say you lost the will. When?"

"Before we got to Boston."

"Well, did you report the loss to Mrs. Gould's sister?"

"Report it?" Gentry snorted indignantly. "Well, I guess not."

"And why not, pray?"

"Why? I'll tell you why, by the Flying Dutchman!" And Gentry's face was growing red. "Because I'm no fool—that's why! I had the same reason I was going to tell you about— same reason I didn't tell *you.* There was Davy gone, Norton gone, baby gone. Soon as I missed those papers, I says to myself: ' I'm lucky my throat wasn't cut in my sleep, or that I ain't been knocked on the head and thrown out the stern port.' And why should I have yipped to you? I never thought you'd know about it, for one thing. What's more, where would I have been if I had told you? I hadn't no proof, had I? No, by thunder! I hadn't. And that ain't all."

"Well?"

"Why, what would you have thought, if I *had* told you? Look at my position. Wasn't it quite the reasonable thing for any one to believe that *I* might have knocked them two— Davy and Norton—overboard? I stood a show to profit by it, didn't I? Well, that's what you would have thought—and if I'd told you I lost them papers—had 'em stolen off me—you'd've thought just what you're likely thinkin' now. You'd've thought I sold that will to Gould, and was only trying to cover up, like, in case something leaked out some day."

And Gentry placed his head to one side, and nodded slowly at my father, watching him through narrowed eyes. "That's what you would have thought, by the Flying Dutchman!" he resumed. "So I didn't tell you—no, nor Mrs. Gould's sister, either. Why should I report such a loss to her, especially when I thought she'd never know it? It'd only be a good way to get my head bashed in some foggy night! Mum was my cue—and mum I keeps. I'm only a mate as yet, and I has a job to keep."

My father eyed the man a full half minute before speaking again. "Well," he said then, "I'll grant there's something in what you've said—if it's true. But, by God! I think you're lying."

Gentry's neck swelled, and his face reddened.

"Maybe you think because you're ship's owner I have to swallow that!" he roared. "By the Flying Dutchman! But I don't, though. I—"

"You're guilty as hell, that's my belief!" my father roared, in equal anger. "You either sold that will, or have it still." And he aimed a tremendous blow at Gentry's chin.

The big mate promptly sidestepped, and countered; and the ensuing battle lasted for over an hour, wrecking the office, and ending in the street, with a howling mob about.

It ended only after the battered and ghastly combatants were forced to stop by sheer weakness. Father had to be taken home in a carriage, and he breathed with difficulty for a month. His face was battered out of all recognizance. But Gentry fared little better. For once he had met his match.

As for Captain Randall, that worthy spent over a month in the hospital before emerging.

Meanwhile the mystery remained unsolved; although Gentry and Randall left Boston, and were eventually listed as shipowners on their own account, the circumstance left the legal aspect unchanged. The assumption that they received the money from Gould to invest in ships could not be regarded as proof. So there the matter seemed to rest for a long period of years.

CHAPTER V.

A SALEM INN.

THOUGH both Gentry and Randall selected Salem as a home port after the revolution had ended successfully, I did not come into direct contact with them again until I had passed my thirtieth birthday. Then my father extended his holdings by the purchase of Warren McClung's shipyard in Salem, and I went there to take over its management. This not only placed me in touch once more with Randall, but gave me news of Gentry's passing.

"The old Cormoran was put in here for reconditioning by Randall," said Mr. McClung. "Yes, she's Gentry's old ship, but he went ashore with his mate, Blackburn, in Havana last trip, I understand, and never came back. Neither did the mate. Food for fishes, I suppose, after a brawl in some waterfront dive. Well, his boson—named Bagby—brought her back and Randall put in a claim for her. Gentry had no wife and no relatives, 'cept an aunt in Boston, they say; anyway, Randall made his claim good and he's got her."

Being still a bachelor, I took up my quarters in the Sign of the Anchor, where Mrs. Webb, the landlady, assigned me to a comfortable suite of two rooms, located on the second floor, and this placed me in daily contact with old Randall himself, for he was living in quarters just below me, on the ground floor.

He was then past sixty years of age and stooped and withered. He no longer sailed the seas, but sent others instead, inasmuch as he now owned three schooners, in addition to the Cormoran. Yet in spite of his worldly success his eye was more furtive than ever, while his gaunt features, pallid now and deeply lined, were those of a man who would be better off without a memory.

And I noted an odd point or two about him. Where he had been aloof and taciturn, he now seemed to seek company eagerly. The long, low taproom, with its beamed ceiling, its latticed windows, and its clean, sanded floors, took up the whole front of the house, and he spent more time here than he did in his own quarters.

All evening he would sit there drinking, ever quick to speak up with a leading question or purchase another round for his seafaring cronies whenever the conversation lagged. I put it down to a pathetic eagerness to drown memory in rum and camaraderie.

Another point I noted had to do with the seaman Bagby, who was known as "the boson," just as though no other man of that rank had ever put to sea. He was a huge, hulking, sullen man, with a bullet head and piggish eyes; and his square, smooth-shaved face had been turned blue from an excess of rum.

All day—so my garrulous landlady told me—the boson prowled about the beach or went afishing, with no attempt to get another berth at sea; nor had he performed any other work since his return to Salem with the Cormoran. Yet, she informed me, he occupied a good room at the front of the house, on my floor, and for the past six months had paid his bills regularly. Usually he would not answer when addressed; only look up with a flame in his small eyes and growl, and few seemed to care for his company.

Though he and Randall met frequently, they exchanged mere grunts, or spoke not at all; but on two different occasions, when the big boson was drunk on rum, I saw him summon Randall curtly with a jerk of his bullet head. Nor did the old shipowner linger long in stays. Both times he arose—albeit with a frowning face—and accompanied the boson to his quarters.

What this portended I did not at first surmise; but Mrs. Webb came into my sitting room one evening at the end of my first week and stirred up the old fire anew.

"It ain't that I should be talkin' about a payin' guest, I suppose," the little woman began, apologetically. "Cap'n Randall, I mean. But just the same—and I'm not asking just out of curiosity, Mr. Waltham—I wonder if you'd give me the straight of that mixup on the Mary Louise, years ago."

As I hesitated her little black eyes snapped with ready comprehension, and she hastened to explain.

"I'm asking," she declared, "because I think the old devil had some'at to do with Cap'n Gentry's taking off—so there! I'm a friend of old Mrs. Peabody, Gentry's aunt, who might've claimed the Cormoran and had enough to last her the rest of her days, poor old thing, only Cap'n Randall produced a note from Gentry and took the ship over.

"Now I don't think Bill Gentry ever signed any such note; no, nor I don't think as he ever would have borrowed a shilling from Cap'n Randall under any circumstances. He used to stop here when he was in port, and I know he had no use for Cap'n Randall.

"But all that aside—there's something else I'll tell you if you'll help me get the straight of the Mary Louise business."

With my curiosity aroused, I complied with her request. Her eyes, which reminded me of little black buttons, never left my face during the recital.

"There!" she exclaimed when I had

finished. She leaned closer to me, then, and declared: "*I don't think that will ever left Gentry's hands while he was alive!*"

I straightened, eagerly. "Why?" I cried.

"He had a little strong box, all polished, with brass bound corners and an inlaid top. He never left it aboard his ship when he came here. Well, sir, that box wasn't on the Cormoran when she was brought back. I had told Mrs. Peabody about it, you may be sure. But when she asked about it, why, this boson, he ups as bold as brass and says: 'Sure! Cap'n Gentry never left that box aboard ship no place he anchored. He took it ashore with him there in Havana—and that was the last I see of him.'"

"Then what is your theory?" I asked.

"I think Cap'n Randall got the contents of that box," she declared. "What's more, I think the will was in it. If not, why would a man named John Gould be coming here from England?" And she leaned back triumphantly.

"How do you know that?" I cried.

She eyed me shrewdly, then tossed her head a bit defiantly. "Oh, I've been looking around. Found his letter, among other things—his letter to Cap'n Randall. It was just a short letter, saying he would sail from Bristol on the Atlanta her next trip. She's due in Boston some time this month. Anyway, I think Randall has that will, and now he's going to sell it to this Gould."

CHAPTER VI.

A PLEA FOR HELP.

I DIGESTED her words for a moment in silence.

"I'll grant it is not at all unlikely," I said at last. "Still, it's only a guess."

"But you'd be willing to help, wouldn't you, if there *was* a chance to prove it?" she cried eagerly.

"Most assuredly."

"Well, then, I'll tell you this: it isn't *all* supposition on my part. You see that chimney there?"

I glanced at the chimney in the east wall. It was now the middle of July, and the stove had been removed from the room, but the chimney contained an aperture for a stovepipe, now closed by a plate.

"That chimney," she said, "runs down to the grate in Cap'n Randall's sitting room. Pull out that plate, and you can hear what is said in that room fairly plain. Well, I wasn't above trying to catch something that way, a time or two when the boson and Cap'n Randall was down there. And I *did* catch something. I know he—Cap'n Randall—*did* get Gentry's papers out of that box."

"Ha!" I cried. "That's more definite."

"Yes," she said. "But I couldn't find them. Oh, I searched, all right, times when he was out—but his chests are under heavy locks, and 'twasn't much use. But here—I've thought it over, and I've wondered if you'd think it advisable to swoop down on him with a search warrant from Magistrate McCullom."

"But you can't swear Randall actually has the will, can you?"

"No," she replied, "I can't. All I heard was something about 'them papers.'"

It was necessary, I judged, to have definite knowledge of the document's existence and location, before trying anything drastic; and, after some further discussion, Mrs. Webb agreed with me. We decided to wait for John Gould's arrival, with the intention of trying to overhear something more definite at that time; for, even though we were correct in assuming that Randall had the will, a bailiff's search might not only fail to disclose its whereabouts, but would cause the frightened conspirator to destroy it at his first opportunity. And so matters were standing when, three days later, a young woman was ushered into my private office at the shipyards.

She came toward me with a quick, springy step and her keen eyes full on mine.

She was about twenty years of age, with an exquisitely tinted countenance, eloquent of intelligence and fire; a woman who gave the impression of tallness, though I topped her by half a head; a woman with a strong figure, molded in long, lissom curves.

Her clothing was of inexpensive material, such as might have been worn by a maid or governess, and she wore a high-crowned, beribboned bonnet which came down to the tips of her ears and which covered her temples and shadowed her features. Those strands of hair visible to me were shot with the rich reds and browns one sees in the sheen of a turkey's wing; but her eyebrows were very black, with a habit, as I was soon to discover, of twitching humorously.

Just then, however, there was nothing humorous in her aspect. She had the chin of one who would dare say anything, and a wide but firm mouth; and she had an air of sophistication, though there was nothing suggestive of impropriety about her. Yet she was not quite assured as she faced me. Instead, she seemed a bit nervous; her color was quite high, and her eyes could not wholly hide the fact that she was laboring under excitement.

"Mr. David Waltham?" she said— a bit hurriedly and even somewhat tremulously. "My name is Mary Channing."

I BOWED and placed a chair for her. Her voice was very pleasing in tone.

"I know you'll think this most unusual," she went on quickly. "But doesn't the name recall anything to you? And—do I look like any one you have ever seen?"

2 A

"No," I said slowly, studying her closely. "I can't say—"

A shadow of disappointment fell over her face.

"Well," she said, "I was in hopes you might see some resemblance to the woman who died on your father's schooner—or so I've been told—many years ago. You see, I'm a niece of Miss Gertrude Channing."

I sat up then, abruptly. "A niece of Mrs. Gould's sister?" I cried.

"Yes!" she declared excitedly. "And oh, Mr. Waltham, I've come to ask you about the happenings on board that schooner."

"I wasn't aware that Miss Channing had any relatives on this side of the water," were my first words.

"You know her, then?" she asked, quickly.

"No," I replied. "My father had some letters from her, years ago, but I never met her."

"Neither have I," she said. And when I eyed her curiously at this statement, she blushed deeply and hurried on:

"But let me explain. I was born on this side of the water, and my parents died when I was young. Then—comparatively recently, I heard the Mary Louise story, through the woman who raised me. And she had heard it through a sea captain who was discussing Captain Gentry's death in Havana.

"I've come here from New York just on the strength of what I've heard —but it may be that I've come on a wild goose chase. I can tell, though, if you'll answer my questions."

"Why, I'll be glad to tell you what I know," I said. "But don't you think you might be a bit more explicit? Why do you want to know the exact facts?"

She dropped her eyes, and flushed anew. But in the next breath she raised her head, and eyed me with a faint trace of shame, and some defiance. "Suppose you were a girl, Mr.

Waltham, and circumstances had made you a barmaid—"

"Not a *barmaid?*" I cried. "You don't look—"

"Thank you, Mr. Waltham!" she said, rather dryly. But she went on, almost at once, "I didn't want to tell you of that. But suppose you were a barmaid — or had been a barmaid— and you heard there was a will which might change your whole life, and you you had been raised by a woman who ran a grog shop, who thought the life of a barmaid was quite good enough for you—well?"

"Why, I'll gladly tell you anything I know," I said.

"Oh, thank you!" she cried, smiling radiantly. "Then there *was* a will?"

At once I plunged into the Mary Louise story.

She quickly became serious again, and through it all she sat forward on the edge of her chair, with her eyes snapping, her hands clasping and unclasping, and her color ebbing and mounting. Now her eyes filmed with tears; now her lips closed grimly. But when I came to the latest developments her excitement increased, and her eyes shone like stars.

"That *does* put a new light on the matter!" she cried, when I had finished. "Why, I came here only expecting—" But here she broke off, abruptly, and stared out of the window, with her hands clenched. Suddenly she wheeled on me. "I feel sure that the will must still exist, and if I can I'm going to stay here and at least *try* to get it!" she declared.

"It's only a supposition, you must remember," I pointed out. "The baby is dead. Mrs. Gould's sister, your aunt, may be dead also. There'll be litigation and delay, even if you should get this will. You'd have a long, laborious process, too, in proving your identity—"

"I can prove that when the time comes!" she cut in. "And I'll take all the other risks. I realize it's a long

chance, but who ever won anything in this life without trying? I—I'm wondering if you'll help me?"

"I will do anything I can, Miss Channing."

She thought a moment. "You've said Mrs. Webb appears sincere in her desire to help Gentry's aunt regain her rights. You are sure of this?"

I nodded.

"Then will you give me a note to her—just a little introductory note, saying that I'm interested in the Mary Louise story, too?"

With this request I complied readily enough. I would have detained her for some explanation of what she had in mind; but here she begged my temporary indulgence, saying that she intended to ask Mrs. Webb for a place at the inn, and would gladly take anything that offered, even though she had to work as a scullery maid. "Further plans will depend on Mrs. Webb's attitude."

That noon, when I entered the inn, Mrs. Webb followed me to my sitting room.

She always wore a shell-back comb at the back of her shapely head, with a little lace cap atop her coil of gray hair; and this was now somewhat disarrayed, while the stiff little curls beside her ears fairly shook in her excitement.

"Mr. Waltham," she cried, "you sent that girl to me this morning. Do you know anything about her, 'cept what she told you?"

"Not a thing," I said—and I briefly outlined our conversation. As I talked, pink spots glowed in Mrs. Webb's stiff, parchmentlike cheeks, and her little piercing black eyes watched me closely. In their depths was a twinkle which I could not quite understand.

"Well, sir," she declared, "you get hard as nails running an inn, and don't trust much—but I'm taking *her* in on her say-so. You wait till you come home to-night, and you're apt to get a surprise." With which enigmatical statement she whisked away.

CHAPTER VII.

THE MASKED BARMAID.

THE surprise was waiting for me when I returned that evening, for I found Mary Channing behind the little semicircular bar—wearing a narrow black mask.

Her merry gray eyes, with flashes of green in their depths, twinkled at me through the slits; but when I seized the first opportunity for a word alone with her, and asked the reason for the mask, she said, demurely, "It's Mrs. Webb's idea. Ask her." Nor was Mrs. Webb very explicit. For when I asked her, she smiled at me, roguishly, and cried:

"Why, it's killing two birds with one stone. Causing a lot of talk, isn't it? And that makes trade."

"Are you two planning to rifle Captain Randall's quarters?" I asked.

"Why—I've already tried that. No use. But I'm going to do whatever I can to help her get that will, if it still exists."

It piqued me to sense that they were not taking me wholly into their confidence: and I found myself growing more and more curious about this masked barmaid. She had manifested an abhorrence for the calling — if it may be termed such—when she first talked to me; yet now I found her apparently enjoying it.

Of course I realized that she had a motive; but it irritated me strangely to see her serving other men with drinks. On the other hand, it pleased me when she came to serve me, and irritated me anew at the very fact that I had allowed myself to be pleased! For, after all, whether she was related to Miss Channing or not, the fact remained that she had been a barmaid, and was a barmaid still.

I determined to be no more than or- dinarily courteous when she came to serve me. But events so shaped themselves that my name was linked with hers before the second night had passed.

Her advent had caused a deal of talk. Questions about her and the mask flew quickly from tongue to tongue on the first night. And even the boson came out of his sulks, revealing his yellow, broken teeth in a grin.

"What mought I call ye?" he asked her.

"Why," she replied, laughing pleasantly, "you might call me Miss Teerious."

He slapped the table at this, and his grin widened. "And *when* mought I call on ye?" he cried.

"When you want a drink, and have money to pay for it!" she retorted instantly.

This was greeted with a guffaw from the onlookers; all the others took her chaffing in the best of good nature, but the boson sulked under his rebuke. So, on the next night, when he grew more than ordinarily drunk, he lurched up and attempted to snatch off her mask.

Turning so quickly that I could hardly follow her movements, she tripped the man, and sent him sprawling, full length on the floor. He came up again immediately, and I thought he was about to strike her; but by this time I had started toward him, and, coming at him side-on, I caught the tipsy brute with a shove that knocked him over.

He started up again, and whipped out his dirk; but I kicked this weapon from his hand, and knocked him unconscious with a blow to the chin.

In the hubbub that followed this, Mary spoke quickly into my ear.

"Thank you, Mr. Waltham," she said. "I'm sorry, though, you had to be dragged into a brawl over a barmaid."

Cold perspiration broke out all over me. Knocking down a bully in a woman's defense is one thing; engaging in a public brawl over a barmaid *was* quite another thing. I made some inarticulate rejoinder and hurried into the outer darkness.

THE boson apparently had no desire to seek open revenge, though he glowered whenever I came near him thereafter; but the brief affair caused a deal of talk, nevertheless, and I found myself the target for a deal of good-natured chaffing, particularly from Mrs. Webb.

My cheeks flush easily, and she seemed to find amusement in twitting me about the affair; nor did she seem to be impressed when I told her, rather heatedly, that I would have done as much for any woman.

And well she may have smiled! Before another week had gone by, the expected arrival of John Gould, and the Mary Louise mystery were secondary considerations with me. Mary assuredly made no attempt to thrust herself upon me; but there was that in her smile, or the demure flash of her eye, or her chuckling, infectious laugh which haunted me.

So matters were standing at the end of the week when, as I was sitting late one night in talk with a skipper, I noted Captain Randall being helped off to bed by two of his cronies. It was an unusual circumstance, since the old rascal seemed able, as a rule, to down great quantities of rum without showing the effects.

Mary had left the room, and Mrs. Webb had been serving Randall's table; but at the time I gave this little thought, and, shortly afterward, took leave of my friend, and went upstairs. There, as I turned into the dark hall which ran from north to south past my room, I bumped full into the masked barmaid.

"Heavens!" said she.

"Hell!" said I—though I had intended to say nothing of the sort.

She laughed low. "Well, Mr. Wal-tham," she said, "that is where all barmaids are headed for."

My hands had leaped up, at the moment of contact, so that I had caught her arms. Her tresses had fallen, in a thick cloud, down across her shoulders and breast, and I winced inwardly at the thrill their touch gave me.

"You seem to find me a source of amusement!" I said, with some heat. "That would be excusable, perhaps, if I had ever made any silly advances—"

"Silly, sir?" I felt her shoulders stiffen a bit. "You mean it would be silly of me to think you would ever make advances to me—a barmaid—don't you, Mr. Waltham?"

"I didn't mean anything of the sort!" I declared, heatedly. "I simply meant I haven't made any advances—"

"Then," she cut in, "perhaps we are to waltz?"

I lowered my hands instantly—and I wonder my ordinarily dark features did not illumine the hallway.

"That," I stammered, "was involuntary!"

"I understand," she said, quite primly. She started to move—and then stopped, with a little gasp. "I believe," she whispered then, "that my hair is caught on your coat button, sir."

In confusion my hands came up, and so encountered hers, groping for the button. My head whirled, and I seized her fingers, pressing them against my breast.

"Those involuntary hands!" she murmured.

"See here," I cried, "do you think you have treated me fairly?"

"A *barmaid*—treating Mr. Waltham *fairly?*" she whispered with a chuckle.

Knowing full well that she had read me as easily as a sailor judges the weather, I nevertheless hated to admit that the difference in our positions had been the cause of my resentment after that brawl. So I hastened on:

"I mean in the matter of the Mary Louise mystery. I know you two women are scheming. Won't you tell me what you have in mind?"

"Oh!" she whispered, quietly disengaging herself. She listened for a moment. "We have something in mind," she admitted. "But we weren't sure you would approve of it."

"But I want to help all I can."

"Well," she whispered, "had Captain Randall gone to bed when you came up?"

"Yes," I said. "He was very drunk."

She drew a sharp breath. "Mrs. Webb said she intended to put a drop in his grog," she whispered, excitedly. "And when he's fast asleep we're going to open the big chest in his quarters. We've found out that he keeps the key hanging from his neck. Now, sir, do you want to help in *that?*"

"I do," I said instantly. "I think it's justifiable in this case."

"Then come with me," she said, "to Mrs. Webb's rooms."

CHAPTER VIII.

BURGLARY.

GAINING admittance into the captain's quarters did not prove very difficult. After waiting until we were certain all the guests were in their rooms, and I had secured my derringer, we went down the back stairway and into a hallway which lay between the dining room and the quarters on the east side of the house.

Mrs. Webb produced a passkey, and we entered an empty room adjoining the captain's bedchamber. Here we paused and listened for the man's snores; and, assured that he was sound asleep, Mrs. Webb unlocked the intervening door, and we entered the bedroom.

"That drug'll hold him for some few hours," said Mrs. Webb, in low tones. "So we ain't got to worry none about *him.* But we've just got to have a light."

Forthwith she made haste to lower the windows, and draw the curtains; whereupon I busied myself with flint and tinder, and lit a candle.

Captain Randall lay on his bed, breathing stertorously. His friends had not troubled to undress him, having merely removed his shoes and his coat. So he lay flat on his back, with his arms outflung, and one leg dangling over the edge of the bed, pallid, unwholesome, disgusting.

It was the work of but an instant to open his shirt and disclose the string around his neck. Two keys—one small, and one large—were attached to it. He merely groaned a little when I lifted his head and slipped the string over it.

The captain's big locker was under his bed. It was a heavy box, painted blue, with a brass name-plate screwed into the top, and the corners were also bound with brass. With some difficulty I pulled it out beside the bed, and unlocked it.

"We must be careful now," Mrs. Webb warned, as I threw back the lid. "We've got to replace every article just so—'specially if we don't find that document."

"Ah, but it *must* be here!" Mary whispered. Her breathing was very rapid now, and her eyes shone feverishly.

"Well, we'll see, deary," Mrs. Webb rejoined, pressing the girl's hand.

Not much of interest to us was disclosed in the top tray: three account books in one compartment, and in the others some twists of tobacco, a brass telescope, an image of Buddha, several small, highly polished seashells, a Chinese fan, a silver-mounted pistol, a sailor's sewing kit, a bundle of charts, and some works on navigation.

Nor did we find any papers in the next tray, where the captain had spread a blue coat, almost new, decorated with brass buttons. But in the bottom of the locker, under an old waterproof coat, we found a small strong box.

" That small key!" Mrs. Webb whispered excitedly.

My fingers shook as I unlocked this box, for my hopes had been mounting with each passing second; and I scanned the contents eagerly. There were several letters, one bundle being tied with ribbon—a strange thing to find in this man's possession!—and a canvas sack filled with coins. There were also several folded papers. One of these proved to be a note from William Gentry to Andrew Randall for the sum of ten thousand pounds. But the packet we were seeking was not there!

" It just *must* be here somewhere!" Mary whispered, with a little catch in her voice.

" I'm not beaten yet!" Mrs. Webb declared grimly. " The old curmudgeon! What would he be wanting to see that Gould for, I'd like to know?" Whereupon she began a search of the bureaus and a closet in the captain's sitting room.

" More'n once he's shut hisself up here for a day at a time," she said vindictively. " That old fox! I think he's got another hiding place here somewhere."

We searched for a half hour or more, even trying the fireplace for loose bricks; but at last we were forced to acknowledge ourselves beaten, and I reluctantly replaced the contents of the locker, shoved it under the bed once more, and slipped the string over the captain's head.

" You see that?" Mrs. Webb whispered, pointing at a loaded pistol under the man's pillow. " He's never at ease, that man. Allus has that around. But there, deary, don't you give up."

She took Mary by the shoulders. *" That will was still around a year ago and Gentry had it."*

" What?" we cried in unison.

" Yes," said Mrs. Webb. " It was in that box of Gentry's I told you about," and she tossed her head with some little defiance. " I ain't a brag-

gin' of it, but I had my reasons for doing the same with Gentry as we have with this man to-night. That's how I saw that will. The whole packet you told me about, too.

" I didn't know just what it all meant. 'Twas only afterwards, when I got the Mary Louise story straightened out, that it all got clear to me. But I didn't say anything—just put it back and said nothing. I'd rather have crossed a typhoon than that Bill Gentry, anyway—and I've learned to think a deal before I put an oar in. But there you have it. It stands to reason that thing's here somewhere, doesn't it?"

" It certainly does!" Mary exclaimed, with manifest delight. " But where, where?"

" Looks like we'll have to wait until that young Gould gets here," said Mrs. Webb. " So let's to sleep."

This time, after listening carefully for signs of movement, we emerged into the lower hallway with the candle still lighted. And, when Mrs. Webb had preceded us, and Mary and I were standing on the second floor landing, near the stairs which led up to the servants' quarters on the third floor, I detained her a moment.

" Please take off that mask a minute before you go up," I pleaded. " I haven't seen you without it save once, and then you had that bonnet on that shaded your face."

" S-hhh!" she whispered, finger on lips, and quickly blew out the candle. Some one had started up the front stairway.

Whoever it was went directly to one of the rooms at the front of the house, but my chance was lost.

" Damnation!" I muttered.

She laughed low in her throat and I caught her by the shoulders.

" If I made you believe I didn't *want* to make advances, it was a lie," I whispered. " I'll not let you go until you promise to meet me somewhere."

" Why, you see me every day, sir."

"But, if you could slip out to the beach—"

"Where we can't be seen by others?"

"Why," I said, "isn't it the custom, when a man would talk to a maid, to seek seclusion?"

"And a mossy dell, I believe."

"Or a stile, perhaps," I rejoined, trying to meet her on her own ground.

"No!" she declared. "I tried that once, and, climbing over, I caught a splinter in my stocking."

"So!" I gripped her very fiercely. "You have had affairs!"

"Also pangs, Mr. Waltham. Those stockings cost me a crown."

"Please be serious!" I cried.

She laughed. "Well," she conceded, "if you'll escort me from here, I'll go with you to-morrow night, after I come off duty. That will be at ten, to-morrow night."

I groaned inwardly. Walking away with the barmaid from this inn! Unthinkable! And then, because the aroma from her hair was too alluring and too maddening for me, I buried my face in it and cried, "Kiss me!"

"Ah!" she whispered. "But osculation with barmaids is dangerous, Mr. Waltham."

I choked.

"But you may," she went on, "kiss my hand if you wish."

Her hand! A barmaid's hand! Shades of Cæsar! But I, David Waltham, kissed that hand, and counted it a privilege.

CHAPTER IX.

BILL GENTRY RETURNS.

NEXT morning, at the breakfast table, a serving maid told me that Mrs. Webb had been summoned during the night to go to Boston, where her son was very ill, but this news was quickly driven from my mind. For, when I stepped into the taproom on my way out to my office, there stood Roaring Bill Gentry, leaning on a pair of crutches!

He was now fifty and a bit gray, but there were the same tremendous shoulders, the identical beak of a nose, and the same keen, twinkling, crafty eyes, with the long eyebrows twisted upward, like a devil's horns.

He was wearing a smooth broadcloth blue coat, with shining brass buttons, and a fine cocked hat was tipped back on his great head; and though the leathery folds on his cheeks showed more cross-webbed lines, the years had made but little change in his bronzed, craggy features.

Sight of him brought me to a full stop, whereupon he spoke up.

"You seem to know me," he boomed out in his deep, melodious voice. "But I can't quite place you, somehow."

"It's been many years since you saw me," I said, rather curtly. And I told him my name.

"Not *Davy!*" he cried, with a start. An odd flicker of light appeared for a second in his shrewd, half-closed eyes. But in the same instant he had recovered himself and was smiling. "Well, by the Flying Dutchman, if it ain't, may I be scuttled! Tall as me and nigh as heavy, I should say, too."

And he chuckled. "Why, I'd ought to have known you—though it's a long time. Same long, dark face; same black eyes; same stubborn chin. But here, this ain't shipshape, this ain't! Let's have a wring of your flapper, Davy—unless you still feels like the old man did?"

"A handshake between us would be an idle pretense," I told him, thrusting my hands into my pockets.

He looked hurt and eyed me reproachfully.

"Does you and your dad still think I knocked you overboard?" he said.

"It looks very much that way," I said bluntly. "Appearances are certainly against you. The man who threw me over didn't have to hunt very far for me—though I admit I yelled and gave my position away. It might have been Captain Randall, of course; but with all that aside, how do you explain your ownership of the Cormoran?"

"Explain it?" he cried testily. "You, a builder and shipper, ask me that? With conditions the way they've been at sea the past twenty years or so? Why, by the Flying Dutchman! thousands of ships have changed hands at sea—and you know it."

"You got her before the war," I pointed out. "If you mean to infer that you captured her, I know better. The record of sale shows you bought her."

"Never denied that, did I?" he retorted. "But you see here: they called it privateerin' during the war, but I never saw much difference in privateerin' than flying the Jolly T. Roger out and out, by thunder!

"Well, now, I ain't denyin' I made a haul afore the war, when I got funds to buy that Cormoran—and I knows, too, I didn't have no piece of paper with me from the Continental Congress when I did it, 'cause there weren't no Continental Congress. Maybe"— and he became sarcastic—"I *shouldn't* have grabbed a chance to feather my own nest. King's ships was grabbin' cargoes right and left on the pretext of punishin' smugglers o' contraband; but maybe I should have overlooked them things, and let old King George grab it all. And when it comes to the pot callin' the kettle black, Davy, you and your father had several privateers out during the war, didn't you?"

"Exactly," I replied. "And ac-

counted for every capture, as well as the losses."

"Well," he shrugged, "that's neither here nor there. Point is: here we are bow on. Now you look old Bill straight in the eye. Do I look like one who would bring a slip on your cable?"

"No," I admitted, "you don't. But I'm older now, Bill Gentry, and looks don't mean as much to me as they did. But see here: there's your old Cormoran, riding out there beside the Elsie, taking on salt fish and some lumber for the sugar islands. We finished reconditioning the Cormoran this week. Have you heard about that yet?"

"Yes," he said with an oath. "My old aunt told me. I'll have her back afore sundown, and you can lay to it."

"Why," said I, "they told me Randall had your note."

"I never signed no note!" Gentry declared.

"Then," said I, looking at his crutches curiously, "it would appear that some one tried to have you put away, there in Havana."

"Maybe they did," he said shortly. "Knife stab in the back hurt the spine, and now I can't rightly use this right pin yet. But I'm making no charges, you understand—I'll deal with *him* first."

Just then the little hallway leading into Captain Randall's quarters opened, and he came out. Sighting Gentry, he stopped. All color fled from his face, and his jaw sagged, while his eyes were black and staring, for all the world like some guilty soul who has been brought, quite suddenly, face to face with the devil.

TO BE CONTINUED NEXT WEEK

" Then I'll get going again. Good night—and sorry!"

" Send Me the Bill "

It wasn't only the smashed bumper on his new car, but being gyped—
and before his best girl at that—that made of peaceful
Wilbur Grant a demon bill-collector

By ALBERT CHENICEK

IT wasn't Wilbur Grant's fault at all. He was driving along very carefully, mindful of the printed warning stuck to the windshield to the effect that a new car should not be driven faster than twenty-five miles an hour for the first five hundred miles, when —z-i-p-p!—this fellow in the big Pioneer Eight tried to pass him from behind.

It was a crazy trick, because there was a car coming fast from the opposite direction, and the man in the Pioneer tried to remedy his mistake by cutting in quickly.

There was a screech of metal scraping metal, and with consternation and dismay Wilbur saw his shiny new bumper bent hopelessly out of shape. Marge Potter, sitting next to him, let out a gasp and muffled scream. Wilbur said a number of things in an earnest way that made Marge look at him with a touch of admiration in her hazel eyes. She had been engaged to Wilbur for a considerable time, but never before had he so aptly said the right thing at the right time. Marge, you see, was quite modern.

The Pioneer stopped a short distance farther on and a man descended. Wilbur halted his car and got out and went to meet him. Wilbur was mad, very mad. He'd tell this bird something! It was no joke to have a brand-new car messed up that way!

But the stranger—a middle-aged man, nattily dressed, with a strong, clean-shaved face—didn't give Wilbur a chance to explode.

"My fault entirely!" he exclaimed, speaking very rapidly. "A shame, too —new car, isn't it? I'm mighty sorry. Tell you what you do—take it to some good shop and have it fixed up and send me the bill. I'll pay it. That's fair, don't you think? Here's my card."

Wilbur accepted the bit of pasteboard. He was somewhat flabbergasted. Usually, he knew, wordy arguments followed such incidents. This frank and complete acknowledgment of carelessness left him little to say. Still, he had a right to be angry.

"A fine way to drive," he began.

"I'm usually more careful," the stranger said, with a smile. "But this evening I'm in a big hurry. Mind— let me have the bill. There's nothing else, is there? Then I'll get going again. Good night—and sorry!"

He nodded his head and ran to the Pioneer. A second later the car moved off.

Pretty nice sort, Wilbur said to himself as he returned to where Marge waited. Neat dresser—probably well off. He glanced at the card and read:

S. SHANE
414 North Kilroy Street
Chicago

"Well, he's certainly going to get the bill," stated Wilbur emphatically, after they were on their way once more and he had told Marge what little there was to tell. "And it won't be any cheap, patch-up repair job, either!"

"That's all you have—the card?" Marge asked. "You didn't take down his license number?"

Wilbur frowned. Golly, he should have done that. Suppose—

"Suppose it wasn't *his* card he gave you, Wilbur!" As usual, Marge read his thoughts. "What are you going to do if he doesn't live at that address?"

Wilbur's momentary misgivings passed. "Pshaw!" he said. "Did he look like a petty cheap skate to you? There wasn't anything small about him that I noticed. See his car? A Pioneer Eight—that means money. And notice how he was dressed?"

Marge was not at all impressed. "He was dressed like a snappy sport, *I* think," she returned. "And that car —you told me yourself that every other Pioneer car in Chicago is owned by a bootlegger or a bandit—not many other people can pay the price."

"I was just kidding when I said that, Marge."

"Well," said Marge, "maybe Mr. Shane was just kidding, too."

"If he was he'll certainly regret it!"

She looked at Wilbur's determined face and said, "Big mans!"

Wilbur relaxed at that and colored. Kidding him again! "Well," he remarked, "I've been in Chi six months and nobody's put anything over on me yet. And nobody's going to. I know you think I'm just a hick in a big city, Marge, but—"

"Now, Wilbur!" she interrupted, snuggling closer to him, "I don't think anything of the kind!"

"You do!"

"Don't! But sometimes you are so —so careless. You don't use your head. Now this Mr. Shane—"

"I suppose you've met lots of smarter men since you came up from Brandon. Anyway, I used my head enough to pick you for Mrs. Wilbur Grant. But maybe you don't like that idea so much any more."

Marge said nothing.

A half mile of silence. Wilbur looked at her lovely profile and spoke contritely.

"Gee, Marge, I'm sorry. I'm just a dumb idiot!"

She was smiling again, her eyes aglow with a soft light.

"Do you suppose," she asked, "you

could kiss me without having a wreck?"

"Oh, well," said Wilbur, "I've got a bent bumper already."

DURING his lunch hour the following day Wilbur drove his little coupé to a garage and ordered repairs made.

"Don't mind the expense—do a first class job," he ordered the garage man. "The fellow who ran into me is paying the bill. I'll give you his name and address, and if you'll send him the statement he'll settle up."

The other looked at Wilbur and then scratched his head. "Well," he began, "I'd like to oblige you, but it's against our policy. We generally deal direct with the man who owns the car we fix. Just the policy of the house, y'understand."

"But—" said Wilbur.

"Look here," broke in the man, "your bus will be ready to-night. Suppose you come in and square up and then take the bill to this fellow. That way you can have the bus right away, see? He'll pay you and everything'll be jake. You see, if we deal with him by mail it'll take a couple of days, and a garage ain't no place for a young fellow's car to be parked these swell evenings. Especially if he's got a nifty girl, eh?"

Wilbur hesitated. "All right," he agreed. "Make it that way—not much difference. It'll be ready to-night? At about six? I'll be in then."

When he arrived at the place at the appointed time he found the bill was higher than he had expected.

"We checked up the front axle," said the garage man, "and found it was a little off, so we straightened 'er up. And the radiator had a couple of leaks that had to be soldered. Those side-swipes generally do more damage than a guy would think. But you should worry—it ain't nothing out of your pocket. And the car's good as new."

Wilbur paid somewhat reluctantly.

Twenty-two dollars and thirty-seven cents. He'd get the money back, of course, but he didn't like the idea of paying out that much personally, even for a short time.

When he saw Marge—they lived at the same boarding house—she asked a number of questions, but after she had learned how the matter stood she made no comment. Wilbur had the uncomfortable feeling that she was keeping an "I told you so!" poised on her lips.

Consequently, when they started out in the car after supper, there was too much elaborately careless confidence in his words:

"First thing on the schedule is a stop at 414 North Kilroy. Won't take a minute to get the cash or a check from Mr. Shane."

"And then," said Marge, "we'll go for another nice drive out of the city, like the one last night!"

The house, when they reached it, after several apparently rational Chicagoans had given them conflicting directions as to the location of Kilroy Street, proved to be a two story brick building of modest appearance.

With a queer, tense feeling in the region of his heart, Wilbur left Marge in the car and went up the stone stairs. In the vestibule he found two buttons over two mail boxes, and he felt immensely relieved when he saw the name, "S. Shane," on a card.

"I knew he was all right!" he told himself cheerfully, and vigorously applied a finger to the black circle.

As he waited, a door to his left opened and an elderly woman came out aud extracted some mail from the box that wasn't Mr. Shane's. Her glance at Wilbur was curious, and then she asked:

"Are you calling on the people upstairs?"

"Yes," said Wilbur. "Mr. Shane."

Her eyes went to the box. "That's the name. But he doesn't live here any more—moved out this morning."

Wilbur stared. "Moved—out?" he repeated.

"Yes. I don't know where he went." Her voice became sympathetic. "I imagine you'll have a difficult time locating him. Several gentlemen, who looked like bill collectors, called this afternoon."

In a half daze Wilbur returned to the car and Marge. She saw that something was wrong, but she said nothing. Wilbur started the car and then turned to her.

"He moved to-day," he stated grimly. "You were right—I'm the original dumb-bell! But this ain't the end of it! I'll find him and—"

Marge patted him on the arm. "Never mind, Wil," she said. "That old swindler will meet his Waterloo some bright day. Let's forget him."

DURING the next two days Wilbur was a man of one idea, and that idea was to find a way to catch the elusive Mr. Shane. Somehow he managed to get his work at the office done satisfactorily, but routine habit was responsible for that.

It wasn't so much the twenty-two dollars and thirty-seven cents, though the loss of the money hurt; the real wound was the fact that he had been so easily "played for a sucker." Undoubtedly, had not Marge been aware of how he had let himself be tricked, Wilbur would not have felt so badly about it. But, as he had said on the night of their first drive in the new car, he felt she thought him less keen, less able to take care of himself than other Chicagoans, and this confounded affair would strengthen her belief, whatever she might say to the contrary.

Perhaps Wilbur was entirely too sensitive on the point. And perhaps that sensitiveness proved that Marge was not far wrong.

Though he had lived in Chicago less than a half year, Wilbur liked to think himself a real big city man, and he never told any one, when it could be avoided, that he had been born in a small town.

When Marge had come to Chicago to be near him, and landed a job as a stenographer, Wilbur, from the very first, had discouraged any conversation about their earlier days in Brandon. All that was in the past, he said; small time, Main Street stuff.

Marge undoubtedly had been impressed by his manner and bearing, those first weeks after her arrival when he took her around and showed her the city. But later she had apparently decided that, at bottom, he was just the same Wilbur Grant she had always known, and thereafter she frequently made comments that deflated and depressed him.

Defensively—as in the case of Mr. Shane—he had boasted that no slick Chicagoan had ever fooled him. And now he felt that he appeared ludicrous in her eyes.

It was a well-nigh intolerable situation, and Wilbur was desperately resolved to find a remedy. It never occurred to him that he had really asked for the blow by his unnecessary bragging; nor did he realize that Marge's kidding was entirely harmless, and that she liked him even though he was just a Brandon boy in Chicago.

Wilbur was making a not uncommon mistake; he thought her opinion of him had been lowered, whereas it was only his wounded ego crying for the salve of revenge.

No way out came to him until the second evening, and even then it took some time to disclose itself. He was reading a newspaper when his eyes came to rest on an editorial rebuking the police in scathing terms for their failure to catch a murderer and liquor racketeer named Stroop—"Snappy Sam" Stroop.

His attention was held by the alliterativeness of the name. Stroop—Snappy Sam. Stroop—Stroop—

And then his memory furnished a bombshell.

A week or so before he had seen a picture of Sam Stroop on the back page of a morning newspaper—and the man in the picture had been Mr. S. Shane!

Almost overwhelmed, Wilbur excitedly acquainted Marge with his belated discovery of Shane's true identity.

"But Wilbur," Marge exclaimed, unconvinced, "are you sure?"

"Absolutely!" he told her with conviction. "Why, I can shut my eyes and see that picture plain as anything! 'Snappy Sam Stroop Wanted for Murder in Bootleg War.' And there were a couple of other pictures of the detectives hunting him.

"'Nother thing," he went on. "Don't you remember you said he looked like a snappy dresser—a sport? And then think of the name he took— S. Shane. A couple of S's. His real name has the same initials. I read somewhere that when crooks take aliases they often use their right initials. It's—it's psychological!"

"It's probably because their baggage has their initials," said common sense Marge. "But I imagine you're right —he did seem to me like a man who would like to be called Snappy Sam."

Then she added: "Knowing he's a bootlegger and a murderer doesn't help much, though, does it? The police haven't been able to find him, and so you haven't much of a chance, and I wouldn't want you to anyway."

Wilbur's sophistication came to the fore. "Oh, that doesn't always mean what it seems to mean. If some cops heard certain whispers, they'd be unable to find Lake Michigan. Shane— Snappy Sam—was driving right along the road like a respectable citizen when we met him, wasn't he? I mean, he didn't look as if he was scared of being arrested."

"But Wil, he's a murderer! Suppose you should find him, and he began shooting—"

Wilbur rose to the occasion magnificently. "Let him shoot! Nobody can get away with what he tried to put over on me, as if I was a simple-minded hayseed!"

"Isn't your life worth more than twenty-two dollars and thirty-seven cents?"

He closed the net about himself by saying: "It isn't the money, Marge— it's the principle of the thing."

Wilbur's plan developed rapidly after that. It was on Ogden Avenue, leading southwest out of the city, that the collision with Snappy Sam had occurred, and Wilbur intended to patrol that stretch of concrete every night. Sooner or later Shane—or Stroop— would drive that way. There were a number of road houses in that section, and Sam was interested in road houses, according to the newspapers. He'd probably been on his way to one the night of the meeting.

Wilbur believed that Snappy Sam was not exerting himself in an effort to elude the police, because such exertion was unnecessary. Sam would drive along as openly as any law-abiding citizen; to spot him would require only patience. And the fact that he drove a Pioneer Eight would help.

Wilbur's plans went no further than that; what would happen when the meeting took place he did not know, and he tried to keep his mind a blank on that point. Tried—but did not entirely succeed. There were times when he visualized a battery of six-guns spattering lead in his direction.

Wilbur wished he'd never bought the new car.

THEY saw Snappy Sam Stroop— alias Shane—late the third evening of their watch on Ogden Avenue.

Marge, who had insisted on accompanying Wilbur, saw the Pioneer Eight first. Wilbur immediately gave chase, forgetting entirely about the dangers of driving faster than twenty-five miles per hour in a new car, but the big sedan would have got away had not a red light abruptly halted all traffic.

Wilbur, pulling up as close as possible, discovered that the driver of the car was really S. Shane, and his pulse accelerated. When the light changed to green and they started off again, he gave the little coupé all the gas it would take.

Even so they lost the big car—but saw it again five minutes later. It was parked in the court of a road house. Though no one was in it, Wilbur knew it was the same car, because he had noted the license number. Without delay he stopped alongside it and prepared to get out.

But Marge sought to restrain him by grasping his arm tightly.

" Wilbur!" she pleaded, genuinely alarmed. " Don't go in there!"

Then hurriedly, when she saw he was still determined: " Wil, it's foolish —unnecessary! We know he's here— why can't you telephone the police? They'll make a raid and catch him!"

Just for a moment Wilbur hesitated. He might do what she suggested. Then abruptly he shook his head. Twenty-two dollars and thirty-seven cents had to be collected. Stubbornly he insisted on that. He wasn't going to be played for a sucker.

Fear and near-panic gripped Marge as she watched him strike toward the entrance of the road house. But then when he disappeared from sight she relaxed, became calmer, and began to feel a definite pride in him. Whatever his faults, Wilbur was no coward!

As for Wilbur, it could not be said that he had the appearance of a conqueror when he stepped into the glittering interior of the building. Nor did he feel like a conqueror. The lights, the chattering of the people at the numerous tables, the barbaric tempo of the music coming from an unseen orchestra—all these momentarily confused him.

Just as a sleek-looking man in evening clothes approached him, he caught sight of the man Shane sitting alone at a table in a secluded corner. On the instant Wilbur lost all his indecision. His jaw set, he resolutely strode across the floor.

Shane saw him coming, and appeared to be a trifle puzzled, as though he were trying to place him. Wilbur stopped, leaned across the table, and said belligerently:

" I want to see you a minute, Mr. Shane!"

Shane frowned. " Keep your voice down!" he snapped. " If it's important, I'll—"

" You bet it's important!"

The other stood up. " Follow me," he instructed, and led the way out of the dining room and down a narrow hallway that was lighted by colored globes hidden in silk flowers. Numerous doors were in the walls, and before one he stopped.

" We'll go in here," he said.

The sleek gentleman in evening clothes had followed after them, and now he protested. " Not in there!" he exclaimed. " That is reserved. Down the hall farther—"

Shane had opened the door and looked inside. " Nobody here," he interrupted. " This will do. We'll use it only a few minutes. Beat it, sheik."

Inside the private dining room, Shane closed the door and turned to Wilbur.

" Now what the devil do you want?" he demanded.

Wilbur flared. " I want what's due me, you crook! Thought you could get away with something, didn't you? You're going to pay up—"

He reached into his pocket to get the garage bill. After that things happened rapidly.

Shane leaped backward and his right arm swung to his hip. Wilbur then realized the man had thought he was going for a weapon—and knew that if he didn't act fast he was done for.

He jumped and was just in time to force Shane's gun hand up in the air.

Breathing hard, they tussled, lurched about the room. Then Shane, raising a knee quickly, caught Wilbur in the stomach and drove the breath from him. Wilbur lost his grip. In a flash the man had him about the throat—flung him away.

Off balance, Wilbur skidded across the room and hit the wall with a terrific jar. And the panel he struck caved in with a ripping sound!

From out the ragged aperture leaped a man. Gun in hand, he sailed over Wilbur. The latter never had a very clear recollection of what followed.

The roar of guns—flashes of fire—a shrill ear-splitting whistle—the smell of powder—shouts—from somewhere, far off, the hysterical screams of women—pounding feet—hoarse orders—and then suddenly comparative silence and cessation of movement.

As Wilbur struggled to his feet he became aware of the fact that the small room was crowded with men—men who bore all the marks of plainclothes detectives. And then the man Shane stepped up to him.

"Not hurt?" he asked. "That's good. I don't know who you are or why you came here to see me, but you certainly were a big help, young fellow! I never thought this dump had double walls—we never would have caught Snappy Sam if you hadn't smashed through!"

Wilbur reached for a chair. "Snappy Sam!" he repeated. "Why—aren't *you* Snappy Sam Stroop?"

"Me? Hell no! I'm Sam Shane, and I'm a detective. I—"

He stared at Wilbur intently. "Say, I make you now! You're the fellow whose bumper I smashed the other night!"

"Yes," said Wilbur, "I wanted to have you pay the bill—that's why I came here."

"My God!" said Shane. "And the joint was surrounded!"

Considerably embarrassed, Wilbur explained, and his explanation appeared to stun the detective.

"You thought you were coming to face Snappy Sam—and you weren't armed? Boy, you had guts! But why the devil didn't you send the bill by mail—that's the way I expected to get it. I told the mailman where to forward my mail."

"Well," said Wilbur, "I never thought of that. I guess I didn't use my head."

"You used it plenty going through the wall," Shane returned. "We got a hot tip that Sammy was going to be here to-night, but I couldn't see him anywhere when I came in. I think," he added, "that maybe I'll be able to get you a little slice of the reward. If that was your girl you were with the other night, I guess you'll be able to use a couple of hundred bucks, eh?"

"I guess so," said Wilbur.

HE told Marge everything while on their way back to the city. "You were right," he concluded. "I'm dumb—but I'm a fool for luck!"

Marge looked at her engagement ring thoughtfully. Then she smiled.

"No," she said, "but I think I am!"

THE END

"Kill Him, Jimmie—or I Will"

By W. WIRT

Author of "Take Him for a Ride"

Chicago and the rum ring! A story of the underworld—and of a Federal agent who searched out its darkest and most dangerous corners on a relentless trail of vengeance

Novelette—Complete

CHAPTER I.

THE BLACK SEDAN.

THE three men sitting in the closed car parked along the curb of one of the quiet residential streets north of Wilson Avenue, Chicago, were watching the infrequent passers-by. It was in the middle of the afternoon and there were not many people on the street. One or two nursemaids with children—a woman or two going shopping—a canvasser going from door to door.

The man sitting at the wheel turned a little, "I sure hope he don't show," he said, uneasily, "I don't give a hoot about any ordinary guy, but puttin' a Federal dick on the spot is something else again."

"You and me both," answered one of the men on the rear seat, who had a Browning sub-machine gun resting between his legs. "They will chase you from here to hell—this lad's buddies. I got two minds to lam it, right now."

"You better get three minds, feller," sneered the man beside him. "What do you care who this bird is? You must want to get beat to death with a couple of nightsticks, don't you? Do ya' see that window, with the shade up an inch, across the street? Well, the big boys are right there to see that we go through. Laugh that off. You better come clean with that gat—or you'll be huntin' for a whole bone in you by night."

"Aw, I ain't got cold feet," protested the other, "only I wish these damn elbows would do their own killin'—they got practice enough. This here—"

"Heads up," said the man at the wheel. "Here he comes!"

2 A

As he was reeling he fired once, straight into the open window

The two men in the rear eased down on the floor of the big limousine and to all appearances it became simply an expensive car with a chauffeur.

The well-dressed young man who had turned the corner from the elevated station, sauntered down the sidewalk toward the car. That there was absolutely no thought of danger in his mind was apparent. He stopped just before reaching the car and lighted a cigarette, tossing the burned match almost under the wheels.

He was a well set up, tanned young man, with laughing blue eyes and a swing to his shoulders as he walked that told of days in the service. As he passed the car he looked carelessly at the driver, who returned the look, just as carelessly.

He had passed the car by about six feet, when the back window slid down noiselessly on oiled sashes and the muzzle of the Browning sub-machine gun came out, also a heavy automatic pistol held in the hand of the other man.

There was no warning—no fair play —no giving the young man a chance of any kind. But some sixth sense must have told him of deadly danger, because

3 A

he whirled, his hand went under his left armpit and came out with a Colt .45 just as the heavy, steel-jacketed bullets from the Browning and the automatic began tearing and shattering his body.

As he was reeling back, he fired once, straight into the opened window. Then his dead body crumpled to the pavement. The window went up, the big car started and disappeared around the corner. As it did, the man who had handled the Browning said, "My God— he got Tony—between the eyes."

Old ex-Ranger Captain Yancey of Texas was visiting his niece in Chicago on his way back home. She lived in the 600 block, and he was sitting at the second floor window comparing Chicago and all big cities very unfavorably with Texas, when it happened. As the shots came, he stood up and his right hand flashed down to his side, only to stay there. There was no much-notched old ivory-handled .41 to meet his grip.

"Doggone," he said, plaintively, "I could have got me—" and he turned and ran to the door.

When he reached the body, there was

already a little crowd, standing back, watching the blood seep slowly out on the concrete sidewalk from the body of the young man, whose blue eyes were no longer laughing.

As the old Ranger captain bent over the shattered form, two burly men were still peering out of the window across the way, through the inch the shade was raised. One of them whispered, "Here comes Hogan," as a uniformed copper came running up. "He'll tend to this—let's go, Mac. That'll teach those buzzards to lay off us."

"What's this?" said Hogan, as he came up. "Get back, there, you people. What came off? Did you see it?" he demanded of Yancey.

"Well, suh," drawled Yancey, "I was sittin' in the window yonder and I heard the shots, that's all. I reckon it happened too fast for anyone to see much. The young gent here, he fell down and a car drove off."

"Yeah?" said Hogan. "Ring for the dead wagon, Bill," to another officer who got off a motorcycle. "Some guy has been taken for a ride. Did you get the car number, now?" to Yancey.

"No, suh," answered Yancey, who could still put a bullet in the heart of a man at sixty yards. "My eyes are plumb bad. I reckon I was looking at the young gent a lot."

"What's your name?" demanded Hogan.

"My name is William C. Yancey," answered the old Ranger captain, mildly. "I'm from the country, I don't reckon I'll stay much longer with such goin's-on. 'Taint safe to—"

Hogan sneered. "Better get back to the sticks," he growled. "Go on, now —the bunch of ye. Move on—or I'll take some of ye to the station house."

THE driver of the death car was sitting in one of the back rooms of what used to be Powers and O'Brien's saloon and gambling house on Madison Street. The two men who had watched from the window were with him. They were hard-faced, hard-eyed men; one had the baggy pouches under his eyes that told of disordered living. Both were well dressed and had the arrogance and command that goes so often with official authority. They were detective sergeants, working out of the ' front office.'

"What did Tony want to butt in for," snarled McGinnis, the man with the pouches under his eyes. "Smith could have done it without him. Now he's croaked, the damn fool."

"It saved us the trouble, Mac," said Haven, his partner, with a sneer. "That wop was due for a ride pretty soon himself. Here's the jack for you and Smith, Johnnie."

The driver looked at the two fifty-dollar bills flung on the table. "What's this?" he growled. "Fifty dollars— for killin' a—"

"Perhaps you'd like to come over to the Harrison Street station with us, instead?" purred Haven. "Down in the little room."

"Put it back in your pocket," said Mac. "This rat is due for a fanning, anyway. Let's take him down and give it to him. He's acting like he was hot —he needs it."

"No—no—" stammered the driver, shrinking back from the cold, hard eyes boring into him. He knew what it meant down in the little room. He knew of strong, well men taken in there in the basement of the old Harrison Street station, with three or four big detectives or policemen, night sticks and blackjacks swinging idly—and knew how they were carried out, a broken, bloody, cringing mass of broken bones and torn flesh.

"Sure, it's plenty," he gasped. "I ain't kickin'. For Cripes' sake, fellers, don't do it. I got lots of good dope for you! I'm right, ain't I? Mac—you know I'm right! I'll do anything you say. What's the use of beating me up? I'll drive any car and—"

"That's something else again," said

Haven, putting the two fifties in his pocket. "As long as you feel that way about it, we'll put off the little room stuff for a day or so."

"Aw, hell," said Mac, his eyes showing the cruel, almost insane desire that always possessed him to see suffering and pain—and to inflict it. "We can get plenty of drivers, Ted. This heeler is overdue, right now."

"Honest, Mac," implored the driver. "I ain't done a thing except work for you fellers. Please, Mac— Hey, I want to tip you guys to something. If I'm right, will you lay off me?"

"He's gettin' good," sneered Mac. "Propositionin' us. What do you know —rat? Come on with it, quick!" and the burly detective took a step forward toward the much slighter, shorter driver, who cringed back, throwing up his right arm.

"Don't," he pleaded, "I—Smith, he began beefin' about knockin' off a Government cop and how you guys ought to do your own killin' and that he was—"

"What was that you said about knockin' off a Government cop? What Government cop? When? Where was he knocked off? What the hell do we know about it, you damn snowbird?" demanded Haven, angrily. "Mac, I guess you're right. We better take this mack in with us."

The driver shivered. He knew that his own life, that would be beaten out of him, depended on what he said.

"I don't know nothin' about it," he said. "I just come up from downstate and I heard some lads talkin' and one of them was this Smith guy. He was drunk and shoutin'—"

"Yeah?" interrupted Mac, "and did he mention our names?"

"Not while he was talkin' about the cop. He did when he began to beef about things in general."

Haven began to whistle softly "and they brought a little star dust down to make the shamrocks grow." Mac started to say something, then closed his mouth. He knew that when Haven began to whistle that old tune, his evil, clever brain was planning. The driver had heard that Haven did that, and almost always right after, men were killed. He could only hold his breath and hope.

Mac knew that Haven had the brains of the partnership—what Mac didn't have in that respect he made up for with brute courage and cold mercilessness. Haven was not behind him in either of those respects. They both looked upon Chicago as their legitimate hunting ground—and hunted in it as two black jaguars would in the South American jungle.

Haven stopped whistling. "I think that Johnnie here is a good kid, Mac," he said, smoothly. "He don't do any running around. You live with your wife and kids, don't you, Johnnie?"

"Yes," said the driver. "I live out in Morton Park. I tend to my business and then go home—honest, I do."

"That's what I thought," answered Haven. "You're all right, Johnnie. That was a good tip-off you gave us about Smith. I'll tell you what you do —you go and—here, you take this jack," and he took the two fifties from his pocket, "and give it to Smithie— tell him we said that he did a good job, see, and that we will let him cut in on that Hammond stuff in a day or so. Then, Johnnie, to-morrow morning, you bell him around to Mike's—we'll drop in and give you both a job to do out on the road. When you get out there—put him on the stop and you can keep the money yourself. Don't be afraid of the little room, Johnnie. Mac and I were only kiddin' you to see how much nerve you had, weren't we, Mac?"

"Certainly," said Mac, promptly. "We know you're right, Johnnie."

"I'll have him there," said the driver, wiping the sweat from his forehead. "My Gawd, fellers, I thought you meant it. I'll take him for a ride."

"All right, Johnnie, get going. To-morrow morning at Mike's. Don't forget, Johnnie?"

"I won't," said Johnnie from the door.

"And then what?" questioned Mac, after the door closed.

"Why, then," said Haven, softly, "at the place where these two desperate gunmen and gangsters are waiting to commit a cowardly murder, there will come along the brave and fearless Detective Sergeants McGinnis and Haven, accompanied by several other equally brave and fearless police in the strict performance of their duty, and I am very much afraid that the two gunmen, who will put up a resistance to arrest, will be killed by the officers." He smiled at his partner.

Johnnie had gone down the stairs, half blindly, praying almost aloud, his parched lips moving. "Oh, God—let me get home in time. If I can get Nett and the kids out in the country, the old man will take care of them. I can duck somewhere if they're safe. I know what they're going to do—they didn't fool me, the dirty—"

He reached the street and made his face resume its usual reckless air. His car was parked in front and he stood by it for a moment, watching the crowd go by, lighted a cigarette, got in unhurriedly and drove west, out of the loop. Once clear of the traffic, he stepped on the gas and drove recklessly.

CHAPTER II.

CONSEQUENCES.

LATE that night, as Johnnie swung his car in to the curb in front of his house, a man got up from the steps and came sauntering out. "Hello, Johnnie," he said. "I been waiting around for you a hell of a long time. Misses and kids away?"

"Yeah," said Johnnie, getting out. He knew that in coming back to the house he had lessened his chance to get away by about ninety per cent, but he had not figured that Haven and Mc-Ginnis would put any kind of a cover on him before morning. He had thought that he could come back to the house in safety to get some clothes he would need on his trip South—as he had left most of his money with his wife in Indiana.

The man who had been waiting for him was a deputy sheriff named Cohen, whom Johnnie knew was close to Haven.

"I took them down in the country for a spell," Johnnie went on indifferently. "Her old man is sheriff down there and is kinda sick. Let's go in and get a drink. I got some of that last beer that come up."

"Good idea," said Cohen, "only I don't go much on beer. Got any hard stuff?"

"Yeah, plenty, any kind you want," and as they walked toward the house Johnnie asked, "What do you know?"

"Not much," said Cohen, with a yawn. "Met Haven and he said that he wanted me along on one of them things to-morrow, and for me not to get tied up no place. They're goin' to bring up a shipment from the South, I guess, and he wants me to ride it in, maybe."

"An' you get half a grand for it," said Johnnie. "I sure wish I could get me a piece of tin to wear and get in on some of the heavy jack. I'm satisfied though, now."

"Yeah?" said Cohen. "Well, I didn't have a damn thing to do, and I didn't want to hang around the office. Old McMullen might send me out with a warrant. Thought I'd come out and play around with you."

"Glad to have you," said Johnnie, as he opened the door.

He knew that Haven had sent Cohen to see that he kept his appointment at Mike's, and that if he couldn't shake him his chances of living beyond the next day were few, but he grinned cheerfully as he brought out bottles and glasses, trying to decide whether or not to take a chance and try and kill Cohen that night or let it ride until morning.

He knew that Cohen, for all his seeming carelessness, was watching his slightest move and that his gun swung in a holster just below his right hip. He could get to it faster than Johnnie could to his, in his back pocket.

"We'll make a night of it," said Cohen. "Your missus is away. I'll call up a couple of skirts I know and we'll pull a party."

"Not for me," said Johnnie. "I'm off that stuff, boy. Let's you and me just stag it. I'll play you some stud after awhile. I got me some drivin' to do in the morning."

"Fair enough," agreed Cohen, affably. "I'm getting sick of molls myself."

Johnnie, who had driven many a death car, spoke the truth when he said that he had some driving to do in the morning. He could not shake Cohen, and all through the night he had no chance to kill him. Cohen matched him drink for drink and more, his little beady eyes never losing their alertness.

In the morning he drove with Johnnie to pick up Smith, then to Mike's, where, a little later, Haven and McGinnis came in. Johnnie and Smith were told to be on the Sheridan Road at noon, near the corner of a certain street. A gray roadster with an Indiana license would come slowly by and the driver would ask them the road to Milwaukee. They were to kill both the driver and the passenger.

The driver of the gray car, Haven said, would get out to look at his engine, thinking that the passenger was the one to be put on the spot; but they were to kill both—the driver having, as Haven said with an evil sneer, "become a flying jib," a talkative drunk.

Smith, not knowing that he had talked any while drunk, grinned cheerfully and said, "Leave it to us, chief." This kind of killing he liked to do.

Johnnie had joined in. He would kill Smith, and keep on going north until he reached friends in Milwaukee, who would hide him and pass him along.

If Haven or McGinnis ever got to him, he'd claim that he got scared and ran; that some men in a passing car had seen him. For Smith's life he didn't care. He was a gangster and a crook like himself.

He drove with Smith out on the Sheridan Road to the place ordered, drew in to the side of the road, turned to Smith, who sat in the rear, the Browning sub-machine gun again under his knees, and said, "Hey, Smithy, we're early. I don't like to be here with all these cars comin' by. Let's unload and walk down to the shore. We got an hour, anyway."

"Suits me," said Smithy. "Wait till I pack this cannon," and he stepped to the gun. As he did, Johnnie shot him through the head. The young killer straightened up, his gun still in his hand, and turned to the wheel. His foot was already down on the gas when a sleet storm of lead poured into the car, shattering glass and woodwork. From all sides it came, front and rear, as pitiless and accurate as had the rain of death that had poured on Federal Agent Wilson such a short time before.

As Johnnie sank over the wheel, hit in a dozen places, dying, he saw the flash of brass buttons and police uniforms and heard Haven shout, "Go in, men! Don't let them get you! Shoot to kill!"

Johnnie raised his head amid the flying glass and lead and lifted his gun. His last thought was—if he could only shoot square into the face of Haven, he would be—then the light went out for him forever.

JIMMIE HOWARD sat in the living room of what he called his bachelor apartment on H. Street in Washington, his sleeves rolled up, winding a silk line on a reel. His thin, serious young face, with solemn black eyes and bony "Duke of Wellington" nose, lighted up with the happiness known only to a fisherman who has a place to go where the fish are biting, and plenty of good tackle, friends waiting for him, and thirty days' leave—all at the same time.

His friends called him "Sad Parson," or "Sad," or "Parson," just as it happened, because of that serious, melancholy look, half sad, half sleepy. Jimmie only grinned. That half asleep air had badly fooled several men. His friends all knew that inside "that medieval monk's mug" of his, as one of them expressed it, there was a gay, careless, laughing spirit, who thought life a huge joke to be laughed at and lived.

He was from Maine, and, as he used to explain in defense of his "medieval monk's mug":

"One of my great-great-granpas was a Presbyterian elder, darn him. He used to go around with a Bible and convert the Penobscot Indians, and when he couldn't convert 'em he'd smack 'em down. He tried to convert a female of the tribe, some relation to old Powhattan, and instead of his doin' her, she made the old boy lay his Bible down, they tell me.

"Anyway, that accounts for my mug. It's the elder's map, with a little dash of Injun that crops out once in awhile. Yeah, he married her, you poor fish. And darn lucky to get the chance. Boy, you ought to see a picture some artist painted of my great-great-grandma. She was one bearcat for looks."

Now, he sat at the long living room table, his spirit singing to him of fish biting and the cool of the north woods.

He heard a key turn in the outside door and rose. There was only one person in the world that had a key to his door beside himself, and that was Sally Wilson, the girl he was going to marry. When Jimmie was away, she would come over and give his rooms a

straightening up, with loving little pats for his coats and things as she hung them up.

She was chief of a stenographic section in the Treasury Department, and there were few afternoons after four thirty when she could not be found with Jimmie, if he were in Washington.

Jimmie looked at the clock. "What are you doing off so early, woman?" he called, as the door opened. "Andy'll be tying a can to you. Come on in. I'm fixing my tackle and—"

Sally Wilson had stumbled into the room, her pretty face drawn and white, her blue eyes dry and staring, her lovely tremulous mouth already working with the grief she had so proudly tried to hide while coming to Jimmie.

"Jimmie," she said, in a cold, strained voice, unlike her usual slow amused drawl and gently soft tones, "Charley—is—is dead!" And she held out her slim young arms to him.

Jimmie had her in his arms, was holding her tight in an instant. "Steady, old girl. I've got you safe. Steady, stop shivering so, Sally, darlin'. Come and sit down with Jimmie." He picked her up, carried her to the big old rocking-chair by the table and sat down with her in his arms.

"I—oh, Charley, my big brother. They killed him. He used to take care of me when I was little. They said his body—was—" Her voice began to rise and she clung to Jimmie like a frightened child.

"Cry, Sally," commanded Jimmie, holding her tight. "Cry, you must. Be a brave girl now—Charley would want you to be! Put your head on my shoulder and just cry."

The relieving tears came finally and with her soft, warm form tight to his. Sally between sobs told Jimmie what Major Scott had hurried over to the Treasury Building to tell her.

"Tighten up, Sally," Jimmie said, patting her heaving shoulder and kissing the top of her proud little boyish head. "I loved Charley—next to you

—better than any one in the world, and I know that he wouldn't want to see you grieve so. You're a Wilson from Kentucky—thing to do now is to plan to get them. Child—stop crying for Jimmie—Charley would want us to be getting them—you can cry a lot and everything later."

"Do you—do you think he is really just over the hills, Jimmie, dear, waiting for us?"

"I don't think anything about it—I know it—and I'll bet that he's madder than nine hundred dollars right now at us for not getting busy. Listen, Sally —he's just the same as gone on one of those long trips of his—I tell you."

Jimmie Howard soothed and petted her for a long time before Sally became anywhere near normal. Finally, she said: "Yes, Jimmie, I'm better now—see? I'm not crying any more, honest, I'm not. Major Scott said to tell you to go to Chicago and—find out—who—who killed—"

"Steady, old-timer. You told me how the Wilson women used to send their men out in the old feud days with the cross already marked on their gun stocks. Are you any less a Wilson than they?"

Sally's head came up at last. "No," she said proudly, "I'm one of them, Jimmie, dear. Will you go and—"

"I'd have gone anyway—division chief or not—and now I'm being sent. I'll get 'em for you—and uncle, Sally."

"Then," said Sally Wilson, firmly, "I am going to take my thirty days' annual and go, too."

"What?" said Jimmie, in alarm. "No, you're not. You'd fog me up and you couldn't help me, Sally."

"I won't interfere with you, Jimmie. I'll—I want to be there when you—get them. I'll just get a quiet place and—it might be that I can help in some way. I'll—I'll change my name, Jimmie."

Jimmie looked sternly at the lovely tear-stained face held so close to his. He knew that she would be in no danger, and that he could give her some things to do that would keep her well on the outside. He hoped that it would take her mind off her grief.

"All right, Sally," he said gently, kissing her. "You can be my partner in this. You get to Major Scott in a way that won't attract notice and tell him I asked to have you sworn in as a Federal officer and given credentials and everything with them. When you get to Chicago, you go to the Drake Hotel and register in as Miss Sarah Coudray—wasn't that your mother's name?

"Well, then you get one of the money envelopes from the desk and wrap your credentials and badge up in some flannel or soft stuff and seal it up and give it to the clerk to put in the safe for you. It's your money and jewels—sabe, Sally?"

Sally Wilson nodded her head. "Yes, Jimmie."

"Then I'll make contact with you. My name will be James Henry Tucker —that's a good old New England name. My grandma was a Tucker. Now, are you going to be a good girl and stop grieving about Charley until we get whoever did it?"

"I'm—I'm going to be a good girl, Jimmie, dearest," said Sally with a little quaver in her voice, "and I—I won't let you see, but my heart will keep on grieving, I'm afraid, and—"

"That's all right," said Jimmie, taking her in his arms again. "You're a good, brave girl right now. You go and wash your face and get to Major Scott to-day. I'm leaving on the night Pennsy train."

After Sally had gone, her head up now and the light of the old Kentucky feudists in her eyes, Jimmie swept the fishing tackle on the floor and in spite of his brave talk to Sally about Charley's being just over the hill, he sat somberly for a moment, seeing the face and laughing eyes of his best friend in the service instead of the shining top of the table. "Well, old kid," he said aloud, very slowly, "they got you. —but I swear that I won't rest until I get them," and his arm and head went down on the table and he cried unashamed.

CHAPTER III.

ON THE TRAIL.

"IT'S for you, Uncle Willy-um," called little Mrs. Beach from the telephone seat, gayly. "You better come a running—it might be a telegram from Ma telling you to come right home. Don't you go, Uncle Willy-um, will you?"

"Honey," said old Ranger Captain Yancey, as he put down the paper, "Ma don't have to wire me to come right home a runnin'. I was doin' that runnin' to where she was long before you was born. Yes, suh," he said, as he took the receiver from his niece, "this is William Yancey talkin'."

"This is James H. Tucker talking, Mr. Yancey. I'm a reporter for the Theodore N. Scott information bureau. We have been told that you are an exponent of the theory that Company B's horses must be fed on pork and beans and would like to have an interview with you on the subject."

"Well, suh," drawled the ranger captain. "I reckon you got me wrong. That was Captain Jinks of the Horse Marines' way of doin'."

"I see. Well, there is some mistake; but the Scott Bureau is very anxious that I get in touch with you. Would it be possible for me to see you for a few moments?"

"Well, suh, I was aimin' to go out and get me some exercise. If you-all want to come down to the Wilson Avenue beach, I reckon you can. I'll be up at the north end."

"Uncle Willy-um Yancey," said pretty little Mrs. Beach, firmly, as Captain Yancey put the receiver down, "don't you dare tell me you're going to get mixed up in anything up here.

Ma said that you were to take a rest. I'll wire her," she threatened, a smile on her lips. She had been raised on the big Lazy W ranch by her uncle and Ma; and her father having been a ranger, she knew from Captain Yancey's answers and the light in his eyes that there was "Ranger business" in the offing somewhere.

"Shucks, honey," said Captain Yancey, reaching for his hat, "you know I'm getting along right smart for that foolishness. That feller wants to know about hoss feed, I reckon."

"This isn't the range country, Uncle Billy," said Mrs. Beach, a worried little frown appearing on her forehead. "Up here is altogether different. Bob says that they all don't trust each other and—"

"Sugar," said ex-Captain Yancey of the Rangers, as he started to open the door. "That no-'count scoundrel of a husband of yours is plumb right, I reckon. Only one thing up here is the same as down in our country and that is, a Colt forty-one bullet placed right will still stop 'em, one place or the other."

James H. Tucker had no trouble in locating Captain Yancey at the south end of the beach—not the north. In certain circles, on fixing a compass point of meeting, north means south and west means east. The beach was crowded and no one paid any attention to the two men lying on the sand back in the shade.

"The major got to me with a special delivery before I left," Tucker had said, after introducing himself, and he handed Yancey a sheet of paper on which was scribbled in longhand:

Jimmie—my old partner in the Rangers is staying with his niece, named Beach, at 620 Rosemary Street. His name is Yancey. He may be able to help you some.

There was a scrawled picture of a very bony pair of legs in a kilt at the bottom.

"I phoned him from the depot," went on Jimmie, solemnly. "He gave me a sort of general working description of you. We have to be pretty careful on account of wire taps, even in Washington. There's quite a few people would like to know just where a Federal agent was going—and why —and what he looked like."

"Well, suh," smiled Yancey, "if that old cross between a polecat and a sidewinder gave you any kind of description of me, I reckon it wasn't what you could call right complimentary."

"It wasn't," said Jimmie, idly tearing the note into small pieces and sticking them down in little holes in the sand here and there. "But I used my own judgment."

He told Yancey of Wilson, and then was surprised to hear that Yancey had been an eyewitness to the killing and had later in the day wired Major Scott in the old Ranger telegraphic code to that effect, adding that he might be of some help.

"'The mills of the gods,'" quoted Jimmie. "This gang plans a killing— with all details covered—and then do it under the eyes of an old partner of the man's chief. Tell me exactly what you saw, captain, please."

Yancey told him and wound up with: "Son, I saw the face of the man with the machine gun—and the car was a big blue Carton with an Indiana license number 265,784. What was your buddy doin' up here on Rosemary Street?"

"A former Washington girl lives up there," said Jimmie. "Charley was sending in his reports to the major through her. She'd mail them to a girl in Washington. Captain, it's as I told you. We have to take all kinds of precautions. Major Scott had a private secretary once that was wrong—and it cost the lives of three good men.

"That car license doesn't mean a thing. They probably changed it before they had gone ten blocks, in some garage they had hired. This man with the machine gun, captain? What did he look like—a wop?"

"SON," answered Yancey, sitting up cross-legged on the sand and rolling a cigarette, "I don't reckon that he'll do you much good—he's dead."

Jimmie, who had been punching little holes in the sand with his finger, looked up. "Dead! How do you know?"

"It's thisaway," answered Yancey. "This here young buddy of yours was sure game. He turned and got one of them when he was the same as dead himself, and I was all for him. After they took his body away I figured that maybe-so the old man could sort of pay off a little on his account and I knew that some report of the deaths must go in to the coroner's office. Dr. Rienhardt down there is one of the assistants and he and I had got right friendly the time he was in Texas a long time ago.

"So I drifts down there to make him a little visit. Shore enough, in comes the report of the killin' of your buddy, and that the body was at the Augustana Hospital. Well, suh—I didn't reckon I could do any good by seein' him—so I just hung around with Doc some more.

"Then later in the day there's a report from police headquarters that the body of an unidentified man was found on the corner of a North Side street, and that he had been shot between the eyes; had evidently been thrown from a car. I told Doc that I was lookin' for a man that might have got treated thataway and the Doc he said that he'd drive me over to the morgue and let me take a look."

The old Ranger captain, his deeply bronzed old face as impassive as that of a wooden Indian, stopped, snapped the cigarette butt away, produced tobacco and brown papers, slowly rolled another, lit it, then drawled: "It was the man your buddy killed, son."

" He got one," said Jimmie. " They unload any of the gang that gets knocked off. Well, how about the man with the machine gun? How did you line him up?"

" About the same way, son. I figured that Doc would be the best one to hang around with for a day or so, because everything regardin' any killin' comes in his office. Well, suh, pretty soon in comes a phone that some of the police had shot it out with a bunch of these city bad men up on—now—oh, yeah, the Sheridan road. I tells the Doc that I'd admire to see how it come off right away and me and the Doc we drives out, pronto. We gets there before the bodies had been taken away—or the car, Jimmie.

" There was a right smart lot of the police there—and the car was the same one—and the young gent that had used the machine gun was there, dead, and with him was another young gent; and he was right dead, too."

" Double cross, or maybe a triple," said Jimmie promptly. " They were sent out there to get some one—then got it themselves instead."

" By the police, son," pointed out Yancey, " I got me the papers home about it. This other gent's name was Johnnie Adams."

" Wait a minute, captain. Let me get this. We know how the first man got his. Then the rest of the same outfit that put Charley on the spot get theirs —from the police!"

Jimmie looked out over the placid lake for a little while, when he said: " Captain, Wilson was here on that mail car robbery on the Illinois Central, working with the Post Office Department men. I wonder if—

" Here—how's this? Charley gets on a hot trail—the higher-ups get tipped that he's warm. They don't know who he is, perhaps—or perhaps they do, and don't give a damn—anyway, they get some gang that they've got a toe-hold on, and make them bump him off.

" That's easy, so far. Then they get the idea that the men they used aren't the right ones to know about it, and they frame a little double cross, intending to bump them off, and the police horn in, and—not so good. I was going to say that the cops did the job for them, but, by gosh, it's the cops that did the work for themselves. What papers had the most details of the thing?"

" They all had extras out, son. They had the most interviews with the officers and such like—and pictures and all, in their yellow sheets, I reckon they're called."

" Captain, I never worked here in Chicago before, and I don't know many people. I don't want to go within nine hundred miles of the district attorney or the marshal's office. I know there are square cops here that don't stand for any kind of crooked stuff at all, just as there are straight deputy sheriffs and marshals."

" There's lots of different insides up here, son. They all got their pet grafts, I reckon. I know one square cop up here and that's old Cap'n O'Reilly.

" He's been down my way. Son, he was captain at the old Harrison Street Station when Jack Mallory was inspector and Luke Colleran had the front office. Kipley was chief then. They were all square cops. That was years ago, but I reckon that Cap'n O'Reilly sorta keeps in touch with things—anyway he could give us a lot of workin' information. I used to know him right well, and I reckon he'd like to favor me."

Yancey didn't tell Jimmie that once just over the border in Mexico he had shot his way through a crowded Mexican gambling hall to reach the prone and wounded figure of a young Irishman named O'Reilly, who had come down from Chicago to get a man and had been decoyed over there by some of the man's friends.

Yancey had reached him just as a Mexican stooped to put a knife in his heart. The Mexican finished his stoop toward the floor, but with a bullet in his heart, and Yancey had coldly and efficiently shot a clear path to the door and carried O'Reilly to safety across the line before the *guardias rurals* could arrive on the scene.

"This here O'Reilly," he went on, "has right good sense, Jimmie. I reckon he could tell you a lot."

"Do you think he's covered in any way?"

"I don't reckon so, son. He ain't active no more. No reason why any outfit would want to cover him that I can see. Him and me go fishin' a lot when I drift in here for a visit. If I was to call him up and tell him the pickerel was bitin' up on the Flambeau River, out of Ladysmith, Wisconsin, I reckon he'd let go all holds and come. It's a night's ride on the Soo Line out of here."

"How soon can you reach him?" asked Jimmie.

"Why, I reckon if I went right back home and called him up, I'd get him about this time. We'd be leaving on the night train, I bet you."

"I'll be on her," said Jimmie, rising. "I'll get these papers that tell about the Sheridan Road thing."

The next morning Miss Sarah Coudray at the Drake Hotel found several letters slipped under her door when she woke up. Most of them—in fact all but one—were announcements of various shoppes that solicited the patronage of the guests.

The other was a Sherman House envelope, and in it was a little torn off piece of newspaper:

One of the gangsters killed was identified as John Adams, a chauffeur, evidently the driver of the car. He had been for some time a resident of Morton Park. The dead man's family, consisting of a wife and four children, had been taken to the country by him the day before the killing.

From neighbors it was ascertained that Adams's wife was the daughter of Sheriff Gordon of Newton County, Indiana. On receipt of a wire she came at once to the city with Sheriff Gordon and claimed the body of her husband. Mrs. Gordon stated that as far as she knew, her husband was making his money as a legitimate chauffeur, owning his own car. The police state that they believe this to be correct and made no effort to detain her in any way. She left with the body for Newton, last night.

There is no reason to doubt that Adams had been the driver of several death cars, according to descriptions furnished by people who had been near the scenes of killing——

On the sheet of paper was written:

DEAR SALLY:
Run down and see her—another old friend of yours is staying at 2103 Halstead Street.

Sally Coudray tore the letter up into tiny pieces and then burned them on one of the ash trays and blew the ashes out of the window. She packed up, checked out. She stopped on her way to the depot to buy several woman's magazines and a blank receipt book; and went down in Indiana, soliciting subscriptions.

CHAPTER IV.

THE NEW DEPUTY.

"INDADE 'tis a hard game to buck, down there," said Ex-Captain O'Reilly reflectively, as he reeled in his line. "Hard fer enny wan—an' if he's a square cop, 'tis harder. Time was in the owld days that every gambler paid fifty dollars a week fer each table he had in his house, and saloon-keepers accordin' to their means. The sportin' houses on Custom House Place and Fourth Avenue was run accordin' to law and order, and each paid so much.

"Each district had its authorized collector, and while I misdoubt but what there wasn't bigger graft goin' on, it was a rare cop that stood in with a crook.

" I had me own troubles, keepin' me fingers clean. I did as I was told an' kep' me district tight as ordered. Thin there was no beer-runnin' gangs and bootleggers and all. The force was mostly Irish. Dom few else except a few Dutchmen, who are good men to have wid ye in a scrap, them square-heads.

" Now there is everything from Polacks up and down. 'Tis a Kilkenny cat affair entirely. The front office bucks the police end. The sheriff's gang and the county dicks are out for thimselves. The United States marshal's gang is all scrambled up, which it never used to be, and every dom mother's son of them mostly have their fingers in the pie in some way and fight the others.

" Let a man lift a loaf of bread, and they all go out and get 'em—sure; let a poor girl take a pair of silk stockin's now, and—throw her in the coop for life. But these dom murder cars and bootleggers' wars and what not—sure 'tis told me that wan outfit had wid 'em wan of the assistant state's attorneys; and all them dicks from hell to high water are playin' to get their bit, and they double crossin' and triple crossin' each other like a mad crew. 'Tis so, be Judas.

" If Luke had the front office and Jack Mallory and me the old district, and Kipley was back, and old Carter H., sure there'd be—well, maybe not. Chicago's gettin' pretty big and times have changed. Maybe we'd be doin' the same. There's straight cops and straight deputies and all still, never fool yourself, young feller."

" It's about the same everywhere now, captain, at least, as far as we know," said Jimmie. " What I want to get is a line on the best way to horn in."

" Best way I know," answered O'Reilly, " would be for ye to get on wid the sheriff as deputy. Them boys seem to play wid 'em all. Sure now, let's see. McMullen and I pounded the

pavement together for miny a mile before into politics he wint and finally becomes sheriff. 'Tis little that owld divil won't do for Pat O'Reilly.

" I have it! Wait, now, I'll give ye an easy one. Ye look some Irish, anyway. Yer name is Murphy—James Cardogan Murphy, the same as yer pa's, and yer mother was me favorite sister Maggie, that got married and wint 'way to hell-and-gone to live—one of me sisters did that thing years ago—now where the divil did she go to live? 'Twas up in Maine. First it was—"

" Holden, Maine," suggested Jimmie, with a grin, almost the first since Sally had come stumbling into his rooms.

" No—Portland; do it be ye know that place? 'Tis a bigger city and all. Ye came down from Portland to see me and what does me bowld Captain O'Reilly do but git his nephew in on the sheriff's gang of hijackers. Sure, her two boys was killed in France, but she might have had six for all any one knows around here."

" Hold 'er a minute, captain," interrupted Jimmie; " when the knock-off comes, it may be that I'll be uncovered. How'll you stand then?"

" The same as I stand right now," said the doughty old Irishman. " 'Tis afraid of no man I am or no gang, and well they know it, all of them, may the black curse of Crum'el be on their dirty double-crossin' yellow hearts. The same as I stand right now, young feller. I have a few friends left of me own high up and low down. Good men and straight, and all of them gangs lay off 'em. They know better than to fool wid us."

" I hope I don't have to show in at the finals," said Jimmie, " but I thought I'd better say something about it."

" Son," said old Ranger Captain Yancey, " that's comin' clean. This here old doggone fightin' Swede here is—"

"Swade is it?" bellowed old Captain O'Reilly. "Sure now, ye poor skinny piece of tripe, I can take the both of ye right now and trun ye in the river."

The old ranger, who had killed a dozen men, and Jimmie Howard, who had killed a few himself and had the chilled steel nerve of all the Howards, both hastily admitted he could, without any doubt.

"WHO'S the new lad?" asked Cohen, who was sitting in the front office of the sheriff's.

"Old Pat O'Reilly's nephew," answered one of the deputy sheriffs sitting with his feet up on the window sill. "I was in here the day the captain brought him down. Comes from Maine, I heard O'Reilly tell McMullen. He looks like he lost his wad or something, don't he?"

"Yeah, maybe he has. Has he been out yet?"

"Nichols told me that the old man sent him out with them on that Stanton warrant. He said that this guy Murphy was there. Carries his gat under his left arm."

"Guess I'll go over and see what he's got," said Cohen, rising.

"My name is Cohen," he said, as he held out his hand to Jimmie Murphy. "I've seen you around for a couple of days. Let's go and get some lunch."

"All right," answered Jimmie. "I ain't found me no good place to eat yet. I paid a dollar and seventy-five cents for some bum chuck last night in one dump."

Cohen laughed. "You don't know where to go? Boy, I'll take you to a place where you can get good stuff— all kinds," and he looked closely at Jimmie, whose face lighted up.

"I wish you would," Jimmie said earnestly. "I'm a stranger in a strange land. I asked Cap'n O'Reilly where at was a good place to go and get a glass of beer and he said, 'Lay off that dom stuff—'tis the curse of the O'Reillys!' My gosh, he's the only one of the fam-

ily that thinks so, I bet. My ma was his sister and she didn't feel like that. The old lady liked her cup of tay, boy."

Cohen grinned. "I've heard that old Cap O'Reilly was pretty tight about lots of things, but a wildcat in a scrap. Come on, I know a good place."

They went down Clark Street toward Adams Street, Cohen nodding or saying "Hello" several times in a block, it seemed to Jimmie. Just after crossing Adams, two men standing in a doorway of an old building looked up and saw Cohen and Jimmie approaching. One of them stepped inside the door and disappeared. The other stood where he was.

Cohen stopped within three feet of him. "What's the idea, Sam, and where did Whitey duck to just now?"

"We're off watch," the man answered, looking at Jimmie, who stood a little to the right and back of Cohen. "The big boy said he might be along here about noon. We were waiting to see him."

"Yeah? Well, he won't, because he's in Hammond this morning. I can tell you that—and something else. Come on out of the door, Whitey; this is for you, too."

The other man stepped out of the shadows. "Had your hand on a rod, didn't you?" sneered Cohen. "Feller, you sure hanged yourself doing that. Well, here it is, you birds. You're all done and washed up, see. I was told to pass the word. The first rattler out of town is yours—for keeps. The feller you was waiting for must be getting soft to let you get away, at that. You ought to get taken for a ride, you—"

"Aw, hell," said Sam, "what have we done? We wasn't in that."

Cohen laughed. "Well, there it is for you. Use your own judgment. Come on, Jimmie." He started to turn away.

"Wait a minute," said the man called Whitey, his mean, scarred, broken-nosed face and hard eyes showing his rage. "We ain't no cheap knucks to be chased outta town when any one gets through with us, and I don't give a damn if it is—"

"I wouldn't call any names out loud," interrupted Cohen; "and keep your hand in front of you, feller—or you'll get yours, right here!"

Whitey looked at the passing crowds, at the two traffic cops on the intersection of Clark and Adams, then back at the sneering deputy. "It's you," he snarled, "that's put us in wrong, you skunk! You played us dirt and then—" He appeared to notice Jimmie for the first time. "Who the hell is this guy?"

"Me?" asked the sleepy-eyed Jimmie, mournfully. "I'm just a hungry lad he was takin' to lunch. Don't hesitate on startin' anything on my account—because the quicker we kill you rats the quicker we'll eat."

Whitey laughed. "I wouldn't want to stop no preacher from eatin'," he said. "All right, Cohen. Tell the big boy we're on our way, you dirty mongrel half-breed kike!"

At that word Cohen flamed into a deadly rage, and his right fist flashed up at Whitey's jaw. They were standing so that Jimmie and Cohen were practically in front of the others, who were now half in and half out of the doorway of the old building, which had one low, broad stone step leading up from the sidewalk. The two deputies were on the step.

Cohen's blow was fast, but Whitey's head swerved an inch back and to the left, and his counter was faster. His left fist crashed full in Cohen's face. With split lips and blood pouring from his nose, Cohen reeled back, halfway across the sidewalk.

The passing crowd at once made room for him and ran in either direction, seeking cover behind anything they could. Cohen's coat was open and they could see his deputy sheriff star and cartridge belt. He staggered to a halt, blew the blood from his nose and mouth as a swimmer would water, and drew his gun.

There was a more desperate effort by the bystanders to get under or behind something. In Chicago, even the children knew enough to scatter like a flock of quails, on the sight or sound of a gun.

AS Cohen started back across the sidewalk, there was the sound of a shot and Whitey's body, the hand still clutching an automatic, fell across the doorway almost at Cohen's feet. Sam came in view, his hands high above his head, Jimmie Murphy behind him with the muzzle of his Colt .45 pressing into Sam's back.

The two traffic policemen were running towards them, tugging at their guns. From across the street came two plain-clothes men, guns in hand. Cohen's bloody lips twisted into a cruel smile and he deliberately raised his gun to kill the defenseless man within two feet of him.

Jimmie shouted at him, "Hold 'er! He's my meat!" and as Cohen's gun still came up, he slid the muzzle of his Colt up over Sam's shoulder, straight at Cohen's heart, stepping in front of Sam and crowding him into a narrow space between an iron railing and the window of the next store.

"'Tis me that has 'im under arrest," Jimmie said firmly. "Cohen—put that gun down now." Just then the coppers and plain-clothes men arrived. Cohen stood for a second, rigid, looking full in Jimmie Murphy's eyes, then lowered the gun.

The two coppers recognized Cohen, as did the plain-clothes men, and at once began to drive back the milling crowd that had begun to come around, now the shooting was over.

"What the hell's comin' off, Abie?" demanded one of the detectives, the other stooping over the body of Whitey.

Cohen started to say something

when Jimmie interrupted. "These two were tryin' to stick up the jewelry store here when me and me partner come along. Sure, I had to bump off the wan on the sidewalk; and here's the other. Me brave Abie Cohen here, he tries to take 'em both alive wid his fists."

"Yeah?" said the detective, looking at Cohen, then at the dead Whitey and the living Sam behind Jimmie, "and who the hell might you be?"

"I'm a deputy sheriff," said Jimmie with pride.

"He's my partner, Valletti," said Cohen, "old Cap O'Reilly's nephew."

"Oh—I see," answered Valletti. "You take after old Pat, I guess."

More police had arrived, uniformed and plain-clothes men—also the patrol wagon and a couple of reporters. Most of the officers were engaged in keeping the traffic moving, holding back the vast crowd. The two corner officers had gone back to their posts. "You better get over to the Emergency, Abie," said one of the officers. "We'll take care of this for you. What were they trying to do?"

"Hold up Swanson's here," answered Cohen quickly. "We come along just in time. Take this guy to the Harrison Street station and hold him for Haven and McGinnis. Mac wants him, I think."

The man called Sam had been standing in the little space behind Jimmie, with two or three hard-faced detectives and a police lieutenant almost touching him. As Cohen said 'Harrison Street' and ended with 'Mac wants him,' Sam dropped like a stone to the sidewalk, rolled under the iron rail to the foot-wide space between it and the store window, around the feet of the officers and rose to his feet, whipping a little .25 calibre automatic from his vest pocket. Jimmie had taken the larger one from his hip pocket when his hands went up. Sam knew of the little room at the Harrison Street station and had decided that he would go out on top,

with the chance of taking one or two with him.

There was an automobile parked at the curb and he ran for it, firing over his shoulder. The closeness of the police to one another helped him for a moment.

There are straight police in Chicago just as there are crooked police, but no one ever accused either the straight or the crooked with lacking nerve to stand up to a gun fight or any other kind of a fight, at any time.

They drew their guns and stood where they were, those behind the others stepping to one side or the other to get clearance and returned his fire with their .38 police specials. Cohen, almost blinded with blood, stood with his heels together, firing as rapidly as he could pull trigger.

It happened so quickly, without any warning that the people crowding the windows on both sides of the street hardly had time to shrink back, when it was over. Sam never reached the automobile—alive. His body rolled to it, actually propelled by the stream of lead that was driving into it.

One of his bullets hit the police lieutenant in the chest, another lodged in a detective sergeant's shoulder and a third grazed Jimmie Murphy's cheek, drawing a thin line of red across it up by his ear. Those shots were all Sam had time to fire.

———

CHAPTER V.

SPEAKEASY NIGHTS.

ON the way to the hospital Jimmie told Cohen that Whitey drew his rod just after he hit Cohen and on Jimmie's command to drop it, had started to swing it on Jimmie—so Jimmie killed him. Sam had not had time to draw before Jimmie's gun was on him.

"Why the hell didn't you let me kill the snake?" asked Cohen through the handkerchief he was holding to his lips.

"Sure now, I would have," answered Jimmie, placatingly. "Only thing, I was fussed up and I thought he was me own meat and like all the Irish, I guess, I wanted to do me own killing. What it was all about I dunno and I care less. Next time now, Abie, yer name is, isn't it—you can kill 'em all yerself. Me first name's Jimmie."

Cohen laughed. "All right, Jimmie. You and me ought to make good side-kicks—an Irishman and a Jew."

"And the best fightin' men in the world, once ye get 'em started," said Jimmie, gravely.

After one of the doctors at the Emergency had fixed them up, Cohen said, as they were waiting for a taxi, "Well, I don't know how much I can eat with these damn lips all gummed up, but we'll go and get a drink, anyway—that is—if you drink any, Jimmie."

"D'ye ever see an Irishman who wouldn't?" demanded Jimmie. "Lead me to it, feller. 'Tis not much I drink I'll admit. That lad I knocked off must have packed an awful wallop, Abie, darlin', to cut ye up like that."

"He was one of the best heavys in the business," answered Cohen, as they got in the taxi he had flagged. "Before he slipped."

"An' you swung on him," said Jimmie, with a grin. "Sure now, Abie, ye must have, though he slipped a lot."

"I'm pretty good myself," said Cohen, returning the grin as best he could. "Besides he called me a kike and I don't take that from nobody but my friends when they're kidding me."

"Upstairs by me lives kikes, hey, 'Abie?" grinned Jimmie. "Well, every man has his fighting words all right. Cap'n O'Reilly was telling me the other night that in the old days if any one called him an Irish potato, he'd start moppin' up. They could call him Irish or Mick or flannel mouth, but if they added the potato thing it got him."

"I guess that's right," said Cohen. "Are you living with him, Jimmie?"

"Naw—he's too straight-laced—I mean that all he wants to do is to go to bed early or play whist with a lot of old-timers. Me, I take after the Murphys a lot, I guess. My pa was a regular guy, Abie."

"Yeah—where do you live then?"

"I got me a swell room over on Halsted Street near Madison."

"This the first time you been in Chicago, Jimmie?"

"Yeah, boy. I was in Portland and then another guy and I went up in Canada and worked between there and New York a lot. I was just fussing around and—"

"Did you say down around Montauk Point?" asked Abie with a grin, "or Atlantic Highlands, which?"

"Who wants to know?" answered Jimmie, with a grin. "Boy, some day I'll tell you some tales about big jack. I seen ten grand notes lying around like snow on the table."

"Better not let Cap'n O'Reilly hear you telling it. He'd crown you, feller."

"Ain't that the truth," said Jimmie, earnestly. "When my ma got me to come out here she warned me about telling him anything. There's one good, straight guy, Abie, and I can lick the man that says he isn't. He may look at things different from you and me, but he's there, forty ways from the jack."

"He is," answered Cohen, promptly. "Old-timers tell me that there wasn't a gamer man on the force than old Pat O'Reilly. Well, here we are."

The restaurant was one of those that show a chop or a fish on top of a cake of ice in the window. There was a small gilt sign down in one corner, Bowen's Steak and Chop House.

In the front room Jimmie saw several tables on both sides with a narrow passageway between, hardly wide enough for two men to walk abreast. At the back there was a cigar case and a desk with a cash register on it. Two waiters were serving the tables which were fully occupied by men. A fat, jolly-looking man, with a big red face came from behind the cigar case as soon as he saw Cohen.

"I just heard about it," he shouted in a jovial voice. "Been getting ready for another medal, hey, Abie? Ain't you goin' to leave me no customers at all?"

"Here's the guy that did it," answered Abie. "Shake hands with Jimmie Murphy, Jack. Where's the rest of the bunch?"

"Some of them in back," answered Jack Bowen. "Glad to meet you, Mr. Murphy. The boys was talking about you. Make yourself at home. Go on back Abie, with Mr. Murphy, here."

Cohen led the way past a man standing at a locked door beside the desk. He unlocked it as he saw them coming. As Cohen passed he grinned and said, "O. K." The man smiled and answered, "O. K., me good lad," as he stood aside. Cohen paused a minute. "This is Jimmie Murphy, outta our office."

"Right," the man answered. "Come in any time, Mr. Murphy."

THE door opened into a room large enough for fifty tables seating four, and a regulation bar running the full length across the rear. Every table was full, and men were standing three and four deep at the bar. Four bartenders were serving drinks as fast as they could.

"Hell of a crowd in here," growled Cohen. "Let's get one of those little rooms on the side."

He led the way over to the left where there were several doors. A waiter hurrying by stopped. "Go into number two, Mr. Cohen. They're just going. I'll be right in."

"Bring a couple of Manhattans with you, and hurry up," answered Abie.

"Yes, sir," the waiter grinned. "I'll be right there."

Cohen spoke to a couple of the men going out, and then as they sat down at a table, said to Jimmie: "Boy, wait

4 A

till you see the chuck they hand out here. Want anything else besides that Manhattan, Jimmie, to start off with? I ordered them without thinking."

"Is it good booze?" asked Jimmie. "Some stuff I got the other night was rotten."

"Here?" asked Cohen in amazement. "Feller, this stuff is real, no foolin'."

A meal was served by Adolph, the waiter, with all the drinks he could persuade them to take. At the finish Jimmie sighed. "My gosh," he said, leaning back, lighting one of the big fat cigars from the box that lay on the table. "Boy, if I could afford to eat like this all the time, I'd get fat."

"Yeah," answered Cohen with a grin. "It does cost a lot," and he tossed a dollar down on the table. "Come on, Jimmie, if you're ready, fill your pockets with those cigars. Wait a minute, want any cigarettes?"

"No, I got a pack. Hey, what's the idea, Abie? That buck wouldn't pay for three of the cigars, let alone anything else."

"That ain't for the stuff—that's a tip for Adolph, and he's damn lucky to get it. Get wise, boy. You don't suppose they'd take any jack, do you? I'll take you to fifty places, old kid. All you got to do is to say what you want."

Jimmie's eyes widened. "Yeah— so that's it? Ain't life grand?"

"It is for the guys who are right," said Cohen.

The door opened and two men came in. Cohen looked up and grinned. "Hello, Haven. Hello, McGinnis," he said. "Sit down and have a drink. This is Jimmie Murphy, a new man at the office. Jimmie, this is Haven and McGinnis from the front office at the hall. They're two regular guys."

Haven and McGinnis both shook hands with Jimmie, eying him shrewdly. "Captain Bate was telling us that you two got Whitey Smith and Sam Norton," said Haven. "I'll take a little Three Star, Adolph," to the waiter who had followed them in. "And so you're Pat O'Reilly's nephew," he add-ed to Jimmie.

"Yeah, my mother was his sister."

"He was before my time," went on Haven. "He retired before I went on the force, but I've heard a lot about him. He was one square cop."

"That's right," said Jimmie, with solemn emphasis. "He was that. I've heard my mother tell about him for years. The old boy fought 'em all, and sent many a man to salt creek. He's full of lead right now, and all he got out of it was—his pension."

"If he'd catch you in this dump," said McGinnis, with a grin, "he'd damn near murder you himself."

"Ain't that the truth," said Jimmie, returning the grin, "but it's still catch-in' before hangin'. When he got me the job he said, 'Sure I misdoubt the Murphy blood in ye. If ye get caught in any jam now—don't be squawkin' to me fer help. Ye won't get it.'"

"He's a rare old cockaloo," said Haven; "he don't realize that times have changed. Well, Abie, what about this Whitey and Sam thing?"

"Why, nothing much. I was taking Jimmie here to lunch and met 'em and passed the word a feller had given me to tell 'em. Whitey got hard all of a sudden and began rambling about some nut stuff, and finally he called me a kike. I swung at him, but he beat me to it, and I went out on the sidewalk for a minute. Then he tried to get his gat around on Jimmie, and Jimmie got him. Then Jimmie came out with his gat in Sam's back and the gang be-gan to come up. Jimmie here gives out the office that they were trying to stick up Swansons!"

"Yes, we read about it in the ex-tra," answered Haven, "so Whitey got ratty, did he?"

"Yeah, so much so that—"

"Well, that's the way it goes," in-terrupted McGinnis, and he turned to Jimmie. "Those birds were bad ac-tors. They been pullin' a lot of crooked stuff, and needed killin'. Abie, if you ain't busy, drop around to Mike's to-night, will you?"

"Sure," answered Cohen, rising. "Jimmie and I were just going. We gotta go over and make a report on this here holdup."

JIMMIE trailed around with Cohen for a week or ten days, never forc-ing his company on him, simply giving Cohen a chance to ask him to come along, which Cohen did at every opportunity. The word gradually seeped around that 'Jimmie Murphy was a good boy to have along." The sheriff's office had several deputies who seemed to do all the regular work, and a great many like Cohen, who came and went as they saw fit.

Jimmie became known as a tight-mouthed bird, who was always good-natured and absolutely fearless.

He went with Cohen, and also three or four others, to all the speakeasies and dives, did as they did, ate and drank his fill, tossed out a tip for the waiter, and went on his way.

One night he and Cohen were in one of the South Side road houses. Cohen had been gambling since noon in a joint not two blocks from the city hall, and had lost heavily. Jimmie had been told where he was, and had persuaded him to quit about midnight and dine out on the South Side on the plea that some fresh air would clear his brain and later he could come back and mop up. Cohen agreed.

They were sitting on the veranda of the road house, which sat back among a grove of trees, within a few miles of the Indiana line. Cohen was drinking steadily and still cursing his luck.

"I held three kings, Jimmie, before the draw, and I made those bums pay heavy before they could draw any cards. The guy next to me hikes it for fifty, and the man sitting next to him lifts it again. I was sittin' in the golden chair, I tell you.

"I tilts it again, and so does Wilton, who was next to me; the other guy, a dick named Lawson, stays right along. I boosts it once more, and they both stay. Well, there we was with half a grand in the pot before the draw. Fair enough, ain't it? I draws down to mine and gets another king. Picture that, me with four kings!

"The next lad, Wilton, he draws one card. I know his play—he holds a kicker to threes—well, I figure him at the worst, a full. Lawson, he stands pat. We bets 'em. Wilton he drops out after I shoves in a grand—all I had on the table. We was playin' table stakes—nothin' back, see.

"Lawson, he covers my grand and squawks about it only being table stakes, and I'm runnin' a sandy, see. So I says, 'All right, feller, you think you got such a hell of a good hand. We'll lift the rules'—and I calls Kentucky George over and gets five grand outa him and puts it down on the table. Lawson, he has hard work raisin' that much. All he can touch for with what he's got makes forty-five hundred dollars, so I drags five hundred dollars and he calls me. Listen, Jimmie, old kid. I shows down four kings and an ace. Pretty good hand, ain't it?

"Yeah, boy," said Jimmie. "What could he have been holdin', now?"

"Jimmie—true as I sit here at this table that hyena put down a straight flush. He had 'em *pat*. It wouldn't happen once in a million years, and it had to happen to me."

"Who was dealing?" Jimmie snapped.

"That's the worst of it," answered Cohen, draining his glass. "I was myself. I dealt him a straight flush and myself four kings. How's that for Jew luck, Jimmie?"

"Pretty bad, old-timer," answered Jimmie.

"I'll say it's bad. I lose two grand of my own, and borrow five more from Kentuck." Cohen stopped and looked intently at Jimmie, who leaned back in his chair and grinned at him. "How game are you, Jimmie?" he asked.

"Me—I run from a rabbit, why?"

"Aw, I don't mean that way—I mean—would you want to make some jack—big jack—to-night?"

"Yeah, boy. I sure do."

"Listen, Jimmie; I know where a truckload of bonded hard stuff will pull in at three o'clock for a change of licenses and drivers. Are you game to hijack it with me?"

"Me? Sure I'm game, but what the hell would we do with that much booze, sell it to some one?"

"Certainly; I know a lad that will buy it the minute we drive it in his place. We can get forty dollars a case for it, and there's five hundred cases. We'll have to stick up the driver and the two guards and the garage men—it 'll be duck soup, they won't be looking for no play. Just you and me, Jimmie. Will we do 'er?

Cohen had drunk enough to make him all weasel and his losses had made him desperate beyond all caution.

"That's twenty grand," said Jimmie. "Ten apiece. Come on. How do we do it—do we just stick 'em up and go away from there?"

"Yeah, only we jump 'em as deputy sheriffs, see—it's in Cook County. We make a regular pinch out of it. We call up the station house and Cap Jones will send over and get the prisoners. We'll have to slip him a grand. They'll get bond right away and we start in with the truck, see—but some one jumps us and takes it away from us. Get it?"

"Yeah, I get it—but listen, Abie, I'm wise enough now to know we're going to start a private war right away. The birds that own that truck ain't going to see that much jack get taken away from them without puttin' some one on the spot."

"Aw, hell, it's the Caproni gang that owns it. Sure, they'll squawk. Whadda we care? There's a war on right now between them and— Jimmie, you're a right guy, ain't you?"

"I am," answered Jimmie solemnly. "But I'm right to me, first. I ain't been here long enough to get the inside stuff. Abie, I don't want to get mixed in anything that I don't know where I'm at, see. I got old Capt'n O'Reilly to think of—as well as my own skin.

"Here, I'll tell you something," and Jimmie reached for the bottle. He was talking a little thickly now himself and his eyes were tightening to slits; his voice became thicker and a brogue began to creep into the words. He poured out and drank a whisky glass full of the brandy.

"'Tis me that was payoff man for Doyle and 'twas me and Mike Daugherty that handled the unloadin' at Montauk Point and 'twas me wid Larson and Big Tim that served miny a good man wid sand for breakfast on command of our superiors—Doyle got his finally and so did Mike and Tim and here I am, wid me skin wid a few holes in it, but still wid me skin. 'Tis enough for ye to know. An' now—I'm asked if I'm right.

"Sure, I'm right, Abie darlin', right as a golden guinea, as they say up in Canada—but to meself first and to others as long as I think they're right wid me—an' no longer, me bowld Cohen."

"Sure, Jimmie, sure," answered Cohen, placatingly. "You and me are partners, ain't we? I knew you were a right guy the first time I saw you."

"'Tis so," said Jimmie, solemnly, looking like a wise old owl. "Go on from there. Sure, I'll help you hijack a truck of booze, or diamonds, for all I care. But first, ye fool, who's who an' why is it—tell me that before we turn robbers."

"There's a hell of a lot of who who's," said Cohen, looking at his watch. "It's like my old father used to tell of the Jews. Him and the Rabbi. There's captains of tens and captains of hundreds. I'll tell you on the way to—"

The proprietor came out on the veranda and up to their table. "Sorry, gentlemen," he said, "I'll have to ask you to pull out. Just received word that the prohi dicks are going to pay me a visit about two o'clock."

"Now, may the foul fiend fly away wid them," said Jimmie. Sure, we was just gettin' right."

Cohen laughed. "Never mind, Jimmie. We gotta be leaving, anyway. Take good care of them, Pete."

"I will," answered the proprietor, grimly. "It'll cost me a couple of grand, I suppose—Well, come again, gents."

CHAPTER VI.

HIJACKERS.

HOLDING up the truck in the quiet private garage of one of the big old mansions on the South Side near Sixty-Ninth Street and Drexel Boulevard was easy. Jimmie and Cohen lay in the darkness beside it and when the truck entered, they did also, right behind it.

A garage man slid the big doors shut and switched on a light; new license plates were lying ready on the floor. Two men rose from cots over in the corner, stretched and yawned, ready to drive the truck on after the change. Three men climbed down from the driver's seat, all of them young foreigners.

"Duck soup," said one. "Not a touch in the road at all. Them damn John Laws must have been sleepin'— what the hell!"

Jimmie and Cohen came around the truck one on each side, their guns in hand.

"Up wid 'em!" shouted Jimmie. "Ye are all under arrest! Up—or I'll start shootin'!"

The only resistance offered was that one of the young foreigners, the one nearest Cohen seemed a little slow in obeying. Cohen struck him a hard blow just above his ear with the barrel of his .45 automatic, and he went down like a poled ox.

"Get over against the wall," he commanded. "Quick, or we'll make cold meat outta all of yer."

The five men obeyed, their evil faces and hard eyes showing they were like cornered rattlesnakes.

"Hold 'em, feller," said Jimmie, "till I get their gats."

"Keep that way," commanded Cohen to the line facing the wall, their hands high above their heads. "Frisk that bum on the floor and get his gat, Mister Sheriff, then go to the phone over there in the corner and phone the station house, Drexel 10100 and tell Cap Jones to come over here with a squad."

"You'll get yours for this," snarled one of the men without changing his position. "You guys can't pull this stuff with Al and—"

"Wan more squawk outta you," said Jimmie, "an' 'tis little ye'll need fuss about it. Sure, I'll blow a hole through ye like a subway tunnel, ye wop."

Captain Jones arrived with four men in his car and came charging in, night sticks much in evidence. Jimmie had just said over the phone—"Sheriff's office men have a truck in the garage at the corner of Drexel and Vinton Street. Come over."

Cohen greeted him. "Captain, we have seized this truck full of booze. Will you take these men in and hold 'em until morning for us? I'll phone about it later after we deliver the truck to the U. S. warehouse for safekeeping. You'll be home probably by then, your home phone is Y. C. 1000, aint it?"

"It has just been changed," said Captain Jones. "Ring for the wagon, one of yez, and the rest go over and put the bracelets on them. My phone has been changed to—I can't remember, look it up in the book, I know it's 2000 or something," he continued to Cohen.

"That's right," said Cohen. "I remember now, 2000. Well, we'll be getting in with the truck."

"Do you want a couple of men to ride it in wid ye?" asked the captain, solicitously. "Sure, there's a grand lot of booze there for the two of ye to—"

"Naw," said Cohen. "Some of the boys are just outside waitin' for us."

"All right," said Captain Jones. "Remember, now, if anything happens to ye, I offered protection in."

"You did," said Cohen. "I'll remember it"—climbing up to the driver's seat. "Come on, buddy, let's go."

"An' now what?" said Jimmie, as they rumbled down the street.

"Easy," said Cohen. "Here we sit, if anybody stops us—we flash our tins, we seized this truck—called Captain Jones, put the prisoners in his charge, and are taking the truck to the warehouse. If it's Federal dicks, which is plenty unlikely at this time, and on this route, same story. Most they could do if they're not open for a cut would be to trail us to the warehouse to make sure. We're regular officers, ain't we, Jimmie? Sure we are."

"Trail, hell," said Jimmie. "Are we to lose twenty grand now? Them prohibition guys may be good snoopers, but few of 'em will stand up to a gun fight. We'll shoot the living lights outta them and their car, and it won't be the first time, either."

Cohen laughed as he swung the truck around a corner.

"They got to do it inside of three blocks then, Jimmie. I don't care nothing about knocking off Federal dicks myself. You got no chance if they pin it on you."

"That's right," agreed Jimmie gravely. "I'm just talkin', Abie; that brandy was heavy stuff. I ain't never killed one either."

Cohen laughed again. "You Irish," he scoffed. "Damn good fighters, hey, Jimmie, old kid?"

"Upstairs by me lives kikes," Jimmie grinned. "Is this the place?" The truck swung into an alley and alongside what looked to be an old stable.

"Yeah, you sit there with it for a couple of minutes. I'll bring the lad out."

In twenty minutes, just as dawn was breaking, Jimmie and Cohen flagged a nighthawk taxi on Indiana Avenue, each with nine one-thousand-dollar bills in their pockets. Abie set aside two grand for Jones's cut.

"Not so bad," said Cohen, softly. "Not—so—bad."

"Tell me the rest," said Jimmie, just as softly.

"Why, in the morning we report in that we seized a truck load of booze and turned the prisoners over to Captain Jones and on the way to the warehouse with it we were stopped by a lot of boys who flashed prohibition agents' tins and they took the truck away from us. The old sheriff will raise hell with the prohibition outfit—get it, Jimmie?"

"I do," said Jimmie. "Us being law-abiding deputy sheriffs, we turns it over to the Federal dicks widout question."

"Sure we did," said Cohen. "What else? Now, we go and get us nine drinks and something to eat at Bowen's. Boy, if I didn't gamble, I'd have all the money in the world."

WHEN Jimmie finally got back to his room, he took several pieces of heavy, white paper, wrapped the nine $1,000 bills carefully between them and put them in an envelope addressed to Theodore N. Scott, 1998 H Street N.W., Washington, D. C. He scrawled on a half sheet of paper "Take care of this collection for me—Jimmie" and tucked it in the envelope also.

On his way out the landlady stopped him and said, "Mr. Murphy, there's a letter for you at the desk upstairs. I put it up there so's I wouldn't lose it. It come yesterday."

It was from Sally and said: "It was my old friend. She told me all about her troubles. Where can I see you? She sent a message to you."

Jimmie sat down and wrote another letter:

"I'm going to drive up to a little hotel—the Beach Tavern, at Lake Bluffs—for a rest, to-night."

Going out, he mailed them both, then called up Captain Yancey and told him that Captain Jinks was driving north that night and would like to have him come along.

Jimmie knew that there wasn't one chance in a thousand that he was being trailed or that any wire-tap was operating, either on Captain Yancey or Sally; but he also knew that a Federal agent who wanted to live long took no chances whatever that could be avoided.

He had bought a roadster and Cohen had gone with him to the license bureau, where the license was issued to him then and there without even a verbal examination.

As they drove through Evanston, Jimmie told Captain Yancey how he was gradually inching his way in and becoming known as a "right guy" in the whirlpool of the underworld.

"I got me a little information myself," Yancey replied. "This here holdup on the I. C. that yore buddy was workin' on—Capt'n O'Reilly and I have been kind of nosin' around. Two or three of his side-kicks still on the force who are straight coppers are keepin' their ears open, and a couple of them old—what was it he called 'em, son? Them jaspers that tell things?"

"Informers?" supplied Jimmie.

"No, that wasn't it. It was—doggone if I can remember. Anyway—"

"Oh, stool pigeons," said Jimmie.

"Yeah, that's it. Well, Capt'n O'Reilly, he's got him some old-time stool pigeons that most of these young fellers never heard of. Ain't that a hell of a libel on a pigeon, Jimmie? That's the flyin'est bird that—"

"It sure is," said Jimmie with a grin. "So you and Capt'n O'Reilly have some lines out? I thought you two had retired?"

"You hadn't ought to interrupt the old man that away," said Yancey, but he smiled at the keen young face beside him. "You was tellin' me to get back on the trail. Well, suh, it's hard to cure an old dog, I reckon, from picking up a scent. These here gents they tell the cap that from what was dropped here and there that a couple of detective sergeants named Haven and McGinnis seem to have been pretty close to that holdup, son, pretty close."

"Yeah?" said Jimmie. "They are the birds that got the credit for knocking off those birds in the car out Sheridan way." Jimmie stopped talking and drove silently for quite a little while, his lips tight.

"They are close to the holdup," he said, thinking out loud. "They uncover Charley Wilson in some way—they have him killed—then they kill the man that killed him."

"That's A B C, son," drawled Captain Yancey; "but how you goin' to prove it in court?"

"In court?" said Jimmie, surprised into a grim smile. "What court? Why bother Uncle and run a bill up, Capt'n? When we're sure of it, we'll invite them to a necktie party—only we'll use lead instead of neckties."

"Shucks, son," said ex-Ranger Captain Yancey, "I'm plumb surprised at you talking thataway, an' you a Federal agent."

"That's right," said Jimmie. "I was going to invite you and Capt'n O'Reilly to be present, but now I—"

"Son," said Captain Yancey, "I saw them sidewinders kill your buddy without givin' him a break at all. Don't you go leavin' the old man out now."

"I'm shocked at your talking thataway," grinned Jimmie. "An' you a Ranger captain! Here we are."

Sally "Coudray" came down from the veranda of the hotel as they drove up, and they made room for her slim little body between them, then drove toward the quiet lake shore.

She told them of taking a room in the little Indiana town and of meeting Johnnie's grief-distracted young wife. Before two weeks Johnnie's wife had told her about Johnnie and how, on the way down, he had confessed to her what he had been doing, and how they had planned that he was to go to South America and later she would join him.

"She loved him, Jimmie," Sally said. "She just loved him, in spite of what he had done, and she cried and cried. Finally I told her who I was and—"

Jimmie's eyes tightened a little at that, but he didn't say anything. Sally saw it, though, and said: "Why, Jimmie, did I do wrong? I didn't tell her anything about you or Washington. I just said I was—was Charley's sister and that we came from Kentucky, and that I wanted to get revenge on whoever did it."

"Honey," said Captain Yancey, "you did just right. She could understand that, being as how she loved her own man."

"I guess that's right," said Jimmie.

"Well," said Sally, "it turned out to be, anyway. She said she'd help me—that it would be revenging Johnnie, too. Jimmie, she told me that her husband had told her that he was afraid of two detectives, named Haven and McGinnis; that they had made him drive the car when—Charley was killed," and Sally's little hands clinched into tight fists.

"She said that Johnnie told her about the train robbery and everything. It's those two men, Jimmie, and a man named Cohen, who's a deputy sheriff, that are the ones. She said that the neighbors told her when she was waiting for Johnnie's body out at Morton Park that the man Cohen was waiting all that day for Johnnie when he got killed."

"All right, Sally," said Jimmie. "You're a good girl and you have done it all. You go back to Washington now and I'll—"

"But, Jimmie, I want to stay. I want to be here when—"

"Please, Sally—for me? It would

only worry me and it might affect my
—aim."

"Oh, Jimmie, are you going to—"

"I am," interrupted Jimmie. "And
after I'm going to have the word
passed that for one Federal man, there
were three collected, maybe more. You
go home now, Sally, and watch the papers. I've got to get Haven and Mc-
Ginnis and Cohen and some of their
buddies together some way—doing
something that will let us catch them
with the goods on 'em. They'll be
jumped for that, but the right word
will go out what happened. It may
stop the next gang from getting ambi-
tious."

"Well," said Sally, "I don't—"

"Honey," said Ranger Captain
Yancey, "you jest do what this here
scoundrel of a Jimmie says. You done
found the trail—let the men folks tend
to it now. When you-all get to Washington you tell Major Scott to send me
a Federal agent's commission so that
this here man of yours can't be cutting
up any didoes without the old man. I
ain't shot me a gun for so long I'm
plumb distracted."

"Yeah," said Jimmie. "You look
it, captain."

* * *

CHAPTER VII.

IN DUTCH.

"WHEW, Jimmie, I'm glad you
showed up," said Cohen the
next morning as the latter
came into Bowen's. "Come on back."

They went back in the little room,
and after Adolph had brought in
bottles and glasses, Cohen said: "Boy,
there's particular hell poppin' about
that truck."

"Yeah?" said Jimmie. "What
now?"

"Why, it seems that— Aw, hell,
you'll know it sooner or later anyway.
Listen, Jimmie, I run with Haven and
McGinnis, see? They're in the biggest
stuff in this town."

"Yeah," said Jimmie, indifferently.
"What of it?"

"It's this," said Cohen. "That
truck belonged to Caproni, see. I knew
there was a war on between them and
Haven and Mac, and that the big boys
wouldn't give a whoop if we knocked
it off; but what I didn't know was that
Caproni had come through to Haven
and Mac and the war was off.

"It only happened that afternoon
while I was being made a sucker of
over in Kentucky George's. The two
gangs threw in together—and then that
same night you and me knock off that
truck."

"How did you know the truck was
going to be there?" asked Jimmie.
"According to what you say, there was
war."

"Aw, I got friends in their gang,
same as they have in ours, I guess.
Everyone knows that's one of their
stations. Listen. Here they all are
sitting pretty and bingo. We knock
off a truck that they was bringing in to
the tune of fifty grand—we only got
twenty, but they was getting fifty
outta it."

Jimmie laughed. "An' now all hell
can't make the wops believe that Haven
and McGinnis weren't double crossin'
them. 'Tis good, Abie, darlin'!"

"Not so damn good," objected
Cohen. "It's brought the war back
on again, and Haven and McGinnis are
foaming at the mouth—first, because
we didn't cut them in, and, second, because I didn't go to them first and tell
'em what I was going to do."

"What do you care? Ain't ye man
enough to take care of yerself, now?"

"Sure I am—but against them two
is something else again. I don't want
to do it; I've got some sugar from those
lads and want to be in with them."

"Well then, tell them how come—
all the way through an'—"

"I did, every bit of it. How I lose
the money and we was drinkin' and all.
They said, 'All right, Abie. You and
Jimmie Murphy ain't to blame, but you

got us in a hell of a fix. Let it go at that."

"Well, then, what are you beefing about? That ain't no foaming at the mouth that I can see."

"You don't know them guys, Jimmie," said Cohen earnestly. "They've patted a guy on the back and put him on the spot an hour later for a blame sight less than that."

"I dunno," said Jimmie, frowning. "I don't want to have 'em think that we pulled a boner, either. I'd like to work with them meself. What can we do, Abie?"

"How do you think I know?" said Abie. "All I can think of is to be careful where we go and what we do for a long, long time. Maybe they'll get over it.

"An' maybe they won't," said Jimmie solemnly. "If they are that kind of men, Abie, we better do something ourselves."

"What could we do—against them? Talk sense, Jimmie."

"Sure now, the fright is driving ye nuts. Not against them, Abie. Something that will show 'em we meant right. Wait now—till I got me good Irish brain working. First, 'tis the starting up of a war again, ye say. Well, both sides wanted peace, didn't they, when they came together?"

"Sure, Jimmie."

"Good so far. Now, who wanted it the most?"

"Why, Caproni, of course. Haven and Mac had them on the run, having all the cops with them, more or less."

"Good agin. Then this guy Caproni, he thinks Haven and McGinnis double crossed him and now the war is on—bitter war."

"It sure is. Last night Doughface MacGuire and Splint Kelly got theirs, and we put Angelo Serefino and a couple more wops to the cleaner, already."

"Yeah, well, foller me close now, Abie, darlin'. Supposing you and me would go to this Caproni and tell him just what happened and offer back the twenty grand. Would he believe us, now?"

"He might at that, they say he is a well educated guy. But where are we going to get twenty grand—outta thin air? I ain't got a nickel."

"Me neither," said Jimmie. "I was up in Milwaukee wid a moll· and she cried it outta me to go to Ireland wid, what was left of it, after I cut me old lady some—"

"And besides," said Abie, "I wouldn't stick my head in that dago's place for a million—not now. We'd get no chance to do any explainin'."

"Supposin' I went to this Caproni now and told him. Then if he was believing me, I could tell him you and I would cut him in on a little thing that would get him back his fifty grand and then some more. Would he patch up the war now?"

"What thing, Jimmie?"

"Whist now! 'Tis me and a bank cop knows it and no one else."

"Bank cop—say, Jimmie. You and me are partners, ain't we? Tell me, if there's enough in it, we could mop up and go to Paris. I ain't seen that burg since 1917."

"So quick, hey? Forgot all about squaring yourself with Haven and Mac! No, Abie, listen. It'll take more men than two, this thing. Let's get straight with Haven and Mac first."

"Hey, wait a minute," protested Abie. "How are you going to get straight with them by letting Caproni and his gang in on a big clean-up?"

"NOW, you wait a minute," said Jimmie. "First, does Haven and McGinnis want to have Caproni and his gang to play with, or would they rather mop up on as many as they can all at once and clear the roads for their own bunch?"

"What a foolish question," said Abie. "Sure they'd rather mop up, but how—"

" Never mind now, answer me questions. Then, if that's the case, I go to Caproni and tell him what happens. I tell him if he'll square us wid Haven and Mac, I'll cut him in on a big wan, he and his gang, to make up for the twenty grand. All right—he gets to Haven and Mac and declares peace agin."

" Yeah? Like nothing at all. First thing he'll ask is why you don't pull this thing yourself with your own gang and he'll be thinking all the time that it's a plant of Haven and Mac to get him and his gang on the spot. That wop's got brains, feller.

" You'd be pushin' daisies before you got two blocks away from his flower store. You're all wrong, Jimmie. Haven and McGinnis don't believe we double crossed them—only that we pulled an awful boner. I wish we could square it. Listen, Jimmie, if you got something ribbed up, why not cut them in—that would show them we're right."

" It would make too many in," answered Jimmie. " Me and the bank cop—then you and Haven and Mc-Ginnis and three or four others. It'll take five or six men to do the job, Abie, countin' five outside men and the bank cop, that's six, and if we add Haven and Mac that's eight, and it's only a hundred and twenty grand. Too many in the cut, Abie."

" Aw, we can get plenty of men for a grand apiece that would help stick up the mint if they knew their get-away was covered.

" Yeah, and one of them cheap rats gets caught and squeals. Not in any of my jobs I don't have them lads. That's what got Doyle track thirteen and a washout. Some of the hand-painted shoe strings got rapped for something else and the dicks made 'em come through with all they ever knew. Not. me, feller. Forget it. I, guess that Caproni thing is no good. We'll have to show Haven and McGinnis some other way that we're wid 'em."

" And we better hurry," said Abie, grimly.

" You said they knew we didn't double cross 'em," said Jimmie.

" Yeah, but lemme tell you, feller, it ain't healthy at all to pull boners when it affects them; and another thing—we didn't slip them anything of the twenty grand either, remember that."

" Well, what of it?" said Jimmie. " I didn't know a thing about their being in it or entitled to a cent. You ought to have told me, Abe. They could have had half of mine. I want to work with them lads. They got things right here."

" Aw, there was a war on, I tell you; how did I know that Caproni had come clean?"

" That's right, Abie, you couldn't. Well, if you think they know we didn't mean to double cross them, we better let it go at that as long as you think the Caproni thing is wet."

" I do," said Abie. " Nothing doing on that line, Jimmie."

" All right. I'm going out with Adams and the Terrible Swede with some warrants. See you later, Abie."

After Jimmie had gone, a panel of the wall slid back and Haven and Mc-Ginnis stepped in the room and sat down.

" See," said Cohen, " I told you the straight of it."

" We believed you, Abie," said Mc-Ginnis, " but we wanted to hear what Murphy had to say."

" Did you hear that crazy Jimmie wanting to go to Caproni! That would be a swell way to get himself put on the spot all right."

" Never mind about Caproni, we'll attend to him," said Haven. " What you do, Cohen, is to get close to Murphy and find out what it is he's got that's good for a hundred and twenty grand. We must be careful. I'm not afraid of old Captain O'Reilly, but there's no use getting him heated up. He's got too many friends among the old-timers. If we could get some toe hold on Murphy, he'd make a damn good man for us," and Haven began to whistle softly.

Cohen and McGinnis poured themselves out a drink and began talking about other things.

"Abie," Haven said finally, "I'm going to tell you something—one reason that Mac here and I got sore about that truck thing was that Caproni had agreed to cut us in for some big jack, and that lost it for us. We know you lads didn't know anything about it, so that's that. Well, Mac and I have been under a heavy drag for months, building houses and all and in a deal where we've been putting up, and we need money badly.

"If you can get Jimmie Murphy to come across with what he's got and it turns out as good as he says, it 'll help a lot. What I'm trying to dope out is a way to put him where we want him after it's over. I think I got it, but it's up to you, Abie, shill him along."

"He talks a lot," said Cohen, "but he don't say much. He's tight as hell and high water, that guy. Say, I can tell him that you two are still sore and I'm afraid I'm going to get a ride, see, and the only way to square you fellers is to come across with ten grand. He ain't got it and neither have I, and then I'll coax him to cut you in on this bank thing."

"All right, Abie, do the best you can, as quick as you can. If Jimmie agrees, tell him I aim to plan it out so that there will not be so many men needed. Come on, Mac, let's go."

ONE afternoon later in the week Cohen asked Jimmie to drive out on the West Side with him while he served a subpœna, and Jimmie lazily agreed.

"Anything new in that bank thing?" Cohen asked, after he had cleared the loop and was on Jackson Boulevard.

"Gettin' hot," Jimmie said. "It's a payroll, Abie—it goes down once a month to a big plant in the country. Paymaster comes in with bags and guards and everything and comes out of the bank with the bags—you know, one car ahead, one behind, everybody with guns out—that kind of stuff. Then, in an hour or so an old flivver, with a delivery body on it, marked Furniture New and Secondhand, drives around to the side entrance and a couple of men load an old bookkeeper's desk on and away they go."

"And in the desk," said Abie, with an evil grin, "is the real jack! Pretty good, hey, Jimmie?"

"Yeah, boy, who would be looking for one hundred and twenty grand in an old desk? Well, the flivver drives up to the plant and the desk is taken up to the bookkeeper's room and there you are. Sometimes it's chairs or a typewriting desk, see?"

"Why, ain't there no bank down there in that burg to get the jack from, Jimmie?"

"No, it's a new plant, branch of one of the big companies, Abie, and the town isn't built yet. That's why they can't pay off in checks."

"It ought to be soft," said Abie.

"It is," said Jimmie. "I been thinking it over. If Haven or McGinnis can dope out some way that the four of us can put it over, I'll cut them in. We can croak the bank cop—he's no good to us after."

"Sure," said Abie, "I'll see Haven to-night, Jimmie."

They drove up to a little house out beyond Washington Park. As they pulled into the curb a white-haired ruddy-faced old man, with a white, close-cropped mustache, sitting on the next porch, leaned over the railing and shouted: "Hello, Yid, did ye come to pinch me now?"

Cohen looked up. "Hello, sergeant," he called. "Not to-day. When I do, I'm going to bring all the sheriff's gang along with me."

"You better," bellowed back the old

retired police officer. "Who is that ye have wid ye?" and he got up and came down the steps of the neat little bungalow.

"It's old Sergeant Cassidy," said Abie to Jimmie. "Friend of Haven's —you stay out here and gas with him while I go in." Then as Cassidy arrived: "This is Jimmie Murphy, sergeant, one of McMullen's men and my side kick. He's a right lad—and strong with Haven and Mac."

"Glad to meet ye," said Cassidy, climbing in the car and sitting down with a grunt. "'Tis seldom any of the boys come around now to see the old man. Murphy, is it? What Murphy now? Ye have a look of old Terrance Murphy—him they called Skip Murphy on account of the way he dragged his leg and missed a step. He was me partner down at the Harrison Street station when Jack Mallory was inspector and O'Reilly was captain. Jack Flanerty had the saloon on Clark and Van Buren, do ye mind—" and the old talkative Irishman rambled on telling of the days when Jack Flanerty was collector, and of Vina Fields and Carrie Watson. Finally, he repeated: "What Murphy are ye, now?"

"I'm Capt'n O'Reilly's nephew," said Jimmie, with a grin.

"Are ye now? 'Twas Maggie O'Reilly that married a Murphy and went away somewhere. I was—"

"She went to Maine," answered Jimmie. "I'm her son, sergeant, I came on and Capt'n O'Reilly got me this job."

"He did? Sure, he was always a great wan to take care of his own. Is your ma still alive now, Jimmie?"

"Yeah, alive and kicking. My pa is dead, though."

"Yes—so I heard. Sure, Maggie and me were sweethearts in the old days. I thought of marrying her once meself—but she thought different," the old sergeant added, with a grin. "Sure now don't be telling my owld woman that—she'd make me life miserable, she

would so. And 'tis a friend of Haven's, ye are, too? Come on in, I have some fine owld stuff hid away."

"Let's wait for Abie," said Jimmie.

"We will. So you're Maggie O'Reilly's boy—well, well. How long you been here, Jimmie?"

"About two months, I came right down from Portland."

"So—that's right, I remember now, 'twas to Portland they wint. You must come out and meet my owld lady, but mind ye, now, no word about me and Maggie."

"I got clam blood in me," said Jimmie, with a grin, as Abie Cohen came out.

They went in with Sergeant Cassidy as he insisted and finally got away after several rounds of drinks.

Cassidy came out on the porch with them and watched them as they drove away.

"So," he said out loud as the car turned the corner, "Ye are Maggie O'Reilly's son from Portland, young feller me lad, ye are—like hell."

The old sergeant, who had been deep in the "pickin's" while on the force, went to the telephone, and after trying several places, got Haven on the wire.

"'Tis Cassidy talkin'—Cassidy— Sergeant Cassidy of No. 21— Oh, ye do—why the divil don't ye take the wax outta yer ears? Oh, ye can hear now—can ye—all right thin, listen to me. I dunno what ye are doin' or how close ye are to the lad that's in McMullen's office running around wid Abie Cohen, but this, I'll tell ye. Maggie O'Reilly — she that married Murphy, had two boys—an' both of them was killed over in France—

"How do I know? Never mind how I know—I'm tellin' ye somepin. If that owld devil O'Reilly introjused him as his nephew—guard yerself well, me bowld detective sergeant— Ye will. Never mind the applesauce as me flapper of a daughter do be sayin' all the time. Ye might see that a couple of cases gets dropped off for the old man once in awhile. Ye will—fair enough," and the old police officer hung up.

CHAPTER VIII.

FOREWARNED.

JIMMIE was just leaving the sheriff's office about, five,thirty the next afternoon when one of the deputies called after him: " Hey, Jimmie! On the phone, boy! Take it in Sam's office, he's gone!" Jimmie turned back, went into the room, closing the door behind him and picked up the receiver. "Hello," he said curtly, thinking it was Cohen or one of the deputies. "This is Jimmie Murphy, what is it?"

A thin, half hysterical voice with a peculiar whine in it came faintly to his ear. "Jimmie! Is it you, Jimmie, no kiddin'? Jimmie, I got to know sure. Quick, tell me, where is the old apple tree—hurry up, tell me! Don't stall, Jimmie!"

Jimmie's face tightened and his face set in hard lines, but he answered promptly: "Down in my ole pappy's back yard—by the well."

"Oh—that's right, Jimmie, come down here as soon as it's dark—go round the rear in the alley an'—"

"Wait a minute," Jimmie said. "Tighten up, feller. Where is it?"

"Back of Tsi Wang's laundry on Clark near Polk—go round the back and climb up on the shed, I'll be there at the third window. Will you come, Jimmie? Oh, if they find out! The minute it's dark—"

"Steady," drawled Jimmie, " I'll be there, old timer, keep your shirt on. Tell me something."

"I—oh—he may be back any minute, listen, Jimmie, I used to be M. I. G. 2—" and the connection was broken.

Jimmie put the receiver slowly back on the hook.

"I think," he said softly to the telephone mouthpiece, "that right here is where old man Howard's son Jimmie

calls up the reserves in the shape of Texas Rangers and police captains."

When Jimmie crawled up on the shed built against the wall in the rear of Tsi Wang's that night, Ranger Captain Yancey stood at the corner of the alley, his old slouch hat tilted back on his head, a more or less silly grin on his weather-beaten old face, swaying a little on his feet, already marked down by two or three pair of wolfish eyes as being an old hick that a couple of more drinks would make ready for killing.

In front of Tsi Wang's and down a couple of stores stood ex-Police Captain O'Reilly in a hot argument with two other retired policemen who had met each other there and at once halted and began the old argument as to who had been the best chief in Chicago.

A young policeman walked by them and grinned, conscious of his youth and of the fact that he was on the way up the hill that they had climbed.

He knew Captain O'Reilly, and saluted respectfully as he passed, walking to the corner to give the old rube a look over to see if he could take care of himself.

A thin, wasted hand opened the window as Jimmie raised up from the roof and he threw a leg over the sash and entered the room.

The man that had opened the window had gone back to a cot against the wall of the little dingy room. The smell of opium was distinct to Jimmie's nostrils.

"Jimmie," the man whispered, "don't look at me like that! Quick, Jimmie, you're uncovered! Those thugs took me in a car and pointed you out, and made me tell them—see what they did to me, Jimmie?" and he tore open his shirt. His body was covered with red and dark blue welts.

"In the old days they could have beat me to death, Jimmie, but now I couldn't stand it. I crawled down to old Tsi Wang's room and got to his phone when he was sleeping off a pill."

"All right, old kid," Jimmie said softly. I know—it's all right, Fitz, you're coming back, though. Tell me what it is. How long you got?"

"Old Tsi Wang is hitting the pipe, and the two devils that are guarding me are down below with a couple of skirts. The Chink that's on guard in the alley sneaks around to play a little fantan about this time. I'm all in, Jimmie—my God, once I was an officer and a gentleman like you. This damn stuff got me and—"

"Steady," said Jimmie; "get through first, Fitz, and then I'll get you out of here."

"No use, I'm done, Jimmie. I couldn't live without it, now. It's been six years, Jimmie." He raised himself up with an effort to a sitting position and with clenched hands, holding his head up, spoke as if making a report.

"You were tipped in some way to Haven and McGinnis. They know I used to be an agent, and came down here and got me. They beat me up here, and then took me in a car and showed you to me, and beat me some more. I denied ever seeing you until McGinnis began—I couldn't stand it, Jimmie—and I told them who you were!

"I heard Haven say you were a deputy sheriff—if it had been in the old days, Jimmie, they could have beaten me to death before I told, but now—I thought I had sunk to the bottom—but to betray my own outfit!"

"Under torture, old-timer," said Jimmie; "and even then you wouldn't if your nerves hadn't been shot to hell. You've redeemed yourself, boy. Can you climb out of that window, or will I carry you?"

"Have I, Jimmie? Have I, honest? Tell me."

"You have," said Jimmie, positively. "I wouldn't tell you if you hadn't. It clears your record, no matter what you've been. At the risk of your life, you warned me. Now, come on."

"Jimmie, you go—I can't—that beating I got broke something in me. I was clear when I resigned, Jimmie—I had sense enough left for that. Am I clear, Jimmie?"

"I'll report in that former Federal Agent Fitzmorris worked on the case with me, and was of great assistance," answered Jimmie, absolutely ignoring the fact that any moment might throw him into a death battle. "Come on, Fitz, old kid. Buck up—you're not done yet by a damn sight."

Fitzmorris shook his head. "Jimmie, you've made me feel clean again; but I'm done. Do you think Peggy will know, Jimmie? Thank God she went west before I slipped and—"

"Certainly she knows, fool of the world," said Jimmie; "she's waiting for you up there somewhere. You'll catch it from her for the way you've been acting, but that's all. Come on—let's get out of this dump. We'll give them a fight and make 'em like it."

"Jimmie—can I—"

"Sure you can. The major will do anything I ask him. Boy, I'll have your badge and credentials here in three days, and a thirty-day sick leave along with 'em, so you can straighten up. Get goin', feller, we're overplaying our luck right now. We'll mop up on this gang in the open."

"Sure we will," said Fitzmorris, standing up. "Why, Jimmie, why not? In the game again, and clear!"

Then his knees gave way under him and he would have fallen to the floor if Jimmie had not caught him in his arms.

Jimmie carried him to the cot and laid him gently down. The room was unlighted except for the light that shone in from the arc light in the alley below, that had come on a moment ago, but there was enough for Jimmie to see that the man he had worked with when they were both rookies had gone to explain his conduct to Peggy.

Not touching the body, or in any way arranging the clothes, Jimmie went softly to the window and out through it, closing it carefully. He got out on the shed, and in a moment was sauntering carelessly out of the alley to hail a passing taxi.

Captain Yancey walked slowly past the still arguing coppers, then stopped, turned and came back to them. " Can any of you gents tell me the best way to the West Side?" he asked.

"Well, now," answered O'Reilly, " it's a large order. What part of the West Side do ye be lookin' for?"

"Why—I reckon it's the corner of Madison and Paulina that I want."

"Ye do? Sure 'tis right by that corner I'll be goin' in a minute, as soon as I tell these scuts wan more thing. It's home I ought to have been a long time ago, instead of standin' here gassin' wid these flannel-mouthed terriers. So long to ye, boys," and he walked along with Yancey to where his car was parked.

AN hour later, Jimmie, sitting in the rear seat of O'Reilly's car with the curtains down, was telling them of Fitzmorris.

"He was one of the best men on the force," he wound up, " and then, after his wife died, dope got him; how, I don't know. He dropped out. Just how Haven knew he was a Federal agent in the old days I don't know, either.

"It was just by chance that Fitzmorris knew me; there are so many agents, and I only know twenty or thirty myself. Just luck, I suppose, that he could tell them who I was. The curse of Crum'el must have been working against me that I'd be one he knew. He rambled a lot, and all I got was that Haven knows who I am — and that's that. Also it's one more to square accounts for with the gang."

Yancey stirred in his seat. " Son, I'm gettin' right well fed up with these here killin's and beatin's like you tell about. I reckon we better close in on them snakes, right now."

" Wait, now," commanded the canny old Irishman. " 'Tis waitin' for them, don't be in a hurry. They'll be puttin' Jimmie here on the spot, but not at wunst. They'll be tryin' to find out if enny wan else is in wid him. They know that Federal dicks generally travel in pairs, wan to cover the other —didn't this Wilson lad have a buddy, now, Jimmie?"

" No—he was working alone with the P. O. Inspectors. There was a lot of Uncle's mail taken in the I. C. thing."

" Well, this Haven and McGinnis will try and decoy ye some place, Jimmie, to get outta ye what ye know and who's wid ye, that's sure. They don't know how deep I am in it—and, be Judas, they're still afraid of the old man, say what they will among themselves. Wan thing right now, young fella, and that is ye go nowhere at all wid any of them unless ye pass the word to us. Ye hear me, now, Jimmie?"

" Well, suh," drawled Yancey, " down in my country we aimed mostly on doing the decoying ourselves— it's going to be right hard to cover Jimmie in a way that won't make them plumb suspicious. From what I saw of the way these here gents work, a car might come along any minute."

" Cover nothing," said Jimmie. " I could wire and get twenty men here from Washington in twenty-four hours. This is my picnic, and I'm going through as is. I can—"

" Sure," interrupted O'Reilly; "sure, Jimmie. But ye don't mind a little help now, do ye, from the old men?"

" Mind? I should say not. I mean that we're men enough to knock these birds off, and in the way they deserve —the three of us."

" We are," said O'Reilly gravely, " if there was twinty of them instead of three—not countin' the understrappers."

" We'll get them later," said Jimmie.

"The capt'n here ought to know his own hunting ground," drawled Yancey. "I reckon he's right about them not putting you—on the spot, as you jaspers say—for a little while. I got me a plan that might work."

"Ye have?" said O'Reilly. "Ye have, hey? Come across wid it, then."

"Well, suh, have you got you any right good burglars among your friends, capt'n?"

"Sure, miny av them, in the pen what I put them in, and out av it when they done their time. What the divil now, Yancey, ye owld fox?"

"Well," said the old Ranger captain, "I got me an idea that we might give 'em a chance to try Jimmie here out on that tellin' thing and save 'em a lot of plannin'. It's thisaway." And Yancey began to drawl out a plan of action.

CHAPTER IX.

IN THE BOMBPROOF.

HAVEN'S new house was a pretentious one, on one of the prominent northwest side corners near Fullerton Avenue. His wife and family had gone away for the season. The only servant left to take care of him, the few times he came home, was an old negro, husband of the cook who had gone with the family to the beach.

He was a big, brawny negro, with a deep scar running from his cheek bone to over his ear on the left side of his face and a twisted nose. When the knock came at the kitchen door he was sitting with his feet up on the table, a bottle with an Old Crow label on the table beside him.

"Dawgone it," he grumbled as he got up to answer, "these heah no-'count peddlers don't gib folks no rest, nohow."

He opened the door, after reaching over and setting the bottle down by one of the table legs.

An old man in shabby clothes stood there. He was wearing an old black slouch hat, and his clothes, though worn, were neatly pressed. "I'm sellin' some stuff hyar," he began, "that will shore make the best beer — boy, you sho' smell like you-all don't need no beer malt."

"What dat?" growled the negro. "Does you— What you want, white man? Dis heah ain't de—" he stopped, looking into the frosty blue eyes of the old man standing at the door. "No, suh, capt'n," he went on, "Ah don't need me anything. Ah got me plenty good lickah, yassuh. Is you from de South, captain?"

"Texas," said the old man. "Boy, the colored people up hyar are right snippy. I almost had to kill me seven or eight already since Ah been up hyar. Wheah you from, boy?" The old man leaned against the doorsill, evidently in no hurry.

"Me? Ah come from Kentuck a long time ago, capt'n. Ah used to run on de L. and N. for yeahs, capt'n. Ah was de chef on old seventy-five. Capt'n, Ah don't want none of dat stuff. Ah got me all de good stuff Ah want."

"Yeah? An' that bootleg licker 'll kill you, boy."

"Dis heah ain't no bootleg licker Ah got. Capt'n, Ah got me in a crap game las' night an' Ah loses heavy. Ah knows you-all is from de South and Ah knows a gentmum when Ah see one. Ah seen lots of gentmum like you down in Texas. Capt'n, does you want to buy you a bottle of de real stuff?"

"Where are you goin' to get the real stuff, boy? I got me a ten-dollar bill for a bottle of good Bourbon if I plumb stahve to death aftuh."

"Dat's just what Ah need, capt'n, to get in de game wid to-night. Capt'n, mah boss am away—does you come in, Ah shows you some real stuff—does you—capt'n, you-all ain't no prohibition officer, is you?"

"Me? One of them snoopers? Boy,

I reckon I better kill me a nigger, right now."

The big colored man laughed. "No, suh, capt'n. Does you do dat, you don't git de Bourbon. Come in de kitchen, capt'n."

When the old man came out, he had a bundle under his arm, and the old negro, reaching for the bottle under the table, said aloud: "Now Ah gets me back in de game an' Ah mops up dis time."

The old man didn't seem anxious to sell any more of his stuff, although he tried several more houses in the vicinity, then giving it up as a bad job, took a street car toward town, and within an hour was with Captain O'Reilly.

"Here's a present for you," he drawled, as he put the bundle down, "from Haven's private stock."

"Take it away wid you," answered O'Reilly firmly. "I don't want it. Jimmie is set until the thing is ready. I had McMullen send him wid a square deputy out in the sticks on a job the owld boy thought was for me. 'Tis no wan will know where he wint either. Now, what have you, and when do you need me bowld burglar?"

"Well, suh," drawled Yancey, "I reckon we won't need him at all." He told O'Reilly of getting into Haven's house and that the colored man had taken him down in the basement, in his anxiety to get money to gamble with, and had unlocked a room that seemed to be dug out beyond the walls and showed him tier after tier of cases of liquor in a room at least thirty feet square.

"That nigger," drawled Yancey, "said that he had a key that Haven didn't know nothin' about and that Haven would skin him if he caught him. He said that he had found Haven's key ring one day when Haven forgot to change it with his pants, and he took a wax impression. Since then he's been snitchin' some right along from the back cases."

"So! He has a key, has he?"
5 A

"To that room anyway. And I saw something else, capt'n. There's a table in there and three or four chairs; and on the table was a piece of rubber hose, wire hose—an' on top of one of the lines of cases was one of them night sticks."

"Look at that now," said O'Reilly. "'Tis the eyes of a hawk ye have still, ye owld divil."

"This nigger," went on Yancey, "told me that he used to be a chef on the L. and N., and that Haven was a Pullman conductor once on the same road."

"He was, before he came here and got on the force, I'm told," answered O'Reilly, "and bad cess to the train that brought the murderin' divil. Wait a minute—why, 'tis the same, I bet ye. Is this coon a big wan, wid a bad scar on him by the cheek bone?"

"Yes, suh, he sure has a bad one—and his nose is twisted around. It looks as if he'd been hit mighty hard some time."

"He was," said O'Reilly grimly. "Twice, before he would behave—wanst by Jack Mallory and wanst by me. Sure now, I got him—'tis as ye say, chef on the L. and N. he was, then burglar and stickup man, then to Joliet for twenty years. Wid good time off now, he'd be out these five years.

"Sure 'tis him—and where better would he be goin' now than to Haven, who railroaded wid him. Gimme room, till I get to that phone. He shoots craps, does he? 'Twill be in Yaller Jackson's place widout doubt, but I'll make sure. Yaller will do what I tell him and kape still about it. Go on home now, me brave malt peddler, an' leave it to me. 'Tis no burglar we'll be needin', as ye say."

WHEN the negro who was called Scarface Mose entered Yaller Jackson's place, Yaller called to him: "Hey, dare, Scarface, ole kid. Easy money upstairs—niggers in from de country wid rolls. Up in de back room—go on up and you cleans you a bank roll."

"Dat's what Ah aims to do," grumbled Scarface, turning to the stairs. "I gotta get me some jack, yaller boy."

He opened the door of the back room and had stepped inside before he realized that there was no crap game in there.

Instead, he saw the grim, hard old faces of Ex-Police Inspector Jack Mallory and Captain Pat O'Reilly.

O'Reilly shut the door as Scarface moaned: "Oh, mah Lawd!"

Mallory thrust his face almost into that of the trembling Scarface: "Ye did that Martin job last night," he snarled.

"Ah sweah Ah ain't!" stammered Scarface, his face getting a waxy gray. "Ah been straight."

"Haven can't save you, you con," rasped O'Reilly. "Come clean or we'll beat you to death right here. You did it."

"Ah knows dat nobody can save me, capt'n," said Scarface hardly above a whisper. "Not from you two gentmums. Ah'm done."

"Well, now," said O'Reilly, "ye may not have done it after all; but ye know if we say so, ye go back for life, don't ye?"

"Yessuh, Ah knows dat. Capt'n, honest to God, Ah never—"

"Shut yer mouth," snarled Mallory. "Pat, we started to kill this blackbird once before. We'll just finish the job now."

"Oh, Lawd, Lawd!" moaned Scarface. "Don't do 'er—don't do 'er."

"Has Haven anything on ye?" demanded O'Reilly.

"No, suh, capt'n. Mah wife dat Ah married when Ah come out from de pen, she's de cook, and he gib me a job, dat's all. When Ah was on de L. and N—"

"What could Inspector Mallory and me do to you?"

"Capt'n," answered Scarface, ear-

nestly—and he fully meant it—"you gentmums could skin me alive and nobody pay no 'tention to it, yassuh."

"'Tis so," said O'Reilly grimly. "Before we do that—which won't take a minute any time—listen to me, Scarface Mose, and listen well, and see that ye get it the first time—there'll be no second. First I'll tell ye what will happen to ye if ye even look like ye was goin' squawk to any one. Now then—"

"HELLO, Jimmie," shouted Abie, as Jimmie came into the sheriff's office. "Where've you been for two days? Boy, I got a hot one, and I've been looking for you all over town. Let's go over and grab us something to eat, and I'll tell you about it."

"Aw, the old man sent me out in the sticks. Nothing doing on that grub stuff for me. I got a hot one of me own to handle. Come over here, Abie. Listen now," he went on as they walked over to one of the unoccupied windows of the big room. "That bank thing comes off to-morrow morning. I got to beat it right now and see the bank cop. You tell Haven and McGinnis that I want them in, see, and that I'll meet them at Haven's to-night about twelve thirty. You be there, Abie, and we'll frame it."

"What! You want to see Haven at his house? Sure, Jimmie, I'll have 'em there. I was surprised that you decided to cut them in. Stick around with me, Jimmie, after you get to the lad at the bank. I'll be over to Bowens."

"I will not. I'm going right now, and when I get through with him I got to go with Capt'n O'Reilly to see some old bird that's sick. I'll be there, Abie, between twelve and one."

"I'll have Haven and McGinnis there," answered Abie, and as Jimmie walked away he added under his breath: "What luck for us—we didn't have to—"

It was twelve thirty when Jimmie

pulled up to the curb in front of Haven's brilliantly lighted house. Two uniformed policemen were standing on the corner talking, idly swinging their night sticks, and quite a few people were passing. Jimmie rang the bell, and Abie opened the door. "I'm butler," he said with a grin. "Haven's family have gone away, and there is only an old smoke in the kitchen. Come on in, Jimmie. They're in the dining room. Boy, they broke out some fine booze."

Haven and McGinnis greeted Jimmie as ever. "Sit down, Jimmie," Haven said, "and pour yourself a drink. Abie tells me that your thing is ready and you want to cut us in. We're right guys, Jimmie, and we'll stick and slug to the finish."

"I know that," answered Jimmie, sitting down. The dining room was a large one, with French windows leading out to the veranda. The people passing on the sidewalk could be seen from the table.

"Well," he continued, "here it is for the four of us—an' no more. The bank cop we can knock off."

For an hour they discussed it, Haven taking the leading part in figuring ways and means. At last he said, "Well, it's jake now, the way she lies. Have another drink, Jimmie, before you go," and he picked up the bottle that Jimmie had been using. Just as he was going to pour it, he stopped and held it up to the light.

"Say, there's some cork or something in this, boy. Abie, go down and get a fresh bottle. Wait a minute— Jimmie, you want to see a regular licker storage? I'll show you some booze that came from the bonded warehouse. Come on, Mac, and you, too, Abie. Let's show Jimmie some real stuff."

"Sure," said Jimmie, getting up and easing his heavy cartridge belt, filled with forty-five shells. "This blamed belt is wearing a sore spot on me. I got to take it off for a minute or two." He unbuckled it and laid it on a chair, with the holster and his Colt hanging from it.

"Leave it there," said McGinnis. "It'll be all right."

"That's what I was going to do," answered Jimmie. "It's a relief for a few minutes, anyway."

"I thought you packed your rod under your arm, Jimmie?" said Abie.

"I used to," answered Jimmie, opening his coat and rubbing his side under his left arm, "but it wore me raw down here, too."

Haven led the way from the dining room to the big, lighted kitchen. "Hello, Mose," he said to the negro, who rose hastily from his seat as they came out. "You can go out if you want to. I'll lock up."

"Yassuh, Capt'n," said Mose, promptly. "Ah gits me some fresh air and den—"

"Go shoot craps," supplied McGinnis. "They'll clean you, Mose."

They went down through the roomy, deep basement, Haven pointing out specially built features to Jimmie; past the furnace, through a laundry room to a door set in the masonry. Haven unlocked the door, reached in and switched on a light, holding the door open to let the rest pass him.

The room contained tier after tier of cases, marked Old Crow, Pebbleford, Four Roses, Three Star and other brands well known in the days when the whisper of prohibition was a thing to be laughed at.

In the middle of the room was a table, on which lay a wirewoven length of hose, about four feet long. There were three or four chairs, no other furniture, just the long rows and aisles made by the cases, brand by brand.

Haven shut the door after them. Jimmie heard the lock click as he walked to the table and half sat down on it, picking up the hose and swinging it idly.

"This room is built out under the lawn," said Haven, as he walked toward Jimmie. "There's fifteen feet of dirt over the roof. I made it burglar-proof. That's what I use to siphon off with, Jimmie," he added, as Jimmie looked down at the hose.

Cohen picked up a chair and went over by the door and sat down tilting it against the wall.

"And now," continued H a v e n, smoothly, "before the pleasantries of the evening commence once more," he took off his coat and drew a long, heavy blackjack from his pocket. Cohen's gun had slid into his hand as Haven started to speak and he rested it in his lap, the muzzle straight at Jimmie's heart. McGinnis laughed, his eyes showing the insane gleam of cruelty and reached up on top of one of the cases, bringing down a night stick.

"We will now have a few words from Mr. James Howard, Federal Agent," Haven went on, swinging the blackjack by the loop, "working under Major Scott from Washington."

"Aw, hell," snarled McGinnis, "beat the lousy spy up first. Let me at him a minute, Ted."

"Don't be impatient, Mac," answered Haven. "There's plenty of time for that. It might take Mr. Howard's mind off of what he will no doubt be glad to tell us—if he wants to live."

"It would," said Jimmie with a grin, still sitting on the table.

"I saw what you did to Fitzmorris. He told me you birds were experts. You mustn't take too much credit for that, though. He was all in—time was when he'd have killed you three rats before breakfast any morning."

Haven's impassive face broke as Jimmie mentioned Fitzmorris. McGinnis swore viciously and stepped back a step. Cohen's chair came down on all four legs and the evil smile faded from his lips.

Haven recovered first. "You know Fitzmorris?" he asked, suavely.

"You mean—did I know him?" corrected Jimmie. "He's dead, you know, from the beating you cowards gave him. I knew Charley Wilson, too."

"Wait, Mac," said Haven sharply, as McGinnis stepped forward, the night stick raised. "That will do us no good, I'm afraid. Fitzmorris got loose in some way and made contact with this young gentleman. Get it—you fool—this is a plant and we've swallowed it, hook, line and sinker. He wouldn't come out here knowing his hand was tipped unless he's covered in some way."

"Covered, hell," snarled McGinnis. "What's eating you, Haven? We got him, same as we got that other dirty spy, Wilson, and that hophead. Supposin' he is covered outside—so are we, all the time. We'll beat him to death and throw him down the well, like garbage. Get out of my way. I'll start on him, the——"

He stopped in his bull-like rush at Jimmie.

FROM one of the aisles made by the cases, stepped old Ranger Captain Yancey, his ivory-handled .41 Colt in his hand.

"He's covered inside, too," said Yancey, mildly. "Put 'em up!"

Captain O'Reilly, with a United States deputy marshal's star on his coat stepped out in sight from the other side, his police .38 special in one hand, a night stick in the other. "Ye dirty rats," he bellowed, just as Abie Cohen, cornered, knowing that the death he had given others was on him, but game as the weasel he sometimes resembled, raised his gun, which he had lowered when McGinnis started his rush. He meant to kill Jimmie before he went into darkness himself.

Yancey's gun roared and Abie Cohen, deputy sheriff and cold-blooded murderer, pitched forward, a little hole in the center of his forehead—the back of his head almost blown to pieces.

Jimmie's hand went under his soft shirt and came out with an automatic and pressed against Haven's side, in one flowing motion so fast that it was there before the sound of Yancey's shot had died away. McGinnis looked at Yancey and O'Reilly advancing on him, then, in the face of their two guns, snarled like a jungle cat. He dropped the night stick and continued his hand around to his hip pocket. It reached there and then fell away. Ex-Police Captain O'Reilly, now United States deputy marshal, hater of crooks and crooked coppers, himself a "square cop," had shot him through the heart.

Faint sounds of running feet could be heard from the outside for a moment, then they stopped. The two uniformed policemen who had been standing on the corner came running up on the porch followed by one from the alley. They ran up the steps together —to stop, confronted by the grim faces of Jack Mallory, ex-inspector of police, a man known to fear no one man —or twenty—and United States Marshal Bob Bostweck, who had been a "killer" before they were born.

"Are ye boys goin' somewhere?" demanded Mallory, coldly. "If ye are, think twice of it, young fellers. 'Tis Government business goin' on down there. Onless ye be wid Haven and McGinnis now, are ye? If so, me and the marshal will take ye to jail—and ye needn't bother to be runnin' down no steps to the basement."

The three young policemen vehemently denied any connection whatever with either Haven or McGinnis.

"Go on, Jimmie," said O'Reilly. "What the divil are ye waiting for, I dunno. Ye have him, go on, kill him."

"Just a minute," said Haven smoothly. "I know I'm overdue, but I've got a wife and family. Is there any—"

"So did Johnnie Adams and a lot more," answered Jimmie. "Make it snappy, Haven, if you want to come across with anything."

"He's stalling for time," said O'Reilly. "'Twill do ye no good, me murderin' bucko. If it 'll ease yer mind now, me old inspector, Jack Mallory is out in front wid the marshal himself

and some of his boys. Ye have no chance, Haven—'tis the same as ye handed out to miny a lad. Kill him for the snake he is, Jimmie—or I will."

"He can't kill me this way," said Haven. "I surrend—" As he spoke he took a desperate gambler's chance to win clear. There wasn't one chance in a million that he could get by with it, but he took it.

Jimmie was standing close to him on the left side, his gun pressed into Haven's side on a line with his heart, his elbow and forearm on a right angle. Haven's left arm was forced out a little backwards. As he said "surrend—" he slapped up with his left hand at Jimmie's elbow, intending to knock the gun away from him, at the same time circling Jimmie's body with his right arm, drawing him in front of him. Whether he figured he could use Jimmie as some kind of a shield or hostage, once he had him between himself and Yancey and O'Reilly—or that he could, in the confusion, draw his own gun and fight his way clear, no one knew but himself.

As his hand hit Jimmie's elbow, it did what Haven had not foreseen. It rapped Jimmie sharply on the funny bone and Jimmie's whole arm and hand jerked. His finger tightened on the trigger and Haven's grip relaxed. As Jimmie stepped back, Haven slowly sank to his knees, blood spurting out of his side where Jimmie's bullet had torn through an artery. Then, his fighting, merciless spirit whipping him on, he staggered to his feet, his eyes glazing and drew his gun.

Jimmie waited, a little frozen smile on his lips, until the gun muzzle began to come around. It seemed ages to the two men watching the play. At last— Haven's lips tightened, his body stiffened and the gun began to slowly move to a line with Jimmie.

As Yancey raised his gun, Jimmie fired twice. The gun jumped from Haven's hand with the first bullet. The second went through his evil brain.

"Wan for each," said O'Reilly, calmly, as he looked at the three dead men. "And 'tis wan more than the two buddies av yours, Jimmie. Stay here now till I go up and let Jack Mallory and the marshal in. I do be thinkin' that I'll bring down the young coppers wid them—to teach them an object lesson."

"Well, suh," said Ranger Captain Yancey, mildly, "I reckon I'll go on home to Ma to-night. She's plumb li-

able to raise Cain with me playin' around up here, thisaway. Son, when you and that right pretty Sally Wilson girl get hitched up, we'll be lookin' for you down in Texas for a visit."

"We'll come," answered Jimmie, looking down at the men who had killed Charley Wilson and Fitzmorris. "I think that Charley is resting easy —now."

THE END

Campbell's Black Reports

CONTRARY to the general notion, savages do not kill senselessly. Nine times out of ten, when a white is murdered by Africans it is through misunderstanding or fear on the part of the blacks. The writer has been through the most savage parts of Nigeria without a gun or any sort of weapon. Trouble comes mostly of the superstitions of the blacks. The case of Captain Campbell is one.

Campbell was doing survey work back of the Pagan Belt. He had gone there unarmed. He knew the natives, knew Africa, and thought he could get through with tact and patience. A few weeks after his departure his black appeared at government quarters with word that his massa "done be bush-chopped," killed in the bush. Questions as to where it had happened, and the how and why of it, drew from the excited black a strange tale.

"Sah, Massa Campbell go nine days where sun come up—went east. We come from country dat go up into de sky on one side, and if you fall down you go die one-time, and country go up into de sky on de ober side, and if you fall down you go die one-time all same." (Campbell had reached a cañon, whose sheer bluffs meant sudden death if you fell down them.) "Massa Campbell put sticks wid flags in de ground." (Survey stakes with bits of white rag to mark them.) "Bera well. Plenty nigger come. Make talk. Massa Campbell no savvy. He shut his head, go on wid de work. Bera well. Niggers talk loud. Get heap angry. Massa Campbell no savvy. Niggers run to their village. Come back wid spears. Kill Massa Campbell. Bera well."

An officer left with two Housa constables to inquire into the murder, and mete out what punishment he should think fit. He did not punish the murderers. The palaver brought out that, from the point of view of the savages, the killing was a necessary evil.

This tribe had recently lost a brutal chief through death. For two weeks after his death they had kept up a furious din of tom-tomming, shouting, shaking huge hand rattles and beating gourds, to scare away the brutal chief's spirit. If it had been a friendly spirit they would have hung out rags to show it that it was welcome to stay around.

And there came the white man, hanging out rags and luring back the spirit of the bullying chief. They had expostulated with the white man, pleaded with him, but he would not heed. So in fear of a return of the dreaded spirit they had put the white man to death.

T. Samson Miller.

There flashed to me the vague horror that this was a coffin

A Brand New World

*Invaders from Xenephrene! Armed with terrible weapons they
land upon an Earth that is struggling to adjust itself
to a new and demoralizing climatic upheaval*

By RAY CUMMINGS

LEADING UP TO THIS INSTALLMENT

A NEW star swims into our heavens in the fall of 1952, steadily growing larger and brighter as it approaches the solar system.' Xenephrene, as it is named by the great astronomer, Prof. Vanderstuyft, is almost as large as the earth, and swings into an elliptical orbit around the sun, between the earth and Venus.

Strange climatic disturbances arise, with record cold throughout the United States. Astronomers are making discoveries and calculations, which are withheld by government orders, until February. Then it is admitted that the earth's axis was shifting till the south pole will, in April, point toward the sun. The northern hemisphere will be plunged into six months of darkness and Arctic cold, which is already being felt, while the southern hemisphere will have torrid daylight. Then conditions will be reversed during the next half-year. The equator will be the only temperate zone.

Immediately business, industry, agriculture collapse; transportation southward is overcrowded, and millions perish in the swiftly increasing Arctic cold, trying to make their way along deep, snow-drifted roads toward the sunlight. New York is abandoned,

This story began in the Argosy-Allstory Weekly for September 22

Miami is made capital of America, and there is a world-wide scramble for the equator and southern hemisphere. Peter Vanderstuyft, who is telling the story, and Freddie Smith, both of the Amalgamated Broadcasters, start south. Peter's sister, Hulda, is visiting the Cains in Porto Rico; Dan Cain, Peter's schoolmate, is in love with Hulda. One night the Porto Rican houseboy sees a "ghost." Dan and Hulda go out and discover a strangely beautiful pink-white girl with long, white hair, standing near a 20-foot silver sphere. Timid, she springs lightly over them in a high arc; at last she lets them approach, calling herself "Zetta."

Meantime, while the southward panic is at its horrible height, comes the discovery that a hostile race in human form has come from Xenephrene, landing near New York!

CHAPTER IV.

ZETTA.

THAT midnight of February 10th, Hulda and Dan stood on the small Porto Rican trail, facing at a brief distance the white girl in the moonlight. She answered Hulda's call; in a queerly small voice her words came to them:

"Zetta! Zetta! Zetta!"

There was a brief silence. Dan murmured, "Let's go nearer."

Slowly, carefully, they advanced; fearful of again frightening her. But this time she did not move. She stood watchful, trembling slightly, but held her ground. And presently they were confronting her. She was shorter even than Hulda; very slim and frail. A young girl just reaching maturity. A rose, not yet full-blown. The thought occurred to Dan. But the comparison was wrong. Not a rose, for this was a flower of young womanhood of a species no one of earth could name.

She seemed, aside from her snow-white hair, no more than a strangely beautiful girl of earth. But to both Dan and Hulda came again, more strongly than before, the feeling of her strangeness. There was something singularly unusual in her aspect. And this they both recall clearly: as they stood there for a silent instant confronting her, both were conscious of sensations indescribable, as though they were feeling something within themselves — something vague, elusive— something no mortal of earth had ever felt before. And, perhaps, hearing something—so faint, so ethereal they could not define it—faint as though it were sound heard not by their ears, but by their minds.

And they saw something, too, which perhaps no mortal eyes had ever seen before. An aura, a dim, very faint red radiance shone around the three of them as they stood there together in the moonlight. Hulda and Dan remember it was something like that.

They stood for a moment, stricken with wonder at their sensations; and perhaps the strange girl was less timorous as she saw their attitude of awe. She stared up into Dan's face, and smiled. Queerly wistful; trusting. A gentle little creature! And he stared down into her dark eyes and found them shimmering pools of iridescence. Then again she spoke, other words in a strange, liquid tongue, soft, with curiously clipped, intoned syllables.

Dan shook his head. "We can't understand you. Can you understand us?" He smiled; and Hulda smiled.

"She's not afraid of us," said Dan. The girl was waving a hand with what they knew was a gesture of negation. She could not understand their language; and when Dan tried Spanish —realizing it was futile; and tried his imperfect French—her gesture continued.

He tried again. "Dan! Dan! Dan!" he said, and struck his chest. And Hulda indicated herself with "Hulda! Hulda!"

The girl's eager face brightened.

They had established communication; the first communication between Xenephrene and our earth!

The girl cried, "Zetta, Zetta," and laid her hand on her breast.

It was the first communication between the worlds. What dire events, tragedies, amazing things to transpire before the last communication was over!

IT is not my purpose, and again, I have no space in which to narrate all the details of these days. The girl was persuaded to follow Dan and Hulda, and through all that February she lived with the Cains in the plantation house, guarded and kept hidden, though the news of her presence could not be entirely concealed.

The silver ball in the coconut grove was a vehicle in which, by some method unknown to earth, this girl—this Zetta, as she called herself—had come from her world, to ours. And she had not come alone A man had been with her —he seemed to be of middle age. He lay dead near the vehicle. Perhaps the victim of an accident; or perhaps the girl had killed him.

There was no one, as yet, to say. Zetta could not, apparently, understand any earth language; and her languge sounded hopeless to fathom. She seemed intelligent, docile, willing and anxious to be kept with the Cains; eager, it seemed at first, to be in the room with them—to hear them talk. But after that first night, she did not speak again; and they thought she had fallen into a sullen silence.

There is so much I have to tell! Astronomers at Quito had seen this silver vehicle enter the earth's atmosphere that night of February 10th; and had seen another, infinitely larger, which they believed had started from the surface of Xenephrene.

Dan notified father of his strange visitor, of course. Father sent instructions. The authorities of Porto Rico buried the man's body, and set a guard to watch constantly over the vehicle as it lay in the grove. Scientists came to inspect it, and could understand but vaguely its mechanism.

Two weeks passed. Father was in Miami then; and near the end of February he started by government plane for Porto Rico.

Conditions all over the world were far worse now. We only had a vague picture; the radio and television were operating intermittently—but all the regular channels for the dissemination of news were paralyzed. And, too, the governments withheld, or distorted to a less terrible aspect such reports as were available.

Europe was enveloped in snow to the Mediterranean; the Barbary coast was jammed with refugees. London and Paris, like New York, were threatened with complete abandonment.

In Canada, they said—like Scandinavia, north Interior Europe and Asia of the far north—there was less panic, less disaster. These people were accustomed to intense cold and equipped to withstand it.

In the Canadian rural districts, the farmers shut themselves up with their winter fundamentals of food as had been their custom, and were said to be making out fairly well. But the big centers of population, dependent upon transportation and industry, were devastated. Greater Montreal was abandoned in February.

Transportation everywhere in the United States was kept partially open, but only by efforts born of the frantic desperation of necessity. The new Arctic airplanes, recently developed, were being hastily manufactured in quantity, in government plants established in Florida and Southern California, and were as hastily put into service to bear the people southward. The railroads of our northern States kept open for a while with snow plows loaned by the great Canadian trunk lines which had long since succumbed.

Steamship service along the Atlantic

Coast ventured no farther north than Charleston, South Carolina. The North Atlantic was filled with ice floes driven south by the constant storms; the Polar ice field was reported now as extending nearly down to the former New York—Liverpool steamship lanes.

The St. Lawrence River was frozen solid, from Montreal past Quebec and down to its mouth, before Christmas. In January the middle Mississippi was solid with an ice bridge which one day broke and swept away three railroad bridges. The Hudson, from Troy to New York harbor, was solid by mid-February. Within a week after that even the Savannah River became impassable, and the port closed.

Yet, for all that, by whatever desperate expedient possible, the people were being transported south, and were cared for in their new locations, in the best fashion that could be managed.

What formerly had been our tropic zone was thronged with new arrivals. Daily they poured in from the north. And from the far south, as well—in spite of government's pleadings and commands to the contrary; from Buenos Aires, Rio, Santiago, people were striving to get north, nearer the equator, fearful of this new heat and blazing daylight which was coming upon them.

Nor was it only a disturbance of the world's normal temperatures. With the abnormal climate came other inevitable disturbances. From widely divergent localities, devastating windstorms were reported. A typhoon, wholly out of season, swept the China Sea. A hurricane in Central America. From Peru and Chile they told of heavy rains flooding the arid coast. Rain fell at Biskra with torrential rainstorms sweeping up and across the Sahara.

I had been saying that father, near the end of February, went to Porto Rico. The two weeks previous to his arrival there were weeks of amazement growing daily into awe as Dan and Hulda were brought into closer contact with their beautiful, unearthly visitor.

IT came upon them gradually, the strangeness, weirdness of this girl so like themselves at first glance, yet obviously a being wholly different. They treated her as a visiting guest, though in reality she was a captive. Upon father's advice—for he guessed, at least partially, what the outcome was to be—the Cains were content to do nothing with Zetta save to have her live with them in seclusion; and to make her comfortable.

That she was extremely intelligent, Dan saw at once. She evidently realized that they were wholly friendly. Whatever her purpose, living there with them seemed all she desired.

She had her own room, next to Hulda's. She seemed to appreciate Hulda's efforts for her comfort. She ate with the family, making whimsical faces at the food which she obviously disliked at first. For the rest, she seemed content to sit in the living room, watching them, listening to them talk.

To Dan, her constant presence was at once fascinating and disturbing. Fascinating, for Zetta's beauty was queerly magnetic, but disturbing, too, for there was about this girl always that uncanniness indefinable. For hours she would sit in the living room, apart from the family group. She did not like chairs, preferring to sit cross-legged on the floor, on a cushion. She was very silent, although she would answer when spoken to, with a smile or a strange, friendly gesture, and with her eyes following each person who spoke.

Her complexion was the creamy, pink white which we of earth call beauty. She blushed, or flushed, readily. For no apparent reason a wave of rose color would suffuse her face, throat and neck. It even extended sometimes to her arms, and to her legs as they showed amid her half-revealing drapery—the smooth white of her skin flushing with deep rose color. For no reason; and then Dan noticed that it generally happened when the outer door was opened and a rush of cold air swept in. Nature automatically protecting her against the cold!

Dan often would furtively watch her. He was sitting in a far corner of the room one evening; the elder Cains and Hulda were gathered about the radio.

The small, clear voice of the announcer was giving a summary of the world's tragic news, this middle of February; on the small tel-vision screen which the Miami Central Office was connecting with various localities to illustrate his words, vague, fleeting pictures were mirrored.

Zetta was seated on the floor, in an opposite corner from Dan. He saw that she was not listening to the radio. But she was listening to something! Her head was tilted alert; across her face a succession of her emotions was mirrored—a frown; whimsical pleasure; a smile.

She was listening; and Dan realized suddenly that she was hearing things he could not hear! A world of things, perhaps; something displeased her, she gestured disapprovingly; and then smiled again.

Uncanny! She was wholly absorbed, unaware that Dan was watching. Hearing things no mortal of earth could hear! Like a dog, Dan thought, which hears faint sounds denied its master. But Dan knew it was more than that.

And then his heart leaped. Zetta was seeing something he could not see! Something in the room. Her eyes followed it, as evidently it moved. She turned her head to gaze after it; she smiled, with breathless parted lips, and then she laughed.

Was she, perhaps, irrational? Conjuring visions in an unbalanced mind? The explanation occurred to Dan, but he did not believe it was so. Rather, it seemed to him, this girl's perceptions were more acute than ours.

She saw and heard things beyond the range of our human senses. Here on earth they were things strange to her. She was listening and watching them; surprised, often pleased, as one with normal senses gazes upon new sights and finds them interesting.

Dan found opportunity to regard the girl more closely. Her eyes, when she looked at him, seemed normal. But at other times he saw that her pupils became suddenly abnormally large; or again, contracted to pin points, even in the dimness of indoors. And once, a dark veil—a film—seemed to creep over the eyeball; but she became aware of the scrutiny, and it was gone before Dan could make sure.

Her ears, in outward shape a trifle rounder than ours, were generally hidden—pink shells in the waving mass of her white hair. Dan fancied that they moved at her will — that sometimes they expanded.

Her fingers, and her toes, were long, slim and tapering, with pink-white, pointed nails. The joints were more numerous than with us; it gave them a prehensile aspect; and Dan fancied, too, that the arch of the bottom of her foot was cup-shaped as though it might serve as a vacuum for walking upon inclined surfaces.

Father had told Dan that Zetta probably was from Xenephrene. But no one could be sure. An idea occurred to Dan, and a few days later, just before dawn, he and Hulda tried it. Xenephrene, on clear days, was visible just before sunrise. The weather, here in Porto Rico now, was generally below freezing. Once it had snowed. The Cain's fruit groves were killed; but with all the world's catastrophe for comparison, Dan and his father thought little of it. The Porto Rican day now was about two hours long. The sun made a low arc in the south, descending within two hours, not very much to the west of where it had risen.

It was mid morning when in the darkness before dawn, Hulda and Dan stood with Zetta outside the plantation house. To the south Xenephrene would soon rise.

"Do you think she'll recognize it?" Hulda asked.

Dan smiled; how could one guess? Zetta stood between them, puzzled, looking first at one, then the other. She had walked out with them quietly. She always walked quietly, carefully, as though trying to imitate their own slow steps. And though Dan, with gestures, had often tried to make her leap into the air, she never would.

It was cold, this mid morning before dawn; Dan and Hulda were dressed in heavy, northern garments. Zetta wore the filmy robe in which they had first seen her. She seemed to prefer her own garments, a number of which had been brought from the vehicle, and installed with 'her at the Cain's. To the cold she was utterly oblivious; the cold of outdoors, or the warmth inside—she seemed not aware of the difference.

They stood on the knoll. The sky to the southward was brightening. The stars there moved in a low arc. Then Xenephrene came up. Blazing, purple-white star.

"Look!" said Dan. "Zetta, look! We call that Xenephrene. Can't you understand me? Do you recognize that star? Your world? Did you come from there?"

At sight of the great purple star, a queer emotion swept her face. Dan pleaded: "Zetta, haven't you learned anything of our language? We call that Xenephrene. Your world? You came from there? Speak, Zetta!"

She said slowly in English, with an accent quaint and indescribable: "Yes. My worl'—I came from there."

"BUT what's the matter with you, Hulda?"
"Nothing."
"But there is!"

"Not at all, Dan. Why do you say that?"

"But there is! You're angry, or hurt. At me? What have I done?"

"Nonsense. You haven't done—" She stopped; and he saw that her eyes were filled with sudden tears; she tried to protest, but the words would not come.

They were sitting alone late one evening in the Cain's living room. Dan had noticed that for some days Hulda was abnormally quiet, and she no longer treated him with her usual comradeship. A reserve had come to her. And now, when he asked her why, she burst into tears!

"Hulda! What's the matter?"

She sobbed openly; he tried to put his arm around her, but she pushed him away.

"Hulda!" A light broke on Dan. "It's Zetta—why, you silly little girl—"

"You were—were kissing her this morning!"

"I was *not!* Nonsense!"

"Well, I s-saw you, with her in your arms, l-lifting her up—"

"Yes. Lifting her up. But not kissing her. But I'm kissing *you!* Now—like that! And *that*—Hulda, darling—"

It is not my part to reconstruct the scene that followed between them, although both have described the wonder of it to all of the family who would listen—wonder and awe at the voicing of love which all of us knew they had felt for a year or two. They were engaged when ten minutes later they thumped on the elder Cain's door to tell them the wonderful news.

Dan maintained that to Zetta he owed a great debt of gratitude; for without Hulda's jealousy of Zetta, Dan says he might have been too stupid ever to propose. The episode with Zetta was simple enough; Dan explained it readily to Hulda's entire satisfaction.

He had been alone with Zetta that

morning, trying to make her talk more of our language, which now he knew that she was learning. With a mind wholly different from ours—this Dan now realized—she undoubtedly was learning with extraordinary rapidity. But, quite evidently, she had her own method. She would not speak again; but when he began naming objects in the room, trying to aid her by systematic teaching, she showed approval and listened attentively.

During the course of this lesson, Dan had touched her. He laid his hand on her arm. Curious sensation! He felt at once, not a lack of solidity, but a seeming lack of weight. She had risen to her feet as though startled by his touch. He stood, from his much greater height looking down at her. Still holding her arm.

And this Dan confessed to me, but most assuredly he did not confess it to Hulda. As he stood there, staring into the glowing dark depths of Zetta's eyes, it occurred to him that he should release her. But he did not. Instead, he caught her in his arms. Lifted her up. Not, to be wholly truthful, because scientifically he wanted to test her weight. Rather was it because, at touching her, an instant of madness swept him.

It passed. She was pushing him away, smiling, startled, but unafraid. And, with the madness gone, he tossed her into the air as one would toss a child. Caught her; tossed her again to the ceiling and let her fall, to land lightly on tiptoe as her feet came down to the straw matting of the floor. And in the doorway, he became aware that Hulda was standing, silently watching them.

When father arrived at the Cain's he weighed Zetta. Had she been a normal girl of earth, by her appearance she would have weighed some ninety or a hundred pounds. Zetta weighed eighteen pounds!

There were several scientists in Porto Rico who, at father's invitation, came to see Zetta. They were with her hours each day. Dan and Hulda were excluded. Father's manner, Dan said, was very solemn, and he seemed to be laboring under a suppressed excitement. Then came the news of March 2, that invaders from Xenephrene had landed on the earth near New York. The scientists at the Cain's house hastened to San Juan, but father remained.

One afternoon—it was the afternoon of March 4—Hulda and Dan listened at the door when father was with Zetta. She was talking to him now! Talking in low, slow tones; haltingly, and often he would question and prompt her. Abruptly he rose to his feet and came out.

"Hulda! Dan, where are your father and mother?"

Dan called them; they came bustling in. The excitement of these days was too much for the elder Cains; they lived in a constant confusion and bewilderment.

"Sit down, all of you," father commanded. "Zetta—come out here, child."

She came at his call, wide-eyed, gentle; but she, too, was trembling with excitement. Father seated her gently on a cushion. He said:

"Our earth, lashed into turmoil by this extraordinary change of climate, is far worse off than that. These invaders—well, what Zetta has to say will at least give us information—aid us in doing what we can to repel them! It is a bad condition—it may prove serious—possibly complete disaster!"

He regarded Zetta with a gentle tenderness. "This girl has come from her world to help us. Yes, she has learned our language, with what strange qualities of mind, and senses so different from ours you will be amazed to hear. A very gentle little creature. I think all of you have grown to love her—she says you have been very kind to her, and she loves you very much, particularly Hulda."

It struck Hulda with a guilty pang, hearing this after her own jealousy of Zetta; for Hulda was no more than human, and there had been days when secretly she hotly resented the strange and beautiful girl's presence in the house with Dan. But that was over. Hulda exclaimed impulsively, "I do love her!"

The two girls' glances met affectionately. "Yes," said Zetta suddenly. "We do love ver' much."

Father went on: "She is here—came here to help us. All this time, in her own way, she has been striving to learn our language that she might tell us. She has told me everything. Zetta, tell them—just what you told me—"

Father stopped his nervous pacing and sat down abruptly. And without preface, quietly, sometimes haltingly, in her strangely small voice and curiously clipped syllables, Zetta began her amazing narrative.

CHAPTER V.

CRIMSON SOUND!

ON the afternoon of March 3, Freddie and I, in Miami, were summoned by the War Department, which was installed here in temporary quarters after the flight from Washington. We were greeted by the secretary, who introduced us to a dozen or more grave-faced officials who were seated around a large table in a cold, badly illuminated room. They were under the impression that I had recently been to Porto Rico with my father; they wanted further details from me, as an eyewitness, to supplement the information which had been furnished them concerning the captive girl from Xenephrene.

I had not been to Porto Rico; I could tell them nothing, but I remained at the conference with Freddie. Of him, they wanted a demonstration of his invention. The War Secretary

laughed, but it was a very hollow, mirthless laugh.

"You see, young man, we are almost in the position of grasping at straws."

By the general public, who reads of war conferences and grave official decisions given with calm dignity in times of national crisis, the inner workings of a government are never understood. The people naturally picture men of great intellect, calmly, judicially weighing problems of international law, and quietly giving their decisions, as though the whole matter were controlled by some giant, insensate machine of precision, incapable of error, undisturbed by human feeling.

It is not so. Or, at least, I can vouch for the fact that in the darkness of this afternoon of March 3, 1953, in the United States War Department at Miami, it most certainly was not so.

These gray-haired men were very human. Most were unshaved, with rumpled hair and reddened eyes. Distraught, harassed; undecided; doubtful of everything; striving to do the best they could, with the welfare of millions of their people at stake. Conditions of unprecedented disaster had for weeks assailed them. Under this culminating blow—invaders from another world landing to attack what once was our greatest city—they were all but broken.

Very human indeed! The Secretary of the Navy sat savagely chewing on the stump of an old cigar, blowing on his hands, cursing the cold at intervals. The Air Secretary was pouring hot coffee at the end of the table, shoving a litter of papers out of his way to make room for the cups. The stooped, middle-aged, haggard gentleman pacing the floor was our President.

"Grasping at a straw," said the War Secretary.

In a sudden silence, through an open doorway to the room adjoining, I could hear the clatter of the southern telegraphs, telephone bells, the hiss and splutter of the radio and tel-vision instruments.

"Close that door," the secretary added querulously. "You've brought your model, Smith? Put it here on the table—tell us about it."

Freddie opened his apparatus and explained it briefly. His so-called thermodyne principle. Though ultimately he had hoped to adapt it into a motor of revolutionary design, his present model was merely a small projector.

"Projector of what?" demanded the President irritably.

"Of heat, sir," Freddie answered. "I'll show you. This is a very small model, of course, but it demonstrates the principle."

They did not want any technicalities from Freddie. He explained only that his apparatus, in this present small form, took a tiny electric spark and built it up into a new form of radiant heat.

"It is," said Freddie, "heat of totally different properties from the kind with which we commonly deal. It travels—radiates, by the diffusion of its electrons, more like light than heat. At a great speed—I think possibly, at over a hundred thousand miles a second."

He opened his apparatus. It consisted of a small, flat, metallic box, curved to fit a man's chest. A disk, like a small electrode, to be pressed against the skin. Freddie bared his chest and strapped it on.

"I use," he said, "the tiny electrical impulse which the human body itself furnishes. This, I amplify, build up and store in a battery." Wires from the generator led to a small box which he opened to show his audience—a box of coils, and a tiny row of amplifying tubes. He put this in his pocket, with wires leading to the battery and the projector. These were both in one piece—the projector a small metallic funnel, with a trigger; a grid of wires was across its opened end; it had a long metallic handle, in the hollow interior of which was the battery where the charge was concentrated.

"Electrons of heat under pressure," said Freddie.

"Show us," said some one.

Freddie erected a screen across the room—an insulating screen to kill the heat-beam so that it could not injure the wall. The men moved aside.

Freddie, after a moment to generate and concentrate the charge, raised the muzzle.

The thing hissed slightly; a dull violet beam sprang like light from the projector. It struck the screen, some twenty feet away, in a large circle of fluorescence; in the dimness of the room it seemed like phosphorescent water, landing in a spray and dissipating as it struck, like a dissolving mist.

Freddie cried, "Peter, hold something in it!"

I took a sheet of paper, held it carefully into the beam. It shriveled, blackened and burst into flame. Then a lead pencil—it melted off midway of its length as I held it up.

Freddie snapped off the apparatus. "That's all, gentlemen. With a large model, I would use a high voltage current for my original impulse, instead of the tiny impulse of the human body."

"How far will that beam carry?" the President demanded.

"This one?" Freddie asked. "Or a maximum, full-sized projector?"

"This one. Why talk about what you haven't got?"

"About thirty-five feet, sir. Further, perhaps, if I concentrate it—keep it from spreading. Say fifty feet. But at that distance its temperature would not be very great."

"How great?"

"Two hundred degrees Fahrenheit."

"How much is it at the muzzle?"

"About twelve hundred."

An effective range of thirty-five or fifty feet! They were all disappointed. "We can't," said the War Secretary, "figure this thing in the light of a large model we some time might be able to build. What good is that?"

The man beside me said abruptly: "This thing is useless to help us now, gentlemen. But, in the future—do you know, I wouldn't say but what this young fellow has hit upon something not unlike what our enemies seem to be using—"

The door from the adjoining room opened. A man said: "Davis has started his flight. He's almost within sight of them now—shall I bring in the screen?"

"Bring it in," said the President. "Get these lights down—put that away, Mr. Smith—we'll discuss that some other time—it's been very interesting."

Freddie hastily gathered up his apparatus. The lights in the conference room were turned out; it was illumined only by the blue reflection through the doorway. Men brought in a tel-vision screen some two feet square; placed it upright on the table and we all gathered before it. The instrument room door was closed. We were in darkness save for the vague silver radiance that came from the screen.

FROM the whispers around me I soon knew what was transpiring. The invaders had landed on the east bank of the frozen Hudson, near the suburb of Tarrytown. Xenephrene was at its closest point to the earth now, which is what doubtless prompted the invasion. Xenephrene was passing us; beginning to-day, the distance between the worlds would grow greater.

Presumably the invaders had landed on the night of February 28. It had been snowing around New York City steadily for a week; but that night was clear. Reports said that a great silver ball had been seen floating down from the sky; later, from the ground, strange beams of colored light were seen, moving slowly southward. And strange sounds were heard.

But the information was confused and unauthentic. This last blizzard had cut off all the New York area from the world. There was practically no transportation; no wires remained standing; no radio-sending stations were operating within all that region.

How many people remained on Manhattan Island, no one could say. Very few, probably. A deserted, congealed city, snow-buried, with its huge buildings nothing now but giant monuments to a greatness which once had been. The cold was worse than scientists prognosticated. Nothing could get to New York now, save possibly dog-sleds, and the new type Arctic planes; and very few of those were available.

War against the invaders from Xenephrene!

Our government bulletins of the day had assured the public that these invaders would be held in check, attacked, held from moving further south, and very soon exterminated. What deaths to our people they had already caused, was not known. But it was evident that they were hostile; a plane carrying refugees had passed near their lights. Confused stories were told of melting, vanishing snow under red light; and stories of another refugee plane attacked and destroyed by red light and strange sound! Meaningless news! Yet terrible!

The British Empire, from its capital in North Africa, offered us aid. They were building the Arctic planes. The French government from its headquarters in Tunis, preparing to move again south to the lower Sahara, radioed its desire to help. Argentina and Chile, harassed with their own problems in the new tropic heat, wanted to help if they could.

Magnificent gestures, but they all meant very little! So far, nothing had been done. A few of our planes had ventured near New York; and none had so far been heard of since. Now, a huge Arctic plane, commanded by this Davis, equipped with modern aircraft artillery, with radio and a tel-vision image-finder, was making an experimental flight. A companion plane, flown by the famous Robinson, was with it. Robinson had the longest-range airplane gun of modern times; and he carried bombs. His purpose was to try and get above the enemy; and Davis, with his tel-vision and radio would report conditions as best he could.

This attempt, then, was what now we were to witness. I have never been present at so dramatic a scene as this one which took place on the tel-vision mirror, and in the room around me.

In the darkness the silver light from the screen vaguely illumined the tense crowding figures. The highest officials of our government! No calm judicial conference here! Tired, cold, anxious men, watching and listening with bated breaths and thumping hearts. There had been a buzz of whispered comments; the shifting of chairs; shuffling of feet. But now there was silence.

The screen image blurred for a moment as it was brought in from the other room; but soon it cleared. I saw the cold, frosty stars in a field of blue-black; far below, the dim vista of gray-white snow shining in the starlight—a panorama of snow-laden country at night. The image-finder was in the front of Davis's plane, pointing diagonally downward. A swaying scene, diminished by the mirror, and by the two thousand-foot altitude at which Davis was flying.

Some one said: "Where are we? I don't recognize that landscape."

"Long Island. He's heading for New York City. Hush! We'll throw in his radio-sound." It was the voice of the War Secretary. "Grant, you said you had connection."

A man was fumbling with the miniature audiphone beside the mirror. We heard the drone of Davis's plane; and then heard his voice, with words indistinguishable as he spoke to the gunner with him.

6 A

The President's voice said nervously: "Have you sending connection? If we want to give him orders—where is the other plane? Isn't Robinson around here?"

Grant said: "Yes. He was visible awhile ago. Davis is going to fly over New York—the enemy, he thinks, is still up in the Yonkers district."

I sat staring at the screen. Half an hour? Or two hours? I could not have said. Swaying stars; a dim white swaying landscape. Then the horizon dropped; stars covered everything; Davis was mounting. He leveled at last.

Dimly, far down, I could see the white configurations of Long Island Sound, frozen into solid ice, white with piled snowdrifts, black where the wind had swept it bare. A blurred, shifting scene, dizzying, but sometimes steady and very clear. It tilted up—all land for a moment.

I saw, momentarily as the plane swooped down, the great bridges over the river from Long Island to Manhattan. Gaunt, ghostly in the starlight. Small as a child's toys. Broken toy bridges, with ice piled upon them; cables dangling—the older Brooklyn Bridge lay askew. A jam of river ice had wrenched at one of its piers.

It was a motionless world; the river of tangled, motionless ice-floes, the frozen, motionless bay with hulks of vessels caught in it and abandoned; and the great city—all congealed, stricken of motion in every detail.

And then we were over lower New York. The parks were wan, white blobs; the streets were black cañons; the great buildings with their archways and pedestrian levels in the crowded lower district stood like frozen headstones—Davis swooped—I saw a great office building in which, it seemed, the water system must have burst and flooded it when still there was warmth inside; its façade was a mass of ice. The plane zoomed up and only the stars were visible.

Above the motor drone from the audiphone, the President's voice said: "Ask him about Robinson. Where is he?"

Then we saw Robinson's large quadruplane, with its helicopters folded, its cabin hanging like a silver bullet beneath the lower wing. It came swinging into our image from one side, and headed north into the starlight.

Abruptly we heard Davis's voice: "Above Central Park. It's piled level as an Arctic snow-field. In the lower city there seemed no lights—saw no sign of any one remaining. The enemy is in the open country up ahead—northeast of the Yonkers district—Look! There now, you see the enemy light!"

AT the distant northern horizon in the background of the image, a dull radiance of red was visible. It seemed a crimson glow standing up into the sky. Not the yellow of a reflected conflagration, but red—crimson red.

"Blood!" murmured the man beside me. "Crimson stain—"

Davis's voice was saying: "I'll keep in sight of Robinson. He's mounting. I'm cutting out my connection with you now—except the image and the continuous one-way sound. You'll hear and see better. Hear and see all that we do—I can begin to hear it now. Good-by to you all."

His voice broke with the snap that indicated his connection was off. The War Secretary cried: "Grant! Stop him! We must be able to talk with him—give him orders! That fool—daredevil—he's likely to do anything just so we may see and hear as much as possible!"

But the connection was broken. Davis, with that ominous, significant "Good-by to you all," had cut out so that we might see and hear in full volume. We could no longer communicate with him.

The mirror was brighter and clearer with its greater power; the drone of the motors came louder; and then dimmed suddenly as Davis evidently threw in his mufflers.

In the silence now, we heard another sound. The sound of the enemy! The sound of that crimson radiance in the sky ahead! A low whine. It did not seem electrical. A whine—more like a giant animal in distress.

I listened, with a shudder thrilling me; and I know that every man in the room must have felt the same. A queer thrilling shudder, as though the very sound itself were physically affecting me with its vibrations. It was very soft, now at first; and I was only hearing the faint, radio echo of it; yet upon my senses it laid a singularly weird, uncanny feeling of the diabolical.

The minutes passed. As the plane flew northward, the crimson stain in the sky seemed spreading. And the whine increased; grew louder, resolved itself now into a myriad undertones. Cries, muffled, faint, aërial, yet somehow clear; screams, checked and then begun again; a low, tiny throbbing—a myriad unearthly sounds, weirdly abnormal, like nothing I had ever heard before, all blended as undertones to the one great whine.

The crimson radiance, screaming into the night! Light and sound intermingled. Was this some strange weapon of a strange science which the invaders from Xenephrene had brought to attack us? There was something deadly in the aspect of that crimson radiance. And something equally lethal in the gruesome sound which split the night around it.

My thoughts were whirling in this fashion when I heard the muttered words of the man next to me—murmuring to the man on his other side: "God! That's weird! Vanderstuyft says that the girl from Xenephrene can see and hear below the human scale! This is it—the infra-red made visible, and its sounds brought up to our human ears! Weird—"

Some one else was asking: "Is that light and that sound their weapon? Where's the Robinson plane?"

And the War Secretary said: "Hush! He's there—ahead. We're mounting."

Nothing but sky again. A blood-red, night sky. The stars gleamed like crimson jewels through the radiance. Then again, the Davis plane leveled. We saw now that the invaders evidently were encamped in a snowy stretch of what had been comparatively open country. The houses which once were there, lay now under mounds of snow. A blank rolling landscape; fences, roads, all gone beneath the billowing blanket of white; the trees only were left, stark black sticks in patches.

In an oval, perhaps a mile across its greatest diameter, the red beam stood up into the sky. A barrage of crimson—not light, but sound! It throbbed and screamed and whined its defiance!

The two planes circled the radiance, some ten thousand feet up, and several miles away. The Davis plane fired a shell; we heard the dull muffled report, saw a yellow glare where it struck the red beam and harmlessly exploded. But it struck low, where perhaps the sound-vibrations were too intense.

The planes mounted higher. We could see Robinson's ahead and above us; he was closer to the crimson barrage. Trying to climb over it—to drop a bomb.

From this greater height, within the oval other lights showed, far down on the snow. Tiny moving spots of vivid color. The enemy's encampment. Davis was now at least at the twenty thousand foot level, Robinson was still higher. In that deadly cold it seemed incredible; but still they struggled up.

At this height the crimson barrage was thin; once, overhead, I seemed to see where it ended. The whine of it was fainter, but every gruesome undertone still sounded clear.

"He's trying it!" The man beside me blurted it aloud. Startled movement sounded in the room; a chair pushed back with a rasp; tense murmurs; shuffling feet. We stared. Robinson's plane darted in—

There was just an instant when I thought it was safely through. I could see it clearly—the black outline of a bird stained crimson. It seemed to hang motionless; then it fluttered; falling—and as it fell, like a mist of black vapor it suddenly expanded; a black wraith of a plane expanding, dissipating. It did not seem to reach the ground. It was gone, dissolved into nothing visible, with only a howling, mouthing sound from the crimson monster to mark its passing!

A shiver swept me; I was cold, trembling. I heard some one near me cry in horror;: "Davis, he's—" and check himself. The screen was a blur of crimson, with lurid spots of light on the ground showing through it. Davis was heading downward in a swoop through the red beam! It spread until the whole image before us was a crimson stain.

The lights on the ground seemed coming up, leaping up, growing in size as the plane dived at them. The room was a chaos of gruesome tiny screams! We were in the crimson! It snapped with a myriad sparks. It howled, squealed, screamed! An instant, but it seemed an eternity. Then the red vanished. We were through it! By Heaven, through it! Safely through! Diving at the ground!

I saw that one of the spots of light had broadened to a green ghastly glare on the snow-surface. Figures of men in human form standing there, foreshortened by the overhead perspective to huge heads and dwindling bodies. Human forms: men of almost naked bodies, standing in the snow, bodies painted green by the glare. Apparatus of war erected in the snow—a bare spot where the snow was gone, and rock and earth showed clean—a shimmer that seemed a pool of water lying warm with ice around it.

A glimpse—no more than a second or two undoubtedly. Then the scene, rushing upward, was fading. The confusion of sounds and blurred lights suddenly grew faint—faded—vanished into darkness and silence!

The tel-vision screen was dead—a blank silver surface staring at us like a corpse. The audiphone was mute.

Davis's plane had vanished like its fellow into nothingness before it reached the ground!

This was the afternoon of the 3rd of March. That night, while Freddie and I were at our boarding place, the news reached us that a silver ball of invaders from Xenephrene had landed in the twilight of the Venezuelan coast —the heart of the region which in all our western hemisphere we had come to prize most dearly!

CHAPTER VI.

"IF I HAD BUT KNOWN!"

"LOOK here, young man," said the War Secretary, " can you operate a plane of the Arctic A type?"

I could, and so could Freddie, I said. The War Secretary continued his pacing of the room. It was about nine o'clock of the morning of March 14 —black as midnight outdoors; cold, with clouds scudding low over the Florida keys, clouds which promised snow. The War Secretary had sent for us.

Conditions were worse everywhere, it seemed now by this morning's news —as though each day brought its disasters worse than any which had gone before. The invaders from Xenephrene were obviously almost impregnable to our attack. The efforts of Robinson and Davis had proved it, if nothing else. It was obvious also that the invaders at New York City so far had made no offensive move. Their barrage—the crimson howling sound, or light, whatever it might be—was merely their defense.

"God knows," the secretary exclaimed, "what weapons they may have to loose against us when they begin an attack!"

And now, another huge silver ball had landed in Venezuela—on the coastal plain near La Guayra. In the deserted frozen wastes of New York State the invaders were not an immediate, serious menace. But in Venezuela it was a far different condition.

La Guayra was the main receiving port for all our refugee ships. A twilight had fallen there, but the temperature still was mild. It was colder up in Caracas, but the people thronged there, and with heroic efforts the Government and the citizens were doing their best to receive them.

It was not a wholly unselfish effort. With the new climate, Colombia, Venezuela, the former jungles of the Amazon basin of Brazil; Ecuador, Peru, even the mountain fastnesses of Bolivia, and the arid coast of north Chile —this was the land of promise. It was the best, the only tolerable all-year climate left to the Western World. Here the new great cities would spring up—centers of industry and commerce; here would be the new great fields of grain; the cattle ranges.

But here, in the midst of the confusion of arriving settlers, the enemy from Xenephrene had landed! We had no details; we only knew that around the silver ball a barrage of red howling sound was standing up into the sky. Within that circular mile of the red barrage, all that had been evidence of our human life—houses, trees,. people —all was vanished!

The War Secretary stopped before me. " I've radioed your father this morning, Peter. Told him to send that Xenephrene girl up here to us at once! We've got to do something. We must learn if we can what these unearthly enemies are like—do scientifically what we can to oppose them."

He gestured at me vehemently. " You Hollanders are very stubborn, young Peter. Your father told me he was very busy—he'd have full information for me in a day or two! That's the scientist for you! Taking it methodically, with that damn scientific routine, when a day or two is an eternity just now!"

I regarded Freddie. We did not smile; in these terrible days there was not a smile left in us. But Freddie nodded.

"That's father's way," I said. "But—"

"Well, I told him I was sending a special plane down there at once to get him and the girl. The Venezuelan Government is demanding details of us. Every thirty minutes Caracas calls me up. Makes a fool of us—a girl of this unknown enemy race right in our hands and we don't produce her! Your father said, 'Good! Send Peter and young Fred Smith—I want to see them anyway.'"

There was nothing that could have pleased Freddie and myself better. The secretary offered us a pilot, but we did not want one. We started that morning, armed with legal papers, given us jocularly, but with serious intent, nevertheless, and commanding father's presence with Zetta in Miami the next day.

It was eleven o'clock when we got away in the big Arctic A plane. A black morning with swift, low clouds, and a wind from the north. Flying southeast, we had scarcely left the Bahamas behind us when the weather cleared. Cold starlight shone on a dark, cold ocean. Icebergs had been seen down this far, but we did not chance to pass any now. But we saw many scurrying steamships.

In some four hours we raised the Morrow light of San Juan and I turned southwest, to strike the coast beyond Arecibo. Flying low, we headed in, over the line of breakers on the white beach. Columbus landed near here, not so many lifetimes ago. Yet how different was the world then!

The tumbled mountains rising behind the sea which Columbus had described to Isabella rose before us now. The same shape; every tiny peak undoubtedly the same. But they were not the vivid warm green which had so enchanted the mariner. These were cold and blue gray, and the tops of them were white with snow.

It was mid-afternoon when, in the darkness, we dropped with a roar upon Dan's landing stage at the foot of the knoll. We leaped from the plane and hurried up the hill, to see Dan and father, and Hulda and the Cains waving at us from the veranda, and a small, strange white figure of a girl standing among them.

If one could only glimpse the future, even for a brief moment! It makes me shudder sometimes to think how blindly we are forced to tread our way through life, raising each foot without the knowledge of what will happen before it reaches the ground! That afternoon, for instance, I was very happy to burst in upon father and Dan. If Freddie and I had known what was impending, we would have done anything rather than arrive at that moment. If we had delayed our arrival even an hour! Yet, even in a seeming tragedy, there is evidence of some all-guiding purpose. We may not see it, we may deny it, but I think that always it is there.

We came upon the plantation house within a moment after Zetta had begun her narration. She had told it to father; she was beginning it for Dan and the others, when the sound of our arriving plane checked her.

The few remaining hours of that afternoon and evening were crowded with the confusion of our arrival, our exchange of news and ideas, and listening to the world news from the radio. Zetta did not tell her story that afternoon or that evening. Father, with a quizzical smile, looked over the legal papers with which we served him.

"Good enough, boys! I'll obey.

We'll take Zetta and go up to Miami to-morrow morning." He turned to Dan. " You come with us. Zetta will tell her story to the authorities in Miami, just as she's told it to me. And I'll have some interesting scientific data for them, I promise you."

He gestured with a voluminous sheaf of papers—his scientific notes on Zetta's narrative and on the girl's mental and physical being. He gestured with the papers and then stuck them back in his pocket. Fate! Providence! Call it what you will. He did not hand them to Dan or to Freddie or to me— he stuck them back in his pocket!

The news of Hulda's and Dan's engagement brought me pleasure. I shook Dan's hand warmly and kissed my sister as she flung herself into my arms. Little Hulda was radiant. Dan's handsome, tanned face was flushed as he received our congratulations; and when they were over, he stood towering over Hulda, with his arm around her as she clung to him.

Happy lovers, snatching at their happiness even in the midst of the world's turmoil! Happy that afternoon and evening.

I SHALL never forget my meeting with Zetta as they introduced me to her that afternoon. She stood in the center of the room, and something momentarily diverted the rest of them from us; for an instant we were alone. I stared at her.

What futile words of greeting I may have uttered I do not know, and I think that she said nothing. I saw a quaintly beautiful young girl, curiously different in a way not to be defined from any girl I had ever before beheld. A strange, weird beauty. I took her hand as she held it out in the gesture they had taught her.

I have mentioned Dan's feelings under similar circumstances. Dan was in love with Hulda; the instinct of all that was upright and true within him rose to cast out this surge of alien emotion. Not so with me—I was wholly fancy free.

I took Zetta's hand. It seemed then as though the contact might suddenly become beyond my power to break. Her gaze held mine. I saw a sudden startled look in her eyes, and then saw something else—the mirrored play of emotions like my own.

Her body seemed to sway toward me; I could see and feel her withstanding its sway. An attraction between us. Do I mean that literally? Scientifically? I do not know. There is, perhaps, between the sexes on earth such an attraction. Or it may perchance be psychological, emotional, nothing more.

I felt it with Zetta, and I could see that she felt it and was startled. But in her eyes there was more than surprise—a swift melting look of tenderness.

Mrs. Cain bustled up to us. " Isn't she a darling little thing, Peter? We all love her. Oh, dear me, these terrible, strange times!"

Our hands broke apart. Was it love we had felt in that instant? Could love be possible, could it be right between a man and a woman so different? Does the Creator intend the worlds thus to be joined, or is the isolation He has imposed upon each of them an evidence that such cannot be?

Love between Zetta and me? I do not know. But all that afternoon and evening I found my eyes turning to her, and found her somber gaze upon me.

We chanced to approach each other several times, and always I was conscious of the attraction of her nearness. Not so strong as at first. All my instinct, my reason, was prepared for it now; a thousand barriers of conventionality and time and place and circumstance contributed subconsciously to resist it. But it was there, invisibly, intangibly holding us.

The evening's radio news brought a measure of relief to the world. From

New York came the report that the invaders had vanished. Moved somewhere else, perhaps—but where it was not known.

Father made one comment; his words, which proved to be true enough, linger clear in my memory. " They left New York yesterday afternoon, after the attack by Robinson and Davis. There are not two vehicles—only one! It left New York and landed last night in Venezuela! It may leave there presently." His glance turned to Zetta. " I have reason to think that the invaders will voluntarily withdraw from the earth. Very soon, I imagine —while Xenephrene is still comparatively near us."

" True enough! At midnight that night the radio told us that the Xenephrene vehicle, with all its people, had left Venezuela. The night was heavily overcast, with a rain and wind storm all up through Central America and the lower Caribbean; and north of sixteen degrees there was snow. Where the invaders had gone, no one knew. The world was anxiously awaiting news of their next landing place.

We sat up for perhaps an hour. It was snowing outside, with a howling wind that swirled the snow about the eaves of the little plantation house. At about one o'clock we all bade each other good night and went to bed.

Ah, if we had but known!

I awoke to find Freddie shaking me. He and I had slept together. It was four in the morning, and the house was noisy with the storm outside. Freddie was alarmed—he did not know why. Something had awakened him—we decided it was a thumping which we now heard in the living room, a door banging in the wind, with a queer, broken rattle to it.

There is a sense of evil which comes to any one awakened unexpectedly in the night. I felt it very strongly now. And Freddie's face was very white and solemn in the glow of the night light which he had switched on.

" The door to the porch," I said. " It's blown open—it's banging."

We went out to close it. The living room was very cold; snow was blowing in through the outer doorway. We turned on the light. The door was not only open, it was hanging askew, half torn from its hinges. More than that, part of its wooden framework was gone. Not broken—vanished—as if melted off. A leprous wreck of a door, hanging there, banging with a thump and rattle in the wind!

No need to tell us what had happened—I think we both knew then. The door to father's bedroom stood open. He was not there. The bed had been occupied; there was no sign of a struggle, no abnormal disorder anywhere about the house, except for that dismembered front door, which had been locked.

Our light and our voices awakened Dan and his parents. They came out from their rooms. But Hulda did not come, nor Zetta! Their bedroom doors, like father's, stood open; but the occupants were gone.

Horrified moments followed, during which we searched the house and the buildings near it. There was no evidence of any kind of how, in the noisy night, while the rest of us slept, father, Hulda and Zetta had been spirited away.

The terrified elder Cains remained in the house. Hastily dressing, Dan, Freddie and I rushed to the corral. The chilled little ponies welcomed us. We saddled, and in single file, slowly against the wind and the driving snow, we rode out into the night.

There was no surprise left for us when we reached the " Eden tract " in the valley by the caves where once the Cains' treasured fruit trees had grown so luxuriantly. It was all a dim gray expanse of snow, with the naked tree branches showing in black, forlorn rows.

The trunks of the coconut trees stood like huge black sticks in a patch

of white. But among them there was
no small silver vehicle. The guards
had been withdrawn a week before.
There was no evidence here of anything.

The heavy falling snowflakes would
have covered up even recent footprints;
there was only the depression in the
sand and snow to mark where the
vehicle had been.

The last communication was broken.
The last remaining evidence of Xenephrene upon our earth was gone!

CHAPTER VII.

MYSTERIOUS STAR, IMPERTURBABLY SHINING!

MORE than twice seventeen
months went by. For me and
for Dan the progress of the
world, it seemed then, must always be
in cycles of seventeen months. That
is the length of time which Xenephrene
took periodically to overtake and pass
us in our orbit. Almost between us
and the sun, every seventeen months;
and at such times she was at her closest
points to us, some sixteen to nineteen
million miles away. Not very far, in
terms of astronomical measurement,
but to Dan and me very far indeed.

Two of these passings came and
went. We had hoped there might be
some sign from Xenephrene; even
something hostile would have seemed
to us better than nothing. Dan and I
often sat in the night, gazing at the
great purple-white star.

Romantic, mysterious world, imper-
turbably blazing up there! It held captive for Dan the woman he loved; for
me, a beloved sister and my dear father. Held them captive—if indeed
they were alive, which is the best we
could hope—held them, and it gave no
sign! Beautiful, mysterious world—
and sinister! Gazing up at it, my fancy
roamed.

What strange sights and sounds and
beings were there! We had had but a

little glimpse, no more—and then it
was snatched away.

It is not important now for me to
recount what these months brought on
earth. The adjustment to new conditions, new climate, new night and day.
Volumes of history describe it fully—
the myriad shifting events over the
world's great surface, the new nations,
new mingling of races—everything
new, it would seem. Everything but
human nature; the old characteristics,
love, hate, jealousy, friendship, greed,
envy—nothing on earth has ever
changed them, and nothing will.

We did not know why father, Hulda
and Zetta were abducted; but that they
were captured by the invaders and with
them returned to Xenephrene we felt
sure. Why the invaders came at all, and
then so hastily withdrew, we could not
guess. Zetta knew, and she had told
father. But the secret went with
them. Perhaps, we decided, the Creator
intends this veil of mystery between
the worlds? If that thought could be
spiritual consolation to Dan and me,
we tried to make the most of it.

Dan was distracted. Vainly he and
I sought some way by which we might
get to Xenephrene. It seemed impossible. Before that terrible winter
when what they now call the " Great
Change " began, any serious talk of
going to a neighbor planet was always
laughed at. But no one laughed now.

Scientists told Dan and me that at
present, for us of earth, the thing was
impossible. If father had left his
notes, perhaps, instead of putting them
in his pocket that fatal afternoon; if
some vestige of apparatus had been left
behind by the invaders; if only we still
had even a portion of the mechanism of
Zetta's small vehicle, that our scientists
might study it, try to learn its secret—
Ah, those ifs! They are all encom-
passed in the one phrase, which each
of us mortals at one time or another in
life has murmured sadly to himself:
" If only I had known!"

I was far older now in spirit than

that winter thirty-five months before. We do not age in regular progression, but in spurts of stressed mental and physical suffering. I aged, for though I lost a sister and father, something else I lost, less tangible but unforgettable. The girl Zetta—the loss of what might have been, for me and for her.

Love born of a glance, now to stay with me always? It was not that. I was not so youthful that I could cherish such romantic illusion.

But this I knew. Something, that memorable afternoon when she and I first joined glances, sprang into being. 'As though over the gap from one world to another, from a man to a woman and back again, it sprang and clung reluctant to be broken. And it left its mark upon my mind and spirit. It was not to be; I believed that fully. But, had it been, the consciousness was within me that it would have been a thing very beautiful.

And I was older; and, I think, a better man, just for the memory.

Thirty-five months! A dreary, hopeless interval to Dan and me. Dreary, for in the midst of all the world's turmoil we seemed to stand apart; not actors, spectators merely, with our minds and spirits up there where the great purple star was shining. Thirty-five hopeless months, for it seemed that what we had lost was forever gone.

ON February 4, 1956, Dan and I were living in Porto Rico. Freddie was in Miami. Father's post in Southern Chile was taken by one of his fellow scientists. The world rolls on! Father was lost, his post filled, and himself almost forgotten. How fatuously we mortals attach importance to ourselves! We strut our little moment upon the stage, some in the spotlight, some shrinking in the shadows by the back drop. We miss our cues, fumble, and are abashed or terrified. But in a moment no one cares. The curtain rings down; up again, with the old play, but new scenes and other actors; and the changing audience forgets we ever were on the stage at all.

Father's post was filled. Freddie and I had been down there to Chile one summer, but we did not like it and we came back. Summer! The very word had lost its meaning. They were beginning now to call it the Day.

We came back in June, chasing the daylight, and located in Porto Rico. Dan and his father were engaging in the new agriculture. The daylight and twilight months in the West Indies were found favorable for the raising of vegetables. Every one was groping. What could or could not be done was as yet scarcely known. But it promised to be a profitable business. Food of any kind, anywhere in the world, at any time, found a ready market. All the world governments were engaged in its purchase, its storage, and its distribution.

A new era was beginning; and in it some saw a more rational order than in the old. I am no economist; yet now I could see quite clearly the fallacy of much that the world had previously thought was best. Tariff walls between the nations were gone now. The world in its necessity became one big family, working to maintain itself as best it could.

In the daylight in Porto Rico, we were raising vegetables to feed the people who were living in the darkness and cold of the south. Six months later, they would be doing the same for us.

It is not my purpose to indulge in economic theories here, though Dan and I often discussed them. Freddie was not interested. We wanted him with us; but though he came to Porto Rico, he stayed in San Juan, often going up to Miami. The National Capital was still there; and Freddie had interested the government in his invention.

The world catastrophe had brought a great stimulus to scientific invention.

New devices, born of the necessity of totally new world conditions, were being developed. Every government was ready to help with funds. Freddie had perfected his motor, financed by our government.

More important than that, however, they were interested in producing his heat-ray projector in more powerful form. His new projector, he told us, was very nearly ready. Not for war purposes, of course. With characteristic thoughtlessness, the world had already almost forgotten the brief invasion from Xenephrene. Such a thing as that naturally could never happen again. And after what the world had been through, war between our own races was unthinkable.

Freddie's heat-ray, he said, would be used in the six months' Night against the cold. It had a myriad uses. With it, a ship might blaze a path down a frozen river. Water power might be utilized further into the long Night; why, a city might even be sprayed with its beams and be kept spring-like despite the cold! Visions! But by such visions science moves ahead into the realism of achievement!

That long Night of '55 and '56 Dan and I spent housed in, with the comparative comfort of our newly rebuilt and heated plantation house. Throughout January and February it snowed heavily; the tumbled little mountains of Porto Rico were solid white.

Sometimes the leaden sky would clear; the stars and moon would glitter on the snow, so bright one could almost read outdoors. Our winter moon was magnificent. The moon's orbit about the earth was very little changed from before; its plane had shifted with us, scientists said, and the moon was pursuing very nearly its old path relative to us.

Dan and I had a small Arctic A flyer, and sleighs. We did not use the plane much. The indolence of the long night of enforced idleness was upon us. Most of the world was learning how to work hard in the daylight months, and to do nothing gracefully through the months of darkness. We read our books; listened to the radio; studied, planned and talked.

It would have been very pleasant, had there not been that constant sense of what we had lost. Father, Hulda—and Zetta. I had spoken very little of Zetta to Dan. The dreams of what might have been, were my own; even with him, I could not share them.

And then came February 4, 1956. The long night was fully upon us, the twilight days were passed—midwinter was in early April. Dan and I had been out after breakfast for a drive in the sleigh. We had returned for luncheon with Dan's parents; and I was on the veranda, enveloped in furs, pacing up and down in the snow. Dan, with his cigar, came out and joined me.

There is sometimes a very queer directness to the fate which governs our lives—and a very great unexpectedness. We walk in the dark, with an open road or a chasm yawning before us, all unaware of which it may be. Or we may be standing at the threshold of a shining garden of hope and happiness, walking in the dark toward its gate, with heavy heart because we do not see it, or realize it is there.

Dan and I were like that now. January, 1956, had been the second time that Xenephrene passed at its closest point to earth. We had hoped that something might happen to give us news of father. But nothing did.

Gradually our hope had been dying. The January days dragged through their brief twilights into the solid winter night. We gave up hope. Xenephrene was drawing ahead of the earth again, with millions of miles of lengthening distance between the worlds. No sign from the great purple star; and we both felt that now all hope of hearing from father was gone.

Thoughts like these possessed me as I paced the veranda that afternoon. They were in Dan's mind too, I am sure; but when he joined me we neither of us spoke of them.

IT was clear and cold. The snow on the veranda crunched and creaked under our tread. Beyond the incongruous coconut railing the knoll-top showed white, with a blue-white beam of light from one of the side windows slanting out on it. There was no moon; a deep purple sky, with the sharply glittering silver stars. To the south, below the horizon, we knew that the sun at this hour was hovering. But it was too far down even to pale the stars now. Xenephrene was down there near it, invisible to us of the north—

Dan and I paced in silence; or talked idly of the now commonplace things of the new era of our world.

"They claim they can keep the falls of the Iguazu open all year," said Dan. "And send the power by radio—even up as far as here."

The distribution of electric current by wireless had been recently greatly improved. It seemed really practical now. In a few years Niagara, in the Day, might supply power and light to the dark, frozen cities of the south throughout their Night.

There had been most disastrous floods throughout the world when, with the coming daylight, the snow and ice had melted. Watercourses were unable to handle the sudden, abnormal flow.

But new channels were forming; nature and man alike were making adjustments to the new conditions.

"If they could send us heat from the south," said Dan. "I mean direct, natural heat. These new transformers of the power-waves may be all right, but—"

"Freddie can—I don't mean send it, but produce it, at any rate—"

"Some day," said Dan, "we'll be able to spray all our land here with that contrivance of his. Hah! That would be a great idea, wouldn't it?" He chuckled with an ironical gibe at the absent Freddie; but still he was more than half serious.

"Imagine us, Peter, getting out in the June twilight, helping the snow to melt by spraying it with heat—warming up the frozen soil, getting it plowed and planted a month earlier. If we could get our perishable vegetables down to the Argentine ahead of the others, they would bring mighty big prices—I was reading what might be done with tomatoes, Peter—"

He checked himself abruptly, gripped my arm with a force that whirled me around. We stood at the veranda rail.

"Heavens, Peter, look at that!"

From overhead near the zenith, a shooting star came blazing down. I had never seen one so brilliant. A great yellow-red ball of fire, with a flame of tail. It seemed to take long seconds as it soundlessly fell across the sky before us—down with a blaze to the northern horizon where the Caribbean lay, a dim, dark purple in the starlight.

We breathed again. "That didn't burn itself out," said Dan. "I'll wager that was a meteorite—actually came down somewhere—"

"Northwest," I said. "Florida way. It certainly seemed close to us, didn't it?"

We went back to our pacing. There was nothing particularly unusual in seeing a meteor fall across the sky. But we were both silent, wondering. We had caught just a glimpse of the gateway to our renewed hope; we did not know it, but we both sensed it.

An hour passed. From within the house, old man Cain called, "Oh, Dan —come here, listen to this."

The radio announcer was relaying an item from Curaçao. In the twilight at Willamstadt they had seen what seemed to be a meteorite fall into the sea near the Venezuelan coast.

"Another!" exclaimed Dan.

An hour later, still another meteorite was reported. It had fallen somewhere in the region of Victoria Nyanza— in the lake, perhaps, or along its shores.

Still, this seemed nothing remarkable. But about five o'clock the radiophone rang with our private call. It was Freddie, in Miami. The gateway to our hopes swung wide to receive us. Dan answered the call; I stood at his elbow, trembling with excitement—at first premonitory, then justified.

In the silence I could hear the tiny sound of Freddie's voice.

"On, Dan? Dan Cain?"

"Yes. That you, Freddie?"

"Yes. Listen—I'm in Miami. A meteorite fell—they've got it—Okechobee region. Listen—it cracked open. Was pretty well burned—but a big one. Hollow inside! They cracked into it—they found— Oh, Dan, they phoned me from Moorehaven just a little while ago. They "—Freddie's voice broke with his excitement.

"They—what, Freddie? Take it easy—can't understand you."

"I'm coming, Dan. By plane—I'll get away about eight o'clock. Peter there? Good! See you about midnight —soon as they bring it here to me, I'll bring it to you."

"Bring what? What, Freddie?"

"The cylinder. Whatever it is— haven't seen it. They're bringing it— they've got it. Heat-proof, insulated metal cylinder—they say it's engraved 'Peter Vanderstuyft, Porto Rico— Rush.' I'm bringing it, Dan. Tell Peter. It's a message from Xenephrene! It must be! A message from Peter's father!"

CHAPTER VIII.

FROM ACROSS THE VOID.

WE helped Freddie unload the cylinder from his plane. He arrived about midnight, flying alone with his precious burden. It was a cylindrical metal container, some ten feet long by three feet in diameter —a strange-looking, purple-brown metal, smooth and shining like burnished copper. White metal handles were on the cylinder—and down one of its bulging sides was crudely engraved the inscription " Peter Vanderstuyft, Porto Rico. Rush."

The thing weighed perhaps two hundred pounds. It was warm, yet clammy to the touch, as though sweating. And though it appeared smooth, under my finger tips I could feel that it was pitted and scarred—blistered as though by tremendous heat.

We labored up the hill with it, and deposited it on the floor in the Cain's living room, gathering over it, wondering how it might be opened. The message from Xenephrene! It had come at last; and abruptly I seemed to feel that this was not remarkable. We had been waiting for it; and here it was, at our feet here, strangely fashioned— mute, but waiting passively to give up its secret.

We were all trembling. Freddie had discarded his furs and helmet, but his hands were stiff with the cold.

"How do we get into it? They didn't want to open it—I didn't try either. It's the message, Peter."

Dan was on the floor beside the cylinder, running his hands over its surface. His father and mother crowded upon him. Old man Cain's jaw was dropped with his awe; Mrs. Cain chattered, "Land sakes! What next! Dan, what is it? Is it from Professor Vanderstuyft? Is he all right? And dear little Hulda? She's all right, isn't she, Dan? That's what this means, doesn't it? My heavens, these queer times that have come to the world—"

Dan jumped to his feet. "Yes, mother, that's what we hope it means." He kissed her; pushed her away; firm, but very gentle. "You go to bed, mother. Father, you go too. We'll be working here some hours—in the morning we'll tell you all about it."

Freddie, Dan and I were left alone. The double doors and double windows were closed against the cold; a broad coal fire burned in the grate; the room was warm and silent; and blue with the light-tube, which cast its beam down upon the cylinder. Freddie said, with a hush in his voice: "We'd have been afraid to try and open it anyway, in Miami. You—you don't suppose it would explode if we pound at it, do you?"

The sweating thing was strangely sinister, for all its friendly inscription. Dan was again bending over it. Freddie added:

"It was in a meteorite—some strange rock, or metal. Evidently not natural—artificially made. It was burned, fused and shapeless by the heat of its fall through our atmosphere. You can see where the heat has burned the cylinder—"

"Hush!" said Dan abruptly. "Listen!"

With our ears close to the metal a tiny hum was audible. The thing was humming inside. Alive! Vibrant! Humming with that strange, almost gruesome whine which brought to my memory the crimson sound of the Xenephrene invaders when Robinson and Davis had attacked them.

It was half an hour before, with the utmost caution, we got the cylinder open. Upon one of its sides we found four slightly raised circles and four small depressions, numbered from one to eight. And the words, crudely scratched on the metal, "Peter, press one, three, five and eight."

A lid came off. We had not seen the cracks where it fitted. It stuck, fused by heat; but we carefully forced it, and at length it came away.

The human mind is subject to queer vagaries. There was just an instant, as we lifted the metal panel, that there flashed to me the vague horror that this was a coffin; that we were about to behold a corpse—wrapped and sent to us like a mummy. Hulda! Zetta! A ghastly gibe, sent to mock us from this sinister unknown world!

"Ah!" breathed Dan. My leaping heart quieted; but the cold sweat stood in beads on my forehead from those fleeting, horrible fancies.

The interior of the cylinder was divided into orderly compartments. Metal boxes; cones; cubes of metal; diaphragms; coils of white wire—packed, wrapped and lashed in orderly array; each piece seemingly set in springs to absorb the landing shock. A white lining was inside the cylinder, smooth as mica—insulation against the heat, perhaps. A strange, vague odor arose; and we could hear the humming now more plainly. It seemed to come from several metal globes the size of a man's head. Dead black metal; four or five of them were packed near the center of the cylinder. Around them a dim radiance was hovering.

"Wait!" admonished Dan. "Take it easy!" Freddie, in his excitement, would have begun rummaging. "Wait! There must be some instructions somewhere. Don't touch anything until you know what you're doing."

We found the box of instructions; it was, indeed, the most prominent thing before us, though we had overlooked it—a flat metal case some twelve inches square and half as thick, packed edgewise. Clipped to its top was a white roll of what seemed paper.

Dan gingerly removed it; unrolled it—a translucent white animal skin, possibly. And with writing on it! Ah! At last the doubts and fears that were within us all were dispelled. Father's handwriting—his firm, smooth unhurried script.

"To my son, Peter Vanderstuyft. In Porto Rico care of Ezra John Cain, or the Amalgamated Broadcasters' Association, United States of America. Please forward at once."

And then the words: "Peter, detailed instructions inside. We are safe —your father, Hulda, and Zetta."

Ah! Zetta! The gates to the shining garden were swung wide for me then! Zetta!

TO BE CONTINUED NEXT WEEK

With a terrific blow Danvers smashed the invader's big hand

Recluses

The story of a dog is this—a wonderful animal bound by generations of habit and training to the ways of man, but thrilling to the irresistible call of the wild

By RAYMOND S. SPEARS

A THOUSAND generations of breeding ugliness out of Black Forest wolves to make them tractable sheep guardians could not fail to eradicate some of the wolf instincts from the nature of these age-long leaders of rapine. Features, appearance, physique remained the same, but by breeding in the docile and friendly dog types while breeding out the lupine frames of mind came down at last to Queen, who belonged at the Cougar Den Club.

Queen was a tall, narrow, smiling dog, that gave returns in friendly interest to the sportsmen who had organized the Cougar Den away out on the edge of things. There they went to revert for a few days or weeks to the killing of wild beasts enduring the privations of a land where only the trails of animals led through the gaps.

Queen stretched with long dignity before the fireplace. She ate at her own bowl, never deigning to come to the table to beg a bite from the humans. She strolled around the camp, corral, and along the banks of Skipping Creek with her head and tail low, catching game to show that a thousand generations of domestic habits had not cost her any of the wolf skill of her wild ancestry back in the nomadic days of humanity.

She also knew where the trout had their spawning beds of sand. Wading in the shoals she would plunge her open jaws into the water and bring up great flopping fish, some of which she ate. Others she carried nonchalantly into the camp kitchen for the sportsmen, making them envy her for the capture of such monsters, their own fish-rod luck bringing no like rewards.

Queen would go to a near-by knoll and sit on her haunches, surveying the surrounding country. She kept her nose horizontal, however, and no coyote howl ever tempted her to point her jaws up, howling in answer. It remained for a dog wolf, a gray roamer of perhaps her own age, to come by at last; and between suns she vanished from the sportsmen's camp. The men knew she had eloped with the wolf. They found the tracks where they romped away together up the dry sand bed of Thirsty Creek.

The wolf was a traveler when he took Queen with him. And she had the gray hide and the magnificent carriage, the swagger and the gait, the silhouette and the voice of a wolf; a thousand humans wise to police or German sheep or Belgian wagon dogs might see her and yet not notice that she was dog instead of wolf.

Of her wild range no one could make even a plausible guess. Whenever in this or that desert terrain, along timber belts, in the lakes or streams regions word was heard of a pair of wandering wolves who played as they ran, and spent their time chasing jackrabbits, hunting squirrels, turning porcupines over to bite them in the bellies, and other familiar pursuits, the sportsmen were glad that Queen had survived the poison bait, the traps, and the far-reaching rifles of hunters eager to slay the savage pair, though they were much more interesting alive than dead.

But when it began to be said that Queen and her mate, who was called President, to fit him in name for so fine a companion, had a superior intelligence, and were too good for trappers and hunters to slay, champion killers of "varmints" made a dead set to stretch the hides of President or Queen just to show how much smarter they were than even a run-wild dog.

The two never occupied the same den twice in succession until Queen went into retirement, to issue presently with a litter of wolf pups. She lived one spring in the Linkum Hills, another in the Goggle timber belt, and a third up at the head of Diamond waters.

She did her duty by the pups. She raised them till they were racing around. Then, with President, she trained the youngsters to hunt game for themselves, taught them according to their ability to learn, and then, when the pups were able to care for themselves, catching cottontails and eating grasshoppers, chewing grass, berries, and nuts for their health and hunger, she would slip away with her mate to run again, untrammeled by matronly cares, during the autumn and winter, through courtship affairs of February and March, again to go into retirement in late spring.

Inklings of her travels and habits were obtained when from time to time she passed through the Cougar Den country.

She had ways of letting the sportsmen at the camp know that she had come there. She was wild and savage, now, and slunk away from men whenever she came upon them. Rifle bullets spraying around her and President as they ran or slipped away, had taught her to shun humanity.

At the same time she still could not quite forego the memories of the sportsman camp ranch, and she would come down among the two or three dogs who had taken—but not filled—her own place in the camp and its traditions. She could nose the dogs without jeopardy, and she would leave a fish on the porch or lug in a big antelope jackrabbit, just for old-times' sake, and the dogs left her tribute of friendship alone, as though she had warned them of the consequences if they didn't.

Summer and autumn in that country was beautiful. She would come with President, who hung back in the junipers, probably anxious and angry that she took such chances around a human cabin. She was clever, however, and the pair steered clear of all camps, ranches, trappers' cabins, and places where men traveled. When they crossed a wagon road they would jump twenty-five feet or so, and high in trajectory. They had no use for humans, and the coming of hunters or fugitives from justice in their temporary locale would see them hurtling for some other place as far away as possible from mankind.

THE man who had brought Queen from the kennels when a few months old was Roland Danvers. Danvers was a manufacturer of brass and copper implements, making a large income and a fine name for the excellence of his products. He overdid his job, however, and a day came when the doctors told him he had nerve, lung, and muscular ailments, and he must retire into some far, high place to regret his industry and bemoan the meagerness of his sins.

Danvers had always been so proud of his strength. He had been tireless in his mountain climbings. He had braved the precipices and conquered the fastnesses. Now, when he went to the Cougar Den, scene of his wildcraft triumphs, he had to hobble around and stop for breath.

He caught the sidelong glances of pity, and heard the false note of assurance and delight that he looked so well. His friends knew that he was done for, so he had himself built a cabin away back up in the timber belt, and as he was not wholly helpless, he ordered his guides down to the main camp, and warned them that if they came to him oftener than once a week he would shoot them.

There, in his cabin, he sat for hours in the sunshine, and learned to watch and know the wild life around him, instead of shooting the big game and ignoring the small.

He asked his old friends not to shoot anything in this particular valley, and so the deer and bears came around his cabin, feeding on his middens and licking salt. At night he heard the coyotes' howl, and by day he learned the languages of ravens, grouse, and other birds.

A long autumn passed. The people wanted him to come down to the main camp, but he refused. Instead, he ordered up enough supplies to last him all winter, when deep, loose snow might keep the guides from coming in to him as often as they ought to, looking after his safety.

Elk and deer went by him on their way into the winter feeding country. Mountain sheep came down into his valley. Blizzards shut him in. Instead of being alone for a week, he was alone for a month at a time. He set out a prodigal feast there every day for the birds. Although most of the big animals had gone away, mountain sheep came to feed at stacks of hay he had had harvested for them on the meadow spreading wide at his feet, lifting into gorgeous granite ranges across the way.

Weak, lonely and yet hopeful, Danvers studied the passers-by through powerful binoculars as well as close at hand. He had never known rest when youth or man, having begun work on leaving the grammar grades, and had carried on steadily. Now that time seemed more precious than ever to him, he relaxed and enjoyed the passing hours as never before. He forgot his ailments. He lived watching the creatures which fed on his bounty. Even a cougar came strolling by his silent figure, stopped to look him in the eyes and then slipped on his way.

6 A

There was a scoundrel who lived away up beyond where Danvers had had his retreat built. His real name was unknown to any one. He was suspected of being a fugitive from justice. That he was bad was obvious when one saw the greenish hue of his sullen eyes, watched the twisting of his lips, and noticed how quickly his hand went to his big revolver at a strange sound or at the fall of a shadow on the ground within his view.

At his door had been laid cattle stealing, a murder on the other side of the mountains, and robberies. Now and again a Carcajou detective made the circuit of the settlements and ranches which encircled the Tehawus country, and the man back in the mountains knew about that, attaching to it the significance it deserved.

The detectives knew him, but the region's population did not know. He went by the name of Skyline Pete, because he was seen so often silhouetted against the horizon along the crests of the bare Alpine heights above the timber stand.

The rumor went around that Roland Danvers had in his peeled log cabin unusual luxuries and supplies of the most tasty kinds. This was near the truth, for the doctors had prescribed for him a great many luxuries to assuage his physical condition. He had a fortune from which he could scarcely spend the income.

His cabin was finely furnished, but he would have been glad to exchange all that he had for the robust health and easy habits of mind of most of those who dwelt far away and in humbler surroundings than his mountain retreat, where at times despair could not fail to mingle its voice with his most determined resolutions. Never before had his courage been so sorely tried.

Drawn into an unnatural shape by his illness, he daily worked against the strains, exercising, reading in the great literature that inspires heroes and re-

cords the transition of human despair into supreme confidence, generally he was content. Though winter was upon him, he refused to obey the portents of the migration of the wild life from the high ranges down into the lower belts.

"No," he shook his head, "leave me here alone. I've enough to eat, more than three pounds a day for the length of the winter season, and a ton of grain and a cord of dried meats to hang out for my wild neighbors. There's plenty of fuel in the woodshed, and lots of oil for my lamps. No! If man can't help me it may be I'll find here in these mountains the faith of mind that 'll overcome my physical ailments."

"We prob'ly cain't git to come up more'n once or twicet this winter, if the snow's loose!" the club superintendent warned him.

"Don't worry about me, boys," he replied. "It doesn't matter what happens. If I go back down now, I'm retreating. I want to stay here and fight it out."

With forebodings they left him, and well they might dislike to leave a man alone like that in such a remote fastness. Danvers was a good fellow. When he had been a stalwart, like his camp mates, he had been one of the kindliest men in the world. Now he was even finer and gentler.

They left him firearms and ammunition. They made sure of every detail, from fire extinguishers to matches, and from venison jerky to long rows of canned fruit. His own solicitude was that he should have plenty of grain and dried meats, great sticks of beef and mutton kidney fats to be hung out for his bird friends, who like himself would rather enjoy the great mountains, despite the cold, than go down to milder climes.

When two of the guides fought their way into the cabin to spend Christmas with the self-exiled man, they found him about the same. He was putting records through his phonograph when

7 A

they came up to the cabin in the evening. The timber above the cabin was splitting with the terrific frost, the ground shaking as the solid granite shrank to the shriveling touch. But within, a red fire blazed cheerily in the sitting room, a heating stove insuring the cabin the ample warmth of comfort. At their hail from without the man threw wide the door.

"Why, boys, you've come?" he exclaimed.

"Sure thing—Merry Christmas!" they laughed, and unloaded bundles of mail, magazines and remembrances which had been sent to him by his friends.

"Thank you, boys!" he said, brokenly, stirred by the affection which was willing to undertake that tremendous trip through the hard going when every step of the snowshoes on the loose fluff let them down nearly two feet in it.

The visitors remained four days. Danvers visibly cheered up under their presence. He was not sorry to have them leave, but from every word that had come to him he knew that his friends were pulling for him. They wanted him to swing up instead of slide down. They couldn't afford to lose him. At the same time they knew he was the captain of his own destiny, and that he must find himself there alone or not at all.

New Year's, January and February were magnificent phenomena in that land. Storms swept the mountains and added snow on the deeps already inundated. There were days so cold that the birds could not face it, and the watcher saw a raven, flying along, suddenly collapse and fall into the snow, frozen to death on the wing.

Wiser birds buried themselves in the loose snow, waiting for the freeze to moderate, and when they came out at last they swarmed in flocks around the great chunks of suet and lean meat which hung in Danvers's trees and scratched and ate the grain till their crops stuck out like pouters. All of them, when stuffed, came with shining eyes to cock their heads to right or left, staring at the muffled human who attended them in their wants.

He even set out dishes of warm water at which they drank damatically. Now and then a foolish young one plunged in to take a bath, requiring thawing operations quickly.

SKYLINE PETE, improvident and a thief, came prowling into the winter hermit's valley. He had failed to lay in enough food to see him through the winter, and, hungry as a bear, emerging from its hibernating, Skyline Pete took advantage of hard snow and bare streaks to sneak out of his own fastnesses into the domain of Roland Danvers.

He arrived near the cabin after dusk. He circled around it, peering through the windows into the fire-lit comfort of the sitting room, where the recluse sat listening to the music of his records, of which he had brought so many that perhaps some had never yet been played. The skulker went, catlike, to the porch to look in. Ravenous, he broke off a chunk of jerky, careless whether it was beef or horse, gnawing it, jealous and envious of the birds, who there had all they needed.

Skyline Pete knew well enough that just one word of his own hungry predicament would give him a back load of supplies, and another lot when he should return. Sportsmen were like that, prodigal in their liberality. He knew that Danvers was one of the best fellows in the world. He hated him for the contrast with his own surly and brutal instincts.

There was loot of firearms, of money, probably, and of innumerable trinkets and valuables. He even saw sparkling on the man's hand the beautiful stone which marked Danvers's allegiance to his wife and sweetheart, now gone.

The visitor turned raider. He slipped to the door and softly tried it. Of course, no one locked a camp in that remote place! Skyline Pete quietly opened the hewn plank barrier and walked in on his toes, feline in his invasion. The cool draft rolling through the room gave the man who had spent the winter there his first warning of the intrusion.

Roland Danvers straightened from the rack of records to look. He saw the whiskery, long-haired scoundrel, who was patched about with furs and hides, the accumulated results of repugnance to cold water, visible to his looks. Skyline Pete had picked up a club of firewood as he came along the porch from looking at the window. Under his grizzly brows his eyes glowed green in their sunken pits. Perhaps he was demented or a reversion to the cave man era of intelligence and habits. In any event murder was his intention, unmistakably.

Roland Danvers straightened up, his brows lifting with surprise. His soul had been tried by his long vigil alone in that high back land. There had been times when he had bent weakly in dejection before the fireplace on gloomy nights, but courage had never failed him. Weak or strong, he was no quitter. He took a step toward the scamp with such a serene and blue-eyed contempt that Skyline Pete flinched, hesitated and took a slight step backward.

The intruder was a much heavier man than his intended victim. He was armed with a club, revolvers, and a knife in his belt. He had every advantage, it seemed, over the slender gentleman who stood with such a feeling of expectant exultation as he had not felt in twenty years, as though youth itself had returned to bless him with its stalwart joy in the beginning of some great feat.

Angered that he had betrayed his own cowardice, the raider surged forward with a savage, incoherent growl, shrill and high in its timbre, raising his club to beat down the smaller man with famine-inspired blows. Side-stepping,

Danvers slipped from under, and the knot struck a dent in the flooring.

Danvers leaped in, driving home a fist blow. Its strength surprised him. He had not known he was that nearly fit.

His physique cleared with his mind. He was largely himself again. He had scant chance against that antagonist, but he took it cheerfully, as though any possibility, however slight, was all he asked.

Much quicker than Skyline Pete, he must, if he would win, keep clear of the club, duck out of the fellow's bear-like arms, and stay on his feet. If caught and seized, he did not forget the guns and knife whose butts jutted out of the bearskin hair at the fellow's waist. Cool against increasing and baffled rage, Danvers had some advantage of which he took the full measure.

Mere cornered defense increased to lively hope for a while, but the ursine quickness and the cat-like bounds of the assailant were soon apparent. Time and again Danvers just slipped clear, and one blow grazed his shoulder, numbing it.

Courage hardly availed in that kind of a contest with the odds so much against him. Cornered, Danvers found himself trying to duck under, but he was thwarted. The next instant they were in a clinch and the chortling exultation of the savage man as he wrapped himself around his victim was accompanied by Danvers' gasping cry —still brave but despairing.

With a glance toward the open door, Danvers gave fleeting thought to the chance of a miracle, and one happened on the instant. He saw a great, fanged, wolf-like creature coming in absolute, instantaneous answer to his shout. The beast was fluffed of fur and white-fanged, light on its paws, with lowered head and tail.

With two short, puppyish springs, as if in play, the animal nipped in, snapping a chunk out of the ham of Skyline Pete. Leaping in again, as the man

shrank away screaming at that unexpected anguish, the beast tore open the
white flesh of Skyline Pete's upper arm,
which had been bared in the struggle.

And then the rescuer tore in and
slashed with faster and more fancy
bites and wrenches. Skyline Pete
struggled clear of Danvers, trying to
seize the wolfish assailant. Then he
reached to snatch his revolvers which
he seemed to have forgotten or felt he
didn't need in the fight with the man.

Danvers flung himself and balked his
attempt to use the firearms. Then Danvers caught up the club from the floor
and with a terrific blow smashed the
invader's big hand, while the animal
charged in, tearing open the calf of
a leg.

Skyline Pete surged toward the doorway. He was tripped by a grab in the
heel. He managed to get outdoors and
go tumbling and rolling headlong, end
over end, down the steep slope in front
of the cabin. The rescuer stood in the
open, breathing swiftly with tongue
out, smiling.

"Queen!" Roland Danvers shouted
as the voice of the whipped man died
away in the distance, cursing and
wrathful in fear and agony.

"Queen! It's you, Queen!"

She turned with her eyes shining to
look at the man who had brought her
into this lofty sky-land. She licked
in her long tongue, and walked with
dignity to him as he dropped on his
knees to wrap her in his arms, glad and
grateful beyond words.

It seemed to him as though in just
these few minutes of terrific struggle
his weakness and his hopelessnes of
ever recovering had both departed. He
had fought a good fight, and then a
friendliness and a companionship out
of the old days had brought him succor
in the moment of his great need.

"Queen!" he exclaimed. "Good old
girl! What can I do for you!"

As if for answer she strolled along
the front veranda and lifting her voice,
yelped and uttered a long-drawn howl.

From yonder there came an answer
in kind, and presently the answering
was farther away.

"Tell him to come in, Queen!" the
man urged. "Bring him in, old girl!
He's welcome!"

But the wolf mate would not accept
that invitation. He lay out in the
ridges and back in the timber, that night
and in the weeks that followed. Queen
took her place by hearth and in the
kitchen. She was there when the guides
broke through into the big country to
the cabin, fearful for what they might
find, and delighted when they were
welcomed by a man in whose eyes were
the full recovery and exuberance of
well-being, mind and body.

Toward these other men Queen lifted her nose and lips, and they respected
her feelings of aloofness—instantly.
Yet presently she let the hair lie down
along her back and curtained her fangs
again, reassured by the voice and explanation Danvers gave her. She did
not know or love them.

Roland Danvers would have gone
down to the main camp, but the dog
drew back from making the journey
even when the way was clear and the
avalanches of the spring melt had
stopped coiling and growling in smok-
ing devastation down the mountain
steeps.

She would not leave the remote cabin,
and so Danvers stayed with her. She
let him play with her pups when they
presently came. She romped with them
herself before the cabin, like a wolf
bitch before her den, watchful, wild
and happy. They grew apace and if
she let them feed on the dishes which
Danvers prepared for them with fond
efforts and varied recipes, she would
also go away alone and bring back a
jackrabbit or marmot or other wild
meat for them to gum with their funny
mouthings and their squeaking little
yelps.

Later she took the pups for short
runs with her, and then Danvers would
see her mate, always wild and keeping

his distance, go to join and run with them, the plump youngsters bobbing along, while with lithe, swift leaps the parents set the pace. And after a time Danvers would hear them circling back, their voices shrill in eager hunting cries, lifting in the wind like wandering wraiths.

A morning came when the family pack did not return. A day or two later Queen came running by, flirting her tail, yelping and on the romp, looking over her shoulder at the man who stood leaning against a post on the veranda. He knew by her refusal to come within a hundred yards that she had gone wolf again.

She was on her way over her long range, jubilant, happy, and wild, not sorry that a thousand generations of civilization had urged her to show gratitude nor regretting that she had turned a man's cabin into her spring wolf-den; but now she would be joining her mate for the jeopardies and the delights of feral freedom on her way! And Danvers with joy headed into his own world to resume his old life.

THE END

ʊ ʊ ʊ

Justice Served by Comparograph

THERE is now coming into common usage by law enforcement organizations—city police departments, sheriffs' offices, and criminologists—a new invention that simplifies the finger-print method of identification.

For years finger-print experts have worked on the one clew—a finger-print, which they check up with their morgue of records of criminals. When they find one in the morgue that is the same as the finger-print left at the scene of the crime they know that they have their man. Convincing the judge and jury is often not so easy.

But the Comparograph, as its name implies, makes comparison easy. It has reduced the tedious matching process to a mere routine detail, one that is fool-proof for the finger-print expert.

The Comparograph consists of two matched microscopes, each with matched objective lenses and matched eyepieces. There is a comparison eye-piece that connects the two microscopes. This eyepiece catches from each microscope half of the object showing on each of the lenses. In the eyepiece each lens object shows as half, and this half is joined to the half in the other microscope lens, thus making one whole of two separate objects—as seen through the eyepiece.

This makes it clear how effective is the Comparograph. A finger-print of a suspect is placed under one lens, while the finger-print clew is placed under the other lens for matching purposes.

Minute adjusting is then gone through by the operator in an effort to match the lenses and whorls of the two finger-print specimens. This definitely determines whether suspicion has been justified or not.

Setting above the eyepiece is a B and L Euscope that has a small prism immediately above the eyepiece. This throws a picture of the matched finger-prints on a screen in the dark box. By looking through one end of this box the operator sees this picture at the other end.

If a photograph of the matched prints is wanted the screen is removed and a photographic plate and holder is installed. The slide is drawn and the exposure is made.

Harold J. Ashe.

" I wonder," said Gillian, " if you're on the level"

The Crime Circus

*With all the forces of corruption pitted against him, Gillian Hazeltine
prepares for the most sensational trial in the history of his State*

By GEORGE F. WORTS

LEADING UP TO THIS INSTALLMENT

GILLIAN HAZELTINE, ablest defense lawyer in the State, is persuaded to give up his criminal practice by his fiancée, Dorothy Murphy. Just then Click Gorner, a gangster client, bursts in upon them in the hunting lodge with the word that Ben Lewis, night club owner, was murdered; he and Nicky Anderson were sole witnesses, and the innocent Violet Dearing, who is being framed, has asked Hazeltine to defend her.

He refuses,. and as Gorner steps outside the gangster is shot down by machine gun fire from rival gangsters. Gillian is warned to stay off the case by Yistle, the State's attorney, by crooked Governor Brundage, and by Mike Rafferty, Brundage's gang leader.

Hazeltine sends Nicky Anderson to Chicago to round up a bodyguard of gunmen. Wally Brundage, the Governor's son, persuades Hazeltine to see the beautiful red-haired Violet Dearing, who has been persecuted by the Governor because of Wally's love for her. She tries to persuade Gillian, pointing out what a " crime circus " he could make of the trial. He refuses.

Dorothy breaks the engagement because of newspaper reports that Gillian is taking the case. The chief of police refuses him protection, so he sends for Nicky. He drives to the capital, and, after a stormy interview with the Governor, tells him he'll defend the girl and " get " the Governor. He persuades Senator McMorrow, leader of the Legislature and foe of Brundage, to push through a bill to hold the trial in the football stadium, charging admission for the State treasury.

This story began in the Argosy-Allstory Weekly for September 15

On his way back to Greenboro, Hazeltine is fired on by Rafferty's gang, who think they killed him. His bullet-proof glass saves him, but he allows the report of his death to go out. Meantime, Nicky's mob kidnap the unsuspecting and celebrating Rafferty gang, and imprison them at Hazeltine's lodge.

Gillian asks Dorothy who suggested getting him to quit his law practice, and when she cannot explain, charges her with complicity in the Brundage plot.

CHAPTER IX.

ON THE OFFENSIVE.

GILLIAN put on a hat and coat and drove down to the jail where Violet Dearing was lodged. Coming down the steps as he was going up was Police Captain Sorrenson.

Sorrenson stopped, stared, and turned pale.

He gasped: "Hazeltine!"

Gillian said affably: "Oh, you thought I was dead, didn't you?"

The police captain made no answer.

Gillian leveled the butt of his cigar at him.

"The only people in this town who are dying violent deaths right now, captain, are the ones who monkey with human buzz saws. I'm a human buzz saw. Hear what's happened to Rafferty and his seven wise men?"

Still Captain Sorrenson was unable to find his voice.

"They're dead," Gillian informed him. "I had them drowned like rats."

With incoherent mutterings, Captain Sorrenson hastened down the jail steps past him. On the lowermost step he stopped, turned and flung back:

"That's a lie!"

"Don't take my word for it," said Gillian. "Drag the river! I'm letting you know I've got a big gang here. And I'm out for blood! Don't monkey with Gillian Buzzsaw Hazeltine, or you're apt to lose your neck! Where did you have those two patrol wagons parked while Big Ben Lewis was being bumped off?"

"What the hell—" began the police captain, and shut his mouth. He vanished in long strides down the sidewalk.

Forty seconds later, Gillian Hazeltine was standing before Cell No. 29, gazing whimsically into the deep blue eyes of the girl accused of shooting Big Ben Lewis.

"'Lo, Red," he said gently.

"My hair isn't red," stated that spirited young person; "it's auburn! I knew you'd come! But, darn your hide, Gillian Hazeltine, you gave me a day of awful suspense. I cried three times. I saw you vanishing over the horizon like a mirage. Now—praise be to Allah!"

"I wonder," said Gillian, still gazing thoughtfully down onto her pretty face, "if you're on the level?"

"Is the correct answer yes or no?" inquired Violet Dearing. "Whichever way you'd love me most, I am, Great Knight!"

"I'd like to meet a woman sometime —for the rare novelty of it," the man pursued his strange topic, "who doesn't try to make a fool out of me, or work me because I am rich and have power, or humiliate me because I treat all women, until they prove they're unworthy, as if they're somehow related to my mother."

"You should not put women on pedestals," said the red head. "We're too tricky."

"You, too?"

"I have lots of tricks—bags and bags," she said brightly. "But so far none of them have worked on you. I tried to vamp you last night. I tried to reach your intelligence this morning, in that note."

"Well, you can congratulate yourself anyhow," he grumbled. "I've decided to take your case."

The red-haired girl drew a deep breath and said "Wow!" in a reverent tone. "You angel!" an octave higher.

"I kept thinking and thinking," he said, "of what you said last night: 'What a fight we could have given them!' It's been running through my mind all day. It happened to be in my mind this morning when Governor Brundage said something particularly nasty in trying to bully me off the case."

"I'd like ever so much to know," said the Dearing girl, "what you meant by that crack at the end of your letter. You said: 'Before you are a free woman, you will have told Wally Brundage to roll his hoop. Why? Because you are too bright. You've made your point!' What did that mean —you've made your point?"

"What do you think it means?" he countered.

"Well," she said, "it means that I either must be what you hate most— tricky—or a fool. I'm a fool to be in love with Wally Brundage, because, so you say, he is such a sap. If I'm only playing him, then I'm tricky. Well?"

"Well?" Gillian mocked.

"Look at it this way," she argued. "Supposing we admit that I fell for Wally at first because he is such a beautiful young animal. Intelligent women do fall for handsome dumb-bells as often as intelligent men fall for beautiful dumb-bells. Then supposing I found that he hadn't a brain in his head and stopped loving him, and at the same time I realized I was being made the victim of vicious persecution by his father? Am I tricky to keep on pretending I'm in love with him?"

"He will be hurt when he discovers the truth," Gillian said.

"I considered that. But remember I am feminine. His father did his best to ruin my reputation. Shouldn't I, being a woman, use any handy weapon to hurt back? Well, Wally was that weapon.

"As for hurting Wally, he needs hurting. He is horribly conceited. He knows how beautiful he is. Every woman he knew until I came along fell for him like tons of bricks. He is, actually, a lazy young good-for-nothing. He needs a jolt. When he recovers from the one I intend giving him very soon, he may brace up, be a man and get to work. No; I don't love Wally. Am I, therefore, the kind of woman you detest most?"

GILLIAN said earnestly: "I think you are one of the straightest thinking women I've known in a long time."

"And you can add," she quickly put in, "the straightest behaving! If you think, just because I became a bootlegger, that I am a moral derelict; that I am any man's sweetie—

"Listen, Silver Fox! I've forgotten more than most of these modern, supposedly wise flappers ever knew about men and wickedness. But I learned it by observation, not from experience. I know my book! But where any man has ever been concerned, I have always considered myself sacred!"

Her beautiful blue eyes, glowing, were looking up belligerently into his.

"I believe you," said Gillian.

She laughed shortly. "You don't have to. Virtue is its own reward! Would you handle my case if I weren't a good girl?"

"Your morals haven't much to do with the present issue," Gillian promptly answered. "In court, it's a great help to know that a woman's slate is clean."

"Mine is spotless. Were you thinking of making love to me?"

"Love!" Gillian blustered. "To you?"

"Am I so dreadful to look at and ponder upon?"

Gillian looked angry.

"Or," she said softly, "does a burned child dread the flame? Did she do you dirt? Did she disillusion you? Are you off her for life?"

"She was crooked," stated Gillian. "She was part of the biggest frame-up I've ever stumbled into. You and I were the goats. As far as I can gather, you were to be framed; I was to be scared out. It seems to me the two of us are in the boat by ourselves, surrounded by angry waves and a first-rate hurricane approaching.

"We're going into court before a fixed judge, and a jury that, very probably, my best efforts can't keep honest. They'll build up evidence, all lies, that will take the hardest thinking of my lifetime to see through and disprove."

He gave her a summary of the situation; mentioning his conversation with the Governor; the attack on his life; the kidnaping of Mike Rafferty; the attitude of the chief of police. She was staring at him with round, frightened eyes when he had finished.

"Mr. Hazeltine, they'll get you somehow!"

"I doubt it. I think I have them buffaloed. I wanted, somehow, to place every one of them on the defensive. I did it by spiriting Rafferty's gang out of town. If that kidnaping doesn't spring a leak, they'll believe by to-morrow that I had those men murdered. I want them to believe that. I want them to know how ruthless I am!"

"You're the smartest thing I ever knew in my life," sighed the Dearing girl. "What do you think will happen?"

"You went before the homicide court to-day, didn't you?"

"I did."

"And pleaded not guilty?"

"Of course. And they denied me bail."

"Did the magistrate appoint legal counsel?"

"He offered to, but I told him I preferred to select my own. He seemed surprised. What will happen now?"

"They'll railroad it through. They'll take you before a special grand jury, and they'll give you an early trial."

"Do you want an early trial?"

"I want a week," said Gillian.

She eyed him curiously. "How about our bets? I owe you a box of cigars and you owe me a box of the purest silk stockings made in the world. That word 'box' is misleading. Any bet with the word 'box' in it always has a catch in it. Some boxes contain one pair—"

"The box I was referring to," said Gillian, "contains, I think, twelve dozen."

"Did you say box car?" queried the lovely red-head.

JOSH HAMMERSLEY, who in older days would have been called a star reporter, but was now merely the highest paid news gatherer on the Greenboro *Morning Journal*, was waiting outside the jail when Gillian emerged.

The age of Josh Hammersley was approximately that of Gillian Hazeltine. The two were old friends. So tried and true a friend, in fact, was Josh Hammersley that Gillian could—and did—speak to him on sundry occasions on sundry topics with the certainty that Josh would use his head, would not write stories for his paper containing statements injurious in any way to Gillian or his causes.

Josh Hammersley was plump, comfortable and bald. He had the wide, innocent blue eyes of a babe.

He said, "Well! well!" in throaty surprise when he saw Gillian descending the jail steps.

"Hello, you big stiff," said Gillian.

"Hello, you big bum," said Josh.

"I heard you were killed. I was just doping out your obituary and now, dog-gone it, I'll have to tear it up."

"Ride up to the house with me, Josh, and I'll give you an earful."

"Anything fit to print?"

"Not much. You can say I'm going to handle the Dearing case."

"Thanks. I'll phone it in from your house."

They climbed into Gillian's coupé. Josh did not notice the splintered left window until they were passing a lighted store.

He said simply: " Bullet-proof glass, eh? Well, things *are* stirring in this town. First I hear you are dead, then out jumps the rumor that Mike Rafferty and his gang were wiped out in a gun fight with some out-of-town boys. I can't find a soul to verify the story." You know all about it, you fox. What's up?"

" They laid for me on the Springton turnpike," Gillian told him. They let loose a burst from a Browning gun and beat it without making sure they'd done a thorough job."

"Yeah? And how about Rafferty?"

" If you want to help a good cause along, spread the news that Rafferty and his gang were captured, had their throats cut and were thrown into the river. You can't print that, because you can't verify it; but it will make a nice, fast-moving rumor."

" I heard that story, too. Is there anything in it?"

" Not for publication. I also want you to spread around that you have, in a safe-deposit box, a complete story of the crooked work that has been pulled off in this city. You can say you are going to print it in case I should be suddenly among the dead or missing. Will you do that, Josh?"

" Sure, I'll do it!"

They drove on through Greenboro and through Riverdale. Gillian parking beside the kitchen door, observed that Toro's battered old flivver was standing there.

He hastened inside and up to his office, followed by the reporter. Gillian rang for Toro, and the Japanese presently entered.

" You know this gentleman," said Gillian.

Toro bowed profoundly.

" You may speak freely before him, Toro."

" Very well, Mr. Hazeltine."

" Did you drive to Lake Largo?"

" I did, sir."

" Tell me what happened."

" I stopped first in Dexter and delivered your cigars and the note to Sheriff Bolton," said the precise Japanese. " I then drove on to your house with the load of provisions.

" At your house I was met by three men with drawn pistols, who took me before Mr. Anderson. I told him you wished to know how he had achieved his sensational victory. He said to tell you that it had been a lead-pipe cinch. He first stole a moving van. He placed his men inside and backed up the moving van at the side door of Lenore's night club, after first ascertaining that the Rafferty gang was disporting inside.

" He told the man at the door he had a load of booze and when the man stuck out his head, Mr. Anderson struck him with a blackjack. His gunmen rushed up the stairs and took Mr. Rafferty and his cohorts completely by surprise. In a twinkling—"

Josh interrupted: " I want to know how long a twinkling is."

"A twinkling," the Japanese promptly responded, " is just two-thirds as long as a jiffy, and just half as long as a trice."

" Go on," said Gillian, impatiently.

Toro obliged:

" In a twinkling, Mr. Anderson's men had your handcuffs on Mr. Rafferty's men, and gags in all their mouths. They threw them unceremoniously downstairs and loaded them like cordwood in the van. Then Mr. Anderson and his men climbed in, shut the doors and drove to Lake Largo. Whereupon Mr. Anderson telephoned to you."

" What happened to the van?" Gillian wanted to know.

" The van was driven five miles back to the main road," Toro answered, "and the man who drove it walked the five miles back to your house."

" Did you see the captives?"

" I did not, sir. Mr. Anderson had locked them all in the large upstairs room you use as a dormitory for over-flow guests. He had placed guards over them, armed with clubs. He told me to report to you that everything is jake."

"That will be all, Toro. You have done an excellent night's work. You may bring highballs for Mr. Hammersly and me, and retire."

"One more point, sir: Mr. Anderson requested that a daily supply of snow be brought in for his men and the prisoners. Most of them are co-caine fiends. Shall they have it?"

"Can you secure it?"

"I have not forgotten my old tricks, Mr. Hazeltine."

"And I don't want you to renew them, Toro; but until this case is settled, you might forget your conscience—for the glory of pure justice! We are waging a war upon the most dangerous vultures who ever got their talons into the political flesh of an American State. Right must prevail! Call it hokum if you wish, Josh, but that's my battle cry."

"You can depend upon my ablest assistance," said Toro, and withdrew.

Gillian remarked: "Toro is a gem."

Josh Hammersley brought his fist down on the desk with a smack.

"Gillian," he burst out, "you're in too deep. You can't right a wrong with a dozen more wrongs. You're breaking every criminal statute in the State! Hired gunmen! Hold-ups! Kidnaping! Dope! and, I'll wager, extortion! Who are you after?"

"Brundage!"

"Don't be ridiculous. You can't get him. He's too slippery. He's too clever."

"I can try. I'm letting you in on this, Josh, so that, some day, you can write the story from the inside. I am going to clean up this State. I am going to make a clean sweep of rotten politicians and city officials in Greenboro, which is the seat of most of the rottenness in the State. Why? Perhaps to purge my own conscience. I'm not overly proud of some of the things I've done.

"Josh, I'm suddenly sick of being the Silver Fox—the craftiest criminal lawyer in this part of the country—the man who can get any crook or murderer off by outsmarting a dumb prosecuting attorney, a sleepy judge and a stupid jury! I've given myself a thorough housecleaning since last night. Now I'm branching out.

"You know what I'm trying to do, Josh. You've got most of the story already. If the Brundage gang gets me—publish the story! Your paper hates Brundage and isn't afraid of him. Come out with me now to Lake Largo and I'll let you listen with your own ears to some more of the story. And on the way out, I'll tell you the inside story of the Dearing girl."

Hammersley put on his coat.

"Come on, kid. I'd walk ten miles over broken glass in my bare feet to see Mike Rafferty with handcuffs on!"

CHAPTER X.

THE FOURTH DEGREE.

THE moon had set when the bullet-proof coupé pulled to a sudden stop with lights extinguished a hundred yards from the Hazeltine summer camp.

Gillian stopped the car because a man with a sawed-off shotgun had sprung out from the bushes. He had forgotten the deputies he had requested Sheriff Bolton to secure.

Holding his shotgun in one hand and flooding the occupants of the car with a flash light held in the other, the man roared:

"Put your hands up!"

Gillian and Josh elevated their wrists. The deputy looked into the car, gasped:

"Mr. Hazeltine! Holy cats, I didn't reco'nize ye! Roll along, Sweet Missouri, roll along!" He winked prodigiously. "Some party a-goin' on up at your place!"

"You bet," said Gillian heartily. And drove on.

Three men with pistols greeted them as they walked up on the porch: Benny the Knife, Hop Smith and Snake Harris.

They lowered their pistols and permitted the two visitors to enter. Cigarette smoke hung heavily in the air of his immaculate living room. Nicky Anderson was descending the stairs when Gillian and Josh entered.

The Silver Fox grasped his hand and said: "Congratulations! You did a beautiful job, Nicky. You know Mr. Hammersley, don't you—of the *Morning Journal?*"

Nicky shook hands with Josh.

"I know him, but he don't know me. Gonna write us up, Mr. Hammersley?" And Nicky laughed boisterously, then sobered. "This gent won't talk, will he, Mr. Hazeltine?"

"He is one of my most trusted friends," Gillian assured him.

"I think we made a clean getaway," said Nicky.

"How are the prisoners?" Gillian wanted to know.

"They ain't said a word—because the gags're still on 'em. Want to look 'em over?"

"We do," said Gillian.

Nicky led the way upstairs to the large dormitory in which Gillian, during large week-end summer parties, often lodged as many as a dozen men at a time. It contained eleven army cots. On eight of these cots lay the cream of Greenboro's criminal element.

Eight pairs of eyes glared murderously at Gillian as he walked from cot to cot, bent over and looked down.

"How are you going to handle this crowd, Nicky?"

"With good heavy clubs!"

Gillian bent over the last cot in the line. It contained the supine, baleful-eyed figure of the gang leader, the man who had with cold deliberation attempted to kill him this afternoon—Mike Rafferty.

"Mike," said Gillian amiably, "I thought I'd never see you reduced to this—trussed up like a hog on the way to the slaughter house! What a sight for sore eyes you are! Nicky, have you had them frisked?"

"Yes, Mr. Hazeltine. We took enough hardware off them to start up a arsenal! There ain't even a penknife among the lot of 'em."

"When do you plan to ungag them?"

"Well, those gags are on good and tight, Mr. Hazeltine. They don't feel good. I figured on lettin' 'em suffer awhile."

"Take their gags off. I want to have a talk with them."

"What if they all yelled? You could hear 'em as far away as Dexter!"

Gillian explained to Nicky his arrangements with Sheriff Bolton. Then Nicky took him into the hall and said in a confidential whisper:

"These boys of mine are O. K., Mr. Hazeltine, but they're weak. I mean, they're human. Let this bunch begin to offer 'em bribes and—well, they're weak and human."

"You'll have to spend all your time up here, Nicky, and see that nothing of the kind happens. My plans take care of that contingency.

"Keep them handcuffed and keep their feet tied together. Only let one of them at a time go to the bathroom. See that he is well escorted. If one of them gives us the slip—we're sunk!"

The two men reëntered the dormitory.

"Take off their gags," said Gillian.

Slug Lenihan, Frisco Joe and Kit Murphy removed the gags from the gangsters' mouths. And for some minutes the air was purple with profanity.

Gillian seated himself in a camp chair beside Mike Rafferty's cot and shouted:

"Nicky, I want this profanity stopped. Use that club on the next man who opens his mouth!"

The profanity ceased.

"That's a standing order," said Gillian. "Not one of you is to speak unless you're spoken to. I believe all of you men know Nicky Anderson. You killed his pal up here last night. He doesn't know which of you did the killing, but he doesn't love any of you. From now until I let you go, Nicky will stay in this room with a long, heavy club. In short, I'd advise you to keep your mouths shut tight—unless it is to answer questions."

HE looked down into the ugly, red, scarred face of Mike Rafferty; and Mike Rafferty's hot, blue eyes glared back at him.

"You, Mike, can talk. I want to know who killed Big Ben Lewis."

The gang leader glared at him without answering.

"Who," Gillian repeated, "killed Ben Lewis?"

Still Mike Rafferty was silent.

Gillian put the question a third time.

"Who killed Ben Lewis?"

The gunman would not answer.

Gillian glanced about the room. He asked the question generally. A pale, pimply faced youth, croaked:

"The Dearing girl!"

"Shall I hit him?" Nicky solicitously inquired.

He had, from somewhere, secured a great club such as our prehistoric ancestors are pictured as having carried.

"Not yet," said Gillian. "Nicky, I didn't have these men brought here because they tried to take my life this afternoon. At the same time, I am, of course, delighted that I have them where I want them. No, I am not revengeful—not a bit more revengeful than a full-grown male rattlesnake that's just been stepped on!

"You think you are a cruel man, Rafferty. In fact, you are proud of your record of brutality. You have made a great many people suffer. You look upon yourself as a thoroughly ruthless individual, beyond all law, entitled to take a life here and a life there as you see fit, or to carry out the orders of a man higher up who has something on you. You like to see blood flow. You enjoy seeing the look of death come into a man's face when you have pulled the trigger.

"Well, I am cruel, too. But I am cruel in ways that you know nothing of—but will soon learn. I am going to torture you, Rafferty. Not with any blunt, stupid police third-degree methods—but with a much more subtle, much more ingenious system. And when I am through torturing you, you will tell me from a full heart who killed Ben Lewis.

"*That's* why you and your friends are my guests here to-night: so that I can find out, as I sooner or later shall, who murdered Ben Lewis."

The blue eyes of the gangster had seemed to turn red. They seemed to radiate venom.

"You," Gillian went on, "are a great talker, Rafferty. You love to hear the sound of your voice. You love to brag. You love to tell how crazy the ladies are about you.

"And you don't even realize that the torture has begun. Before it is finished you will gladly tell who killed Big Ben. If you don't, your men will."

Mike Rafferty spoke. His voice leaped out, a harsh snarling:

"The first one of you who lets out a peep to Hazeltine or any of his gang is goin' to have his guts blown out by me personally—see?"

He stopped with a howl of mingled rage and pain. The club in the hands of Nicky Anderson had landed with a thwack across his chest.

"The golden rule for children," Gillian proceeded briskly, "applies, from now on, to all you men. Gunmen should be seen but not heard! Until you are ready to confess who murdered Ben Lewis, you are not to speak. Any man wishing to visit the bathroom will simply rattle his handcuffs. One man will go at a time.

"Now I will outline my plan of torture," said the Silver Fox. "First, silence! That must prevail night and day, hour in and hour out. Not one word is to be spoken. Breakfast tomorrow is to be your last meal. Thereafter—no food!

"Beginning now—no dope. No cocaine, morphine, heroin or any of their derivatives."

One of the gunmen groaned.

"Day after to-morrow morning, at breakfast time, you are to have your last drink of water. That is my plan. All of you know that it will be carried out. The suffering you are about to undergo, of silence, of hunger, of thirst, of that terrible gnawing craving for stimulants and narcotics—all this suffering can be avoided if any of you cares to speak the truth now. Does any one care to speak?"

The dormitory, save for the labored breathing of the Rafferty gang, remained still.

Gillian addressed Nicky Anderson: "When they are ready to tell the truth, let me know. Phone me and I'll come at once."

"It won't be long now!" said Nicky, gently swinging the club back and forth.

Gillian and Josh took their departure. In the coupé, Josh remarked:

"Gillian, you cannot get away with it! That dormitory is going to be a madhouse before to-morrow noon. Those eight men will be eight wild, frothing animals. They will escape somehow—and where will you be then? Why didn't you torture it out of them to-night?"

"I abhor physical torture," said Gillian.

CHAPTER XI.

STARTING THE BALLYHOO.

THE Greenboro newspapers on the following day pushed all news, including recent developments in the Dearing case, into the second and subsequent pages, whole-heartedly devoting their first pages to the sensational bill which had been introduced by Senator McMorrow in the State Legislature.

In honor of the man who had suggested it, it was given the name of the Yistle Bill. All honor and glory to Adelbert Yistle!

The prosecuting attorney did not know whether to be delighted or terrified. When the front pages of the morning papers were first brought to his attention he was delighted. When he read, as he did in the noon editions of the afternoon papers, that Governor Brundage was vigorously opposed to the measure, he was terrified.

Extras were on the streets at five in the afternoon with the announcement that the bill had been passed by a majority vote of both houses; sent to the Governor for his signature; returned after lunch with his veto—and promptly became a law by an almost unanimous vote of both houses sitting in joint session! Discounting wartime days, perhaps the record for lawmaking in any State in the Union had been broken.

By the terms of the Yistle Bill, the State, represented by the State's Attorney, was to profit hereafter from "such murder trials as attract, to a pronounced degree, the morbid curiosity of the public."

The bill consisted of numerous sections. Briefly summarized it provided that:

The local State's attorney was to be in charge of all arrangements, including the leasing of radio broadcasting rights to the highest bidder, the installation of suitable loud speaking apparatus whereby those seated at a distance from the judge and witness stand could hear all testimony and judicial decisions; the leasing of all profitable privileges and allotting of concessions.

The prosecuting attorney was instructed to consult with the counsel for the defense in order that the State might profit to the utmost.

Editorial writers in the Greenboro papers vied with one another in the flattering terms with which they welcomed the Yistle Bill. They spoke of it as a stroke of genius. They praised Mr. Yistle. They lauded Senator Mc-Morrow. They congratulated the lucky taxpayers. They hung verbal laurel wreaths all over the Legislature. They criticized Governor Brundage for his disapproval. The measure was spoken of as " daring," " audacious," and " revolutionary." Only the sensational Greenboro *Times* condemned the measure! and the Greenboro *Times,* a spokesman of the Brundage political faith, was only lukewarm in its condemnation.

It was the newspapers' opinion that the Yistle Bill had been railroaded through in time to be effective when Violet Dearing's case went to trial.

It was a busy day for poor Mr. Yistle. It was equally as busy a day for Gillian Hazeltine. He had little time for the preparation of his case. Miss Dearing had gone before the homicide court yesterday; this afternoon she would go before a specially impaneled grand jury.

It would not surprise him if Governor Brundage had issued orders that Violet Dearing was to be tried immediately. The Governor would realize that Gillian needed time; by breaking all precedents and bringing the girl to trial without delay, he would hamper Gillian's efforts at building a defense.

At nine thirty in the morning, Gillian was in the jail, saying to a beautiful red-haired girl with a tired smile and scared blue eyes:

" How're you bearing up?"

She answered with a question: " What's in store for me, Gillian?"

In pondering his answer he reflected that she had spanned the chasm from " Mr. Hazeltine " to " Gillian " in perhaps record time, and decided that the name, falling from her lips, took on musical values never before known. He always looked at people's hands for their state of mind; hers, this morning, were white and limp.

SHE was, he realized, frightened. " You're going to be as free as a lark," he assured her.

" I haven't the slightest doubt that I'll be as free as a lark if you have anything to do with it," she said. " But supposing something happens that prevents you from having anything to do with it? I mean, Gillian, you've gone to war with the most dangerous, most ruthless man in the State. You know how he deals with his enemies. You know how he has dealt with me. I stood in the way and—here I am!"

" Don't worry."

" Worry? Knowing that at any moment you might be shot or stabbed in the back? Don't you suppose that Brundage can find other men to shoot at you?"

He countered: " Don't you suppose I can, too? As a matter of fact, I've attended to that. I'm ashamed to admit it, but I have a personal bodyguard. My gardener was a sharpshooter, a sniper, in the war. He is a crack shot with pistol or rifle. He accompanies me wherever I go. Does that satisfy you?"

" It makes me feel much better. Now let's get busy in earnest and decide how we're going to handle this matter of People *versus* Dearing."

For an hour he questioned and cross-questioned her; examined and cross-examined her. At the end of an hour he said:

" That will do for to-day."

Miss Dearing removed from her bodice a slip of pink paper and handed it through the grating to him. It was a check, drawn to his order, for twenty-five hundred dollars, and it was signed by her.

Gillian looked up from it with a quizzical smile.

" What's this for?"

" It's your retainer, Gillian. I don't know what your fee is, and I'll be per-

fectly frank in telling you that this is
every dollar I have in the world."

Gillian was frowning. "Have I
said anything about a fee?"

"You usually collect one, don't
you?"

"When I win this case," he growled,
"we will discuss the fee. This money
I am going to invest for you."

"I want to know," she said firmly,
"what your fee is going to be."

"We will discuss that after the trial.
What are your plans, after the trial?
You will have received hundreds of
columns of newspaper publicity. You
will be more famous than any woman
who ever went on the witness stand.
What's it going to be—the stage—
movies?"

"All the king's horses and all the
king's men," Miss Dearing answered,
"couldn't drag me into the movies—
or upon the stage. Gillian, I haven't
any plans. I will probably assume another name, go West or East or North
or South—and get a job. But I haven't
thought about that."

Gillian put the check away and prepared to depart.

The lovely red-head put her hand
through the bars and nestled it in
his.

"You won't let them shoot you, will
you, Gillian?"

Gillian said to himself: "Watch
your step! They're all alike. They'll
stoop to any trick. This girl wants
you to fall in love with her, so she
can lead you around by a nose ring.
Get this idiotic idea out of your head
of eating breadfruit under a palm tree
in the South Seas! You've been stung
too often, my boy! Don't be an ass!"

So he gave the nestling, soft white
little hand a brotherly squeeze and departed.

The trouble with Violet Dearing, he
assured himself, as he walked rapidly
away, was that she had too much sex
appeal. She was too beautiful. Too
alluring.

"Love," he stated, "is the bunk!"

"I beg your pardon?" said an irri-
table voice.

It was Adelbert Yistle.

THE Silver Fox gazed guiltily at
the State attorney. Mr. Yistle
was pale and he looked harassed.

"You were talking to yourself!"
Mr. Yistle accused him. "You will
be making baskets in the Home for
the Mentally Incurable when I get
through with you this trip, Gillian!"

"Adelbert," Gillian retorted, "if you
didn't always say that, I'd be apt to
be terrified. Have you ever won a
case from me?"

"I'm going to win this one. Look
here, Gillian; what did you have to do
with this preposterous bill—this so-
called Yistle Bill?"

"I'm the father of it," Gillian admitted. "And Miss Dearing is the
mother of it. You, being a strict
moralist, would hardly call it a legitimate child, I suppose."

"Miss Dearing?" croaked the district attorney.

"Sure! It's her idea: hire a stadium,
lease the radio rights, and so on."

"You're up to some of your dirty
work!"

"Adelbert, on my word of honor,
you're wrong. This is not dirty work.
It's part of clean-up week in Greenboro. My name is Gillian Gold Dust
Twins Hazeltine, and I am going to
make Greenboro the Spotless Town."

Mr. Yistle stared at him suspiciously.

"I don't get you."

"You wouldn't, Adelbert."

"You think you're going to get that
murderess off simply by staging one of
your court room farces in a stadium
seating sixty thousand people?"

"No, Adelbert; my getting her off
will be incidental. Doesn't the stadium
idea really appeal to you?"

"It's preposterous!"

"But don't you see it's going to
make you the biggest political figure
in the State? You'll be the logical

candidate for Governor. Beyond that, perhaps the White House! Why are you so suspicious, Adelbert? You ought to be drowning me with gratitude!"

Still the prosecuting attorney stared at him with suspicion. Presently he shook his head.

"Why did you do it?" he demanded.

"Because I love you!" purred Gillian.

Mr. Yistle continued to eye him distrustfully. "What do you expect to get out of it?"

"Not a thing! Not a thing!"

"You know I'm being hounded by people who want concessions. I've had six offers from radio people already."

"Make them submit sealed bids, and give the radio concession to the highest bidder."

Mr. Yistle looked worried. "It says in that bill that the prosecuting attorney and counsel for the defense should collaborate."

"Why not?" said Gillian. "It must be put over with a big ballyhoo, to attract thousands of customers so the stadium will be filled. Naturally, we must work together.

"We must prepare press stories together; we must keep the stadium filled. For example, this afternoon Miss Dearing is to be photographed. Photographers from all the papers and all the news photo services will be here. The public must realize what a beautiful girl she is—and the public will flock to see her. What is more appealing than beauty in distress?"

"I distrust you," said Mr. Yistle. "You have something up your sleeve."

"A wallop in each one," said Gillian. "Nothing more."

"Shall we have a conference?"

"Aren't we having a conference?"

"A jail is no place for a conference. I want to know what you want, Gillian. You always want something. What is it this time?"

Gillian gazed at him as if his feelings were hurt.

8 A

Mr. Yistle proceeded: "All these concessions. What are we going to do about them?"

"The only thing I want," said Gillian, laughing, "is the hot dog concession."

"Stop kidding."

"I am not kidding, Adelbert. I am being serious. I don't care about any of the important concessions, but I would like to have the hot dog concession; I mean, the concession for selling refreshments. And I don't intend to gyp anybody. The idea of supplying all the spectators with good, wholesome, nourishing food appeals to me. You can give all the big concessions to your friends. But let me have the hot dog concession."

"For yourself?"

"Now, Adelbert, you know I don't want the hot dog concession for myself. I'll be too busy defending Miss Dearing. I want it for a very deserving woman, Adelbert."

"Well," wavered Mr. Yistle, "I don't see why you can't have it—as long as you don't want to have anything to say about the other concessions."

"Adelbert, that is noble of you."

"We'll get together later, shall we, to discuss publicity stunts?" inquired the prosecuting attorney.

"Why not hire a good reporter?" Gillian suggested. "Why not give the job to Josh Hammersley? I'll give him a story a day; you give him a story a day. The best story I can think of, to run from day to day, would be that this trial is a grudge fight between you and me."

"It is one!" growled Mr. Yistle.

"Then simply say so to Josh. And I'll say the same. Tell him how you detest me and why. And I'll try to think of some reasons why I ought to detest you. I've got to be running along now, Adelbert. So long!"

"If you think you're going to win this case," was the prosecuting attorney's parting shot, "you're cuckoo!"

Gillian was not smiling when he issued from the jail. Perhaps Mr. Yistle was right!

_____

CHAPTER XII.

FIGHTING AGAINST TIME.

GILLIAN'S next call that morning was on John Walling, the superintendent of the Department of Public Works. Mr. Walling was a robust, gray-haired, affable man of middle age who had, through a dexterous use of politics, occupied his position for upward of sixteen years. Administrations came and administrations went, but he always seemed to know in time which way the flag would blow, which side his bread would be buttered on.

Gillian lighted a cigar, pulled a chair up so that they were sitting knee to knee and said confidently:

" John, did the Dearing girl work for you about eight months ago as a stenographer?"

And Mr. Walling answered affably: " She did, Gillian. I understand you're taking her case."

" I want to know, John, why you let her out."

Mr. Walling looked uncomfortable. He did not answer.

" Was she a good stenographer?"

" Perfect."

" All right morally and so on?"

" As far as I know—yes."

" Then you let her out for some reason having nothing to do with her ability to fill her job?"

Mr. Walling nodded.

" Who told you to let her out, John?"

" Who do you suppose?" growled Mr. Walling.

" I know who," said Gillian. " I'm just trying to make you admit it. It was Brundage. Did he phone you or see you personally?"

" He wrote me."

" Got the letter?"

" I have."

" Will you take the stand, give your testimony and let me submit that letter as material evidence?"

" Don't be humorous, Gillian. I've got a wife and kids."

Gillian straightened up in his chair and looked the superintendent of the Department of Public Works squarely in the eyes.

" Look here, John. As far as I know, you've got a nice clean slate. I don't think you've ever been a grafter, and I'm pretty sure I'd know if you had. You want to keep this job, and I want you to keep this job. But, John, there is a shake-up coming in this State that is going to be felt by every public official from the Governor on down to the lowest office boy in the Sewage Disposal Department. If you want to stay in this job, you'll take the stand and come clean. You know I'm not lying. You know I wouldn't try bluffing an old war horse like you. Give me that letter!"

" So you think you're going to ride Brundage out of the State on a rail!" was Mr. Walling's comment.

" I do!"

" He's wise, Gillian; he's tough and he's clever. He's the strongest man we've had up there for a good many years. Are you sure you're not tilting at windmills?"

" Give me that letter!"

John Walling looked at him thoughtfully. He placed his hands behind his large, red neck and continued to look at Gillian. He teetered slowly back and forth in his swivel chair, without removing his eyes from Gillian's. The sense with which he detected a change in the direction of the political wind was working.

At length, he arose. He went to a small safe in a corner of the office; spun its dial. The door opened. A moment later he placed a letter in Gillian's hand. Gillian quickly glanced through the letter, smiled briefly, and tucked it away in his pocket."

"If you don't lick Brundage," said Mr. Walling, "that letter means I've lost a nice comfortable job."

"You won't lose your job," Gillian assured him.

"That Dearing girl," said Mr. Walling, "is a damned nice kid. She got a dirty deal, and I hope you clear her."

"I'm willing to break my neck trying," said Gillian, and departed.

HIS next call was upon the head librarian at the Greenboro Public Library; a tall, lean pale man, who turned paler and paler as Gillian talked to him.

Another visit kept Gillian fully an hour in the office of the president of the Mammoth Construction Company. Mr. Edward Rice was the kind of man who roared when hurt, or even threatened with harm. At the end of an hour of brisk arguing, he stopped roaring and surrendered.

Leaving his office, Gillian bought an afternoon paper and learned that the Dearing case had been scheduled for immediate trial. The trial would be under way, the paper said, some day this week, and would be held in the Lincoln Stadium!

Governor Brundage was, in other words, bringing pressure to bear on Adelbert Yistle; had, it appeared, ordered poor flustered Mr. Yistle to prosecute the case with no delay. And it would be useless for Gillian to appeal for a postponement. The Governor did not want postponements; the sooner the case could be brought to trial the more handicapped Gillian would be. He needed time to prepare this case. Governor Brundage was aware of it, and would, in short, whip Gillian by every means at his disposal.

How many days, Gillian wondered, would be required to subdue Mike Rafferty and his gang to the point where they would willingly confess? How long could men, inured to hardships as these men were, go without food, water and narcotics—and the use of speech?

He was pondering this problem when Police Captain Sorrenson hailed him on the street.

"I want to know," said the captain grimly, "where Mike Rafferty and his gang are?"

"I told you," Gillian answered, "that I had their throats cut and their bodies thrown in the river. You seem to be a hard man to convince."

"You mean, you had eight men murdered in cold blood?"

"Yes," Gillian fairly purred. "Eight."

"Look here, Mr. Hazeltine. Let's cut out this kidding. If you'll play fair with me, I'll play fair with you."

"You," said Gillian, "are such an infinitesimal speck in my plans that I'd need a microscope to see you. At the same time, you are going down the soapy chute with the rest of them."

A little of the captain's cocksure expression departed.

"Mr. Hazletine," he said earnestly, "I'm perfectly willing to play ball."

"You don't know how to play my kind of ball," said Gillian. "You're too crooked!"

Captain Sorrenson flushed.

"If you get frisky with me," he threatened, "I'll make this town so hot for you you'll think the Sahara Desert is the North Pole!"

"I've laughed out loud," was Gillian's comeback, "when better men than you have threatened worse than that."

It was a worried police captain to whom he cheerily said good-by. He wanted Captain Sorrenson worried. He wanted Chief of Police Bellows worried. He wanted the mayor of Greenboro worried. It was one of Gillian's fighting rules that an enemy worried is an enemy half whipped.

It was late in the afternoon when Gillian visited the Silver Slipper Club, the gambling house where Big Ben Lewis had lived, conducted his notorious business—and been cut down in the prime of his life.

Gillian went over the premises from cellar to garret. One full hour he spent in the dead gambler's office, inspecting every object the room contained. The two entrances interested him most. One door led into a hall from which ran a stairway down to the gambling rooms; the other door gave upon a narrow stairway leading down to the private back entrance on Adams Street.

Through this door had escaped the killer or killers of Big Ben. How many seconds before the other door had been opened by Miss Dearing?

Who had that killer been? Would Nicky Anderson find out in time to save Violet Dearing from the electric chair?

Gillian's last call of the afternoon was upon the State's attorney. The offices of Mr. Yistle were in an uproar, and it was with difficulty that he obtained a consultation with that worried public servant.

Mr. Yistle, in his private office, was stripped for action. His coat, vest and collar were removed. He was perspiring freely. When Gillian entered, he looked up from a cluttered desk with watery eyes and said:

"This is your work! I know it is! How can I prepare my case by to-morrow morning?"

"To-morrow morning?" Gillian repeated.

"Didn't you know it?" wailed Mr. Yistle. "Didn't you know the trial begins in the Lincoln Stadium to-morrow morning?"

"It's news to me," gasped Gillian.

"It's your doing!" Mr. Yistle spluttered. "You know I couldn't prepare my case on such short notice!"

"How about my case?"

"Your case?"

"Don't you suppose I require time to prepare my case, too?"

"It's an outrage," declared Mr. Yistle.

"Who is it going to be tried before, Adelbert?"

"Judge Lorgan."

Gillian made no comment. He had expected that the trial judge would be Judge Lorgan—Judge Lorgan, the wheel horse of the Brundage party, the personal slave of Governor Brundage!

"I dropped up here," said Gillian, "to inspect the revolver alleged to have been found in Miss Dearing's possession after the murder. Can I see it?"

Mr. Yistle opened a drawer of his desk and removed a small Smith & Wesson revolver and a pill box containing the two bullets which had been removed from Big Ben's body. Gillian examined the revolver, took note of the fact that two of the shells were discharged, and surrendered bullets and revolver to Mr. Yistle.

"Have you made sure that these bullets were fired by this revolver?"

"I have," said the State's attorney.

"You seem," commented Gillian, "to have a pretty tight case."

"I have an unbeatable case," declared Mr. Yistle. "But I need more time. I'm giving you fair warning, Gillian! If you pull off any of your sly tricks in this trial I'll have you disbarred!"

Gillian smiled and withdrew.

HE was more worried than he would care to admit. Governor Brundage was a fighter; a fighter who would stoop to gouging, biting and clawing. He was fighting as he had perhaps never fought before in his political life. In his attempts to crush Violet Dearing under his heel, he had met, in Gillian Hazeltine, a worthy opponent.

Gillian's only wish was that he could have met Brundage on more equal terms. He did not object to fighting an uphill fight; he welcomed opposition. Weak opponents did not interest him. But Governor Brundage's strength was disheartening.

What progress Gillian had made so far had been accomplished entirely by his sharp wits. His only weapons were the enemies', which he had seized and turned against them. His only hope for success, Violet Dearing's only hope for freedom, hung on the slender thread of a confession by one or all of Mike Rafferty's gang.

Could that confession be secured from them? Was Nicky Anderson to be trusted? What, Gillian wondered, had happened at Lake Largo to-day? Had the Rafferty gang weakened? Were they ready to confess?

He stopped, on his way home, at the bakery shop of Mrs. Maria Simpson, who was reputed to sell the best bread baked in Greenboro.

Mrs. Simpson, a spry old lady, was one of Gillian's warmest friends and stanchest admirers.

There were customers in the shop when he went in. Mrs. Simpson waited until they were gone, then locked the door and pulled down the shade.

She wore steel-rimmed spectacles, and through these her eyes peered benevolently, giving her a gentle, grandmotherly appearance which belied the facts. She was in reality one of the smartest, shrewdest business women in Gillian's extensive acquaintance.

Mrs. Simpson brusquely informed him: "Gillian, you're worried sick. I understand you're goin' to defend this Dearing girl who killed Ben Lewis."

"She didn't kill him," Gillian wearily protested.

"You mean, by the time you get through makin' a dozen monkeys out of the jury, she'll be a fresh, fragrant little flower of a girl, who never had a thought in her mind beyond bein' a good little girl and helpin' her ma around the house."

Gillian smiled palely. Mrs. Simpson's peppery comments always delighted him.

"She's really innocent," he insisted.

"Then what are you worried about?"

"It's going to be a difficult case. Brundage wants to railroad the girl be-cause his son paid attention to her. She is red headed and fought him back."

"Gillian," said Mrs. Simpson, "I never clapped eyes on the girl, but if you want me to, I'll take the witness stand and swear I've known her all her life!"

"How would you like to become her business partner?" Gillian asked.

Mrs. Simpson eyed him keenly.

"The trial starts in the Lincoln Stadium to-morrow morning," he went on. "I've got the hot dog concession. Rather, the refreshment concession. There ought to be a small fortune in it. I want you to handle it—make sandwiches to feed as many of the sixty thousand people in attendance as are hungry. Can you do it?"

"Certainly I can do it! I've never fed a mob that big, but I've had lots of experience!"

"My idea," said Gillian, "is to sell sandwiches wrapped in wax paper at a reasonable price."

"Gillian, you know there's a mint o' money in this for both of us. But what's the idea back of it?"

Gillian smiled. He removed from his pocket a slip of paper on which he had jotted down a few words.

"Your printer can rush through enough wrappers for to-morrow's supply, if you get after him at once. Will you do it for me?"

Mrs. Simpson chuckled. "Will I pass up a chance to repay some of the favors you've done me, make enough money to travel to Europe in luxury. Now, why wasn't I born as smart as you are?"

"Because," answered the gallant Gillian, "you were born smarter!"

He returned at last to his mansion in Riverdale, too tired, too worried for dinner.

TORO met him at the door and followed him upstairs to his study with a long, gloomy countenance. He was deeply grieved, he said in response to Gillian's inquiry, to report that there had been no telephone messages from Lake Largo. He had driven to the Hazeltine summer residence late in the afternoon in his flivver with a load of provisions.

" Mr. Anderson gave me this note for you," he said.

Gillian fairly snatched the envelope from Toro's hand, eagerly tore it open, removed a single sheet of paper, and read:

DEAR MR. HAZELTINE:

Well, I got to report that things ain't been going as well as we hoped. I cut off their food and water and saw to it that none of them were getting any snow or booze and by this noon they was all just about nuts. They was ready to crack. Then they seemed to calm down a lot all of a sudden and I found that that little louse of a Frisco Joe had been slippin' drinks of water and shots of hop to them all day, also soda crackers.

You can bet your sweet life I gave Joe what was coming to him. Well, we got to start all over again, Mr. Hazeltine, and, believe me, we will get some action soon. I am a tough guy, but you can hardly blame Joe at that. The sufferings these guys went through was something fierce. The gang of them just laid there on their cots and groaned and flopped around. It was fierce. But this time they can groan and flop till they come clean.

Yrs respfy,
NICKY.

Gillian destroyed the note and promptly decided to visit Lake Largo for the purpose of jacking up the morale of Nicky Anderson and his men. Mr. Yistle might, under pressure from the Governor, impanel a jury in a few hours' time; might rush the case through to a conclusion before nightfall.

He entered his coupé and started out. Before he had driven a block Gillian was aware that he was being followed by a long, low gray roadster, and guessed that the chief of police had begun seriously to doubt that story of the drowning of Mike Rafferty and his gang. Would it occur to the chief of police that the eight gunmen might be guests at Gillian's summer house?

Gillian abandoned the project of visiting Lake Largo to-night. He must sit and wait, a form of exertion he detested. But he was helpless now.

It was perhaps the most discouraged moment of Gillian's long, strenuous career when, re-entering his study, he seated himself at his desk to consider the problems of the trial. If he failed to defeat Governor Brundage with the fragile weapons at his disposal, the Governor could be depended upon to crush him.

His mind Gillian presently found obstinately refused to consider the forthcoming trial. It persisted in wandering off to dwell amidst scenes of high romance. He saw himself standing beside a lovely laughing red-haired girl in the bows of a steamer plowing through a phosphorescent sea under sparkling stars and a golden moon. Scent of spices was in the wind. She was gazing up at him with adoring blue eyes, her hand trustfully cuddled within his own.

" I love you," she whispered.

Gillian bent down and kissed that sweet, laughing little mouth; slim and warm and soft, she lay happily in his arms.

The scene abruptly changed. It faded, and now he beheld, in its stead, the most unfashionable piece of furniture in existence—a chair equipped with many wires and plates of metal. For an awful moment he saw the red-haired girl seated in this chair with a mask over her beautiful blue eyes. Some one signaled to a man who stood at a giant electric switch on the wall. The man reached for the switch—

Groaning, Gillian snatched up a pencil and began to write.

" Gentlemen of the jury, it is your sworn duty to ask of yourselves whether it has been proved beyond any reasonable doubt—"

TO BE CONCLUDED NEXT WEEK

*His long arms and
longer legs wrapped the
sleepwalker in their meshes*

Gifford Pinchot's Battle
with a Somnambulist

*He hadn't been warned of his shipmate's peculiarity—but
the governor rose to the occasion—and how !*

By BOB DAVIS

GIVE ear, my hearties, to a tale of
the sea along the Jersey coast, a
tale of dark deeds and black
night, a narrative that will make the
blood run cold and chill the marrow in
the bones of men.

About five years ago, when the tide
runners were coming into New Jersey
waters from the south during the
month of August, a small party of in-
trepid fishermen consisting of the Hon.
Gifford Pinchot, former Governor
of Pennsylvania; Van Campen Heilner, the ichthyologist who has recently
been testing his theories about the ap-
petites of sharks in Bahamian waters;
Eltinge F. Warner, publisher of *Field
and Stream;* Hy Watson, the illustra-
tor; the bucko mate, Captain Bill Rich-

mond, and the writer, set sail to enjoy
an angle.

We tore put of the port of Spring
Lake with a full cargo of delicatessen,
surf casting tackle and the butts flooding with gasoline. 'Twas a fair day
and a merry one. Down the coast we
chugged twelve miles an hour in the
good ship Nepenthe, named for that
rare potation distilled on Mount
Olympus.

While the Nepenthe plunged along
in the blue waters of the Atlantic we
rigged tackle and laid our wagers as
to who would take the first fish, the
largest fish and the most fish.

The soothing motion of the cradling
sea lulled us finally into silence. Captain Bill broke out the bunks and in-
vited us to turn in.

Mr. Pinchot, being the guest of honor, was forced into a lower berth. I took the other lower without being forced.

Heilner and Warner drew the uppers and Hy Watson went on deck with all the loose pillows on board. Just before I climbed into the hay I observed Captain Bill beckoning to me through the forward ventilator.

"There is something I ought to tell you," he said in a low voice as I emerged. "Heilner is a sleep walker. Watch him. He may be quiet all night, and then again he may not. I never can tell when he is going to cut loose and do one of his stunts. If he starts anything just speak to him quietly and put him back in bed."

"Where can he walk on this craft?" I asked, bewildered.

"Oh, he can walk in a cigar box. I've seen him travel two miles in a bathtub. He's a bird when he starts. Don't tell the other guests. I'll keep my eye peeled on the deck and you pipe him in the cabin. Nothing serious ever happens; just a queer stunt, that's all. Mum's the word."

"Does he talk in his sleep?"

"Sometimes. But what he says never means anything," replied Captain Bill.

With that dark secret in my possession I retired almost instantly and the chorus of snoring set in. Charged with the duties of a night watchman, I resisted the inclination to pass away. Through the porthole I discerned numerous dancing stars passing to and fro as the Nepenthe rose and fell with the movement of the sea. "Let him walk," I soliloquized. Good night. Hypnotized, I fell asleep.

It may have been half an hour or an hour afterward when I was awakened by a yell from the upper bunk.

"H-o-l-d me! H-o-l-d me! Here —I come!"

Over the edge of Van's bunk I descried two pyjama clad legs dangling.

"Hold who?" answered Pinchot in a voice that seemed a mile away.

"Heilner!" I shouted just at the moment the somnambulist-ichthyologist came diving from his dreams to the cabin floor. The moment he struck, the lithe conservationist rolled from his own bunk and began to twine his person around Heilner in the manner of an octopus lassoing a jellyfish. It was a swift and terrible embrace, a complete, man sized catch-as-catch-can strangle hold beginning at Van's neck and terminating at his ankles. The long arms and the longer legs of Mr. Pinchot wrapped the sleepwalker in their meshes. No sound save the strained breathing of two gents in a death struggle broke the stillness. In the midst of that appalling drama Captain Bill appeared with a flashlight.

"What's up?" queried the captain.

"He asked for it," said Mr. Pinchot, rising and rearranging his disheveled pyjamas. "Asked for it twice."

Van lay flat on his back, breathing slightly, apparently asleep.

"Don't wake him up," cautioned Captain Bill. "Let's boost him back in his bunk. He'll never know about it." Warner and Watson woke up in time to help the sleepwalker back into his aerie.

I have not heretofore expressed myself definitely on the point, but it is a safe bet that from 2 A.M., when we put him back, until daybreak, Van Campen Heilner, F. R. G. S., owner and skipper of the gasoline launch Nepenthe was actually insensible.

When he came to in the morning he remarked that he had had a bad dream. "I seemed to be walking along in front of a skyscraper, when, without warning, the whole structure from the third to the twenty-first story fell on me. Do I look a bit ratty?"

"Yes, Van, all of that," responded Warner. "But," quoting the mild Mr. Pinchot, "you asked for it."

THE END

"Keep your hand away from that desk drawer!" Morrison snapped

Trouble Ranch

In which Banker Spofford learns a few things about business—and about human nature as well

By GEORGE M. JOHNSON

Author of "Squatters' Rights," "Tickets to Paradise," etc.

LEADING UP TO THIS INSTALLMENT

WHEN Peter De Quincy—known to his friends as P. D. Q. because of his amazing speed—rides into Cactus Springs, he finds it controlled by Spofford, Sr., a shady banker, who has both confidence men and gunmen on his secret roll. Peter soon locks horns with Spofford, Jr., the banker's son; P. D. Q. finds it necessary to knock him out a few times for getting too fresh to defenseless girls.

Meanwhile Pete becomes acquainted with young Newt Winsome, who invites the range rider to come out and visit him and his sister Peggy.

Peggy and Pete get on very well together, and it is lucky for Peggy that she has thus found a young man whom she can trust to help her, for old man Spofford, through a couple of underhanded tricks, is threatening to foreclose a mortgage on her ranch, the Three Star Dot.

Spofford, Sr., wants the Three Star Dot because a syndicate has been quietly formed by some reputable ranchers who want to buy the property to build a big irrigation dam on it. Very few people know about this project.

Pete De Quincy goes around town in Cactus Springs getting a line on all

This story began in the Argosy-Allstory Weekly for September 1

sorts of dealings of the Spoffords, with the help of Aleck Carmichael, an old friend of his, whom Pete finds tending bar in the Red Front saloon.

Also, one night when Mexican Charlie and Carl Davis, two of Spofford, Sr.'s, gunmen, undertake to kill Pete for a large payment by Spofford, Jr., Aleck Carmichael helps work a dummy model of Pete, which Carl Davis shoots into with a Maxim-silenced rifle.

Pete promptly captures Davis and takes him to a deserted cabin in Eagle Cañon.

The cabin happens to be the very one to which Davis and Mexican Charlie have arranged to bring an old prospector named Eb Sanderson, who had boasted, during a drinking bout, that he had just made a strike.

Davis secretly hopes that when he and Pete, his captor, reach the cabin, Mexican Charlie and Davis himself can finish off Pete, along with old Eb Sanderson, the location of whose secret gold strike is to be tortured from him before they kill him.

But when Pete comes with Davis though the cabin doorway, Mex thinks he has been double-crossed, and attempts to shoot, only to have his life wiped out by a speedy shot of P. D. Q.

Pete then leaves Carl Davis locked up in the cabin with his hands handcuffed behind his back, with the corpse of Mexican Charlie and with Eb Sanderson, who is lying there unconscious.

P. D. Q. rides to Three Star Dot and gets Peggy to sell him the ranch on a "straw sale," giving him a bill of sale for the property "for the sum of one dollar and other valuable considerations."

At the same time Spofford, Jr., is in Cactus Springs worrying because he can not find any trace of his hired killers, and because he does not hear any word of the finding of P. D. Q. dead.

While he is worrying P. D. Q. walks along the street past him, and turns in at the entrance to the private bank of Spofford & Son.

CHAPTER XV. (Continued).

PETER COMES BACK.

A CLERK came forward inquiringly as Peter entered the office of Spofford & Son.

"I'd like to consult Mr. Spofford on business," the caller said mildly, "if it's convenient."

"I'll see. What name shall I give?"

"De Quincy's the name," Peter told him. "Peter De Quincy," and the clerk withdrew, returning after a moment.

"I'm sorry," he reported, "but Mr. Spofford is occupied at present and expects to be busy the rest of the afternoon. Would you care to make an appointment for to-morrow?"

"No," Peter rejoined, rather flatly, "I wouldn't want to do that. I'll see him now." His voice had subtly changed, a significant fact which the clerk did not fail to notice. "Tell him it's about the Three Dot ranch."

Again the clerk left, to be gone a little longer than before.

"Mr. Spofford will see you," he reported on returning, and he ushered De Quincy down the narrow hall and into his employer's presence.

"What can I do for you?" the banker demanded gruffly, looking up with a scowl at the caller who refused to be put off.

"I've come to pay the mortgage on the Three Star Dot ranch," Peter nonchalantly informed him.

"What's that you say?" Spofford gasped, as if unable to believe the evidence of his own ears.

"Sorry if I didn't make myself clear. They's six thousand dollars principal and three hundred back interest due on Frank Winsome's note. I'm paying the whole works."

"But what have you to do with the Winsome ranch?" Spofford inquired, glaring at De Quincy from under his shaggy eyebrows.

"Why, I happen to own it," Peter told him, almost apologetically.

"Own it!" Spofford echoed.

"Sure. I bought it to-day—lock, stock and barrel."

"I suppose you have proof as to that?"

"You bet. A bill of sale from Miss Winsome. Like to see it?" and Peter handed over the paper Peggy had given him that same day.

Spofford read, taking pains to conceal the chagrin he felt. This development came like a bolt out of the clear sky, for Peggy Winsome's chance of finding a buyer when the threat of an immediate' foreclosure hung over her property had seemed too remote to be worth a second's thought. Yet the impossible had happened.

"You've got the money with you?" he asked grudgingly.

Peter responded by bringing to light a healthy roll of bills from an inside pocket, and briskly counting forth the required amount.

"You got the mortgage note?" he asked when through.

Receiving the principal on a mortgage was a thing that gave Banker Spofford small joy; he preferred to foreclose, for the security demanded on his loans was invariably worth considerably more than the sum advanced. But this time there seemed nothing else to do. With a heavy heart the banker opened his safe, extracting therefrom the document in question.

"Let's see it." Peter's voice was bland. A hurried perusal of the paper satisfied him. "Indorse that note as paid, you might," said he. "Here's the cash."

Accordingly the transaction was concluded. Peter had the note and Spofford had the six thousand, three hundred.

"What are you going to do with the Three Star Dot ranch?" the banker asked.

"Oh, I don't know," was Peter's careless response. "I might stock her with calves and run the place like it ought to be run. They's a good range thereabouts — that costs money, though." His voice was vaguely regretful.

"You wouldn't care to sell, would you?" Banker Spofford hazarded.

Peter had been on the point of leaving. Now he sat down, quite at his ease. Spofford passed the box of cigars, and they lighted up.

"Sell it?" young Mr. De Quincy ruminated. "I hadn't thought of doing that.".

"This ranch is hardly to be regarded as a first-class investment," the banker said. "Frank Winsome never made much money even when things were right, and in the end lost what little he had made. If you want to buy a ranch there are plenty of better ones on the market."

"But you see, Mr. Spofford," Peter reminded him, "I've a'ready bought this place."

"I might take it off your hands. That would give you a small profit, but a speedy one. A quick turn-over isn't to be sneezed at."

"That's right, too," Peter conceded thoughtfully. "Yes, sir, they's a lot in what you say, Mr. Spofford. A quick profit ought to satisfy anybody. But if the ranch ain't any good, how come you're willing to take it off my hands?"

"A fair question," Spofford admitted, with an open and benevolent countenance. "An eminently fair question —and it deserves a frank answer.

"You're a cattleman, I judge, interested in raising beef. I am what you might call an investment specialist. With the working capital I fortunately have at my disposal I can afford to keep some money tied up indefinitely —on a long chance, that is. You see what I'm driving at doubtless?"

"I ain't quite sure I do," was Peter's cautious concession. He did not appear over bright, but gave the impression of one eager to learn.

"I shall try to be a little more explicit."

SPOFFORD chose his words carefully; he was confronted by the task of allaying suspicion, and without, at the same time, stirring up unpleasant doubts as to his own motives. "As a cattle proposition, the Three Star Dot doesn't impress me," the banker went on. "Frank Winsome demonstrated that."

"Mebby Mr. Winsome wasn't a successful manager," Peter suggested modestly.

"No more than fair," Spofford responded, as if conceding a point, "though personally Frank Winsome was a mighty fine man, and well spoken of by all. But I question whether a better man would have done much more with the place than Winsome did. At best it's a gamble—however, I am interested in the proposition from other angles."

"You mean some time later the ranch might be worth more money than now?" Peter asked.

"There is a possibility of a modest increment, as to which I don't wish to deceive you. I would be willing to hold the ranch for a period of years on that chance, slim though it is."

"I kinda got an idea I'd like to run the place," Peter ruminated. "How about me trying it for a year or two? Would you be willing to buy then?"

"By no means!" Spofford said positively. "I'll buy the Three Star Dot now—or not at all."

Peter seemed sorely tempted, toying with the pleasant idea of a quick profit, and apparently having trouble in making up his mind.

"But I don't believe I'll sell," he finally decided. "I got a hunch I can make a go of that ranch."

Peter again rose to leave, as if the matter had been definitely settled. As he did so a clerk came in with a message, a telegram, which he handed to his employer.

"This was just delivered," said he.

Spofford's face showed no change of expression at the news which met his gaze:

Speed necessary in deal I spoke of. Have ascertained parties backing same are about to approach owner. Fifty thousand if handled right.

BLACK.

The banker realized that the chance to profit on this information was slipping through his fingers. It was now or never, and he would have to play the cards boldly.

"I'm not concerned with the ranch as a whole," he told Peter, no longer beating about the bush. "Would you care to sell part of it?"

Once more Peter sat down.

"What part?" he asked, his face blank.

"Apache Gap."

"Just the Gap alone?" registering puzzled astonishment.

"That's all. The Gap—and nothing else, beyond say—a strip two hundred yards each side of the creek."

"What'll you pay for the Gap and that much land?"

"Five thousand dollars," Spofford said, naming a figure which he believed was high enough to carry his point, yet not too high.

"They's something back of this," Peter insisted, looking Banker Spofford straight in the eye. "You're holding out on me. I bet a railroad's going through the Gap."

Spofford laughed with an air of indulgent superiority.

"Can you think of any reason why a railroad should go through the Gap?" he inquired. "The region is practically a wilderness—off the direct line of transcontinental travel. There is no excuse, even, for a branch line from Cactus Springs. Railroads have to go where prospects of trade and business justify the venture."

"I hadn't looked at it that way," Peter conceded, his face clouding with disappointment. "No railroad, eh? But I don't guess I'll sell—for five thousand. Give me ten and Apache Gap's yours."

"Ten thousand dollars for a barren piece of land like Apache Gap!" Spofford exclaimed. "Man, you're crazy!"

"Perhaps I am," Peter said stubbornly. "But no crazier'n you when you offer five. If the Gap's worth five, she ought to be worth ten. What do you say? I'm in a hurry, sort of. Take it or leave it!" Peter rose and stood waiting, one hand on the doorknob.

Banker Spofford perceived that he would gain nothing by haggling, and capitulated.

"I'll buy," he told Peter.

"Make out the proper papers," De Quincy remarked, "and I'll sign 'em."

The document was duly drawn up, witnessed before a notary, and signed.

"I'll take the cash in big bills," Peter suggested.

Spofford offered no protest to this reasonable request, and a few minutes later P. D. Q. was again on the street, heading for the Phœnix House, where he arrived without mishap.

"Count that roll, Jack," he told the desk clerk. "Then give me a receipt for it, and put her in the safe."

"It comes to ten thousand two hundred."

"Correct. That's the sixty-five hundred you turned over to me a little while ago, and three thousand seven hundred besides. How's that for a quick turn-over? At least that's what these here financiers call the rake-off."

"Mean to say you've cleaned up thirty-seven hundred profit in half an hour?" the clerk gasped.

"Nothing else but! I'm to be a great guy for business."

"Wish you'd tell me how the thing's done," and the desk clerk sighed as he locked Peter's money in the hotel safe. "Must be a gift. Some folks have it—and some don't. You and me are examples of both kinds."

WHEN Peter left the bank young Spofford, who had kept an eye on the entrance, lost no time in consulting his father. The banker explained something of what had happened, telling also of his secret information as to the irrigation project at Apache Gap, all of which was news to Spofford, Jr.

"I hoped one time you might have a chance of marrying Peggy," the older man said, "but a talk I had with her showed your case to be hopeless. Since the Gap couldn't come into the family that way, I was forced to take other steps toward securing it.

"Several of my plans met unaccountable set-backs, but now everything is all right. When the expenses are settled we stand to make a profit of thirty thousand or better—and all the way through, Dud Millbrook's the goat. It might be worse," he added complacently.

"You say De Quincy bought the ranch from Peggy and then sold you Apache Gap?" young Spofford asked.

"That's exactly what he did," Spofford, Sr., chuckled, rubbing his hands together gleefully. "For a moment I was afraid he might smell a rat, but he's too big a fool to be able to see beyond the end of his own nose."

"He's a lot of things I might mention," young Spofford admitted. "But he's no fool, and don't you make the blunder of thinking so. D'you imagine he might have got a tip on that irrigation project?"

"It isn't likely—as long as he was willing to sell me the Gap. That's the key to the whole proposition. If he had been tipped, he'd have kept Apache Gap and cashed in on it himself."

"H-m! Mebby so, but I don't understand this at all. That fellow De Quincy is dangerous."

"Well, I'm pretty dangerous myself," Spofford, Sr., grunted, "when anybody tries to buck me. A lot of people have learned that—to their sorrow."

" Just the same," his son maintained obstinately, " De Quincy is a bad actor He ought to be salted down."

" Why don't you have it done, since he worries you so much?" the banker advised. " Davis and Mexican Charlie would be glad to accommodate, for a suitable consideration."

Young Spofford laughed mirthlessly.

" I thought so once," said he. " But I'm beginning to change my mind."

" What's the matter with you anyway?" his father demanded irritably. " You must be letting this De Quincy get on your nerves. I tell you the thing is all right. That wire from Hollis Black confirmed 'it."

" Let me have another look at the wire."

Spofford, Sr., passed it over.

" I've got an idea," the young man said. " See you later about it."

Spofford, Jr., his mind filled with a tumult of unpleasant thoughts, went down to the local railway station, presided over by a harassed individual who combined in one office the duties of ticket seller, baggage smasher, express agent, and telegraph operator.

" When did that wire for my dad come in?" Spofford demanded.

" What wire?"

" The one delivered a few minutes ago—half an hour, mebby."

" Let's see it."

Spofford surrendered the message, which looked like any ordinary telegram.

" I never saw that before," he was told. " It didn't come through this office, to-day or any other day."

" You're sure of that?" Spofford gulped.

" I wouldn't say so if I wasn't. What's up, anyway?"

" Oh, nothing," Spofford answered lamely. " It's all a mistake, I guess."

His feeling of unrest, of vague dread deepened, though this Spofford tried to conceal from the station agent, whose attention was presently occupied by the arrival of an Eastern train.

Uncertain, ill at ease, Spofford hung around the platform until the train pulled out. A few passengers had arrived, among them a young chap of nineteen or twenty, who glanced about him with a furtive air of sly cunning.

The black suit he wore was new, though obviously cheap and sadly wrinkled, as if the wearer had slept in it. His eyes deep sunken in their sockets burned with a feverish, unnatural glare. Spofford found himself marveling what might have brought a stranger of this type into Cactus Springs.

" Looks like a darn fool kid from the East," he thought. " More'n half nut—from the way he acts. Sick, too, I'd judge."

But Spofford had too much on his mind to pay further heed to the recently arrived traveler; the mystery of that telegram still obsessed him.

" It was a fake, all right," he mused, " but I'm damned if I can understand what's back of the game. Hollis Black wouldn't dare play crooked with dad, we've got too much on him. Where did it come from? And how did it get here?"

" Say, mister, do you live in this town?"

Spofford's thoughts snapped back to the present with a start, conscious that the stranger was addressing him.

" Why, yes, I live here," he replied, uneasy under the burning glance of the eyes which searched his face questioningly.

" I'm looking for a fellow. Might be you can tell me where to locate him."

" Who is it you want?" Spofford asked.

" His name's Spofford."

Spofford, Jr., concealed his growing consternation under a show of indifference.

" There's two Spoffords in town. Which one you want to see?"

"The young one. His dad's the banker here. Do you know him?"

"Why—yes—I know him—a little by sight, that is. What you want of young Spofford?"

"He ain't a friend of yours, is he?" the stranger demanded suspiciously.

"Oh, no—he's no friend," Spofford, Jr., hurriedly assured him. Then repeated his question. "What do you want of young Spofford?"

"I'm going to kill him," was the reply.

"Going to kill Spofford!"

"That's right. I'm going to shoot him down like a dawg, first time I lay eyes on the cur."

Spofford managed to hide the dismay he felt at this fresh danger which loomed on his horizon.

"Why do you want to kill Spofford?" he asked.

"He didn't treat my sister right. Dumped her in a low dive, where she had to associate with all sorts of bad people. I ain't been very well for the last few years, but when I found out what Marie had to put up with in this cursed town, I came here to straighten things. And I'm going to straighten 'em good and proper, you bet!"

A tardy realization of the truth swept over young Mr. Spofford.

"Good Lord!" he gasped to himself. "This wild-eyed cuss is crazy as a locoed steer— Your sister know what you're doing?" he inquired aloud. "She put you up to this stunt?"

"No—nor the rest of the family either. I sneaked out on 'em. Fact is," and the stranger waxed confidentially, "they keep a watch on me, most of the time. Think I'm off up here." He tapped his skull meaningly. "But I fooled 'em. There was some money in the house, and I found out where it was. So here I am. They're all a pack of fools to think I'm crazy. Why, I ain't any crazier'n you are. Am I?" he demanded with unexpected vigor.

"Why, of course, you ain't crazy," Spofford said soothingly. "That's plain enough." A sudden inspiration had seized him—a glorious scheme whereby he might use this addle-pated, callow youth to his own advantage and the confounding of his foe. "Do you know what Spofford looks like?" he queried.

"No. What *does* he look like?"

"Well, he's a bit taller'n I am, and some broader in the shoulders, and he's got red hair; so red you can spot it a mile away. I saw him uptown a little while ago. Come on along with me, and I'll point him out to you.

"But I'd rather you didn't pull the shooting stunt when I'm around, see? Wouldn't be right to drag me in after I've helped you. But Spofford's no friend of mine, and you can kill him and welcome. Got a gun?"

Marie's demented brother proudly produced a cheap, nickel plated pistol, short barreled, and thirty-eight caliber, of the bulldog variety.

"That's no good," Spofford told him. "You couldn't hit a barn with it. I'll fix you up with a real gun.

"Lucky thing you met me, because somebody else might have tipped Spofford off, and he'd shoot you before you knew what happened. He's a bad actor, Spofford is, and you want to keep still about what you're in town for until you get him. Understand?"

The other nodded excitedly.

"Now we'll go up street and I'll give you a look-see at Spofford. Before long you'll have plenty of chances to salivate that guy, who sure needs killing. But watch your step, my boy, watch your step. Stick to me and I'll steer you right."

CHAPTER XVI.

A JOKE ON MR. DAVIS.

CARL DAVIS had been abandoned by Peter De Quincy in a highly embarrassing position, with the unconscious, supposedly drunk desert rat and the corpse of his defunct partner to keep him company.

Davis felt himself caught between the devil and the deep blue sea. Through fear of De Quincy he had betrayed Spofford, but Carl knew that Banker Spofford had a long arm to reach after those who incurred his displeasure, and the knowledge was not comforting.

"Once the old man finds out how much I've spilled the beans—good night!" Davis mused discontentedly. "He'd fry a chap in oil for less. My main hope now is that De Quincy makes a clean job with Spofford, which is a lot to expect of any man."

What Carl most yearned to do was get out of the cabin and put the greatest possible distance between himself and both Peter and Spofford.

"They're a couple of bad hombres," he reasoned, "any way a body regards it; but of the pair that P. D. Q. is a sight the worst. He's got more lives than a cat, and he's harder to keep track of than twenty cats. It was sure one tough day for me when our trails crossed."

In the present distressing circumstances the only hope Mr. Davis had of escaping from the cabin lay in Eb Sanderson, but he perceived little reason to anticipate generous treatment at the prospector's hands.

Davis was handicapped by lack of knowledge as to all that had taken place, and of course he did not know of Mexican Charlie's base plot. But he naturally expected the worst. Sanderson was more than likely to have no doubt but what his two genial companions of the evening before had conspired to steal the gold strike.

Davis could, to be sure, take measures to prevent the prospector ever awaking from his drunken stupor, in spite of the handcuffs. But that left Peter De Quincy still to be heard from, and Carl was not anxious to excite P. D. Q.'s wrath unduly. Accordingly he did nothing.

Time dragged on interminably, while Eb Sanderson lay as one dead. Davis couldn't understand it, not knowing of the fracas which resulted in the old prospector receiving a blow on the side of his head.

"I never saw booze keep a chap down as long as this," he muttered. "He sure had an awful load aboard."

First signs of returning life came late in the afternoon, when Eb grunted and rolled over. A little later he sat up, looking around and rubbing his eyes in bewilderment. At sight of Mexican Charlie's dead body he grunted again, his astonishment increasing when he perceived Carl Davis, who appeared somewhat apprehensive.

Eb blinked, and shook his head, as if to clear away the cobwebs.

"What the hell!" he observed. "How long *you* been here?"

"Quite a spell," Carl replied.

"What happened, anyway? Oh, I begin to rec'lect now. You two skunks was aimin' to steal my strike—dawgone yer measly hides!"

"*He* was," and Davis nodded toward the remains of the late Mex. "Not me. Fact is, *I* saved your life."

"You saved my life!" Eb was skeptical.

"That's right, old-timer," Mr. Davis asserted. "It was like this. That pard of mine wasn't any better'n he should have been, and he had a notion to make you tell where your strike was. He aimed to be mighty rough getting the information, too, but I didn't fall in. Not at all, because I allus was a well-meaning gent.

"That made him mad and we come to blows over the business. He was a better man at scrapping and he knocked me cold. When I woke up I had these bracelets on the wrists."

"I think you're lyin'," Eb stated. "Last thing I remember is him an' me fightin'. You wan't around when he talked about makin' me tell."

Eagerly did Carl Davis pounce upon this helpful bit of information.

"I was outside at the time. That only proves what I'm saying. I heard you two mixing it up, and rushed in. Mex slammed you a good one, and I grabbed his gun and shot him."

"With your arms locked back of you?" Eb inquired sarcastically.

"Why not? That wasn't impossible for a man that knew how to use a forty-five. I did it anyway, even if it don't seem likely and reasonable. Mex lying there proves it."

"Where's the gun?"

"Mex jumped back on me when I fired, and in the squabble his six-shooter fell down that crack. Mebby you can see it if you look."

Laboriously Eb Sanderson hoisted himself from the cot, dizzy but determined. He worked a painful passage to the crack, thrusting his arm in.

"By thunder!" he ejaculated. "They is a gun down here!" and he plucked forth a Colt, one cylinder of which had recently been fired.

Eb straightened up, regarding Mr. Davis with a shade more of cordiality at this seeming confirmation of the wild yarn. Carl began to feel almost optimistic.

"Things are breaking slick," he assured himself. "I got this old coot eating out of my hand."

THEN Eb bent over, picking up from the floor a small object, the significance of which had hitherto escaped Carl's notice. It was the shell ejected from Peter's gun, and Eb could tell that it also had been recently used. One might infer from this evidence that *two* shots had been fired.

"Where'd this empty cartridge come from?" Eb demanded. Davis swore under his breath for having missed a trick.

"I don't know," he said. "Guess it was here all the time."

"Humph!" Eb grunted non-committally, shoving Charlie's pistol into his belt. Then he moved to the door, which resisted his attempts to open.

9 A

"She's fastened, looks like," Carl informed him, rather unnecessarily.

"On the outside," Eb Sanderson added, bending a stern glance on his companion of the captivity. "How do you explain *thet?*" he went on, as if asking a riddle.

Davis was ready for him.

"When I shot Mex," he said ingenuously, "he jumped back, knocking the gun from my hands, like I already told you, before keeling plumb over. Just then I heard a noise, and the door slammed to. A minute later a rider went fanning off on a horse. Know what I think?" Mr. Davis dropped his voice to a confidential tone.

"I know what *I* think," Eb told him succinctly. "I think you're the dawgondest liar the Lord ever let loose. I hate lies thet don't hang together. Was this here the best you could do?" And Eb Sanderson snorted his disgust.

"I'm telling you the truth," Davis insisted. "Some guy happened along and saw me bend a gun on Mex. He shut the door, and beat it for the sheriff, like as not figuring I couldn't get away till he come back with help."

"So thet's what you think happened, eh?" Eb remarked.

"Yes," said Mr. Davis defiantly, "that's what I think happened. Might have been only a kid, one afraid to butt in on a gun play."

Eb tried the door again without success. His glance wandered to a window.

"You might climb out," Davis suggested hopefully. "I can't, with my arms fastened thisaway. Then you could open the door and we'd both get free. It would help me a lot if you'd dig up a file or a hack saw some place and cut these irons."

"Why for would I want to do thet?" Eb queried.

"Why—it would square things, sort of, for me saving you from Mexican Charlie. See?"

Sanderson grunted by way of reply, drinking a dipper of water. Thus fortified he managed an exit through the window. He was gone for rather an alarmingly long time, and Davis, who had dared to be hopeful, again feared the worst. Finally, however, the door opened and Eb Sanderson reappeared.

"I been lookin' around," he explained. "They's a team an' a wagon out back."

"It's the outfit Mex brought you in from Cactus Springs," Carl stated. "Well, old timer, what you think we'd better do?" Davis spoke in a buoyant tone of good fellowship.

"It was you thet shot this greaser?" the prospector inquired. "Was it?"

"Sure, I shot him—to help you out, don't forget."

"All right," Eb stated. "I ain't sayin' a word, then. It was you thet shot him. You admit it, and we'll let it go thet way."

He took the dead man's pistol from his belt, spinning it thoughtfully on his trigger finger.

"I got the team harnessed," said he. "Let's be goin'."

Davis didn't quite like this casual display of the artillery, which augured poorly, but he judged it prudent to hide his qualms.

"That's fine, old timer! I figured you'd not be the chap to throw down a man that had just done you a good turn. Where we heading for?"

"Cactus Springs."

"Well, that's all right by me. And what might be the plan when we get there?"

"I'm goin' to hand you over to Buck Morrison."

"Hey, you don't want to do that!" Davis ejaculated in some alarm. "The sheriff don't need me for anything."

A hint of sardonic amusement lurked in Eb Sanderson's washed-out old eyes.

"You jest killed a man, on your own say-so," he replied. "Thet's murder, ain't it? You belong in the hoosegow, and bein's I'm a law-abidin' citizen what tries to do his dooty, I aim to see

you there. Come along! And no monkey business, see?" He made a threatening gesture with the six-gun.

CHAPTER XVII.

FATE DEALS THE CARDS.

AFTER depositing the money received from Spofford in the Phœnix House safe, Peter De Quincy strolled up to Varney's, feeling that he had earned refreshment. As usual, Aleck Carmichael served him.

"What's new, P. D. Q.?" the bartender asked. "How'd you make out after leaving me?"

"Fine," Peter responded, and he rapidly sketched his adventures at the cabin in Eagle Cañon.

"Funny break, wasn't it, Aleck? Those two polecats and I both picked the same place. I didn't aim to do any killing unless I had to, but Mexican Charlie forced my hand. I wonder who that old rat was that they had on the string."

"His name's Eb Sanderson," Aleck said.

"Good Lord!" Peter gasped in dismay.

"Why, what's the matter, P. D. Q.?"

"I've missed a bet. That desert rat's a friend of Miss Winsome's, out at the Three Star Dot. She told me about him. He'd promised Newt he'd make a strike in time to save their ranch from Spofford, and, by golly, the old chap made good!"

"I was wondering where he picked up the money he was throwing around," Aleck put in. "Mex and Davis must have got wise to what was doing, and made him drunk. I bet they'd have tortured the old fellow to make him tell where his strike was located."

"And I left Davis and the rat in the shack together," Peter said regretfully. "I'm worried, sort of. If I'd only known then what I know now, I would have played a different hand."

"Things do break queer now and then, don't they, P. D. Q.?" Aleck said. "But you're sitting pretty. I wouldn't say they's any cause for worry."

"Mebby not," Peter stated briskly, "but I don't feel right. I'm hitting the trail for Eagle Cañon. Old Eb was flat on his back, and if Carl Davis got nasty to him I'd not forgive myself in a hurry. Any friends of Peggy Winsome's are friends of mine; and I know she thought a heap of the poor old codger. So long, Aleck."

"Good luck to you, P. D. Q.! Likely you'll find everything Jake. We'll hope so anyway."

Peter stopped at Bill's for a hasty bite, not knowing how soon he might have another opportunity. Night was approaching, and there were prospects of much riding ahead. Not long afterward he was on his way.

"I'm glad they's a full moon this evening," Peter mused. "That'll help considerable."

On the route to Eagle Cañon Peter missed, by a narrow margin, an encounter with the wagon Eb Sanderson was driving to Cactus Springs. The cabin he found occupied only by a dead man, with no evidence to hint at what might have taken place since his departure.

"The old rat likely climbed out a window as I figured he might," Peter mused. "But why would he let Davis go? That's something I don't quite get. I'm uneasy, kind of.

"Sanderson might head for town," he cogitated, thinking out loud, "but it seems more reasonable that he'd strike for his camp over in Apache Cañon. The wagon tracks won't help much, because below the mouth of Eagle Cañon I noticed this morning there'd been enough travel both ways to blur the trail past following; I couldn't be certain which direction the wagon went, and night tracking's no cinch."

Peter got this far, and paused to roll a cigarette.

"I sure hate to think Carl Davis might have put something over on the desert rat. Mebby he hasn't, but I can't tell till I locate one or both of 'em. And, of course, I don't even know they're together.

"They's also a faint chance that Davis had other choice friends beside the greaser, who were in on the game and the hang-out. If that was true, most anything might have happened hereabouts to-day."

Thus Peter mused, pondering on the next move in the campaign. Finally he made up his mind.

"I'm going to cut across the shortest way for Apache Gap, and find out whether Sanderson's there or not. If he ain't, all I've lost is a little time, and, besides, I want to look over his place; they's one important hunch I'd like to settle.

"I'm not banking too heavy on it, because she's plenty thin, but a fellow never knows where he'll find pay dirt. Sometimes it ain't always the best prospects that pan out."

Briskly he swung to the saddle.

"I can make town again in good season to-morrow morning. The big show-down ain't far off now."

Though comparatively new to the country, Peter was already beginning to have a very fair idea of it. Two routes to the Gap were available, one much shorter than the other, though it led through a section of broken, irregular topography. This Peter selected, as a time saver over the easier, more roundabout way.

He passed through the Gap two hours before sunrise, continuing on up the cañon; with a warm glow of pleasure he recalled the afternoon spent there in Peggy's society.

"That was the nicest ride I ever took," he thought. "I'm hoping Miss Peggy enjoyed it half as much as I did."

Finally he reached the ramshackle log cabin which served Eb Sanderson as home. The place was deserted, but the owner had made no attempt to lock up when he left. Peter entered, finding a small oil lamp; this he lighted, and glanced curiously about.

"I aim to find out whether that blind hunch meant anything or not," he told himself. "Now's the chance I wanted."

Ten minutes later De Quincy extinguished the lamp and resumed his journey, Cactus Springs the destination. Beyond Apache Gap he passed within two hundred yards of the Three Star Dot buildings, waving at them a friendly greeting.

"Ain't stopping right now," Peter called, as if the silent house could hear him. "See you later, though. Give my best regards to Peggy."

PETER arrived at Cactus Springs in fair season, dusty and hungry, but still going strong. He left his horse in the livery stable, ate a belated breakfast, made one or two visits, and at length strolled around to interview Sheriff Morrison, who was found in his office. The two had met, more or less casually, on several previous occasions.

"Howdy, De Quincy?" Buck remarked cordially. "What's on your mind?"

"Quite a lot," Peter informed him. "Smoke while we chat?" and he tendered the officer a cigar.

"Thanks," Morrison rejoined, accepting the courtesy. He ignited the Havana, rolling it appreciatively between his lips. Then, "Shoot! Let's have it!"

"Not wishing to give any offense, sheriff," Peter began blandly, "I'd like to ask how much dirty work the folks in this town will stand from Spofford and that young whelp he's raised?"

Buck rubbed his chin, surveying the younger man with a shrewd twinkle in his eyes.

"I'd feel sore if some men asked me that, De Quincy," said he. "But I've seen enough of you to know you're a straight-shooter. I'm my own boss, and they's nobody in this town or any place else that dast say to the contrary.

"Speaking of Spofford, he's a cagy old bird that generally knows enough to stick within the law—at least so far as has been brought to my attention. Mebby he's pulled dirty stuff, but it's nothing I can touch him for. Put your cards on the table. What do you want?"

"I want warrants sworn out for Spofford and his son," Peter said, "and I want 'em served pronto."

"Don't want much," the sheriff observed mildly, "do you? What crime or crimes are they supposed to be charged with?"

"The old man is guilty of forgery and robbery, besides being accessory to a holdup, and mebby more. The young squirt hired two fellows to kill me, and we'll put that down as attempted murder."

"Got proof of all that, have you?"

"I have. Take the forgery first." He produced two papers, one of them crumpled, frayed, and almost worn out. The other was the mortgage note obtained from Banker Spofford.

"I got to go back quite a ways to explain what's happened lately," Peter went on. "Four years ago Frank Winsome borrowed six thousand dollars from Spofford & Son—that is, from the old man, who really runs the business—on a five-year mortgage, each of 'em having a copy.

"Right after that Winsome was killed by a broncho, and then it developed that his copy of the mortgage note had disappeared. It wasn't in the safe with his other valuables, and never did show up, though I guess Miss Winsome didn't worry much over the matter.

"Spofford got wise somehow—as I've figured things out, mebby from the lawyer that settled Winsome's estate—that Miss Peggy had no copy of the note, so he made out a new one, with different provisions, and forged Frank Winsome's name to it.

"This new note, which wasn't legal, naturally, gave him authority to foreclose at the end of thirty days if the half-year interest wasn't paid.

"Next Spofford had a man hold up Newt Winsome, when he was riding into town to pay the three hundred dollars interest. Newt fooled the stick-up lad, and turned the cash over to Spofford. But Spofford tricked the kid into thinking he had a receipt for the interest payment.

"A few days later Spofford rode out to the Three Star Dot, denied that Newt had ever paid him, and showed Miss Peggy the forged note. What Newt thought was a receipt turned out to be blank paper. Lacking proof of payment, she had to give Spofford six thousand three hundred by the first of the month—or lose her ranch.

"Miss Winsome had an old friend—a desert rat—that she'd helped from time to time with grub and clothes of her dad's. I had a hunch the lost note might have slipped down inside the lining of a coat Winsome used to wear before he got killed, and that mebby without knowing it, Miss Peggy had given that coat to Sanderson.

"I was up to his place early this morning, and went through some worn-out duds hanging there. Luck was with me. I found the note, and here she is."

The paper P. D. Q. showed Sheriff Morrison was worn to the point of being hardly legible; yet it provided damaging proof of the crime Spofford was alleged to have committed.

"I ain't eggsactly a handwriting expert," Buck Morrison mused, as he compared the two notes, "but it certainly looks like what you say is true. Which being the case, you've got old Spofford where the hair grows short. But that ranch of Miss Winsome's ain't worth the trouble and risk he took to get it. What's behind the game, anyway?"

"That'll come out later, mebby. I ain't through my story yet."

"Don't stop," the sheriff suggested. "It's a good yarn, son."

"Some of what comes now is what you might call conjecture, based on facts I've managed to pick up with the aid of one or two citizens what were glad to help put the greased skids under both Spoffords. I think I've got the main details pretty straight, though a few of the minor points ain't as clear as they might be.

"This desert rat, Eb Sanderson, knew that his friends of the Three Star Dot were in plenty trouble, Newt having told him the whole story after Spofford came out there and showed his hand.

"Sanderson promised Newt that he'd make a strike in time to save their ranch. Peggy had grub-staked him any number of times; so naturally half of what he found would be hers. That was one rash promise, as you'll agree, but I'm a son-of-a-gun if the old cuss didn't make good, though the Lord alone knows how.

"Some place, up Apache Cañon most likely, he ran into a quartz vein or pocket that from all indications looks like a lulu. I saw some of the ore he sold to Clem Bodwell, probably because he needed cash for working capital. Clem paid him sixty dollars.

"If Eb Sanderson had kept off the booze all would have gone well, but he started libating, and John Barleycorn loosened up his tongue. He talked too much, saying among other things that Miss Winsome had a half interest in the strike account of the grub-stake.

"Now young Spofford comes into the story. He'd hired two fellows to kill me the same night the desert rat was in town, but meanwhile they got next to him at Varney's, finding out about the strike from his loose conversation.

"Their idea seems to have been to kill Sanderson, after making him tell where his strike was located. I had their play against me coppered in advance, and then ran into the second, being taken by surprise; I didn't have any idea at all what was stirring until it broke out in gun play."

"Who were those two fellows?" the sheriff demanded.

"Mexican Charlie and Carl Davis. I killed Mex myself, beating him to iron by a safe margin. Davis I had handcuffed. I've lost sight of the skunk temporary, but I don't figure he'll get away for long."

At this point Buck Morrison astonished Peter by throwing his head back and bursting into a guffaw of hearty laughter.

"No, he won't get away for long," the sheriff chuckled, "and he won't get far, either. Why, I've got him locked up in the calaboose right now."

"You have!" Peter exclaimed. "On what charge?"

"Killing Mexican Charlie, the chap you salivated!" and the town marshal laughed again, as at a rare jest. "Can you beat that! Eb Sanderson brought him in late last night, and said that Davis confessed to the killing.

"I talked some with Carl, but couldn't get much out of him. He just kept mumbling away to himself, and acting as sore as hell on general principles. Tell me this, will you? Why did Carl confess to killing his pard —when you'd really salivated him?"

"He might give you the answer, if sufficiently urged," Peter suggested.

"WE'LL let him have the chance. But here's another matter. If Eb Sanderson turned over to Peggy Winsome a big shake of gold, Spofford's plot against her ranch would blow up. I'm wondering if mebby they wasn't somebody else back of that strike business besides Mex and Carl."

"Spofford, you mean!" Peter ejaculated. "By thunder, sheriff! I bet you're right. Why don't we pump Carl Davis and see what runs out?"

Davis was accordingly sent for, appearing after a brief delay in charge of a deputy.

"You're in a kind of mess, Carl," the sheriff said musingly. "The citizens of this town ain't witnessed a hanging for some months, but it looks to me like we might have to stage a necktie party with you on the receiving end."

Davis seemed to have reached a similar conclusion; he was badly frightened, and showed it.

"I didn't shoot Mex," he whispered. "Honest, Buck, I never shot him. Here's the guy right here that did it. I saw him," and he pointed at Peter De Quincy, who grinned cheerfully.

"We've got your confession," the sheriff reminded his prisoner, "and it would save a lot of fuss and bother if we just let things ride as they're headed."

"You wouldn't want to hang an innocent man, would you, Buck?"

"No danger of making that mistake if we hung you, Carl," Morrison said. "I wouldn't call you an angel, 'part from this last business. You're a liability to the town, 'stead of an asset."

"I told that rat I killed Mex," Davis eagerly explained, "so he wouldn't be sore at me, thinking I'd plotted to get his strike. I made him believe I shot Mex to save him. I said Mex and I had a scrap because Mex wanted to torture him, and that's how come I was handcuffed. When he and Mex started to fight I used Mex's own gun on him."

"You thought Sanderson would fall for that!" Morrison observed cuttingly. "Then you sure ought to hang! Who put you two skunks up to killing Sanderson, anyway?"

Davis glanced from one to the other out of fear-haunted eyes.

"Spofford," he finally admitted. Carl had reached the point where he was ready to throw himself on the mercy of the court.

"So Miss Winsome couldn't use the gold from his strike to pay off that mortgage Spofford had on her ranch, eh?"

Davis nodded.

"What did Spofford want the Three Star Dot ranch for? I ain't found that out yet."

"I don't know. All I know is he wanted it, and wanted it bad."

"Bad enough so he didn't stop at murder," the sheriff mused. "That's all we need of you now, Carl. Stick to what you've told us and you may cheat the hangman yet. But I'm telling you this—it 'll be one mighty close squeeze for you."

Davis was led away to be locked up again.

"That clears a few matters that bothered me," said Peter. "Things look pretty rosy right now. Is there any objection to putting the goods on Spofford and his son? I'm yearning for a show-down. Those two skunks have it coming to 'em."

"I guess they have," Morrison agreed. "You were thinking mebby I'd be afraid to do it."

"No, not that," Peter hastened to state. "But, you know how it is. You've likely received favors from Spofford—and—"

"That's all right, son," the official said kindly. "Spofford might have been back of my having this job as town marshal; but I don't owe him anything, and I'm telling you frank, son, they's not a soul in town I'd rather put the shackles on than that slick banker."

"Bully for you, sheriff!" Peter enthused.

"Might be he's at his office now," the officer added. "Come along and see the fun. The sooner the quicker!"

Young Spofford happened to be in the outer part of the banking house when Morrison and P. D. Q. arrived. He was on the point of slipping away at sight of them, but the marshal hailed him peremptorily.

"Just a minute, John! I've been looking for you."

Unwillingly S p o f f o r d, Jr., approached.

"What do you want of me?" he mumbled.

"Your dad out back?" Morrison asked by way of reply, and Spofford nodded.

"I'd like to talk with the two of you," said the sheriff.

"I can't—right now, Buck," Spofford protested. "I'm late for an appointment as it is."

"You'll be still later, then," Morrison declared grimly. "You're coming with me!"

Hooking his arm within Spofford's, Buck dragged the frightened young man down the hallway toward the private office of his father. The trio entered unannounced.

"WHAT'S the idea?" the banker roared threateningly, angry at the unceremonious way his sanctum had been invaded.

"The idea is," Morrison said calmly, "that I'm arresting you and young John for a whole flock of crimes, from breach of the peace down to attempted murder. You can have the particulars later."

"Have you gone crazy, Buck?" Spofford fumed, leaping to his feet. "You must be crazy or drunk!"

"Keep your hand away from that desk drawer!" Morrison snapped, and he pulled his gun as the banker made an inconspicuous motion toward a concealed weapon. "If they's any shooting at this party, I'll do it myself."

"Why, you poor fool!" Spofford was so angry that he frothed at the mouth. "I'll break you wide open for this!"

"The only thing you're liable to break," P. D. Q. spoke blandly up, "is rocks in the State pen. I think you'll be right busy there for a spell of years."

"Where do you come into this?" Spofford demanded.

"Me?" Peter drawled. "Say, hombre, you don't know the half of it all yet. Without stretching the truth a whole lot I might claim credit for blame near the whole works. How about that, sheriff?"

"He's the guy that did it," Morrison stated grimly, "and I'm telling any one who asks me that he did one fine, large job."

Banker Spofford drew in his breath sharply, as if beginning to understand. His complexion became mottled, blotched with unsightly and unwholesome looking ashen spots. Spofford, Jr., gazed at P. D. Q. in a sort of horrified fascination. His lips opened but no sound came forth. It was Spofford, Sr., who spoke.

"*Who are you, anyway?*"

"I'm the guy who swore he'd put you behind the bars if he had to go through hell to do it!" Peter said, so savagely that Spofford instinctively recoiled. "Dud Millbrook's my uncle. Mebbe you've heard of him. Also Cal Whitfield was one of my friends."

Peter's voice became less savage, changing rather to bitterness, combined with poignant agony.

"I never forgave myself for what happened to Cal Whitfield. None of us knew how bad things were by him, and Cal was too proud to ask help of his friends. When we found out it was too late. You had his ranch—and Cal was dead. Later his wife died of a broken heart.

"We couldn't get you on that deal, because you'd kept within the law. So we had to cook up a scheme where you'd step over. This Apache Gap proposition was my idea, with Dud Millbrook, who'd give his right arm to see your finish, backing me to the limit."

At mention of Apache Gap, Spofford stiffened, a look of terror dawning in his eyes.

"One of Millbrook's men tipped off Hollis Black, pretending he was willing to sell out to the enemy of his employer. Hollis swallowed the bait like a hungry shark; and we had you hooked at the same time.

"Black played straight with you, if that information does you any good. The telegram never came from him at all; it was one I faked, to be delivered while I was in your office.

"I didn't really buy Peggy Winsome's ranch—just borrowed it, as you might say. I had you as soon as you took my money and gave me the forged note, but I was glad to sell Apache Gap for ten thousand. It's worth about a hundred and fifty dollars. Miss Peggy gets her ranch clear of the mortgage, and close to four thousand cash profit, besides.

"Guess that's all, sheriff. Do your stuff on these polecats."

"You can't arrest me for the Apache Gap business," Spofford, Jr., babbled, almost at the point of tears. "I didn't have anything to do with it, I tell you. I didn't even know about it, Buck!"

Morrison shrugged his shoulders with superb indifference.

"Nobody said you did, John," he grunted contemptuously. "But the charge against you is attempted murder. You hired Mexican Charlie and Carl Davis to kill him." Morrison nodded toward De Quincy. "Mex is dead and Davis is in jail. He told the whole plot—what we didn't already know—to save his skin."

Neither father nor son had courage to attempt resistance in the face of the sheriff's drawn pistol.

"Hook 'em together with these irons, De Quincy," and Morrison tossed Peter a pair of handcuffs. P. D. Q. obliged. "Now," said the sheriff, "let's march!"

Through the front of the establishment the procession moved, clerks gazing in open-mouthed astonishment. Peter was ahead, and he stepped first out on the street, the two prisoners just behind him. A sudden, frenzied cry rang forth.

"I've got you now, Spofford!" and a six-shooter crashed.

Peter had glanced up at the warning, to see a wild-eyed youth who held in his hand a leveled Colt. In that emergency there seemed just one prudent thing to do, and Peter did it; he dropped flat to the sidewalk as the street echoed with the pistol's blast, vaguely conscious of a strangled cry behind him.

P. D. Q.'s .45 cleared the holster even before he was down, its own report following close on the first. But Peter, moved by an impulse there was no time to analyze, fired to disarm, not kill.

"Nice work!" Buck Morrison grunted, leaping on the assassin, whose weapon had been shot from his grasp. Peter rose, still holding his gun, and then he perceived that Spofford, Sr., was shackled to a corpse.

"May the Lord forgive me!" Marie Avis's brother sobbed brokenly. "I've killed the wrong man!"

"What do you mean, wrong man?" snapped Sheriff Morrison.

"It was Spofford I wanted to kill— for the way he treated my sister!"

"You ought to be satisfied, then," Morrison told him gruffly. "Spofford's the chap you salivated."

"Spofford? Is *that* Spofford?" The boy pointed unbelievingly at the man his bullet had struck down.

"Of course, it's Spofford! Who'd you think it was?"

"*He* told me this man was Spofford," pointing now at Peter De Quincy. The boy's bewilderment was pitiful. "*He* gave me the gun! And *he* was Spofford all the time!"

"Somewhere in this business," Sheriff Morrison observed solemnly, "they's the material for a first-class sermon.

"It shows they's a God, some place, running things."

CHAPTER XVIII.

DOWN AN OLD, OLD TRAIL.

PEGGY wondered and conjectured, and theorized over what Peter De Quincy might be up to when he rode away from the Three Star Dot with the bill of sale.

She felt no resentment whatever that Peter seemed disposed to keep her guessing as to his plans, but just the same she was dying to know. Unquestionably a momentous plot was being hatched at the expense of Banker Spofford, but the details of that plot lay shrouded in mystery too deep for Peggy's imagination to fathom.

What could a lone cowboy, even an exceptional cowboy like Peter De Quincy—for Peggy admitted that he was far from ordinary—accomplish against the wealth and sinister power of Banker Spofford? Peggy surmised all sorts of things, but not once did she strike near enough the actual truth to score a hit.

Newt also did a tremendous amount of speculating, no less curious than his sister.

Peggy smiled. "This will teach you patience, Newt."

"Huh!" Newt grunted. "I don't want to be taught patience. I want to find out what Peter's stirring up—and what he's doing to that Spofford gang."

Fortunately for Newt his waiting powers were put to no great strain; toward the latter part of the next afternoon Peter appeared, breezing up to the Three Star Dot quite as if nothing had happened. Newt spotted the visitor first.

"Hurrah!" he yelled in an outburst of enthusiasm. "He's here, Peg! Peter's come!"

"What's all the tumult over, old timer?" Peter De Quincy inquired, swinging down from his horse with a grin at the boy.

Peggy arrived at that moment.

"It seems good to see you again," she smiled, extending her hand in welcome. "I'd have you know you saved Newt's life."

"How's that?"

"The poor chap's been so consumed with curiosity! I was really worried about him."

"Aw, g'wan, Peg!" Newt protested. " You were just as bad as me, only mebby you didn't show it. Nothing to be ashamed of anyhow.' '

" We have been living under rather a strain," Peggy confessed to Peter.

" Oh, I see." P. D. Q. replied, with a most provoking deliberation. " You were wondering about what I might be doing in town. Well, well!"

"Aren't you going to tell us, Peter?" Newt yelped, fairly dancing up and down. " Come on! Aren't you going to tell us now?"

" I really think you might,", Peggy added, with a demure glance. No one could have resisted it.

"Why, sure," Peter assented. " That's what I came for. Let's see, now—where'll I begin?"

" At the beginning!"—from Newt —" and don't leave out anything!"

" First I've got to give you this," Pete said to Peggy, and he surrendered the bill of sale. " You know, I wasn't aiming to buy your ranch permanent, Miss Peggy. All I wanted was the use of it for a few hours. Much obliged for the loan."

" What did you do with the ranch while you had it, Peter?" Newt demanded expectantly.

" Why—" Peter appeared to hesitate—" I sold Apache Gap. It didn't seem to be any good to you or your sister, and Mr. Spofford wanted the gap so bad I hated to disappoint him."

" Spofford wanted Apache Gap!" Peggy exclaimed. " What in the world did he want it for?"

At the same time Newt asked a more practical question.

" What'd you get for it, Peter?"

" The whole thing's a long story, sort of. He offered five thousand dollars, but I told him it ought to be worth ten, which he forked over."

Sublimely indifferent to Peggy's gasp of unbelieving amazement, Peter went on, " I'll square up now. Here's the mortgage note for your ranch, paid up. It came to sixty-three hundred altogether, and here's the balance in cash—three thousand seven hundred. Likely you'd better put it in the safe, Miss Peggy."

Time was required for the tremendous sensation thus produced to subside. But Newt's curiosity was far from quenched.

" What'd you do to old man Spofford, Peter?" he asked.

" Spofford's in jail." This response seemed to give general satisfaction.

" And young Spofford?" Newt persisted.

" He's dead!"

" Good enough! Did you kill him, Peter?"

" Hush, Newt!" Peggy cried. " You mustn't ask anything like that!"

" Why, it's all right, Miss Peggy. I don't blame Newt for wishing to know. But it was another fellow fired the bullet. Some day, mebby, I'll tell you how it came about. That's another story. Are you glad I didn't kill him, Miss Peggy?"

" Yes," she whispered, " I'm glad you didn't kill him, Peter. Taking human life seems a terrible thing to do. I know it's necessary at times."

" Would you think any worse of me if I had?" Peter insisted. " Suppose it was his life—or mine?"

" You shouldn't ask that," Peggy murmured. " I—I hope you know me well enough to be sure of my answer." Peggy's blue eyes met his honestly, and Peter was quite content at the unspoken message he read therein.

" I'm glad you feel the way you do," he said. " That makes it easier for me to tell what you'd be sure to learn sooner or later. I did have to kill one man, Miss Peggy—a no-'count fellow they called Mexican Charlie.

" He was drawing his gun to shoot me and I beat him to it. He was bad —all the way through. He had a scheme to torture poor old Eb Sanderson to make him tell where his strike was located."

" Uncle Eb really made a strike!" Peggy cried breathlessly.

"Why, yes, ma'am, he certainly did. I forgot to tell you that," and Peter beamed on her with his usual merry twinkle. "They's been so much news I'm slipping up on some of the facts. That was downright careless of me, wasn't it?"

"Oh, dear!" Peggy suddenly sighed. "I'm so happy I'm afraid I'm going to cry." She smiled at Peter, tears sparkling in her blue eyes like diamonds. "I'm so glad for poor old Uncle Eb. This means a lot to him. I wonder where he is now."

"Buck Morrison told me he pulled out of town early this morning. He's probably up the cañon now working on his strike. You'll see him before long, I judge, tickled as a kid. He certainly crashed through when he had to."

P. D. Q. proved to be a shrewd prophet, for at that instant the party was augmented by Eb Sanderson in person, looking—for an old chap—quite chipper and extremely well pleased with himself.

Immediate explanations were in order, and presently it developed that Sanderson had not left Cactus Springs as soon as Peter supposed. From Aleck Carmichael the prospector had learned a number of facts, among them that P. D. Q. had saved his life over in Eagle Cañon, and that Peggy's ranch had been wrested from Spofford's clutches without the aid of his famous strike.

Conversation flew at a fast and furious pace for some minutes as the various details were cleared up to every one's satisfaction.

"This here cow-puncher," Eb at length opined, addressing Peggy, "is my idee of a capable gent. He sure raised hell with the Spofford family and all their dirty plans."

"You're no slouch yourself, old timer," Peter grinned, acknowledging the tribute. "My notion of a capable gent is one that can go out and make him a gold strike to order."

"A feller can do quite some chore when he's got to," Sanderson rejoined modestly. "Between the two o' us, son, we managed to stir up considerable dust."

"I think you're both wonderful!" was Peggy's warm declaration.

"I counted on your share o' my strike savin' the ranch," Eb told her, "but things ain't altered none by what's took place. Half o' all the gold's yourn, Miss Peggy."

Peggy opened her mouth to assure Uncle Eb that she couldn't take any of his hard-earned treasure, but one look at his happy old face bottled up the words.

To refuse a share of the strike would be cruelty, not kindness, leaving to the simple old prospector's mind the bitter thought that after all he had been living on her charity.

"That's fine, Uncle Eb!" Peggy cried gratefully. "I'm awfully glad—for both of us."

"You're entitled to the bulk of the credit, Miss Peggy," Sanderson insisted. "It was what Spofford aimed to do to you that made me really get busy. Otherwise, I reckon, our strike would still be a-waitin' up Apache Cañon fer somebody to come along an' find her."

Supper that evening at the Three Star Dot was a hilarious celebration, a sort of Thanksgiving feast.

MANY questions were asked and answered before Peggy and Newt learned all Peter had to tell them. Then it was time to eat. Later on in the evening, after Newt had finally been induced to go to bed, Peter diplomatically suggested that Peggy join him in a little stroll.

It was, as he said, a large evening—one that should be taken advantage of. Peggy assented and together they walked out in front of the ranch house, following along the trail that led on through Apache Gap.

The moon had risen, a wondrous

full moon, softening with its golden magic the harsh contours of that rugged country. Peggy stopped, held in the spell of the splendid scene.

"Isn't it beautiful, Peter!" she exclaimed, a little catch in her voice. "I've been so worried and frightened —over the thought that Newt and I were going to lose all this. I haven't thanked you yet for what you did. You mustn't think harshly of me—if I have seemed ungrateful. I wasn't— but—"

"Think harshly of you!" Peter said reproachfully. "Why, I couldn't do that if I tried."

Peggy said nothing and for a moment they stood silent, gazing toward the sharp break in the massive hog-back where Apache Creek cut through the resisting layers of up-tilted rock.

"Of course," Peter resumed, quite as if there had been no gap in the conversation, "I wouldn't want to try. It's lots easier to think nice things about you, Peggy."

For the first time he dropped the formal *Miss* from her name. "And I've been thinking of you pretty constant— since the afternoon we rode up Apache Cañon together. Did you enjoy that ride, Peggy?"

"Yes," she whispered, "I enjoyed it very much, Peter." Her heart was thumping so it seemed Peter could not fail to hear.

"I told you this afternoon why I came into the region," Peter resumed. "To get back at the man whose crookedness and evil had ruined a friend of mine. This ranch of yours was a sort of pawn in the game I aimed to play against Spofford.

"But when I got here—and saw you —seems like the thoughts of Cal Whitfield sort of dropped into the background. Cal was dead, and it was too late to help him.

"I wasn't disloyal to my friend exactly, leastways I *hope* not. But there was something about *you*, Peggy—the

smile in your lovely eyes, and the curve of your sweet little lips, and the dimple that danced on your cheek like the flicker of a sunbeam.

"I just couldn't help falling in love with you, Peggy, that afternoon we rode together up the cañon, and I've been getting in deeper and deeper every minute since. Don't you love me, Peggy—a little?"

"A little!" Peggy echoed demurely. In the moonlight her face was tender, despite the roguish, teasing note in her voice. Then she added: "You must think I'm very selfish, Peter, when you expect me to give you a little love —after you've done so much for me."

"I been cherishing hopes," Peter said. "Big hopes, Peggy. But I couldn't be sure—not till I hear you say it. Do you love me, Peggy? Not just a little! *A lot!*"

"Of course I do, Peter!"

And somehow, while the wise old moon smiled down upon them, two figures melted into one, as Peter drew her into his arms.

Some time later they walked slowly back up the moon-lit trail toward the ranch house.

"Know what I'd like to do?" Peter remarked. "I'd like for us to put this ranch where it belongs—thousands of steers on the range, a dozen riders sleeping in the old bunk house, a big round-up every spring and fall, and everything. Just the same as in the old days when your dad was here. How about it, Peggy?"

"I'd love that," she cried. "The money Spofford gave you for Apache Gap will help, won't it? And there's my interest in Uncle Eb's strike. We can do things on a big scale, can't we?"

"Sure we can," said Peter.

"And the Three Star Dot won't be Trouble Ranch any more, will it, Peter?"

"Trouble Ranch!" Peter echoed, superbly. "Trouble Ranch? I don't know any place by that name!"

THE END

Argonotes

The Readers' Viewpoint

CRIME TO-DAY

RECENTLY we published a sketch of part of W. Wirt's interesting and adventurous life. If you read that account you readily understand why "Kill Him, Jimmie—or I Will," in this issue, presents such a fascinating and thoroughly convincing picture of present day underworld conditions.

Mr. Wirt's letters about the story are so interesting and shed so much additional light on the modern crime problem that we are printing part of them here:

The characters in this story are fictitious, but the portrayal of conditions as they exist to-day in any American city large enough to maintain the various "John Law" departments is not fictitious by a darn sight. The story being set in Chicago means nothing—either for or against Chicago. It may as easily have read any city in the country over fifty thousand—and a lot of them under.

Although I was a deputy sheriff, later Federal agent, and for a good many years special agent, in this country and abroad, I in no way attempted this story as an exposure of anything. I have been backed up too many times by straight, hard shooting police and detectives, deputy sheriffs and United States marshals to get even the slightest idea that there are not "straight coppers." There are—a heck of a lot of them—but since the Eighteenth Amendment went into effect there seems to be a train of consequences like the "House That Jack Built." Time was, if a copper was crooked, he could be crooked in only one way—trying to protect some peterman or "caunfort ladran"—master thief or head of a mob—or shaking down some porch climber, and stuff like that. At the worst, he would be getting his from some crooked gambler or "mob"—and he was decidedly in the minority.

Now, with the beer-running gangs, the whisky mobs, the illicit alcohol rings, and what not, with ten-thousand-dollar bills floating around like ten spots in the old days—what the hell, Bill?

But it leads into worse; that's the rotten part of it. The booze game is no man's land—every man for himself. Fine! Let's romance a little. No. 0008000, a good, square copper, by chance runs up on a "hot truck" some night. What night? Any old night on any old road, in any old State. He pulls it down. Now he is getting his little old one sixty or one eighty, or whatever it is, a month, and maybeso his little girl is sick or the payment is due on the bungalow or what not.

He gets an argument like this: "Aw, be a good feller; they're all doin' it. This booze is for some regular lads, see? No one's gettin' hurt, buddy. You ain't no —— —— —— prohibition agent; you're a copper. Here"—and two or three or more hundred-dollar bills are actually shoved in his hand. "You got bad eyesight, see? Listen: the big boy is runnin' this, and it wouldn't be none too healthy for any finger-fattie to lose him twenty grand—would it, now?"

Well, the copper takes it. He'd kill a crook that offered to split the proceeds of a robbery with him for the chance to "make his elegant." He'd go into a dark house alone after a burglar, but: "Aw, every one's gettin' theirs in this game." And right here let me state that he's darn near correct. There have been rumors of bankers backing the shipment, by the shipload, of booze—and not very long ago twenty or more customhouse gents were gathered in for being a little nearsighted.

To continue: next time he demands it and, keno—he's one of the gang. And there comes the part that is raising hell and high water in so many departments. Some gang shoots it out with a rival. Naturally, they call on all help they can, before and after, and the first thing No. 0008000 knows he's in deep with killers and dirty work at the crossroads of all kinds. If a man is getting money from a gang, can he refuse to help that gang when they are in trouble? He could, but does he? Not often. Geraldine, not often—and remain healthy. Trouble is, the gang is composed of all kinds: men who have served time, and men who ought to have if they haven't; and they do other things besides run booze. The copper or other John Law doesn't, but in the protection he tries to give—which is demanded—he gets in over his head. Then, again naturally, he tries to protect himself, because there are always straight coppers and judges and officers who would give their eye teeth to get something on a "right guy" enough to make it stick.

Now suppose No. 0008000 refuses the first bribe and takes in the rum-runners. He sees them at once set free on bond. The truck disappears. He goes home, and the next day is sent out where Seven Hundred and Ninety-Eighth Street meets the wide open spaces—virtue being its own reward.

In my humble opinion, which doesn't amount to a tinker's damn, except to myself, the

Eighteenth Amendment is directly responsible for a whole lot of the graft and crookedness and killing going on all over the country—and I am no ardent wet or dry either.

The old-timers on any force were, and are, straight coppers and nothing else—ninety-nine per cent of them. Sure, once in awhile a gambler paid more than his legitimate share, or some saloonkeeper out of favor was made to come across; a little slip like that wasn't counted.

But now, with the younger men coming on, with ring after ring operating, with backing here and backing there, with gangsters operating machine guns from automobiles, with high officials getting indicted for this, that, and the other, with a member of Congress wahwahing all over the lot about a superintendent of police being far from fragrant as to his breath—what would you?

You can't play with pitch, *et cetera*, and one little thing leads to another. In allowing rum-runners to operate the John Laws have got themselves in " ze one gran' mix," and that goes for more than John Laws also.

Outside of being a picture of what is going on in any large city, " Kill Him, Jimmie—or I Will" was written to point out the one incontrovertible fact that he who knocks off a John Law of any kind, government, State, municipality, or village, shall in turn be knocked off, pronto or twenty years later.

All in all, straight or crooked, the much abused John Law is game, anyway.

W. WIRT.

TO BE SAFE

WITH increasing frequency we hear from readers who have been unable to secure their copies of the magazine. A day late at the newsdealer's stand, or an unusually heavy sale cleaned out his supply on the first day—and some reader must wait to continue a serial at its most interesting part.

We are doing our best to supply enough copies to meet the ever increasing demand, but it is often impossible to anticipate an extra heavy sale. Particularly will 'this be true during the coming fall and winter months, when the excellent feature stories on schedule will be sure to attract new readers and increase the demand.

If you want to be sure of your copy each week, play safe. We suggest that you leave a standing order with your newsdealer.

OF course thousands of ARGOSY readers save their back copies of the magazine, but Mrs. Brown has an in-genious and interesting method for preserving the stories she likes:

Buffalo, N. Y.

In the July 7 issue of ARGOSY you ask the opinion of your readers as to whether they wish four or three serials.

I say four, by all means. When I began to read the ARGOSY in 1923, you were printing five serials. Then you dropped to three and then came back to four. I wanted the five, but did not complain at four. But I really feel cheated when there are only three.

Otherwise please make no changes. My husband and I like all you print; Westerns and all the others. There is only one thing I would like to see changed and that is for the different authors to leave out so many expressions of " My God!" There is such a lack of reverence for God these days, it seems to me the press could help a little by refraining from the use of the expression, even though persons in the situations delineated might be inclined to use it.

Every one of the authors you use, the new as well as the old ones, are favorites of ours and we are especially fond of Kenneth Perkins. Don't see how any one can find fault with any of your selection.

I would like to tell you what I do with my ARGOSYS. I read aloud to the family all the serials and the novelettes, and some times a short story if it is by one of our favorite authors. Then when I get a bunch of magazines on hand, I tear them apart, combining together all parts of each serial, making a finished book thereof. Then I take several novelettes and short stories by one author and combine them under one cover. In this way I have a book of novelettes and short stories by George Johnson, or Charles Francis Coe, *et cetera*. Sometimes I have to hold a collection of stories for some time before I have enough to combine, but they are good when finished. In separating the stories, I type the last page of the story when it interferes with the following story.

Then when my separating is all completed, I keep for myself those stories we have especially liked, and the rest I pass on to a hospital or reading room, where I know they will be appreciated. I have a very fine collection of stories in the past five years, and I hope to continue to gather them.

Your magazines are the cleanest on the market, and I am sure it is your desire and determination to keep them so. Good luck go with you. MRS. NELSON H. BROWN.

AND now, lest we become too satisfied with ourselves, Mr. Leonard has a few kicks to register. Argonotes is not a bouquet department; the brickbats are free to sail in with the more complimentary matter:

Lincoln, Neb.

Why the many typographical changes in the old magazine? Is the paper getting so poor that it is necessary to use synopses, articles, and house ads to fill up the magazine, rather than paying money for stories to put in the same space? For instance, in the current number, in "Six-Foot Lightning," there is over a solid page of review at the beginning of the current story. If it is believed that the average reader, and that is who you are catering to, I suppose, cannot carry in mind what has gone before, at least, put the synopsis in six-point type and cut it short and give the reader something else than what he already knows. If just a few more departments are added, you will get this down to a one-story-a-week magazine. What is the opinion of other readers?

Most of the stories have been O K, with little change from the magazine I started reading twelve years ago. However, when you start adding articles such as "A Legacy of Lead," "Smallest Motor in the World," and "Smashing Through"—then a person might as well pay two cents for a daily paper and read about it there. Would like to see the magazine go back to the old system of one continued story starting and one concluding in every number. L. LEONARD.

ANOTHER fan who is looking forward to the Slater LaMaster serial:

Toronto, Canada.

A friend gave me some old ARGOSIES. I began reading A. Merritt's serial, "Seven Footprints to Satan," which had just started. By the time I had finished ARGOSY had gained another fan.

In my opinion your best authors are Gordon Stiles, Edgar Franklin, Joseph Ivers Lawrence, George M. Johnson, Slater LaMaster, Fred MacIsaac, George F. Worts, Loring Brent—with A. Merritt topping the list.

Why can't we have another story like "Seven Footprints to Satan"? Also some war and scientific stories like "The Call to Arms," "King's Khaki," "Venus or Earth," "The Sunmakers." If you must have Western stories let George M. Johnson and Donald Bayne Hobart supply them, as they are undoubtedly your best Western writers. I am glad to hear that Slater LaMaster is writing another story for ARGOSY. Hoping this petition does not bring a storm of comment about my ears as did the scathing letter of A. J. Corey I will now sign off. One of many ARGOSY fans. T. E. COOKE.

EVERY week dozens of readers write to us ordering back copies of the magazine containing favorite stories. In most cases we can supply these copies, charging the regular price of ten cents for 1927 and 1928, and twenty cents for issues prior to these dates.

For example, "The Great Commander," mentioned hereafter, appeared in our issues of July 3 to July 24, 1926, and can be secured for eighty cents.

Newark, Ohio.

Here is my tenth coupon at last. Edgar Franklin heads the list, with Loring Brent a close second this week. "Every Minute Counts" is fine—much better than "Now We're Rich." *Richard Melton* is the best character ARGOSY has presented for some time. "The Scandal on Kitikat Key" is great so far. I'm sorry, though, that it is only three parts. The fellow from whom I buy ARGOSY is reading both of these and agrees with me on both counts. He also enjoyed "World Brigands" with me. Charles Divine's short story this week, "A Friend of M. Smith," is humorous enough for any one, I believe.

Everything is fine lately. Keep it up. I wish to state also that I am anxiously awaiting that new story by Slater LaMaster, because I know it will be a real masterpiece. I am anxious, too, for a new one by A. Merritt. I bought "Seven Footprints to Satan" when ARGOSY announced its publication in book form.

How much would it cost me for copies of the ARGOSY weeklies containing "The Great Commander," by MacIsaac, or for other of A. Merritt's stories? The first place I look in ARGOSY is the new announcements for serials, and then Argonotes. I am anxious for four serials again, one starting and one ending each week. That's a real system. ROBERT SCHREFFLER.

Looking Ahead!

Mystery—Oriental intrigue—Thrilling adventure—Grim underworld warfare—Romance—Action galore! All these you will find in

THE PAGAN RUBY
by J. ALLAN DUNN

Out of a clear sky they engulf Jack Eastman—just an every-day lad, even as you and I. In a second his prosaic life becomes a mad whirl—and the events which follow give us a thrilling serial as only J. Allan Dunn can write it.

Rustlers—Murderers—Clever liars—Ruthless plotters. Against all these Rex Harden takes up the gauntlet to save a friend—in

LORD OF LIARSBURG
A Complete Western Novelette
by EUGENE CUNNINGHAM

A newcomer to ARGOSY is Cunningham—bringing as his introduction a story that is tense with action and suspense from start to finish — a Western novelette that is "different."

Both coming to you in the
ISSUE OF OCTOBER 6th

ARGOSY
ALL=STORY WEEKLY
"First In Fiction"   *Out Every Wednesday*